THE HINTERLANDS

ALSO BY ROBERT MORGAN

FICTION
The Blue Valleys
The Mountains Won't Remember Us

POETRY
Zirconia Poems
Red Owl
Land Diving
Trunk and Thicket
Groundwork
Bronze Age
At the Edge of the Orchard Country
Sigodlin
Green River: New and Selected Poems

NONFICTION
Good Measure: Essays, Interviews, and Notes on Poetry

ROBERT MORGAN

THE HINTERLANDS

A MOUNTAIN TALE IN THREE PARTS

ALGONQUIN BOOKS OF CHAPEL HILL
1994

Published by
ALGONQUIN BOOKS OF CHAPEL HILL
Post Office Box 2225
Chapel Hill, North Carolina 27515-2225
a division of
WORKMAN PUBLISHING COMPANY, INC.
708 Broadway
New York, New York 10003

LIBRARY OF CONGRESS CATALOGING-IN-PUBLICATION DATA
Morgan, Robert, 1944–
    The Hinterlands / by Robert Morgan.
        p.   cm.
    ISBN 1-56512-021-3
    1. Frontier and pioneer life—Appalachian
Region—Fiction.
    2. Family—Appalachian Region—History—
Fiction.   3. Appalachian Region—History—
Fiction.   I. Title.
PS3563.087147H56   1994
813'.54—dc20   93-33728
                                    CIP

10 9 8 7 6 5 4 3 2 1
First Printing

TO THE MEMORY OF MY GRANDPARENTS
JULIA CAPPS LEVI (1883–1948)
ROBERT HAMPTON LEVI (1877–1955)

CONTENTS

THE HINTERLANDS

I

THE TRACE

1772

T he first time I seen your Grandpa? Why, it was the year everybody was talking about going to Watauga and the Holsten. Then every young girl dreamed of running off to the West. They thought if they could just get there and start over, everything would be perfect, or near about. That's the way girls dream. It was the wilderness of the West they was studying on.

It's natural for a body to think if you could begin over, your life would be better. You would do it different from any of the people or places where you'd already failed or proved to be just ordinary. Every girl has a dream of being carried off to some better place, by a big handsome feller.

It's the appeal of being saved, of being born again, as the preachers say. To start a new life and shed the rags of this old one. Of course, you could change yourself right where you are through hard work and determination. But they ain't much romance in hard work and determination. It's over the horizon, in back of beyond, where things will be different, and better.

That's why the old don't like to pick up and move on. Some of them come across the water when they was young, and cleared up a new place, and even learned a new tongue. You could say they don't have the will anymore, or you could say they know better.

Children, I'm telling you—the day your Grandpa walked into

the Mountain Creek settlement, a wagon train was leaving for the Holsten. Since they had hacked a road across the mountains and through the gaps people had been leaving in little bunches, their things loaded up on carts and wagons, on pack horses. The Shimer Road wasn't nothing but a track, marked by blazes on trees, but I reckon it was wide enough for a wagon to pass. It run from Mountain Creek all the way to the blue mountains of Watauga.

They was leaving by twos and tens. And we'd get word back some stopped on the way, but most headed right on through the gaps into the land of Watauga and the Holsten.

They was lining up in the road, and folks was hugging and kissing their cousins and trading presents. It was a day at the end of winter and the mountains was still bare, though you could see a little green down by the creek. People figured if they left early enough they might get to the West in time to put in a crop.

The women standing by the wagons had tears of joy, some of them, and others tears of grief. I've heard it said men like to up and move on and women want to nest and stay. But I've never noticed it was so. I've seen just as many women with a hanker to move on, to light out and try a new place. Couldn't have been so many people settled here if the women didn't want to come too.

My Daddy worked as a blacksmith, and he was fitting a tire on one of the wagons. That's what they was waiting for, for him to slip the hot iron rim on the wheel and let it cool into a fit before they screwed the wheel back on. Your Great-granddaddy could make anything. He had worked with metal since arriving in the mountains from Pennsylvania. He could shoe horses and oxen, and make any kind of tool you wanted. One of the things he hammered most was the big grubbing hoes we used in them days to chop roots and dig out rocks in the new ground. A heavy hoe sharpened like a razor would cut wood.

Another thing your Great-granddaddy done best was making bells. Mostly cowbells and sheep bells. He had learned it in Philadelphia when he was apprenticed. Though he didn't have no equipment for casting church bells or dinner bells, he could hammer out little bells with the prettiest tone you ever heard. And every bell he made sounded different. The best bells he made for our own cows. They was one bell he put on our lead milker, Old Bess, that truly had the sweetest tone you ever heard. It was made of some kind of brass or bronze, and its tinkle just seemed to fit the cove where we pastured our cows. Its one note was like something in the branch, or coming out of the sky, and it always told us where the cows was at milking time.

I thought at first your Grandpa belonged to the wagon train, 'cause I hadn't seen him before. He was standing by one of the wagons talking to the driver. They's a look real men have, even as young men. It's not so much their size, or height, though they're usually tall, taller than a woman anyway. And their shoulders are broad, it's true. But you see it most in their chest and waist, and the power in their upper legs showing right through the cloth or buckskin.

I saw him standing there and I said to myself, it sure is a shame he's going off to the Holsten and not taking me, 'cause I like the look of that man. And here he's leaving just as soon as I catch sight of him. Ain't fair at all.

Now I had plenty of beaux in my time. I was a popular girl in the valley. And many a boy wanted to walk me home from meeting, I guess. And when there was an infare, somebody always asked me to dance. But your Grandpa was a different sort. You could tell that. He had on this red hunting shirt, the kind you didn't see much back then. It was bright red wool. He must have bought it off a French trader somewhere over the mountains. The thing about wool is how it will shine in the sun. He was wearing buckskin pants like everybody else. Except it was the kind of softened buckskin that only Indians made. The Indian women do it by chewing the skin for days and days and soaking the hide in water with hickory ashes. I remember thinking when I saw him, does he have an Indian wife somewhere back in the mountains?

A lot of men did in those times, especially the traders and hunters. They might have a Christian wife in the settlements, to look after the children and grow crops and keep hearth and chicken roost. And back in the woods, in Tennessee or Georgia, they had an Indian woman raising some of their half-breeds and giving them the kinship with the tribe that guaranteed hunting rights and trading rights in the area. Men always did have it figured out.

Your Grandpa turns around to me as the wagons begun to move off up the road in the early light. He turns to me and says just like that, "Marry me and I'll take you to the West."

I said the first thing that come to mind.

"I don't marry no redcoats," I said. "Unless they have a university education."

That took him back a little. That wasn't what he was used to hearing from the girls he sparked. And I didn't hardly know what it meant myself. He started to answer and then stopped. He looked at me and rared back his head and laughed. His face got red as his shirt. I always did like a man that colored up. It shows their liveliness and their sensitiveness. A big old feller blushing like a kid always moved my heart.

"I'm Realus Richards," he said. "And I'm going back to the Holsten soon as I get me some tools. And this time I'm taking a wife."

"I hear brag bigger than brawn," I said.

"That's as maybe," he said. He tipped his hat and headed

toward the shed where my Daddy had his forge and anvil. I watched him walk away thinking what a nervy body he was, all proud of his red shirt and his big wide shoulders. I wondered if he'd ever seen the Holsten, or if he was one of them boys from the Morgan District that come up there to hunt and amuse theirselves. We was the last settlement before you crossed the mountains to Indian land, and sometimes boys would steal horses and bring them up from Charlotte to sell.

I clutched my shawl and stepped back to the house. Our place was maybe two hundred yards from the road, and my feet was a little wet with dew by the time I got back inside.

"Who was that boy you talked to?" Mama said soon as I got inside.

"Just some windbag said he was going to the Holsten," I said, taking off the shawl and bending to put another stick on the fire. But I couldn't fool Mama. She could read me like a book, always could.

"He's a smart-looking feller," she said.

"Not as smart looking as he thinks," I said. Mama eyed me and grinned. It always irritated me how smug she was, like she could look into my heart whenever she wanted to.

"Daddy won't hear of no girl of his riding off to the West," Mama said.

"He won't never have occasion to hear," I said.

The day before I'd sprinkled some branch sand on the floor. It had been walked on enough to polish the puncheons and clean off the tobacco juice and grease stains. I took the broom and swept out the house, working hard enough to raise a sweat. I dug with the straws down into the cracks, and when I finished, the puncheons sparkled in the firelight like they had been waxed.

"You're going to wear your hands out," Mama said. "You

expecting company?" It was midmorning. That was the time she liked to set in the corner and knit. She liked me to set by her and talk. Or if her friend Florrie Cullen come by, they'd knit, or stitch quilt pieces for an hour and gossip. But that morning I didn't want to talk to Mama no more. I wanted to keep my thoughts to myself. You could hear the hens outside, cackling the way they do middle of the morning after laying.

I cleaned the house and carried the ashes out to the hopper in the back. It was almost soap-making time, and Mama had saved a lot of ashes and fat over the winter. But the harder I worked, the less it seemed to accomplish. I had the idea, even then, that we're always looking for excuses not to do what we're supposed to. Even hard work can be an excuse for putting off the real work we're meant to do. Couldn't have explained it then, but I knowed I'd sweated myself all morning for nothing.

Along about dinner time, when Mama and me had fixed bread and creesie greens pulled on the branch, along come Daddy home with your Grandpa in his bright red shirt.

"This here is Mr. Richards," Daddy said to Mama.

He didn't say nothing to me and I busied myself in front of the hearth taking the cobbler off the fire. Last thing I'd done that morning was stew the peaches for the cobbler. We kept our dried peaches in bags up along the roof. You wouldn't believe the peaches we growed then. And along in August we dried them on cloths on the roof of the house and shed.

Daddy had already built up a rush in his talking. He liked to talk more than anything, and he didn't see too many strangers to tell his stories to. Sounded like he had been jawing all morning while he worked.

"I seen two fellers fight once," my Daddy was saying as they set down in front of the fire. You could smell the smoke of the forge on him. "We was coming back from the war in Pennsylvania, walking all the way back from Duquesne. Colonel Washington asked the English to give us a few provisions from their stores, and we hoofed it down into Virginia and east Carolina and headed west. Long the way these two got to arguing. Everytime one said one thing the other would dispute him. One was a swarthy little corporal named Ward and the other was a red-headed giant of a feller named Lloyd. Lloyd must have been bigger than you, stouter anyway."

While they talked, your Grandpa didn't hardly notice me. I put the cobbler on the table and some pewter and wooden bowls. I didn't go to notice him either.

"Corporal Ward said that the Indians would join the colonies now the French was whipped. He said they had no choice but to be loyal to the Crown. Lloyd took strong exception. He said he hadn't heard of Indians loyal to anything except stealing. He said he didn't have no hope for peace with Indians.

"It was the way Lloyd twisted things that made the corporal so mad. Ward had not meant to say he was certain the Indians would be loyal to the Crown. He was just hopeful. He stopped right there in the road and hollered in Lloyd's face, 'Why do you dispute everything I say?'

"All the men in the band stopped to watch. Lloyd reached over and put his big hand on Ward's face like he was snuffing a candle. Ward whirled around and kicked Lloyd on the leg, tearing his stocking. Them boys went after each other like wildcats."

"Dinner's ready," Mama said to Daddy. But Daddy didn't even stop talking. Him and your Grandpa pulled their chairs to the table and lit into the cornbread and buttermilk and creesie greens. Daddy talked while he chewed, wiping his mouth on his sleeve.

"'I can tell he's a traitor by his long red beard,' Ward screamed, and drove his hand into Lloyd's face. I don't know if he meant to, but somehow his finger went right into Lloyd's eye, and behind the eyeball. Just like you'd root out a tater his hand come up with that eyeball and bloody strings hanging to it."

"What a pretty story to tell at dinner time," Mama said. She always said that when Daddy finished the story.

"Ever after that they called Lloyd 'The Polyphemus of the Yadkin Valley,' " Daddy said.

"Polly what?" your Grandpa said.

"Polyphemus is back yonder in the Bible," Daddy said. "A school teacher said he was a giant with just one eye and liked to eat people."

"Wonder if he ever got that one eye crossed?" your Grandpa said. And we all laughed, including me and little Henry.

I poured your Grandpa a second cup of tea when he had about finished his dinner. Him and my Daddy pulled back their chairs from the table to relax. Your Grandpa had not took off his red shirt and his face was flushed a little from the heat and from eating hot bread and greens.

"How long you been in the West?" my Daddy said.

"Been there twice," Realus said. "Went first with some long hunters when I was just a boy. We stayed nigh two years gathering hides and fur and exploring all around the mountains."

"I hear it's limestone country," Daddy said.

"It's more than half mountains," Realus said.

Me and Henry was listening. Some people have a genius that can't be explained. You take a thousand people and they'll be one of them that plays a fiddle best of all, and one that can survey land, and others that's mighty good shots and storytellers. Your Grandpa's talent was for charming people. It come natural to him.

"They's meadows in the West blue as the blue of the mountains," he said.

"Are they blue as the sky?" Henry said.

"Not bright blue, but blue like the ridge yonder." Your Grandpa sipped his tea and ignored me. But I could tell he knowed I was listening.

"And the game's plenty?" my Daddy said.

"I seen glades in the woods with so many deer grazing you had trouble picking out one to kill," your Grandpa said. "And besides deer there's buffalo in the open country. I've seen valleys full of them. And they's turkeys in the woods like here. And bear all over the mountains. Now the mountains are not tall as they are here. But they go on and on like tater hills one after another, wooly with trees. That's why it takes so long to cross over into the Holsten. The little valleys are crazy and go off every which way. You can't travel long in the same direction till you hit another ridge.

"But the biggest thing I ever seen in the West, bigger than the bears, and the ugly old hog sturgeon in the river, and the buffaloes in the valleys to the west, was the pigeon swarms. Anybody that's been there will tell you the pigeons come over twice a year in flocks so long it takes days for them to pass. I've seen them break down a whole forest where they lit in the trees for the night. And they paint the ground white with their droppings. They'll eat anything that happens to be in their way."

"How come they don't starve?" I heard myself saying.

" 'Cause the land is covered with chestnuts and huckleberries and elderberries, and when they eat out one place, they just move on."

Your Grandpa turned his chair and looked into the fire. "It's near planting time in the West," he said.

"Can't plant corn till the oak leaves is big as a squirrel's ear," my Daddy said.

Your Grandpa glanced at me but didn't say nothing for a minute. Finally he said, "It gets warm sooner over the mountains. The farther inland you go the earlier spring comes. Already it's budding out there, and the grass is green."

"You got some land there already?" my Daddy said.

"I got a place picked out not too far from the river. It's got a spring runs right out from under a poplar tree. And a cove that's covered with pennyroyal along the creek. I've done built a cabin there, but come fall I mean to have a house grooved together. It's the prettiest ground you ever seen. And the soil along the creek is black as the bottom of a skillet."

"And you ain't seen no Indians?" Mama said.

"I've seen Indians pass through in little bands," your Grandpa said. "But most of the Indians has gone on toward Kentucky, and beyond that into Ohio territory. The Holsten was always a kind of in-between land, claimed partly by Cherokees and partly by others. That's why they fit so much over it."

I went on about the business of cleaning up the table and scrubbing dishes in the tub. But I listened to every word your Grandpa said. He leaned back in his chair like he was at home, and him and my Daddy smoked their pipes.

"To go off into the West a man needs a good gun and ax," my Daddy said.

"And a good heavy grubhoe and seeds," your Grandpa said.

"Everything else he can make or raise," my Daddy said.

"Except for a woman," your Grandpa said. "He can't make or raise no woman. He's got to take her with him."

I seen him glance at me quick and return to his smoking.

"I'd be afraid of painters and bears that far back in the wilderness," Mama said. She always did think of the worst things.

"They's bears and painters aplenty," your Grandpa said. "But a man with a good dog and a good gun needn't have no fear. When I first went to the Holsten, I lived in a lean-to of brush and bark. It was plenty comfortable. But late in the winter the wolves found out my little place. I heard howling on the ridge at night, getting closer. You hear wolves in the wilderness any time, so I paid it no mind till one night I was sitting before the fire and looked out in the dark and seen the flash of a pair of eyes.

"I thought of painters, and I thought of deer eyes. But them eyes flashed and moved. And strain though I might looking away from the fire, I couldn't see nothing else. It was a dark night. They was just the firelight reflected from the buckeye trees. You know how high trees look with fire under them, like something steep as the sky falling away in pieces and spots.

"The eyes flashed again, and then again. And it come to me that these was wolves, black wolves, of the kind they have in the West. As my eyes adjusted I could see more of them, coming in close and backing away. 'Yaaaah,' I hollered, and throwed a burning limb at them.

"You could hear them jump away in the undergrowth. But by and by I seen the eyes flash again. It was like the devil out there, multiplied by ten to twenty. I thought, was they like mad dogs, or just starving for game? It come to me they smelled the venison I had hung up beside the lean-to, on a limb too high for any varmint to reach.

"It come to me I could be at my end there in the wilderness by Shooting Branch and nobody would ever know the difference. I was alone in the world. First time I ever felt alone in the woods.

"I got my gun from back of the lean-to, all loaded and primed, and I tried to sight in on one of the devils. But it was so dark their black bodies slipped in and out of sight like fish in a deep pool. I didn't have no powder and lead to waste. I was two hundred miles from any new supply."

"So what did you do?" Henry said.

"I seen how hard it was going to be and how I was almost certain to miss in the dark," your Grandpa said. "So I figured I'd aim at a spot of light falling on a bush, and when one moved in front of it, I'd fire. It took several minutes of waiting. Finally, a form passed in front of the spot and I squeezed the trigger. For a second you couldn't tell what happened because the sound ricocheted off the walls of the draw. But then I heard a snarling and tearing, and a terrible commotion in the dark. Them devils was eating their brother. I reloaded and set by the fire, hoping I wouldn't run out of wood. Finally, when I got down to my last stick, it was daylight. And they was nothing but some bones and a little fur out beside the bushes."

"Why would a woman want to go off to such a place?" Mama said. She usually didn't interrupt my Daddy or a visitor. But if she had a feeling for something, she'd speak out, no matter who was there. I'd seen her argue with a preacher when he spoke against women.

"What for would a woman want to go off into the wilderness away from her kin?" Mama said. "A woman needs her friends and community. She don't want to raise her younguns so far out she can't see smoke from another chimney."

"They'll be other folks in the West," your Grandpa said. "Folks is going there every day, like you seen this morning."

All the time I was finishing up the dishes, I was thinking how pretty it would be to live off in the promised land of the Holsten. The thing I liked best about living off in your own cabin was it was so romantic. You was there with your loved ones and your spring, and the dogwoods bloomed as you put in corn. When the white storms come in winter you stayed by the fire and sewed quilts and taught your younguns their letters. And your man brought home a wild turkey or deer, and fur to make you a coat.

It seemed a pleasure to escape the jealousy, and feuding over boundary lines, and how property is divided up. We know so little of our connection, anyway, as people marry and move on and you don't never hear from them again. It's like in all our blood ties of cousins and aunts and uncles and ancestors and descendants we don't see but those near us. Why children, your children will have children I will never know, and their children's children will never have heard of me. No use to deny it. Looking backwards I don't know more than my Grandmammy and Granddaddy on either side, and all the rest is just a name here, a fact there, a rumor. All the people stretching back two or three generations to Pennsylvania and Wales, and back to Adam, are just lost in the fog and dust. We are isolated in the little clearing of now, and all the rest is tangled woods and thickets nobody much remembers. I always said it's how you enjoy that little opening in the wilderness that counts. That's all you have a chance to do. That's why I'm telling you this story.

Children, I'm sounding like an orator in my old age.

But it was clear Mama seen what was going on. She could read me like a schoolhouse slate. The truth is, I don't think Mama wanted me to ever get married. I was already eighteen, which was old for a girl in those days. You reached twenty and you had a good chance of being an old maid. Maybe it was because she had had so much trouble having her own children out in Mountain Creek that she feared for me. Or maybe it was her own grief of being brought down here from Virginny away from her kin that made her hold to me. Every time the subject come up Mama sulked and got silent. When Mama wouldn't talk to me, I felt the world had turned against me.

"What use has a woman got for the back-breaking burden of

clearing land and raising up a cabin back of beyond?" Mama said. "A woman that has to do the work of a house and work of the field and woods won't live to be gray. Rearing children alone will bring her down, much less the chopping and sawing, the snakes and painters."

Mama had got riled more than she intended, I think. Your Grandpa looked at his pipe, and looked at my Daddy, and looked at the fire. He couldn't say no more about moving to the West and be polite. He was embarrassed to argue with his hostess. Your Grandpa was a big rough feller in them days, but he never could stand no impoliteness. He looked like he wanted to change the subject, but that would be impolite too. He glanced at me and looked back at the fire.

"Nothing ever turns out the way people expect," my Daddy finally said. "Even if you plan for perfection you'll end up doing mostly what you never planned. The thing about new country is it gives a man another start."

"And a woman another burden," Mama said.

My Daddy looked into the fire for a few moments also. He didn't want words with Mama when she was riled up. The fire fluttered a little in the March wind coming down the chimney. "Time to heat up the iron," he said. "Mr. Richards needs him an ax and a grubbing hoe, and a garden hoe, and a spade."

"And I need to look for some seed," your Grandpa said.

"We can let you have some beans," my Daddy said. "But we ain't got hardly enough corn to last ourselves. You can try Wesleys' over in the cove. They might have corn to sell."

Your Grandpa got up and took his hat from the peg by the door. "Thank you kindly, ma'am," he said to Mama.

"You come back and see us," Mama said.

"If it's not too much trouble," your Grandpa said to my Daddy,

"I'd like the first letters of my name cut in all my tools, a double R. Realus Richards."

"Re-alus," my Daddy repeated to himself.

When the men was gone, I thought how strange a name that was. It was one I'd never heard before. While I worked, I said it over to myself. When I went out to throw scraps to the hog in the pen by the branch, I said it for the strange flavor it had on the tongue. It was good to get out of the house and in the sunshine. They was a light wind, warm and chilly by turns.

"Realus," I said again, and the wind seemed to magnify the sound. The name seemed to make things realer.

The old sow—we called her Sally—had laid down in the corner of the pen where the sun reached. I could hear her grunting with satisfaction all the way down the trail. Ain't nothing more easy than a sow laying in the sun with her pigs suckling at every tit. It's like a sound coming out of the dirt. I could smell the new grass crushed by my steps, and the creesie greens growing down by the branch.

Then I heard a louder grunt from old Sally, and a squeal from one of the pigs like something had disturbed it. Sometimes pigs will fight over a tit and I didn't think anything about it, until another squeal come louder and they was a snort from the sow, like she was disturbed and trying to get up with the little pigs holding onto her.

The pen was about four feet high, made of chestnut poles. The pigs was squealing louder. At first I didn't see nothing, and then this man stands up with a pig under his arm. I didn't recognize him at first, 'cause he had this old cap sideways on his head.

"Hey you," I said.

He looked at me in astonishment and started trying to climb

over the fence. It was higher than his straddle and he had trouble getting over still holding onto the pig.

I seen it was the son of that jackleg preacher that lived up the holler, the one named Roopy that didn't have hardly no sense but was caught looking in people's windows. He had a beard down to his chest.

"Hey you!" I hollered again. It looked like he was going to get across the fence and run. He didn't go to drop the pig. I don't know what come over me, for I had no thought of danger. I had the bucket of scraps and slop in my hand and I just slung it around to hit him. He was halfway across the fence and I swung to hit him on the shoulder to make him drop the pig. But he reached out his elbow to stop the bucket and the slop flew out all down his arm and across his face. You never seen such a look of surprise. His face was covered with crumbs of bread and bits of creesie greens, pot likker, and beet juice. He looked like somebody drunk that fell in his own puke.

He turned away and I hit him on the back with the bucket, and more of the slop splashed on his cap and run down his collar. He was in such a hurry of surprise to get away, he forgot to put down the pig. It squeezed out of his arm and fell back in the pen. I reckon he thought I was going to kill him with the bucket. I don't know what I was trying to do.

"I was just going to look," he said over his shoulder. But I slung again and more slop hit him up side of the face. He lit out running through the cobs and manure that slipped out the lower side of the pen. I watched him jump the branch and keep hoofing it, wiping his eyes and face, till he reached the woods.

There I stood trembling with madness and excitement, and most of my slop was gone.

T he next Sunday was the foot washing at the church. It was too cold in the middle of winter to have any foot washing at the meetinghouse 'cause they was no heat at all. When enough people got in the building, and Preacher Reece or another circuit-riding minister got to preaching, the little room would warm up fair enough. And in summer it was too hot, even with the door and windows open.

But along in spring, usually around Easter, when the weather opened up, they'd get water from the spring and fill a barrel by the church house. And from the barrel the deacons and deaconesses would fill their pans. After a long winter the grudges had built up in the community and in the congregation. A church is like a family and sometimes worser, with everybody arguing against everybody for leadership and authority. And the women like to pick at each other, always snipping and gossiping, and hurting each other's feelings.

Come spring it's time to wash it all away and start over. I think that's where they got the idea of a foot-washing service. That, and from the Bible where Mary washed the feet of Jesus and dried them with her hair. And it's a way of showing respect for your brothers and sisters in the fellowship, and humbling yourself. Of course, children, we know people can take pride in their humility.

I never was that religious, but I always went to service when the preacher come through. It was the only time everybody got together. I wondered if Realus would show up on a Sunday. He'd been staying at the tavern down the creek, and my Daddy almost had his tools made.

People had heard of me hitting Roopy up side of the head with the slop bucket. Some kind of grinned when they seen me at the store or along the road. The girls liked to giggle. Margie Travers said she heared I had a new boy friend, said better watch out, hanging around the hogpen with the likes of Roopy. The men didn't say nothing, but they give me curious looks, like they wondered was I a dangerous woman. Everybody seemed to think they was more to the story than just pig stealing.

But I seen Realus twice near my Daddy's smithy. "I'm going to be careful not to steal any pigs," he said to me and grinned. And I found myself blushing as red as his shirt. He was standing at the door watching Daddy hammer. He was so tall he had to stoop.

"Pardon me, sir," I said and slipped past him into the shop.

Women are not supposed to like the place a blacksmith works. But I always enjoyed going down there. If it was a cold day you could feel the glow from the forge, and the warmth of the work being done. The noise of the hammer ached in my head, but I liked the smell of the hot struck metal. Daddy had set up a water trompe to blow air into the forge, and you could hear water pouring down the shaft from the trough, and the hiss of air running out of the pipe to the fire. I never did understand how it worked, but Daddy said it was like a suction of water pulling air down after it.

"It's too dirty here for a lady," Realus said.

"Women has to work in all kinds of dirt," I said. "Men just want them to look pretty and clean, like they don't spend their time scrubbing and washing diapers." I was talking to cover my embarrassment. I didn't have no plan for what I said.

"It'll be the day when you're seen changing diapers," Realus said.

I give my Daddy the knife Mama had sent for him to sharpen. "You coming to meeting?" I said to Realus on my way out. I didn't much care what I said.

"They wouldn't let me in no meetinghouse," he said. "Take me a week to get cleaned up enough to go."

"They'll let anybody into the meetinghouse," I said. He had followed me a few steps beyond the door of the shed.

"Will you promise not to bring your slop bucket?" he said and laughed. He looked so proud of hisself I hauled off and kicked his leg. I ever did have a quick temper.

"Oh, oh, oh," he said, hopping on one foot and exaggerating like I'd half killed him. My Daddy was watching from the door.

"You're a dangerous woman," Realus said. "Was you to go to the West, the Indians would all run."

I walked on back to the house. I didn't want to say nothing else to him.

But your Grandpa come to the meeting on Sunday. He stood outside with the other big boys talking until service started. Then he come in and set on the back bench with the backsliders.

The foot-washing service ain't like nothing else. They's a solemnity and dignity to it. The preacher and the deacons and the deaconesses put white towels over their shoulders, and they fill pans from the barrel of spring water that has been warming outside church. Sometimes they'll build a fire to heat water in a cauldron on a chilly day. Nobody wants their feet washed in cold water, except on a hot day.

It was dark in the meetinghouse, with only two windows and the door, and it took my eyes a few minutes to get used to the gloom. Something about the shadows makes the church seem more sacred. But us kids had always used the cover of the dark to punch and kick and tickle each other while prayer was going on. I don't suppose you grandchildren ever did nothing like that when you was in church? No, I thought not.

Once I got seated by Mama, I didn't turn around to look, but I knowed Realus was watching me. It made my skin prickle all over me, under my dress and down to my ankles. I told myself it was the excitement of the service, but I knowed better.

I set there trying to work out the truth of what my Daddy had said before we come to meeting. "An early Easter makes a late spring," he said when we come out into the chilly air. I'd heard him say it a dozen times, a hundred times. But I'd never paid it no attention before. To keep my mind off your Grandpa I wondered what the saying could mean. How could the time of Easter have anything to do with the weather? Easter, I heard a preacher say once, was based on the Old Testament calendar, on the Passover, which was based on the waxing of the moon.

I could see how something as powerful and heavenly as Easter could have a great effect. But I didn't see how an early Easter would make a late spring, unless spring just seemed later because Easter had come and gone.

I couldn't puzzle it out. Maybe my mind was too much on your Grandpa, anyway. But some things you can't never study out. They remain a mystery, like things of the heart.

The deacons and deaconesses was bringing in the pans of water mixed from the cauldron and the barrel. Everybody on the front two benches took off their shoes. It was customary for the children to sit middle and back of the meetinghouse at foot-washing service. The elders of the congregation only washed the feet of adults. They was no law about it, but it wouldn't look right for men to wash women's feet and for a graybeard deacon to wash the feet of some snot-nose boy.

For the first time I realized what I had done. Thinking too much about your Grandpa and love things, I had set down on the second bench with Mama. And Mama hadn't reminded me. She must have thought I had decided to be one of the adults. Or maybe Mama, who could always read my mind, had decided to let me make a fool of myself. In any case, she give me no warning, and then it was too late. The house was packed full as a box of prunes, and they was no place to move to. I could either stay where I was or get up and leave. Either way was embarrassing.

I glanced back at Realus and he was looking straight at me. I blushed then brighter than I had before. I must have lit up the little church.

The women all around me took off their shoes without raising their skirts or petticoats, and put their feet on the cold pine floor. Mama didn't give me no help; she took off her shoes like all the rest. I had to make up my mind quick. Maybe if I just left my shoes on the deaconesses would pass me by. Or they might order me to take off my shoes in front of the whole church.

The deaconesses Shirley Cantrell and Laura Blaine knelt in front of the first bench, the towels over their shoulders like the sashes of uniforms. On the other side, the deacons Cantrell and Blaine knelt in front of the first row of men. My Daddy stood at the side to follow them, as he was a younger deacon.

The preacher stood up at the front of the room. "Brethren and sistren," he said. "If I have ought against thee, if I have offended thee, if I have raised my voice, if I have held a grudge, if I have born false witness, or if I have in any way wronged thee, let the offense be put away. By this act of humility we wash away our petty differences, our spites and proud words. Following the example of our Lord who washed the feet of his disciples, I ask forgiveness for deeds of malice and omission."

The congregation begun to sing as the foot washing commenced. You could hear the slosh of water as the washers proceeded along the front benches. I sung too, but my heart wasn't in it. I wanted to ask Mama what to do, but she was ignoring me. I had got myself in a fix and she was going to let me solve it on my own. I looked around and everybody was singing. The preacher was singing too. Soon as the deacons finished, he would wash their feet. And then the deaconesses would wash each other's feet.

I turned around again and it was like everybody in church was looking at me and wondering what I was going to do. Mama had took off her shoes and Mrs. Childress on the other side had took off her shoes. Realus was still watching me. And I even thought Preacher Reece was watching me too.

Because of my consternation I wasn't getting no good out of the service. I didn't feel no fellowship, and no easing away of grudges and fears. I just wanted to get away.

"I've got to go," I whispered to Mama. It sounded like I needed to answer a call of nature.

"Are you sick?" she whispered.

Preacher Reece was looking at me.

"I'm going out," I whispered.

I knowed it was bad to interrupt a service. I gathered up my cloak and stood. Every eye at the meeting was on me. They thought I was having some sort of fit or possession and was going to shout, or maybe speak in tongues. Then they seen me hurrying around people's feet and knees toward the door. It was like everybody's feet stuck out in front of me, and I almost tripped myself. Hands reached out to steady me. This is a disgrace, I thought, but I don't care. I had to get out of there.

As I got more desperate to reach the outside the faces blurred and all I could see was the door with people standing in front of it. The way out was blocked. Sometimes during a revival meeting when the preaching gets hot and the preacher begins the altar call a big man will stand at the door to prevent the sinners under conviction from running outside.

But just when I got to the back of the room somebody stood up and pushed the standers aside. I didn't even look to see who it was. I pushed the door back on its leather hinges and rushed out into the cool Sunday air.

It was wonderful to be in the open. The air in the valley was different on a Sunday 'cause nobody was working, burning off brush on the creek bank or pounding iron. I could hear the tinkle of our cowbell off in the edge of the woods. I wiped my face on my sleeve. Hadn't realized I was sweating in the meeting-house.

Somebody stepped behind me. They had followed me out of the service. It was your Grandpa, and he stood there in his red shirt looking at me. It had been him that pushed aside the crowd to let me out.

"I had to get outside," I said.

"I seen that," he said. "I seen all along you was fidgety."

That seemed the most tender thing I'd ever heard a man say, that he had felt for me and seen what I was going through. That was when I fell in love, was right there. If I was falling before, that was when I admitted it. My knees was shaky, and I held onto the rail they tied the horses to.

"You need to cool off," Realus said. And he took my arm. They was nobody in sight in all the valley because everybody was at the foot-washing service.

"Let's walk down to the branch," I said.

"But we'll stay away from the hogpen," your Grandpa said. I didn't feel like teasing or laughing a bit. I took his arm and walked toward the stream.

I never did tell Realus I agreed, but he knowed I had. I wanted to go to the West with him more than anything I had ever wanted. But it scared me to know we was going. Because I remembered how Mama had carried on whenever I mentioned getting married, and how Daddy disapproved of me courting.

Seemed like their attitude was marriage was just for theirselves and not for younger folks. I never acted like that to my younguns. I never stood in the way of my children courting, when it was with decent people. What's that? I always encouraged the young to have a good time. It's one of the blessings of life to go out with those you like when you're young.

My Mama used to have a saying: If you can get a girl over fool's hill she will do all right. I thought I'd got myself over fool's hill long before, walking home with boys after meeting, kissing in the shadows at infare parties, holding hands after corn shuckings. Don't laugh children. Your Grandma was young once, hard as it is to see. I used to think that about my elders too. How had they ever been young and gone courting and had fun? Younguns just see their elders as old people, which is what they look like, and usually act like.

Realus and me walked along the branch, and a little way up the Shimer Road, until meeting let out. By then I knowed I was going with him. I was shuddering too with excitement, and with the thought of talking to Mama.

"Why can't we just go on and go to the Holsten?" I said.

"'Cause I've got to get my tools," Realus said.

"I'm serious," I said. "We don't need to make a ceremony of it."

"You're not serious," Realus said. "It would grieve your Ma and Pa not to know where you went. And it would grieve you afterward to think you had grieved them." We walked up to the head of the holler where the cows was grazing below the spring.

"We'll have our own cows in our own meadow," your Grandpa said. "And our own chicken house with hens and a rooster."

"I want some banty hens," I said. "And some of them little Cornish hens."

"I want a great big Dominicker rooster," your Grandpa said.

"And I want a guinea or two," I said. "I like to hear them pottaracking across the valley of a morning."

We must have stood there talking like that for half an hour, putting off going back to the house. We listed all kinds of things we wanted in our homestead, from spinning wheel to candle molds. We got carried away.

"It'll take us ten years to accumulate and make all that," your Grandpa said.

"Specially if we have to bring it all the way to the Holsten," I said.

"They'll be stores opening up in Watauga," he said. "And besides, we have all the rest of our lives to fix up the place."

We started walking back down the branch. I felt a cold pain down my spine just thinking about my Daddy.

When we got to the house Mama was boiling mush at the fireplace. A chicken was baking on the spit.

"Your Mama's having to fix dinner all by herself," my Daddy said.

"We went for a walk," I said.

"You hadn't ought to run out of service," Mama said.

"I was too young to have my feet washed," I said.

"But you're not too young to go off walking up the branch," Mama said.

"Mr. Jarvis," Realus said. "And Mrs. Jarvis."

Everything got quiet in the house. Young Henry set on the steps to the loft. Realus still stood by the door. Our eyes hadn't adjusted to the dark inside.

"Mr. Jarvis," he said. "Petal and me are thinking about getting married and going off to the West."

"I didn't think you was studying on settling here," Daddy said.

"I've done got a place there," Realus said.

"I never looked for my girl to be took away to the Holsten," Daddy said.

"You said yourself they's wolves and Indians there," Mama said.

"I ain't afeared," I said.

"I'm afeared for you," Mama said.

You younguns laugh at me for talking about courting and such. But you'll be old one day looking back on your youth. Your Grandpa and me was just kids then. Young people always feel like they're making the world new. I guess they have to feel that way. They have to feel they are the first to find the right way. It don't help to know your elders was once young and in love and done outlandish things. Better to think of yourself launching out into new places where nobody's ever been before.

We was planning to go out into the new country. That's why I was thrilled more than I was scared. What young girl wouldn't be excited, to have a man like your Grandpa and the prospect of going off to the new land of the Holsten? Soon I would have my own place. And I was a healthy girl. I wanted to have me a family.

We didn't get nowhere talking to Mama and Daddy. I could see they never would agree for me to go off to the woods of the West. They depended on me as their oldest child, and they hadn't raised me to run off where they would never see me again, and where they would never see their grandchildren.

"Why don't you all come to the Holsten?" Realus said to my Daddy. "They's a need of smiths there."

"I'm too old to pick up and go," Daddy said. "I cleared up land and settled here, and I'm too old to do it again."

"Them that goes now will be the rulers and landowners," Realus said.

"Them that goes now will die of the wolves or the milksick," Mama said. Milksick was something that always come to her mind when they was danger or fear. Where she growed up in Virginny, they was lots of milksick, and places in the coves they fenced off in milksick pens 'cause that was where they thought the cows caught the sickness. Some people said it was a weed like nightshade, and some people said it was a vine or creeper the cow eat that poisoned the milk. But others swore it was some mineral in the ground, or a swamp gas that leaked out and was breathed by the cow. My Daddy used to say there wasn't no such thing as milksick, and that made Mama really mad. That's why he said it. "How come so many have died of it?" she'd say.

"People is always dying of something," my Daddy would say.

"You'll *think* there ain't no such thing if it ever touches your family," Mama would say.

"If milksick will kill you why don't it kill the cow?" Daddy would say. But no matter how much Daddy argued, Mama still lived in deathly fear of milksick. And from time to time we heard rumors of people dying back in the hollers. They was patches all over the mountains fenced off where somebody's cow was supposed to have got the milksick. They was like the Devil's Acre, fenced off to never be used.

"I've heard the water of the Holsten ain't fit to drink," Mama said.

"My spring's good as any on this side of the mountains," Realus said.

"It don't become a daughter to think of leaving her folks forever," my Daddy said.

"A girl has to have her own life," I said.

"A girl that forgets her family will be forgot by her own children," Daddy said, turning the talk sad and grim, like he was quoting Scripture. That's the way my Daddy done things. He would talk around nice as you please, and then suddenly he would take a stand. And they was nothing going to move him from that stand.

Realus didn't say no more. They was nothing to be gained by fussing. I helped Mama bake the chicken, and we had dumplings for Sunday dinner. That was Daddy's favoritest dish. But he didn't seem to enjoy it. The foot-washing service had been ruined by his daughter, and now his dinner had been ruint too. And he had spent the week making tools for the man that wanted to carry her off to the West.

Realus and me didn't say nothing else about going away, 'cause we seen Mama and Daddy would never agree. But parents ought to know you can't stop a girl that wants to get married. The truth is you can't do nothing with a girl in love. A young girl in love has a will to override any opposition. In fact, opposition seems to strengthen her determination. It's the way the Lord has made women I guess, so they'll get married and keep the population going. A girl that's in love don't want to help herself.

We didn't talk no more about the West, but we started planning to get our stuff together and go. We'd have to leave in the night to be far gone by the time Mama and Daddy missed me. That would take some preparation, because we had to carry all our things and travel fast. Besides my clothes and cloth and sewing things, and some cooking things, pots and pans heavy and loud to carry, Realus had to take his tools and seeds. He didn't have but one horse and couldn't afford no more. We was going to have to walk to the Holsten, and let the horse carry everything in packs.

I got me a good pair of shoes. I got Old Man Parker that lived

down the branch to make them. I traded him a sack of goose
feathers I'd saved to make a feather bed. It would have been good
to have the feather bed in the West, but I couldn't walk there
without strong shoes. I don't know if Mama suspicioned anything
or not when she seen the shoes, almost heavy as a man's. If she
did, she didn't say a thing. Women are smarter than men about
situations like that. They know when it's no use to talk, where a
man will jump in 'cause he has to speak, bless his heart. Those
shoes was made of shiny calf leather, and when I pulled them on I
felt I could walk to the far ocean if I had to.

All week I tried to think of things I'd have to have in the West.
We don't notice the things we use because we have them all the
time. Spoons you can cut out of wood, but a thimble and needles
you have to take. A frying pan and kittle you have to take. A bolt
or two of cloth would be worth its weight in diamonds over the
mountains. A gourd full of salt was a must, even though they are
licks in the West where salt can be boiled from the spring water.
Tea I knowed Realus would bring from the store down in Charlotte, 'cause he was fond of his cup more than any man I ever
seen. You start thinking of the things you use every day, and the
list could go on forever, what with little things like beeswax and
blueing and pneumony salve.

But the opposite is true too. It's amazing how little you need to
survive in the woods. All you have to have is yourself and your
man to start over, and your health. A woman carries in her body
everything else she needs to make the future generations.

We didn't have no sweetening then but honey and the maple
sugar they made in the high mountains. Long sweetening didn't
come till later. You could buy sugar, but it wasn't a necessity.

Was I nervous about running away? Of course I was scared
about leaving home. I was a respectful and obedient girl for the

most part. And was I worried about marriage? Every girl is worried about marriage, 'cause it's all unknown to her. If a girl ain't been with a man before, she waits for her husband to teach her about marriage. But a girl has to trust herself and her man. It's the thing she wants to do more than anything else, to get married, and to trust her man.

So I put together two bundles of things, everything I thought I had to have on the Holsten. I put them under a quilt in the attic where me and little Henry slept. Mama never did climb up to the attic, and I reckoned she wouldn't notice one of her thimbles was gone and three needles. Realus was going to get some needles down at the store, but I wanted some spare ones in case he forgot. He was more apt to remember fishhooks than needles.

Four or five times a day I went up to the attic and took things out of my bundles and put things in. They wasn't room for but one quilt, and I knowed it would be a long time before I could piece together another one in the woods. Aunt Docie had give me that quilt for when I was married, and I didn't want to steal none of Mama's. Your Grandpa and me would have to make do with a buffalo robe or such as we could find in the West.

Mama seen me going up and down the steps more times than usual. When Henry wasn't around I'd go up there to sort my things again.

"Why you keep running upstairs?" Mama said.

"It's time for some spring cleaning," I said, halfway answering her and halfway not. I wasn't sure I was fooling Mama.

We made our plans to leave on a Saturday night. They was nearly a full moon then that would be good for traveling. And somehow it seemed easier to get away on a Sabbath day than on a work day. By the time people woke up and got ready for meeting, we could be way up the road.

Realus said he would have the horse loaded up and waiting down by the branch at midnight. I worked all day Saturday thinking, by this time tomorrow I'll be well on my way over the mountains. Everything around the place seemed dearer to me, knowing I wouldn't see it no more. I wanted to hug Mama and Henry, but it wouldn't have looked right. I never thought of hugging my Daddy, because he wasn't the hugging sort of man. I almost cried when I went to the spring, thinking I wouldn't taste water again from the spring that come from under the poplar.

Everybody washed up on Saturday night as usual, and I went up to the loft and pretended to be asleep. It took forever for my Daddy to finish up with his bath, and throw out the water and go to bed. They was a crack in the logs and I tried to look out to see if Realus was down by the branch. I waited and waited for the clock downstairs to ring twelve. Seemed like my heart was going to jump out of my chest if I had to wait another minute.

What do you say? Did we plan to get married?

Your Grandpa said we'd stop at the first settlement we come to and get a preacher to marry us. Or if we didn't see one on the way, he'd get the first circuit rider that come through to say the ceremony. He didn't mean for us not to be legally wed. But it was different then. Being married in the sight of God means you made your vows to each other, and in your heart. Back then you had the official ceremony when you could. That's the way you funeraled people too. You buried them when they died and then when a preacher come through in the spring or summer he performed the service. When a preacher come to some places, they'd be four or five funerals to conduct and maybe half a dozen couples to unite in marriage, though they might already have children.

Finally the old clock struck, and I got my bundles from under the quilt and tiptoed to the ladder. They was a glow from the fireplace, and more light come through the window and laid like a sheet on the floor. I climbed down silent as I could, though the rungs creaked and my bundles rubbed together. When I finally got to the floor I stood for a few seconds listening, and then eased a tiny step at a time toward the door. I just hoped nobody had left a pan or dipper in the way. I could hear my Daddy snoring.

They was a wooden latch and I lifted it gentle as I could. The wood groaned a little. But I got it open and eased through the door. And I was almost outside when somebody touched me on the shoulder. I near jumped out of my hide.

"Shhhh," Mama said, and followed me out into the yard.

"I want you to take this," she said, and pushed a quilt against me. From the cold satiny feeling I could tell it was her best.

"Mama . . . ," I started to say, but couldn't go on.

"You'll be happy," she said. "I pray that you'll be happy." Then she was gone back into the house. I stood there listening to her close the door. She didn't bolt it from inside though, so Daddy couldn't blame her for letting me go. Or maybe she thought I might change my mind and want to come back in.

It was a coon-hunting night, with the moon bright as the light in a dream. I stumbled down the path with my bundles and the quilt. Your Grandpa and the horse stood like shadows beside the branch.

You want to know what it was like the night we run away? Besides the moonlight, which made the mountains look like some place on the moon, in another world, I don't remember much but the excitement.

Your Grandpa took me in his arms when I got to the branch. "This is the start of a long way," he said. I could smell some likker on his breath. He'd had a drink at the tavern to warm him up. Your Grandpa always liked a drink at Christmas and on special occasions, though he wasn't in general a drinking man.

I thought, the Holsten sure is a long way, but he meant the long path we'd go together, all through our lives. The drink had made him think those big thoughts. And he was right, it was the start of a long way.

We didn't use no lantern as we picked our way up the trail by the branch. I thought it was because the moon was so bright. But when we got to the woods your Grandpa still didn't light no lantern, and I realized he hadn't brought one. With all the seeds and tools and salt on that horse he didn't have room for no lantern. We'd have to do without, or make one when we got there. That was my first inkling of what I was in for, learning to make, or make do without.

I found my way trembling along the Shimer Road to the head of the branch and we climbed between the pastures to the start of the next creek valley. I'd been that way to pick huckleberries, but it looked different in the dark. I was already lost when Realus said, "Let's turn aside here."

"Why we turning?"

"To go to the Holsten," he said. "You want to go there don't you?"

"Reckon I do," I said. It didn't seem like we was following the right road.

"Let's be gone," Realus said.

We descended into the next valley and I could smell a creek nearby, and hear shoalwater. They was a damp mossy smell and the thrill of water pouring. Then I heard a mill turning, one that had been disconnected from its stones and was turning fast.

"Is that the Shimer mill?" I said. I'd heard the Shimer Road went to a mill way over the mountains.

"You're all mixed up," Realus said. "We're already on the road to the West, and you're still thinking of places back there."

That was when I come closest to losing my nerve. It was like Realus had accused me of looking back, the way Lot's wife did in the Bible. For a minute I was sad, and my eyes moistened. But Realus couldn't see those tears in the moonlight. I wiped them away and set my face forward. They was going to be no looking back. I would foller my man to the West, as I had promised to do.

Realus was up ahead leading the horse and I walked behind smelling that old horse's smell. When they stopped, I near run into the back of that animal. I stood and listened, and heard first a loud holler, then another. It was like somebody was hurt or in trouble. And then another beller come and we recognized it was hounds. They was after a coon or possum. Or maybe it was a fox hunt. If it was fox they was after, there wouldn't be men with the dogs. The men would be somewhere by a camp fire listening. I could feel Realus stiffen in the dark. He didn't want to meet up with anybody, until we was more distant from the settlement.

"Shhhh," he said back over his shoulder.

But the dogs kept coming on and getting louder. You would have thought the valley was full of dogs, the way their yelps and bellers echoed around. I was getting scared. Maybe Daddy had found me gone and put the dogs after us. But my Daddy didn't have any hound dogs. He'd have to borrow them from the Whitakers or the Jeters.

I walked up and stood beside Realus. "Just stay still," he said. "They may run right by us."

We kept quiet, Realus holding the horse by the bridle. I felt a sickness in my belly as the dogs got closer. I took your Grandpa by the hand, and found he already had his gun out. He must have took it from the horse's pack soon as he heard the hounds.

It was terrible, feeling the dogs coming at you. The air was filled with their yelping and hollering. Men is supposed to enjoy hound music. They become experts at knowing hounds by voice and interpreting the message of the baying. But I took no pleasure in the howls getting closer.

Once the sounds seemed to fade, and I thought the dogs might have turned aside or gone off on another scent. But it was only a pause, like they had lost the trail for a while and found it again. It's hard to judge the distance of hounds in the dark, but you could tell they wasn't far away.

Just the sound of the hounds coming at us made me feel like I'd done something terrible. And it's true I was running away. But just being chased makes you feel criminal. You can imagine how a slave feels with dogs on his tracks.

Realus put his arm around me. "We won't go back," he said. "No matter what." But it was partly like a question.

"I won't go back," I said.

The dogs busted out on the path ahead, and they was lanterns behind them. In no time the dogs was bellering around our feet. One hound sounded like a bull choking. The horse pulled back and your Grandpa had to hold him with both hands. He was afraid the packs would slide off if the horse rared up. Your Grandpa whistled a little to show the dogs we was friendly. But they kept hollering. We had crossed their trail and throwed them off the scent of the coon.

Somebody come running up with a lantern. I couldn't see nothing but a light, and a hand holding it high.

"Who's messing with my dogs?" he called.

"We're not messing with anything," Realus said.

"Identify yourself or I'll shoot," the man said.

I held to Realus's arm while he held onto the horse. Other men was stumbling out of the woods with lanterns.

"I'm Realus Richards, and this is my wife Petal, and we're on our way to the Holsten," your Grandpa said, firm-like, but at the same time friendly.

The men gathered around us with their lanterns and you never seen such wild-looking creatures. They was sweating and panting from running through the woods and their hats looked like dead birds perched on their heads. Three-cornered hats always looked awful when they got old.

"You all confused my dogs," the leader said. The hounds kept circling and barking at us. It was like we was in the middle of a whirlpool of dogs.

"We was just going along the road," Realus said. "We didn't aim to confuse nothing."

"Where you folks going?" the leader said.

"We're on the way to the West," your Grandpa said.

"In the middle of the night you're going to the West?" The man looked us up and down like we was thieves. He looked at me especially.

"We wanted to travel by moonlight to make better time," your Grandpa said. "Long as we could see the road."

"You must have crossed the trail of that coon," the man said.

"We didn't see no coon," Realus said.

"I told you that dog was lying," one of the other men said. He was taller than the leader.

"Preacher don't lie," the leader said. He turned to his companion with a look of hatred.

"Maybe he was just exaggerating," another man said. "They was a coon, but now he's gone."

"Any man says my dog's lying is a cock-eyed liar hisself," the leader said.

The hounds was milling around and bellering and the men got to arguing and it looked like it was coming to fists. They blocked our path ahead, and Realus and me looked at each other wondering what to do. The moon was getting low in the west.

Suddenly Realus pointed to a pine tree just ahead. "There's the coon," he said. Nobody heard him in all the confusion.

"There's your coon," he said, pointing. "I seen the flash of his eyes." The leader watched him point and looked toward the pine. He must have glimpsed the coon's eyes too, for he run that way and the others followed. And your Grandpa and me moved on.

We hadn't gone more than a mile before your Grandpa said, "Here's where we turn off the road and find a place to sleep."

I was getting tired by then and was glad to hear him mention sleep. I could tell your Grandpa was tense, and I was excited too. Ducking under limbs and pushing brush aside he led us out through the woods. It felt like a poplar thicket. The limbs was wet with dew and cold. We stumbled deeper into the thicket.

Finally we got to a place where the ground was level and smooth, but with a kind of steep bank behind it. I could hear water somewhere close. "This is a good spot," Realus said.

"It feels surrounded," I said.

We spread blankets on the ground, and your Grandpa tied the horse to a poplar tree. We didn't even build a fire it was such a mild night. The moon was gone in the west by then.

We spent our wedding night there under the poplars. I hung my clothes on a limb and got under the blanket and quilt. I remember thinking as we got under the covers that this was the best way to start married life, without even a roof over your head and flat on the ground.

Realus used to say loving is the Lord's gift to us, to allow us to share the joy in creation. And I reckon that is so. But it's the surprise that is best. Studying on it too much can make it wrong. But after a day's work of duty, love's an added blessing.

I woke cold, and all the gladness of the night was gone. We had walked so far in the dark in our excitement, and now I was stiff and sore. And the damp had settled right into my bones. That's the way it goes, grandchildren. You do things in the rush of newness and surprise, and in the gray morning you have to pick up and start all over again. It took will, even at the most joyous time of my life, to sit up and look around.

Realus had already struck his flint and got a fire going. I'd heard my Daddy say how a hunter can take the flint from his rifle and strike a spark from it. If it is a wet day, he can sprinkle a little gunpowder on the tinder to make sure the fire catches. Your Grandpa had put two rocks alongside the little fire and had a pot boiling there, and a pan with some bacon frying.

"I always needed a man to wait on me," I said, crouching to the flames. My hair was tangled from the night.

"I always needed a woman to wait on me," he said.

I set down beside him. That was our first hearth I reckon, two rocks by the fire on the little creek bank. I didn't even know what creek it was. We was twenty miles from the settlement by then, and I'd never been that far to the west. And I thought, from these two rocks and this fire, and these two people and the work of their hands, and the loving of their bodies, we'll build a family. We have everything we need.

Your Grandpa poured some tea from a can and soaked it in the boiling pot. Then he poured us each a tin cup full. Children, I never tasted anything as good as that hot tea. I was cold and shivering and sore and stiff. Realus pulled a dead log up to the fire and we set on that and eat bacon and hoecakes and sipped the burning hot tea. We didn't have no cream but I didn't mind.

When good tea goes into your belly and spreads through your veins and fibers it's like lights are turned up. Everything gets sharp and clear. And things seem open and possible.

"Well, old gal," Realus said. "Do you think we're going to make it?"

"We better make it," I said. "'Cause I can't go back now."

I could have set there for hours, but it was time to stir. That was the first time I ever washed pots with sand. We didn't have no soap to waste, and I was in too big a hurry to fill up a pan to wash anyway. I took the pot and skillet down to the creek and scrubbed the grease off with white sand and rinsed them good. White sand will get a pan gleaming in no time, though it will scratch a mug or plate.

I had the things nigh washed when I noticed the creek was getting muddy. I had stirred up the water a little scrubbing the things, but not near enough to make the whole creek cloudy.

"Look here," I said to your Grandpa, who was loading things back on the horse.

"What do you see?" he said.

The creek had started getting dingy, a dishwater tinge, like after a light shower. And then it turned brown, and reddish-brown, like somebody had dropped a bucket of dirt in above.

"Looky there," I said.

"They must have had a gullywasher upstream," Realus said. "But I ain't seen no cloud or heard no thunder."

"That much mud wouldn't wash out of the woods no way, unless they was cleared fields," I said.

We stood there puzzled by the dirty water.

"Could it be one of them siphon springs you hear about?" I said. "The kind that dribbles out and then gushes, almost dries up and then spates?"

"Never heard of a siphon spring being muddy," your Grandpa said. "Besides, this is a creek, not a spring branch."

We loaded up the horse and got ready to move on.

"We're going up that way, anyway," he said. "We'll see what is making such a mess."

You want to know what a siphon spring is? I never really understood it myself. But I've been told they're springs that ebb and flow. They have a big room inside a mountain that fills up and spills through an outlet that tilts up and then down. That outlet acts like a siphon when it starts draining and empties all the water pooled up. Then the hole starts filling up again and nothing runs out till it's full.

We followed the creek up the valley through the poplars. It seemed the stream got muddier the further we went. The water looked bright red in the bare woods. It was like the earth was bleeding toward the head of the valley. It even crossed my mind they might be a battle with Indians, or a slaughter of cattle up there, though I knowed the creek was really colored with mud.

We had gone maybe two miles when we heard voices and banging ahead. I was getting scared and held back. Your Grandpa stopped the horse and we listened. They was banging and ringing.

"Could be somebody making a mill," Realus said. "And they're sharpening a pair of millstones."

"But why would they build a mill where there ain't no fields?" I said.

"Maybe they's settlements nearby we ain't seen," he said.

I could tell Realus was thinking of going around whatever was up there. We was heading for the Holsten and didn't need to be stopped by any devilment going on in the woods. But I think his curiosity wouldn't let him leave without seeing what it was.

We continued up the creek, which got muddier and muddier. Then we seen a clearing ahead, and the flash of bodies working along the creek. I was startled by the sight of bare flesh.

"What kind of heathens are them?" I said. "Are they Indians?"

"No, they're white people," your Grandpa said.

I might have held back from the clearing of half-naked men, but we had been seen. A big man with a black hat and no shirt on stopped shoveling and grabbed a rifle-gun. He run toward us, his hat flapping. "What you'uns doing here?" he said.

"We're on our way to the West," Realus said.

"This ain't no way West," the man said. Others had stopped work and was watching us. The clearing was maybe a hundred yards long, and all churned up with dirt and mud and piles of rocks.

"We may have got a little lost," your Grandpa said.

"Who told you to come here?" the man said.

"Nobody told us to come here."

"You heard about us and you thought you'd come dig some for yourself," the man said. "Next thing there'll be hordes descending out of the woods like buzzards to pick us clean."

"Ain't nobody else coming," your Grandpa said.

"You're the first one to bring a woman here," the man said, eyeing me.

"We was just passing on," I said.

The half-naked man stood on the pile of dirt and rocks and looked at us. The other men in the clearing was watching us too.

"Can your woman cook?" he said.

"Sure she can cook," Realus said.

"Then if she cooks some for us, we will cut you in," he said.

"Cut me in what?"

"Don't act so ignorant you don't know we found gold here last week," the man said. Realus looked at me.

"I ain't no prospector," your Grandpa said. "We was just passing through."

"I ain't no prospector either," the man said. "I'm Jones the Preacher. And that over there's Owens the Peddler. And when we get the gold out of this mud we can all go back to being whatever we was. Except we'll be richer."

Me and Realus was caught. If we tried to leave, they might shoot us to keep us from telling other people what they was doing. If they was gold, we could get a little to take to the West. All around it seemed better to stay and take a cut. At least, that's the way it looked then.

I got out some of my pots and pans and built up a fire at the edge of the clearing, a ways back from the mud and pits. They had set up screens for sifting the dirt. And everybody that had a pan was out in the creek scooping and sloshing. They'd shake the pan a little and look, pick something out and shake the pan again. From time to time one of the men would look at me and make me uncomfortable. Somebody had shot a mess of squirrels for dinner.

Realus got his shovel and tied the horse to a poplar. The man called Jones the Preacher told him to start shoveling in the bank. While I was heating the water I tried to make sense of what everybody was doing. They was men going this way and that, some carrying buckets and boxes and dumping the dirt. It was like watching trout circle in a pool, the way they heaved and hurried, then hunkered over a pan or pile of mud.

Finally I seen the pattern of their work. Some of the men, like your Grandpa, was digging into the banks to loosen the dirt. Then they carried it to the screen and separated the big rocks out. Then in the pans they washed and shook the load until the dirt melted and drained away and only pebbles and sand was left. The pebbles and sand they washed still more, to sort out the nuggets and gold dust from the rest.

I wondered how much gold dust they had found. No doubt Preacher Jones kept it all hid where only he knowed. He seemed like the kind of feller who would look out for hisself.

"I want to show you something," the preacher said behind me. He liked to have scared me where I bent over the fire. I turned around and thought he was taking his pants off. He unbuttoned the top button, and pushing a gallus aside, reached down inside his straddle. Then he pulled out something fat and yellow. I took a step back, and saw it was a deerskin pouch.

"Looky there," he said, grinning at my surprise.

But I didn't reach out and take the dirty poke.

"Don't you want to see?" he said. "Here, let me show you." And he opened the little sack and poured out in his hand what looked like bright sand with little rocks.

"Looky there," he said, and stared into my eyes. "They's enough here for a man and young woman to go wherever they wanted to and live like quality."

He leaned closer to me, looking into my eyes. His beard was black but had streaks of gray. "You and me could go anywhere we wanted," he said and smiled at the pile of gold in his hand. I took another step back.

"Don't you want to come?" he said, and reached to touch me.

"We're going to the Holsten," I said.

"What's on the Holsten?" he said. "Besides snakes and wildcats and hard work?"

"We're just married," I said.

"The Lord can marry and unmarry," he said and grinned.

I backed halfway into the poplar brush to get away from him.
"Just give me a little kiss," he said. "And I will give you this
poke. Just a little kiss to try me out."

He was pushing me back against the poplars. "You'll have to
ask my husband," I blurted out. It was a silly thing to say, but it
was what come to mind. The preacher looked at me for a second,
then he busted out laughing. You could hear him laugh all across
the clearing. I seen your Grandpa look toward us as the preacher
stepped back. I bent over the fire, stirring the stew.

It seemed like each man in the clearing was looking at me every
chance they got. I must have been the only woman they had seen
in weeks. It made me kind of shivery to know all their eyes was on
me. I was making hoecakes on a spade I had washed in the creek
above the digging, and I was making stew from the squirrels they
had already killed. A breeze had come up and besides the ring and
grind of the shovels, and the rattle and slosh of the pans, they was
tall poplars rubbing in the woods behind me. You could hear
them rubbing their necks and groaning. It was a sound like nails
pulling out of planks.

A little feller with a red face and a red beard come up to my fire.
He was streaming sweat and he had freckles all over his shoulders
and chest. "Name's Jenkins," he said.

"How do," I said.

"You need salt," he said. "I got a gourd over here in my bag."

"I got some salt," I said.

He couldn't take his eyes off my skirt. He couldn't help hisself,
though his face was getting even redder than before. I felt sorry
for him. He must not have seen a woman in months.

"I ain't got no pepper," he said. "I wish I had some pepper to
offer you."

"We can do without," I said.

He just stood there, like he didn't know what to say. His pants was covered with mud, and he was dripping with sweat. He must not have been more than eighteen.

"You go back to work," I said. "And we'll have dinner ready before too long."

"You let me know if I can help," he said, and turned to walk back to the pits.

The men worked like Trojans in the gravel and dirt. It always amazed me how men like to move around earth. They like to cut up the dirt and shift it around and reshape it.

But it seemed to me, as I watched them sweat and strain with the heavy loads, digging and carrying, that they was no longer quite human. They had become a power, working beyond will and choice. They could have been a force of the elements, breaking apart and sorting, taking and rejecting. At the very least they seemed like animals working there, doing things they did not understand.

It come to me the piles and puddles resembled a dung heap. They worked like flies on a manure pile, their skin white as maggots bending and twisting. You wouldn't even want to describe the mess that fouled the creek, that touched into the woods and stained every bit of grass and every stick the men had touched. It was like they had turned the woods into a pit of filth. It sickened me as I turned back to the dinner I was fixing.

When I banged on the pot with my spoon all the men come running except Realus. They didn't even wash their hands or put on their shirts. They come dirty and sweaty to the stew pot and dipped squirrel meat and taters onto their hoecakes and eat them like they was tarts. Their faces was dirty and they eat like hogs come to a trough.

I looked back to the creek and your Grandpa was still shoveling mud out of the bank. He had took off his red shirt and his white skin glowed in the sun. I dipped some stew onto a hoecake and carried it to him.

"How come you didn't eat?" I said. He was up to his ankles in the mud and his boots and pants was smeared with the dirty water.

"'Cause I want to get into this vein," he said.

"We want to go on to the West," I said. "Don't we?"

"We can go on to the Holsten with some gold to buy things," he said, out of breath as he scooped up the wet sand.

"Realus, I'm getting scared," I said. "Them fellers look at me funny."

"Ain't nobody going to bother you," he said. He looked at me like I was pestering him. He stopped for a second and took my arm. "We get a poke of gold," he said, "you can buy everwhat you want."

"I don't want nothing but to go to the Holsten," I said.

But he was like a different Realus. He was changed from the man who arrived at the clearing that morning. You could see in his eyes he had a new vision of how we was to live. He was not thinking of getting to the Holsten and starting our crops.

"Ho!" somebody hollered from the edge of the clearing. They was four men leading horses out of the woods.

"What you'uns want?" the preacher said.

"We've come to help you out," one of the new men said.

"We don't need no help," the preacher said.

"They's a whole mountain here," the newcomer said. He tied his horse to a poplar not far from our horse. "You're going to need help to dig out the whole thing."

The preacher talked to the new men. I just heard him say, "Who told you about this place?" They talked in low voices for a long time. I wondered if they was going to fight. As they talked they kept shifting positions, circling each other. The preacher's face was red as wine, and when he took off his black hat the bald spot on top of his head was red also.

But they must have come to some kind of agreement, for the new men tied up their horses and took picks and shovels and pans off their saddles. One man had a kind of pie pan he must have took from his wife's cupboard, and another had a garden spade that wouldn't do much with the sand and gravel. They had grabbed whatever was at hand when they heard about the gold. They was nobody I recognized from the settlement.

The men eat every bit of stew and every bite of the hoecakes.

"That were a mighty feast," the preacher said.

"That were a lavish of victuals," another said.

The preacher come over and stood beside me. He smelled sweatier than a field hand. "You're the kind of woman could make a man happy," he said. "You're pretty enough to be the preacher's wife." I started to move away from him.

"The Lord wants his own to be happy, to have the best," the preacher said.

"I'm sure that's true," I said. "If they are his own."

I turned away to carry my dirty pots and pans up the creek above the diggings and scrubbed them with sand and rinsed them in the clear water. My clothes was getting dirty from walking around in the mud. I thought, how am I going to get Realus away from here before something awful happens? How would I remember to him that we was just married and on our way to our own place in the West? I prayed a little, for the first time since we'd left home. Before that I hadn't felt justified to pray. Not because I had done nothing wrong, but because we didn't seem to be doing anything God would be interested in. I felt like he might not want to look while we was getting away. Then he would be proud of us once we was well married and had younguns.

After that I felt a little better, and gathered up my pots and pans to take back to camp. When I turned around this big feller was standing there watching me. His name was Cyrus and everybody called him Sarse. He was looking at me with this strange look in his eyes. He didn't say nothing.

I thought it better to act cheerful and unafraid. "Evening," I said and started to walk past him. He put out an arm and pulled me around.

"Pardon me," I said, still trying to sound friendly.

But whatever had come over him was too strong for him to stop hisself. He was a big meaty man with hair on his chest, and he gripped my arm to pull me toward the bushes.

"No," I said and tried to twist free. His teeth was clenched with determination. We was about a hundred feet from the clearing and the sound of the digging and the creek made it hard to be heard unless you hollered. I still thought I could get loose and run. It scared me to think how busy Realus was with the digging and not paying no attention to me.

I backed and turned away, and my pots and pans fell crashing in the leaves, banging on each other. But Sarse didn't seem to notice. He took both my shoulders and pushed me toward the laurels. He was trying to grab hold of the collar of my dress and tear it. I must have hollered out finally, or maybe I just made up my mind to. But next thing I remember was your Grandpa appeared just as I fell. He knocked Sarse up the side of his head, and the big man went reeling into the brush.

Realus reached to pull me up from the ground, and then I seen that Sarse had picked up a stick and was coming toward Realus. I must have screamed, for your Grandpa turned just in time to duck Sarse's swing and hit him in the belly with his shoulder.

I'm telling you what's the truth. You never seen such a fight. Both of them was big fellers, sweaty and muddy from the digging. They grabbed hold of each other and rolled on the ground, getting leaves and sticks stuck to their backs. They pulled each other's galluses and slapped and kicked. They kneed each other and bloodied their noses. I was horrified, and set like a fool in the leaves where I had fell.

It turned more of a rassling match than a hitting kind of fight. Sarse tried to grab Realus by the neck and run the top of his head into an oak tree. Realus tripped him up and they both fell down and rolled around kicking up the dirt.

The preacher stood holding his gun and watching. He hadn't said a thing, though the other men kept hollering, "That's it, Sarse," or "Twist his arm, Sarse." It didn't look too good for your Grandpa with all the men pulling for Sarse.

But suddenly Realus got Sarse's head in his arms and swung him around. He slung him against a tree, then he backed up and rammed Sarse's head right into that oak. Sarse staggered all over trying to stand, but he stumbled backward into a laurel bush and looked like the breath had been knocked out of him.

Realus stood trying to get his breath and I run to him. The other men stood looking at us. "Anybody else want to try me," your Grandpa said. His blood was up and he wouldn't have cared who took his challenge. Several of the men stepped closer. I stayed by his side to keep him from fighting anymore.

"That's enough," the preacher snapped. "It was a fair fight." He was looking at me. "Fair enough, leastways."

Sarse rolled over and tried to stand up, but he couldn't. They was blood on the top of his head. He crawled through the laurel bushes till he was out of sight. Several of the men barked after him like he was a coon or possum.

"We got work to do," the preacher said.

I picked up my pots and pans and followed Realus back to the clearing. Two more men had arrived on foot, with shovels strapped to their backs. They was talking to the preacher. When I come back to the fire and put my pots and pans down, one said, "You must be the couple that eloped from the settlement."

"Did they elope?" the preacher said. "Then they ain't married."

"Her Daddy's looking for her," the new man said.

"Your Daddy's looking for you," the preacher said. He stood over me like a slavemaster over a field hand.

"That man could be lying," I said. Realus had gone back to digging in the bank. He was out of earshot.

"You didn't say he was lying," the preacher said.

"It's not polite to accuse people of lying," I said.

The preacher bent close to me. "If you ain't married you're living in sin," he said.

"We are married," I said. "I'm a married woman."

"If you ain't married then you're free to marry me," he said. "I got all the gold we could need. And the Lord will forgive you for your sins. The Lord forgives all who believe on him. You think about what I said. You think real good."

He went back to the diggings and I felt worser than ever. I knowed we had to get away from there, whether Realus knowed it or not. I had to talk to Realus, so I took a gourd for a dipper and started off to get water. On the way back I stopped in the mud and give Realus a drink. While he was drinking I said to him in a low voice, "We got to get away before night."

I smiled and looked past him so the men wouldn't think I was saying nothing. "I'll lead the horse up the creek and tie him," I said. "And while the men are eating I'll slip away like I was going for water, and we'll run."

Realus didn't look at me and I wasn't sure he heard me. But

I had to believe he understood and would go through with the plan.

That evening I worked hard as ever I had to make a meal beside that mud hole. The dirt and standing water had been tramped through and spit in so much it stunk. It turns my stomach just to think of the smell of all those sweating bodies, and the mud and rotten things, and manure where the horses stood.

But I washed my hands and stewed some coon meat the men had brung in, and I roasted sweet taters in the fire. I even took some of our flour and made biscuits. I wished they was some sourwood honey. My plan was to keep them all busy eating for as long as possible, so I used a good bit of the flour and lots of sugar and salt. Hungry men are not going to go chasing through the woods as long as they have good hot food.

I led the horse way up the creek beyond where I had washed the pans. The packs was still on the poor animal. That showed how busy and beside hisself Realus was. He had left the horse standing with his burden. Realus was always good to beasts.

The horse was stiff from all the standing, and I knowed he was thirsty. His name was Dan, our first horse. I let him have a long drink from the creek and I tied him to a tree.

When I got back to the clearing it was only shadows on the heaps of mud. The men come running when I hollered it was supper time. I was happy to see Realus slipped away into the woods.

"I'm so hungry my backbone's rubbing a blister on my ribs," one of the new men said. They grabbed the stewed coon meat in anything they had, a plate, a cup, between two biscuits. The sweet taters was so hot they could just barely hold them to eat.

"Now all we need is tea," the preacher said.

"I'll go get some water to make some," I said.

"No, you wait a minute and serve us some more biscuits," he said. I served the rest of what I'd made. My dress was so muddy I was ashamed to be seen in it. They didn't seem to notice that Realus hadn't come to eat.

As they continued eating they got to laughing, as men will. "Hey preacher," one called from where he set on the ground. "How we going to divide up the gold?"

"Everybody gets a share for every day he's worked," the preacher said.

"Who's counting?" another man said.

"I'm counting," the preacher said.

"How much do you get for half a day's work?" one of the new men said.

"Half a share," the preacher said.

"Then how do you know how big a share is?" the new man said.

"You add up all the gold at the end and you divide by the number of men and days they worked."

The men set around the fire in the early dark. Their eyes glistened. They wrapped shirts and blankets around their dirty shoulders as the air got chilly.

"Show us the gold," one of the new men said.

"Yeah, yeah," the others said.

The preacher wiped his hands on his pants and took the poke out from his waist. He poured the contents on the cloth where I had mixed the dough. The gold glittered like crumbs of light.

"Whoo-ee!" the men said. "That's the real stuff."

"Why don't we divide up now?" one said.

"There'll be no dividing till the end."

"How do we know you ain't hiding some of the gold?" one said.

"You don't know," the preacher said.

I took up the kittle like I was going for water and slipped out of the firelight. I hoped all eyes would stay on the gold.

"Ain't that stuff pretty," the men kept saying.

I darted into the first laurel bushes I come to and walked as quick and quiet as I could. It was that time of evening when everything is shadows and you've not got your night eyes yet. It's hard to go straight in a laurel thicket because you're bending over so much and they's nothing to keep your eye on ahead. You can't see nothing but the limbs all around, and it's hard to look through laurels leaves even in winter time.

I thought I was going toward the creek where Realus was waiting, but after I'd gone far enough to be there I still didn't see no creek. I kept pushing limbs out of my way and running further, and still they wasn't nothing ahead but more laurel bushes. I stopped and listened and all I could hear was my breathing, and the men hollering back at the fire. I didn't hear any creek water.

I thought about calling for Realus, but what if they was to hear me? Above the laurels the stars was coming out, but they didn't help me. I tried to figure out where I had gone wrong. I must have circled back away from the creek. It couldn't be that far away unless I had gone in a complete circle.

After the long walk the night before, and working all day, and the worry and fear we'd had, I must have been awful tired. I felt dizzy and couldn't think, looking around at all the dark bushes. It was like I had sunk into some hole of laurel. I was no closer to the Holsten than I had been the night before. In fact I felt even further from the peaceful life there.

Suddenly I parted two bushes and come out into an opening. And I heard the sound of creek water. They was a man standing by the bank, and I thought it must be Realus, though he didn't have no horse. But just when I got near him I could see and smell it was the preacher.

"Why, looky here," the preacher said. "You're not trying to run away again are you?"

"I was going to get water for the tea," I said. The kittle was still in my hand. I wondered if I could hit him with the kittle.

"All the way through the laurel thicket you was going for water," he said.

"A woman has to answer the call of nature," I said.

"A woman has to answer the call of *her* nature," the preacher said.

I started to step around him. I thought I might be able to run off into the dark bushes again.

"I ain't going to let you go," the preacher said. "You've been sent to me by the Lord and I ain't going to let you get away." He grabbed my arm in his powerful hand. I could smell his tobacco and his sweat.

"The Lord ain't give me to nobody but my husband," I said.

"But he ain't your husband," the preacher said. "You ain't married at all. I'm going to be your husband."

I swung back the kittle and hit him hard as I could. But he seen it coming and throwed up his arm to stop the blow. Except he went down like he had fainted, like his legs just give out.

Then I seen your Grandpa with a stick in his hand. He had hit the preacher from behind just when I slung the kittle. I was so shocked I stood there in amazement.

"Let's go," Realus said. "Let's get away from here."

"He's got some gold. He owes us some gold," I said.

"I want to forget about gold," your Grandpa said.

I bent down over the preacher's body, sickened by the smell of sweat. I felt in his pocket for the poke of gold. But it wasn't there.

Instead I found a handful of sand and pebbles that felt like nuggets and I pulled them out.

"Leave the gold be," your Grandpa said. He took my hand and pulled me along the creek to where the horse was tied.

"We ain't got no time to waste," he said. "They'll come looking for the preacher, and for us. If they can't find the gold they'll follow us to the Holsten."

"The poke of gold is back in the camp," I said. "I seen him showing it to all the men."

"We still have to hurry," Realus said.

Your Grandpa said that since they knowed we was bound for the West they might follow us on the main trail. Best to cut to the north and go a more roundabout way. It would be harder to go through woods on Indian trails and buffalo trails, but it would be safer in the long run.

"We left some of our pots and pans back there," I said after we had gone a mile or two.

"We'll buy some more," he said.

"They ain't no stores in the West," I said.

"They's traders that come through and will trade anything for fur," he said.

The moon come up later and we could see the trail ahead better. But everything seemed stranger even than it had the night before. The mountains looked like a whole other world from the one I knowed. I got my second wind, for we must have walked ten miles before we stopped to sleep on a high-up place, right against a cliff where you could look out on the country below, blue in the moonlight.

"They's liable to be a rattler in this rock," I said to Realus.

"They won't be stirring for another month," he said. The pebbles I had got from the preacher's pocket was still clutched in my hand. I poured them in a rag and tied it up before we went to sleep.

C hildren, the sad facts of life are always sad. You can look at anything in a certain light and it will break your heart. Something that seems perfectly ordinary, going smoothly, will suddenly taste like ashes and swill. I've always been the kind of person that could be overcome by the sadness of everything, for a while. Suddenly the luster and firmness will fall away, and everything shows its naked ugliness.

The day at the gold diggings took some of the vigor out of me. I was relieved to get back on the road, but our mood wasn't the same anymore. Maybe it was the loss of sleep for two nights, and all the work and worry around the preacher's gold mine, and the hard walking. I had been keyed up for too long.

They was something different about your Grandpa the next day too. Or at least it seemed to me he had changed. Maybe it was the fatigue and disappointment of the long day's work in the mud, and the fight with Sarse. He was tired and fretty that day. He'd stop on the trail and listen, and if he heard somebody coming he'd draw the horse off into the trees and I'd follow. We hid there until whoever it was passed.

"I don't want nobody telling which way we've gone," he said.

"But they know we're headed toward the West," I said.

"But I don't want them to be certain," Realus said. "They might follow us."

"Daddy wouldn't do that," I said. "He wouldn't take the time and trouble. He will give up on me first."

"Don't want people to know about my business," your Grandpa said.

So we avoided settlements and stands and taverns, whenever we come upon one. We never even stopped at houses. You never saw such places as we went through. It's a good thing I was a strong girl. We climbed up steep trails and down steep trails. We wound around the sides of mountains under rock cliffs and we surrounded swamps full of mud and briars. Places the growth was so thick we walked in the creek to avoid the tangles. We'd see a little cabin in the distance and your Grandpa would lead us way around the clearing.

"Them people don't care if we're on the way to the West," I said. "They might invite us to stay the night."

"You never know who they might be," he said. "I've heard of people that lived along the road and made their living by robbing travelers. They might kill us just to see what we had." He seemed to grow more suspicious as we went along. Before, he was the kind of man that trusted people. And now he was afraid that everybody was going to rob us. He hadn't seemed like hisself since we left the gold mine. But I think it was his concern for me. To have a young wife made him afraid. Men don't have much confidence in women, and it makes them nervous to be responsible for a wife or daughter. Men feel women expose them to danger.

"They sure is a lot of high mountains protecting the Holsten," I said.

"That's why the land is cheap for the taking," your Grandpa said. "Otherwise the place would be all settled."

It come up the spring rains a few days after we left the gold diggings. I never seen such rain, and we was right in the middle of it. When you're exposed to rain for hours it seems to soak into your bones. Everything we had got wet. After a day or two it was like the rain had washed all the strength out of my body and soul. The rain just kept coming down like a waterfall, and we got slower and slower. With my hair and clothes soaked, and my feet in the mud, I felt like a poor shivering dog.

One night we found a cave and started a fire with some dusty pine wood somebody had left there. Mostly the wood outside was too wet to catch a spark. We'd had to eat whatever we had raw. It was such a relief to get to the cave and cook some corn cakes and a possum Realus had killed. We roasted the possum on a stick. I missed my pots and pans that had been left back at the gold camp.

It seemed like the rain would never stop. I put up sticks in the cave and dried some of my clothes. Everything had a musty smell. It was like the world was going to melt and rot, even if it didn't wash away. The woods floor was covered with mushrooms and moldy patches, mostly these mushrooms that look like jelly and slimy cups.

Children, that was the first time in my life I thought I was going to take the miseries and the all-overs at once. My bones felt sore and the rain on my head had give me the headache. And I felt a cold coming on in my throat and nose. Everything was going wrong, and we still wasn't to the Holsten.

"How much further is it?" I said.

"Petal, I wanted to surprise you," your Grandpa said. "But we're already on the Holsten."

"How long till we get to your place?"

"Maybe in a couple of days, if the rain stops."

That cheered me up a little, even with my headache. We built a kind of ditch at the mouth of the cave to keep water from running in from the rocks above. They wasn't nothing to set on but an old log the Indians must have pulled into the cave. I sorted through everything we had left. We had just a skillet and a kittle, one knife and two soup bowls.

While we waited for the rain to stop, Realus carved me three spoons out of maple. And he made a spatula of oak for turning hoecakes. He killed a turkey and a deer and we eat plenty. I rubbed deer grease on the new spoons and spatula to season them.

Realus sorted through the tools he'd took off the horse. He had left his shovel at the digging and the other tools had rusted in the rain. He went down to the creek and got the flattest rock he could find and sharpened everything, the grubbing hoe, the ax, the adz, the saw. And then he rubbed grease on the metal.

He was afraid that all the rain, and the heat of the horse, had made some of his seed start sprouting. We opened the bags and picked through the grains one by one. Sure enough, some of the corn and beans had started to swell and crack. We picked out all the cracked ones and set them aside. Maybe we could plant them first and they would still come up, if we could get to the place and clear some ground quick enough.

We stretched a cloth on four sticks and put the rest of the seeds on that, hoping to dry them enough so they would stay tight and hard. The danger was the fire would warm them and they'd start to swell even more. Didn't seem like nothing was going right. It was a good thing we was young and in love because older people couldn't have put up with so much. Every day we waited for the sun to appear, but it kept raining.

"This is Noah's flood again," I said to Realus. "It's going to last forty days and forty nights and we're going to be drowned if we don't climb a tree."

"Maybe it's the end of the world," your Grandpa said, trying to joke but sounding sadder than he intended. The truth was, we had started to feel it was the end of the world. It didn't seem the sun would ever show again, or that we would get out of that dark, musty cave. That night I cried. I just couldn't help myself. I'm not the crying sort of woman, but the bottom seemed to drop out of everything. Something just went inside me, and I found myself sobbing. I was ashamed of it, and that made me cry worser.

"Now, now," Realus said. But he didn't know what else to say.

I cried myself to sleep thinking I had run away from home with a man that didn't know what to say to me. We was lost in the wilderness. It was like the Lord had forsook us in that damp cave. I thought I would die of consumption if we stayed there.

When I woke that next morning, the first thing I noticed was how quiet it was. It was like a noise, but the noise was silence, and birds was out in the woods. The light coming into the cave was blinding. We hadn't seen the sun in many days.

"Realus?" I said. But they was no answer. I got up stiff from lack of sleep and crying, and stumbled toward the mouth of the cave where I heard a crackling. Outside, your Grandpa had a little fire going, and tea boiling in the kittle.

"How about some hot tea?" he said.

As I set there on a rock with my hair damp and dirty, sipping from the mug your Grandpa handed me, it seemed like I was being raised from the dead. Children, it's the best advice I can give you, that if you just keep going things will get better. It may take a long time, and seem like they's never going to be no improvement. But I've seen it happen many a time. A few hours before I thought we was going to die in that smelly cave. And here the sun was out and the woods fresh as the day of creation.

Soon as we drunk the tea and eat some corn cakes, Realus said he was going to catch fish for dinner. "It's too wet to travel right now," he said. "Fresh fish will give us strength."

"Then I'm going to wash my hair," I said. I knowed it would make me feel better if my hair was clean. It hadn't been touched since I left home.

I went to the bags we had piled in the cave to find the gourd of soap. The bags had never dried out completely, and smelled a little sour. I had to dig through all kinds of odds and ends to find the gourd. And when I did find the soap I suddenly thought of Mama. Me and her had made it from lye water and beef fat. We made it on the full of the moon like you're supposed to if the soap's going to be pure white.

I took the gourd down to the creek and knelt on a rock and washed all the smoke and grease out of my hair. As I worked the soap into my hair, I remembered Mama doing that for me. Beautiful as it was going off into the wilderness with the man you loved, it was hard to have no other woman to talk to. And I thought, society is people helping other people. That's why people stick together, because they need each other's help. Otherwise things falls apart, and you are back to the mud and animal level.

I had the intensest longing to go back home as I soaped my hair and rinsed it in the cold creek water. I thought of the church and school and blacksmith shop. And people coming over for parties at Christmas time, and the suppers we had after singings. It seemed the most precious thing was a community you could learn from and help out. I thought of the way when somebody died all the women brought plates of beans and chicken. I knowed I would go on with your Grandpa to the clearing, but for the first time it come to me what I had give up. The young is ignorant, and they learn something best by having to do without it.

Your Grandpa caught a whole mess of trout, and I fried them in the skillet before we loaded up the horse and headed down the trail. They wasn't really a trail, but we felt stronger, full of fresh fish and tea. It's amazing what a belly full of hot food will do for your outlook. When we finally got going, the walking was easier than before. They wasn't hardly no trail, but the brush seemed to open up for us. They was always a way between bushes and saplings, though you couldn't see it at first.

"Why ain't we seen no Indians?" I said.

"Indians only come through this country on hunting trips," your Grandpa said. "Or in war parties."

That relieved me some. I was in no hurry to see Indians.

"But we ain't seen no settlements either," I said.

"I told you it was a long way from anybody else," your Grandpa said. "I don't want neighbors to dispute my boundary lines and argue about where the church ought to be."

"But where will we get a granny woman when we need her?"

"We'll find one when the time comes," he said.

"What'll we do if we need to borrow some salt, or some fire?"

"This is the land of make-do," he said. "Make do, or do without."

I liked it when your Grandpa put it like that.

"One more day," he said. "And we'll be there."

"We'd better get there," I said. "If we want to plant anything."

Children, I wish I could tell you about my first sight of the house place. Maybe it was tiredness that made everything look so pretty. When you're tired enough, you get a little out of your head, like you was drunk. So tired you're light-headed.

We had been walking so long, and had been lost so long in the hollers and laurel thickets, and holed up in that rotten cave, that the prospect of having a roof over my head and a bed under my back seemed like the promise of paradise. People will talk about heaven as some city of gold and pearl, where they sing and play their harps all the time. And some people talk about paradise as a place of pure light and happy ghosts floating around. But I think heaven is whatever you need most at the time. If you're hungry enough, some hot biscuits and honey seems like all you need of glory. And if you're cold, a warm spot by the fire seems like Abraham's bosom. And when you're sleepy enough, just a pillow can feel like the sweet milk of mercy flowing in your veins. If you're sweaty and dirty enough, a good bath to relax and clean you up can seem like grace and the best of bliss.

As we come into the little clearing by the creek, leading our tired horse, it was evening and the sun coming in strips across the ground from the tops of trees. A gladness shot up inside me. The red cloth of your Grandpa's shirt seemed to get brighter as he pointed to the cabin, and I loved every inch of his strong figure as he showed me the cleared ground. The prospect of staying put the next day, and the next, for the rest of my life, seemed all of heaven I needed then. I wanted to have a house and hearth. They seemed no happiness but staying in your own place.

I should have been horrified at how little the cabin was. You can't remember, but we used it for a shed when your mamas and daddies was little. That's all we had to live in at first. They wasn't hardly room to turn between the bed your Grandpa had built in the corner and a bench in front of the fireplace, and the shelf that served as a table.

I see you all grinning because I've talked so much of the old hard times. But they was real. Even what I'd had at the settlement was luxury to what I found on the creek. We had to start from scratch, and nobody but a healthy ignorant girl could have done it.

That cabin had been left damp for more than two months. Snow had blowed in and wet the blankets, and a polecat, I reckon it was a polecat, had got in and chewed up everything, and got into the gourds and sacks. It was a scene to quell the bravest soul, much less a girl lost in the woods far from her family.

Your Grandpa looked at me like he wished I hadn't glimpsed

what was inside. "I'll make a fire so's we can see to clean up," he said. "You set out here and rest."

"I ain't going to set out here and rest," I said. The clearing was getting dark fast.

"It will just take me a little while," Realus said.

"It'll take you twice as long if I don't help," I said.

I gathered some sticks in the woods, and just as it got dark he started a fire in the little fireplace. You never seen such a rough fireplace as that. They was a polecat smell in the place, or maybe it was the must and mold that had took on the spilled corn and flour. Everything looked blue and brown with mildew.

I got some water from the creek to boil grits and we still had a little squirrel meat saved from the morning. While the water was heating, Realus cleared away the trash from the floor and throwed it outside.

"Don't throw away nothing we can use," I said. "They's no way to get any more."

"A little mold will spread to everything," he said. "Better to clear it all out before we unload the horse."

"Hot water and a touch of turpentine will take care of mold."

We eat on the bench with the pot of grits between us and the squirrel meat mixed in. The hot grits was better than sweet cake and custard, I was so hungry.

"Wish they was some butter," I said.

"We'll get us a cow this summer," Realus said. "We'll have a whole herd of cows."

"Where we going to get a cow if they's nobody else around?" I said. "You going back to bring one across the mountains? A month going and a month coming?"

"I'll get us one," your Grandpa said. And that struck me as curious, that he sounded so certain of getting us a cow.

Lord, the work we done that spring. Nobody but a young and foolish girl would slave that hard. We didn't hardly have no tools except the broadax and the big grubbing hoe. Realus had brought a plow point from my Daddy's blacksmith shop, and he hewed out a kind of plow from white oak and bolted the point on. But it was just a bull-tongued plow. It wasn't no turning plow.

You just think of starting a place from scratch in the woods with practically nothing but your bare hands. The patch your Grandpa had cleared in front of the cabin wasn't no bigger than a chicken run. Most of it had been a kind of ramp meadow before. A man is not going to clear land in the wilderness unless he has a woman to look after him and help him. A man by hisself will just hunt and go his way. You might say he clears up land for the woman. Either way, it's a mountain of work for both of them.

They was mornings when we started out that it seemed we could move the earth with our own hands. If it was just a matter of digging, we could have dug the ground out level and carried the rocks and throwed them into the creek. I felt like I could shape the dirt with my fingers, the way we did as children, playing in the sand. I felt like the earth was here for us to use, the black soil and the yellow underdirt. The ground just needed cleaning off and flattening to be our play yard.

That spring me and Realus deadened a whole stand of trees down along the creek where Lewis's place is now. We girdled every tree so's it wouldn't put out no leaves. Where we cut the bark, sap kept coming up from the roots and bubbling out, especially the poplars. It looked like some kind of brew soaking out and the early flies and gnats and even some butterflies come to drink the sap before it soured and turned black.

We didn't have time to cut the trees down that first summer. It was corn-planting time, and after we ringed the trees to make sure they wouldn't put out no shade leaves, Realus tried to scratch up the ground under them to plant. But you know what it's like in the woods, with leaves and sticks on the ground, and roots just underneath. You can't hardly plow. The bull-tongued point catched on one root after another. It'll rupture a man if the plow handle hits him in the belly when the point jams on a stob. I've heard of men killed or maimed that way. What you have to do is grub out the roots with mattock and big hoe and pull out the little roots like lacings and gristle. But we didn't have time for much of that.

We done what a lot of people did back then. Stead of planting in rows we put our corn in hills. What you do is pick a good spot and dig it up and plant four kernels. That way you've got hills scattered all over in the best places. And you come back and hoe the separate hills, keeping the weeds away from them.

Ever wonder why we growed so much corn here? It's because corn grows faster than the weeds around it. You plant it in hills, not broadcast or drill it like small grain, like oats and rye. And you can bust corn up in little mills if you have to. You can grind it in a tub mill, or even crush it in a mortar like the Indians. You harvest it by the ear. Don't need no scything or thrashing. And you can eat corn when it's in the milk, which you can't with small grains. And think of all the ways you can use corn, as roastnears, as creamed, as gritted bread, as meal, as grits and mush, as pudding, as hominy.

Once the trees is deadened, the woods will grow up something awful in briars and weeds. And sprouts come up around the stumps. All that powerful sap in the roots with nowhere to go will shoot up in rods and bust out in leaves. Ever notice how much bigger the poplar leaves on sprouts is than on trees? They's so much sap in the roots and so little place to go. We spent the first summer chopping nettles and weeds, vines and poison oak.

You let sunlight into the woods and everything will start coming out.

Around laying-by time a wind storm come up and you seen what else happened to a deadening. The little limbs above begun to fall off among the corn. After a storm the ground would be littered with limbs that had died and broke. It was the second and third year when the big limbs started rotting and coming off, and the bark shucked off the trees and covered the dirt with pieces like shields on a battlefield. Eventually the trees theirselves rotted to the core and fell. The biggest oaks lasted maybe ten years on the trunk until they rotted, and by then we was turning the whole field, plowing around the standing stumps.

It was that first summer I begun to think about what I called the mysteries of our place. Me and Realus worked like we was possessed. I cleaned that cabin and washed out the musty smell with lye. I scoured the base of the cabin and sprinkled lime around to keep the bugs and worms away, and to make the place smell sweeter. By June I knowed I was expecting Wallace, though I didn't know he was a boy. But that didn't stop me from working none. A pregnant woman feels at ease about things, unless she gets sick at her stomach.

I made a broom out of a bundle of birch twigs and swept the yard down to the creek, and the trail back to the spring. We didn't have no chickens then, so the yard wasn't all that dirty. Realus promised he would get me some chickens as soon as he could, and some guineas too, to pottarack around the yard.

Your Grandpa dug a little patch behind the cabin where I planted some beans and squash. And I sowed mint and parsley beside the door with seeds we had brought. And I planted peas and gourds too, and put sticks over the vines when they come up.

I was bent over my bed of cabbage sprouts about a month after we deadened the trees when I heard your Grandpa's ax stop. When he was working I got used to the sound and didn't hardly notice it. They would be a "chop" and then the echo "it" coming back from the ridge across the creek: "Chop, it, chop, it." My heart liked to have jumped into my throat, for I hadn't heard no voices save my own and your Grandpa's since we left the gold camp. I stood up, brushing the dirt off my hands and dress. I couldn't see anything at the east end of the clearing where your Grandpa was cutting logs for a fence. He said the deer would eat up everything in the garden if we didn't fence it.

I walked around the corner of the cabin, where I could see past the sweetgum bushes, and there was Realus at the edge of the woods talking to a man and a woman. The man was leading this old gray horse and the woman was riding. It was one of those horses with mottled gray all over it, the kind I'd seen in Charlotte, and it looked strange there in the woods.

I was almost shaking with excitement for I hadn't seen nobody in such a long time. Or maybe I was afraid that we had been discovered there in the wilderness and our perfect life would be destroyed. I couldn't make out what Realus was saying. I thought of running over there to welcome them myself, and then I thought, no, I'll stand by my door and welcome them.

And I was thinking, now I'll have some other woman to talk to. And maybe they'll have news of what's going on in the rest of Watauga and the Holsten. I wanted to know who was our nearest neighbor, and how far it was to the river.

Realus didn't bring them to the house at first. They talked for several minutes and I was like to bust with curiosity. The voices echoed across the clearing. I started out to them, and then I seen your Grandpa was leading them toward the house.

The woman had on a long gray coat that covered her dress. She looked like she had been rained on and then dried out in her clothes. I knowed how she felt. I reached up to shake her hand.

"I'm Petal Jarvis, Richards," I said. "Why don't you all light and come in."

"They want to make the ford by nightfall," Realus said, like it had already been discussed and decided they wasn't stopping.

"You all are welcome to stay for supper if you can eat what poor folks eat," I said, sounding like my Mama.

But your Grandpa frowned at me. "I was going to give them some meal," he said. "It'll be two months before they's new corn."

He went into the cabin, and I said to the man, who was poor as a whippoorwill inside his dirty buckskin clothes, "You all must be tired of walking."

"We've come down the trail a fur piece," he said. He seemed nervous and itching to be on his way. He kept watching the cabin door, waiting for your Grandpa to come out with the meal.

"How far you going to?" I said.

"Fur as we have to to find good land."

"They's good land around here," I said.

Realus come back with the poke full of cornmeal and handed it to the man. They started across the clearing without so much as a thank you. We watched them skirt the deadened patch and disappear into the woods.

"They wasn't much polite," I said. "They could have stayed here overnight."

"Just as well," your Grandpa said. "They might steal from us or give us some kind of sickness."

"They looked tired," I said. "How come they went on so quick?" My heart was still knocking from the surprise of seeing the strangers.

"I told them we'd had smallpox here," your Grandpa said. "I didn't want them stopping."

"You never was afraid of nobody before," I said.

"They're liable to rob us," he said. "We're alone here and you don't know what kind of people they are."

"They're people just like us," I said.

"We've got to think about the baby now," your Grandpa said.

The prospect of having a family makes some men worry. I was surprised he was suddenly so shy of strangers. It didn't seem like him. But then he was going to be a daddy, and I guessed that had changed him. And maybe being alone in the woods with me had changed him too.

"I wanted to talk to her," I said. "She might have had news."

"Them people wouldn't have no more news than we do," Realus said. "Besides, I don't want them telling people where we are."

When I went back to work in the seedbed, it hit me that what I wanted to tell somebody about was the baby coming. I wanted to talk to another woman and ask her advice. And tell her how I felt and find out what I was supposed to expect. Mostly I felt how much I wanted to tell my Mama the news.

"Here's something the woman give you," Realus said, and pulled a vine from his pocket. It was a sprig of myrtle, what we call periwinkle. I don't know where the woman had brought it from, but it was blooming, and I set it out over there under the hemlocks. You can see the periwinkle still blooming there in spring. Almost every old place in these woods has some around it.

The first summer I worked right through fodder-pulling time and top-cutting time. We had to save every leaf of corn, for it was the only horse feed we had for winter except the corn itself. Didn't have no oats or hay. Didn't have no place to put the fodder till your Grandpa built a log shed. It was really two stalls, one for the horse, and one for the cow we might get. And over the stalls was this loft for the fodder. It was a big, tall, ugly-looking shed, but it served our purpose in them years. You could still see some logs of it over there for years. Realus didn't have time to rive no shingles for it. So he put poplar bark on the roof. Later he nailed cedar shakes on it.

I'd never done real field work before, except hoeing corn. But I sure learned quick. We hoed barefoot in that new ground under the deadened trees, which was foolish, given all the briars and weeds around the hills. Every day we seemed to kill another copperhead. But we had to save our shoes for winter. The awfullest weeds you ever seen growed up around the ringed trees. Big hogweed and queen-of-the-meadow twelve foot high.

They was a black racer we named Zeb stayed around the corn patch. He was so black he glistened in the sun. We'd see him hanging on the limb of a tree waiting for birds, or slipping off into the woods. He liked to catch field mice, and your Grandpa sometimes teased him. Realus would stomp his feet at that snake, and Zeb would rare up and hiss at him. Blacksnakes will guard their territory. When he got mad you'd smell this stink that snakes let out when they're riled. We'd laugh at him and the snake would look at us real mean, then slip off into the brush.

Funny thing was, we didn't see rattlesnakes. I thought I heard one singing off in the weeds one time, but it could have been a jarfly. Back then, in the woods, you could see lots of timber rattlers.

I was getting heavy with Wallace along in late summer when we was pulling the fodder. It was the hottest time, and dusty. I had already been stung once by a packsaddle. They get in the corn leaves, and when I grabbed a handful to bind up I felt this pain like ten points of fire stick in my hand. My hand was swole for days. I was afraid the poison might get into the baby.

We had almost finished with the foddering. The leaves was getting too dry to cure right. And I was trying to avoid another packsaddle. Realus had gone to carry a load to the shed loft. He had made this sled out of sourwood runners and poles which he used for everything. We didn't have a wagon or nothing else.

I was bending down to strip the bottom leaves off a stalk when I seen this thing I thought was a bundle of fodder. My eyes was full of sweat and I couldn't see right. How could I have dropped a bundle without noticing, I thought? And then I seen the tail raise and buzz. There I was, bent over close, before I seen it was a rattler and the thing already coiled.

I was a goner if it bit me close to the head. And the baby was a goner if it bit me anywhere at all. If I jumped back, it would strike, and if I stayed still, it might strike. The sweat was in my eyes so I couldn't hardly see. But I had the sense not to look that snake in the eyes. It's the Devil looking at you out of a snake's eyes. It can put a spell on you and you can't get away. A snake can charm a nursing woman and suck the milk out of her breasts and ain't nothing she can do.

But if a pregnant woman looks in a snake's eyes, it will mark her baby. I've heard of a baby born with little snake eyes that has been marked, and babies born with scales on their backs, and born with no arms. I kept my eyes turned to the side and started backing away, one step easing back after another, hardly steps at all but little movements trying not to touch stalks or weeds. I never worked so hard on nothing in my life. I thought I could smell that old snake he was so close. He could have struck me anytime. He was big around as my leg, I guess. And his scales looked like they had hairs coming through them. Coiled up he would have filled a half-bushel basket.

When I got about a yard back, I jumped far as I could. That snake struck at the same instant, and I bet he didn't miss my leg an inch. A drop of venom hit my ankle and run like spit. A snake can strike his whole length, but he just missed me. I run and got the hoe and hit him before he slid away in the weeds. He was so tough I hit ten times before I chopped his head off. And then that big fat body laid there twitching and striking.

"That thing will weigh twenty pounds," Realus said when he come back and seen it.

Now when my time was almost come I said to your Grandpa, "Is they a midwife near about?" I said it more than once. And he always said he'd go look for one when the time was right.

They was no way for me to be sure when the baby would come. Even if we had seen a doctor, he wouldn't have been sure either. I figured nine months from the time we arrived at the clearing. But the date could be from any time after we left the settlement. I didn't know enough about such things to tell from the look of my belly when I'd come full term. Every woman carries a baby different and the size of the belly won't tell you nothing.

Sometimes I'd feel scared. Any woman approaching her first time will feel scared, even if she's got a doctor, and a midwife, and people telling her what to expect. Because she knows it's going to be a lot of pain, and it's going to take a long time. And they's a danger, both to the baby and herself.

But off in the wilderness like that I had nobody but my husband, and no sign that a midwife was anywhere near. It's a good thing babies is born to young people. The old couldn't stand the fear, much less the strain.

By frost we dug our taters and put them in a hill beside the shed with dirt thick enough to keep them from freezing. I dried a lot of beans on strings we hung from the ceiling. And right at the end of summer I dried some foxgrapes and wolf grapes your Grandpa picked on the river across the ridge.

One of the best things in the fall was Realus found a bee tree. Maybe he seen bees awatering at the creek and followed them up the ridge. But he found this big chestnut that was partly holler and we waited till dark and chopped it down. He lighted some wet leaves to smoke the bees. We got three buckets of honey. I knowed honey would come in good for the baby. You can quiet a baby by putting honey on your finger and letting the baby suck it. Best of all your Grandpa sawed off a holler blackgum log and made a bee gum. He put enough of the honey in the hive to keep the bees through the winter. And we've kept bees ever since.

I didn't have no calendar but I knowed it was coming up toward Christmas time. The leaves was all gone, even on the birches and willows along the creek. And back in the settlements they was probably killing hogs and making sausage. I wished I had me a calendar, but it was one of the things we done without. It had come a hard freeze, and Realus had started hunting for meat. He killed a couple of deer and smoked the meat, and hung it in the loft out of reach of varmints. We lived on turkey in those days. All he had to do was take his gun up on the ridge where he could hear them gobbling, and he'd come back with a bird for me to bake over the fireplace. We had a lot of squirrels in the fall too, but it was turkey and deer meat we lived on in the winter.

"When you going to look for a granny woman?" I said one day when it was nigh to Christmas.

"I'm going out looking for the nearest settlement," he said. "I think they's one about twenty miles north of here."

"Maybe I should go with you," I said. "And if they's a store we could get a calendar and something for the baby."

"It's too rough a road," he said. "I'll go in a hurry and be back in two days."

He was right. I was in no shape to ride over the mountains. Next morning he took the gold nuggets we had saved and some deer hides and a sack of corn and rode off on the horse, holding his gun across the saddle.

"Keep the door bolted after dark," he called back. He had carried in a pile of wood to last me till the next day.

It was a cold, clear day, and I didn't worry none till almost dark when I felt this sharp pain in my belly. It just lasted a second, and was gone. I'd been shelling dried beans and was beginning to boil them. I bent down to stir the pot and felt this wetness on my dress. First I thought it was the steam, or that I'd spilled some water from the kittle.

But then I felt it was too much water coming down on my skirt and that it didn't smell like spring water. Didn't smell bad, just didn't smell like the boiling water either. I got a cloth and put it on the bench where I was setting. Only when I'd set down again did I think I'd lost my water. And that wrench I'd felt earlier had been a birthing pain.

It was near dark, as I've said. I'd have to run to the spring. I left the beans boiling and throwed on my shawl.

It was aching cold, as it gets on a clear night. And they was a big star—I called it the Christmas star—just over the mountain. The last light was reflected from the creek, but it was dark on the path to the spring. I closed my eyes to make them adjust, but I had to feel my way along. I had been watching the fireplace too long. I got to the spring and dipped up the bucket of water, still going more by feel than sight. When I stood up they was this awfullest scream on the ridge above. It was a squall that rose like a woman screaming in childbirth. I stood there froze to my tracks and shivering.

Was it somebody playing a trick on me, or a ghost hollering, or a painter? We'd heard wolves all summer and fall.

Something dropped to the ground up there, something heavy as a bear, or a big dog. I turned to run back to the cabin and this pain shot through me. It was the second pain, and worser than the first. It surprised me as I stumbled along. I thought they was steps behind me, but I didn't stop to listen. Every step I imagined a claw sinking into my leg or back. It was not possible to run with the bucket, but I kind of limped and hopped along.

The door of the cabin was not completely closed and I seen the warm light inside. It seemed to take hours to get there.

When I got in I slammed the door and leaned against it without putting the bucket down. I pushed hard and listened, but they was no sound except my heart thumping and the boiling water on the fire. Beans is supposed to be simmered not boiled, and I'd let them get too hot. But I listened a moment to see if anything was outside. Then I put down the bucket and bolted the door.

I took a rag and set the pot of beans off the hook onto the hearth to simmer. Then I dropped on the bench to rest. What a fix I'm in, I thought to myself.

Children, in the awfullest times you realize you ain't got no choice but to go on. There I was, with your Grandpa gone off for the night somewheres, and a baby coming, and a beast prowling outside. I didn't hardly know a thing about babies, except the stuff that everybody knows. I'd heard a painter is attracted to a mother's milk, can smell an infant miles away. That didn't comfort me none.

I didn't know hardly what to do next. My only light was from the fireplace. Sometimes your Grandpa and me used grease sluts, a rag in a bowl of lard, to light the cabin in summer. And we still had a few candles brung from the settlement for special times. I guessed this was about as special an occasion as I'd ever see.

The candles was in a bag Realus had throwed up on the rafters. I started to climb up there on the bench when the next pain hit me like lightning followed by thunder. I dropped back down to let the pain pass. When the hurting eased I seen the fire was dying down, and throwed on a couple more sticks.

That was the first time I noticed they wasn't enough sticks to last if you kept a big fire all night. Realus had brought in the usual amount of wood for the evening and the morning. But he hadn't thought I'd be up all night. They wasn't enough wood to last much past midnight if I kept a big blaze going.

Just then they was a squall outside the cabin. It was louder than the one I heard above the spring. It was close as the shed, maybe closer to the garden patch. They wasn't no window in the cabin to look out. I got up and tried to see through a crack above the bed, but your Grandpa had filled all the cracks with mud and grass. My eyes was ruined by the fire for seeing out. They was an opening at the eave, opposite the chimney, but I wasn't going to climb there. I got the candles down and lit one.

Something clawed on the side of the cabin and dropped like a sack of meal on the roof. The cabin creaked with the weight. That painter is big as a bear, I thought. The door was bolted with the piece of hickory your Grandpa had whittled to slide in the slot. It didn't look like nothing could bust the door down. But just to make sure I shoved the bench over against the door. If the thing tried to break down the door I'd sit on the bench.

The big cat walked around on the roof and the whole cabin was shaking. The building shuddered like wind was hitting it. Realus had made the cabin strong out of chestnut and hickory logs, and I prayed the pegs wouldn't give way.

The painter seemed to be walking back and forth on the roof, like he was trying to find a place to get inside. First one end of the roof would shake under the weight, and then the other. Splinters fell off the ceiling. He walked along the comb and then along the edges. For a while I didn't hear nothing, and thought he might have jumped off. But then they was a scratching and growling around the chimney, and I saw what my problem was going to be. That painter was trying to come down the stick and clay chimney. He could tear it apart with one swipe of his paw. It was just pieces of wood with clay stuck over them on the inside. That devil was poking his head down the chimney and getting smoke in his face. That would make him mad and he'd slap at the wood. Bits of clay was falling down the chimney, pieces he was knocking off.

I'd have to keep the fire going all night, so that painter wouldn't come down. Your Grandpa had split a great pile of wood out behind the cabin, and thought he'd carried in plenty. I wished I'd carried in the rest before dark. I'd piddled away the afternoon shelling beans and sewing up the edges of a baby wrapping cut down from a wore-out blanket.

It was the time of the longest nights of the year. It would be seven in the morning before they was any light. I looked around the cabin for what they was to burn. Biggest thing was the bench itself, two big planks Realus had hewed, and the stumps they was pegged to. The boards was too long to fit in the fireplace, but I could feed them in, the way they used to do with a Yule log.

They was a cradle your Grandpa had made for the baby from poplar wood. He had sawed out the boards and smoothed them with a piece of glass. That could be burned, much as I would hate to. Your Grandpa had also made a kind of ladder up to the loft with pegs stuck in the logs opposite the chimney. I could pull them steps out and burn them.

I figured all together I could keep the fire going two or three hours beyond midnight, maybe four hours if the chestnut in the bench burned slow. If the painter knocked the chimney down and put out the fire I was a goner anyway.

A pain wrenched through me and it was worser than before. It was the biggest pain I had ever felt, and it seemed to hit me all over. I think I hollered without knowing it, till afterwards I felt it in my throat where the groan come out. But a birth pain is a different pain. It's like something you're straining to get rid of, like you're awful constipated and it's hurting and it's going to take you a long painful time.

I grabbed hold of the bedpost and I held on till the flood swept through me. That seemed to help a little, just to grip something hard as I could. By then I was beginning to sweat. Pain will heat you up like fire in your flesh.

I'd heard tell they made Indian women walk before they had a baby. Now white women don't do that. White women lay in bed and chew a rag when the hurt comes. And they take laudanum sometimes to soothe the pain. I'd heard Indian women walk back and forth along a stream when the baby is coming. That somehow speeds it up or makes it easier. I figured my case was like an Indian's. I didn't have no other help, so I might as well try their method.

I walked to the fireplace and back to the wall beside the bed. It was exactly five steps and a turn. If I walked around the cabin I had to step over the bench, and that was too hard with the weight in my belly. It was five steps toward the light, and a turn. Then five steps in the dark toward the candle and shadowy wall. I was pacing like the painter on the roof. I would stop and hear the pad of feet up there. It was like we was playing some kind of game. Then I started again and counted off my trips across and back. I got up to ten before the pain hit again.

Every time the pains got worser. This time I found myself laying on the bed before I knowed it. I couldn't double over standing so I must have laid down on my side. I tried to hold my breath, but that made the pain harder. I gasped deep and long. I thought if it gets any harder I can't stand it. I kept on counting like I was still walking, and that seemed to help a little. I imagined I was walking to the spring and back, and then to the creek and back. It was so cold outside, the rocks in the stream and the limbs hanging into the water wore little collars of ice. And the ice caught the starlight.

I counted and squeezed my eyes shut and seen the stars overhead that must be out over the roof and painter and trees. The stars was so close and big they shined like falling snow all around me. If the earth was round I was in the middle of stars swishing and spreading and passing.

When the pain weakened I got up. The painter was scratching around the top of the chimney. Bits of sticks and dried mud kept dropping into the fire. Bits of soot and mud had fell into my beans. I didn't want no beans anyway. I moved the pot off the hearth. When I stooped down to move the kittle closer to the flames, I thought I seen the face of that painter up the chimney. Now I don't think I did. The chimney was too far up for me to see unless I was right in the fire. But I thought I seen that devil looking at me. I had a gourd with some grease in it hanging by the chimney, and I throwed that on the fire. The flames leaped up, and I heard the painter growl and jump back. The smoke and flames must have singed him hard for I heard him fling back on the roof to the ground. The burning lard smelled terrible and smoked up the cabin a little. But I laughed to myself thinking of that cat getting grease flames in his face.

I put the last of my wood on the fire. Even the kindling Realus had split from fat pine was gone. It seemed past midnight and so cold outside I heard a poplar crack. But I wasn't cold. I was sweating. My hair stuck to my forehead and my dress was damp. The worst sweating seemed to be down my back. I don't know why a woman birthing sweats so down her back.

Something scratched at the door, high where a man could just barely reach. The door shook and the big hickory bolt in its slot rattled. Your Grandpa had made it strong, but it couldn't hold the weight of that big cat if it lunged at the door. I pushed the bench hard against the door.

The first ladder peg to the loft pulled out easy when I twisted it in its hole. But the second and third stuck hard. I'd need an ax or sledgehammer to break them off. They was meant to hold a man's weight.

That left only the bench to burn, and the cradle your Grandpa had made. That cradle was so pretty it broke my heart to think of burning it. The sides and ends was made of wide poplar he'd smoothed with his knife, and with a piece of glass. The wood shined from the oil rubbed in it. All fall your Grandpa had set by the fire at night smoothing and rubbing that wood before he pegged it together. Now the rockers was made of chestnut. They say rockers out of chestnut won't ever creep, no matter what kind of floor they rock on. Something about the chestnut wood just grips the floor. 'Course that wasn't a problem since we didn't have no floor then. But a good cradle will last a family, and can be passed on through the generations.

If I burned up the bench I wouldn't have nothing to hold the door with, and if the painter broke down the door bolt, me and the baby would die. It wasn't even a hard decision. When the time come I'd break the headboard across the bench and feed it to the fire.

As the painter fumbled around over the door I could hear things fall. The gourds I had hung up, and the hoes, and the horseshoe your Grandpa had tacked there. He had some nails in a bag, and I heard them go flying every which way. Nails was hard to get, unless they was a blacksmith to make them. But a lot of smiths wouldn't make nails. Too much hammering to fashion the little things.

To make the wood last I'd have to measure it out through the night. It must be after midnight, but that still left six hours to go. When you tend a fire it's almost like you're growing a plant or feeding some kind of animal. It's all a matter of pace and timing, not putting on too much wood and not letting the flame die down too far.

When a fire tries to talk to you it'll drive you crazy to figure out what it's saying. You lean close, while you're mending the flames with a poker, turning over a log so sparks shoot up the chimney, and hear a kind of hush and whisper. The blues from wet bark, and the greens, will play around the edges of the flames like pieces of the northern lights. You'll hear what sounds like another word, or just a hiss and puff. But I never did know how to interpret a fire.

When I look into the fire I see all these mountains way back yonder, and shining valleys as far and many as you might imagine. I can see trails leading off into hollers, and houses and bright meadows where you could just keep on walking way out toward some other kind of world you dreamed about when you was a little kid.

The painter was on the roof again. I felt the cabin shake when he jumped back up. More crumbs of dirt dropped into the fire, and I knowed he was pawing around the chimney.

What do you mean, did I pray? Of course I prayed. But I didn't have no time for lengthy prayers. I knowed I had to help myself, and I got on with it. I had to fight.

That night I wished I had a drink to calm my nerves. They was tearing pain inside me and I jumped back from the fireplace. That was the first time I felt the baby shift inside me. It was like the baby turned and dropped. A fire went through my belly and thighs. I was sweating something terrible, and I thought *I can't do this. I can't go through with it.* At the same time I knowed I didn't have no choice. That baby was coming out, and they was a rightness to it. It was like I had felt this terrible pain before. I knowed this desperate pressure and work. Maybe from the time I was born myself.

As the pain scorched through me they wasn't nothing I could do but hold onto the mantelpiece. I looked at the stumps the bench was pegged to. They was white oak, and seasoned by standing near the fire. If I could break them off and use them they'd burn for an hour or more and keep that cat out of the chimney.

Soon as the worst of the pain faded I pulled the bench away from the door. It was a heavy thing, and scraped up the dirt where it went. I kicked it over in front of the fire and pushed on one of the stumps. It was pegged tight to the boards. Your Grandpa had done his work real good. I couldn't just push the bench in the fire 'cause I needed something to prop the door.

When you're scared you take on the strength of two or three ordinary women. I set down on the upturned bench and kicked with both my feet to knock the stump loose. At first it didn't give. Them sourwood pegs held solid. I swung around and kicked at the other stump but it wouldn't budge either. It seemed impossible to loosen the heavy pieces. I set there thinking the next pain might hit me any second. I had to prepare myself if I wanted to survive. That's when I got mad at your Grandpa. It was your Grandpa that left me with not even a gun and no firewood to last the night, and no granny woman to help, and nobody to explain what I needed to do. It was your Grandpa that took me off into the wilderness and got me with a baby and then didn't find a midwife.

My frustration come to a point right then. I seen that stump like it was your Grandpa's head, and I hauled off with both legs and kicked it. It was like I gripped the boards with my back and kicked. I would have killed Realus had he been there. But I felt that stump give a little. I kicked again and the pegs broke and the stump rolled off by the hearth.

Quick as I could, I swung around and kicked the other stump until it give way. Then I rolled both stumps into the fireplace. I couldn't put one stump on top of another. They was too heavy to lift, and they wasn't room anyway. They liked to smothered the fire, and some smoke come out into the room. But the coals was still hot, and they caught the stumps even through the bark.

I picked up the heavy boards of the seat and braced them against the door. It was all I could do to lift the heavy planks. And I tried to dig the other ends into the dirt floor so they wouldn't slide back.

While I was doing that, the next pain hit and I really felt things tearing loose inside me. I dropped back on the bed and rolled over, but nothing would stop the pain. It was like something sharp was going through me. I held my belly and pushed. I pushed inside.

You can't do this, I said to myself. You can't never do this on your own. I propped my legs against the bedposts and pushed, near beside myself with pain. My eyes was full of tears and sweat, and I guess I was hollering. All I could think of in the heat and terrible strain was, this is what it takes to be alive.

My back rolled around on that bed. It was like I was thrashing around in the dirt even though I was on the bed. I had took my best quilt off the bed, the one my Mama had give me, and left nothing but old sheets and blankets on it. I pushed against them sheets so hard it's a wonder they didn't tear.

The big stumps must have caught for they was more light in the room, as well as the candle beside the bed. I guess the room must have warmed, but I was sweating too much to tell. The pains was almost steady. It was new pains, and new levels of pains coming. Every time I thought I couldn't stand it they would come another pain and it would be worse. I didn't know they was such pain. Every pain just kept opening into a bigger one.

I squeezed my eyes closed and pushed against the bedposts, and I pushed against the burden in my belly. It was like a nest of knives was pushing through me. And yet, at the worst moment, they was this solid thing down there that put a deep, sweet feeling inside the awful pain that was working out through me.

I reached down there into myself and felt among the blood and water this greasy thing coming through like a bud out of a seed. That's when I pushed the hardest ever, because I knowed then it might work, that I might on my own get this over with. That was my main wish then, to get it over and done with.

The last push was the hardest. It was a wonder I didn't break down the bedposts. I pushed so hard I could have pushed the cabin up the hill, or pushed the whole earth an inch or two back if I'd had a place to grab hold of it. I squeezed my eyes and pushed away from the fire, and it was like I shot myself through a tunnel of pain and the baby come out in the opposite direction.

I felt down there and held what was coming through. It wasn't no bigger than a Wolf River apple, all slick and greasy. I pushed again like I was trying to push the whole future ahead by a second. I partly set up and pulled on the little head. I still couldn't see nothing. But it was like the baby flopped inside me, worked its back through like a weasel coming out of a burrow.

Then the little shoulders come through and I could see in the mess of blood the little arms. It was the wonderfullest feeling, to see that it had all worked inside me, that the little human being was complete and real. I reached down and took hold of the little feller. He was all slick and covered with the buttery stuff babies is covered with. And the dark cord was all twisted around, attached to the belly and coming out from inside me. I pulled at that thing, and most of it come out, but it didn't come loose from him. They wasn't no way to get it free. So I leaned far as I could and bit that bloody thing in two. And I seen among the blood and all that sticky stuff that it was a boy.

There I was, with the blood and stuff all over me, and coming out of me, and this red little animal of a baby in my hands. I didn't know if he was alive, and I didn't know what to do next. I couldn't get up because I was too weak and I couldn't slap the baby on his bottom like I'd always heard about, 'cause I had to hold him with both hands. So I just shook him a little. I shook him like I was listening for a rattle or a sign. And he started crying. He sounded like a little sheep and got louder. It was a cry that seemed to fill the whole cabin. I was so tired I just set there and held him for a minute while he cried.

We don't need to go into all the details about how I finally laid the baby on the blankets and cleaned myself up a little. That was when I noticed the painter again, still up there on the roof growling. He must have smelled the blood and the baby. The stumps was still burning, and the fire was hotter than ever.

All the mess I wiped up, and put the dirty sheets in a bucket. I poured hot water in a pan and washed myself off. I was almost too sore to touch myself, and was shaky from the strain. The real cleaning up would have to be done later. I just did what had to be done. I washed the baby off careful and wrapped him in a blanket. Then I took us both to the bed and covered us with the big blanket. That's when I felt the soreness and itching in my breasts for the first time. They hurt, but they also itched. I put the baby up next to me, and his mouth just naturally grabbed hold of a nipple. I was tired to death, but I wasn't sleepy.

Of course, I did go to sleep. I dropped off with the baby at my breast. I didn't even know I was asleep. It seemed I was laying there and the cabin was warm and I thought it was summer and green. It was so warm I could take the baby out with me when I went to the spring. It was like I could remember the painter and winter, but it was already blossom time, and birds was fussing in the stubble. They was a scratching somewhere.

Then I realized I had been asleep, for the scratching was coming from the chimney. Dirt and pieces of sticks fell in the fireplace. The stumps had burned down low and the painter was leaning over the top of the chimney. He could smell the milk coming from my breasts. I got up gentle as I could and laid the baby on the blankets. I was so weak my hands shook, and I like to fell back. That woke me up, and I grabbed hold of the bedpost.

They was nothing else to burn but the cradle, and the planks propping the door. If I took down the planks the cat could knock the door down. But at least they was two of the boards. I unstuck one from where it was jammed against the bolt. But I had no way to chop it up. That board was eight feet long and wouldn't fit in the fireplace except if you poked it in longways. The danger was the fire would spread back on the board before the end was burned up enough to push the plank in further.

But I didn't have no choice. I pushed that board in the fire on the coals. I figured if the painter come down the chimney I'd pick up the end of the board and shove it in his face.

Just when I got the plank in the fire, the baby started crying. I had to pick him up and hold him while I watched the plank.

For what seemed like hours, I walked back and forth real slow trying to shush the baby that already had the colic. I guess Wallace was born with the colic, though he growed into a mighty healthy feller. Maybe it was the scare before he was borned that caused it. But he hollered and took on, and I didn't know what to do except hold him and sway to quiet him, which helped a little.

And I kept pushing that plank further in, a little at a time, as it burned. One big piece of wood will never burn as well as little pieces, because the big piece can't get air except on the outside. But I kept the hot coals around the board and it burned enough to give some light and keep smoke going up the chimney. I walked back and forth until my feet was numb. I couldn't hardly feel my toes, or my steps, but my legs just seemed to keep walking on their own.

I might even have gone to sleep while walking. I've heard tell of such a thing. I kept swaying the baby and talking to him and pushing the board further into the fire every twenty or thirty times around the cabin. "Little un," I kept saying to Wallace, "Little un, you better go to sleep."

At some point I come to myself and realized they wasn't no sounds from the roof or chimney anymore. Between times when the baby was squalling, I couldn't hear a thing up there. I leaned over and listened, and they was nothing but a puff and whisper of the fire, like when it's raining and the chimney starts dripping inside. It's too cold to rain, I thought. It was cold and clear when I went to the spring at dark.

With the baby crying, I listened as best I could at the door.

They wasn't no sound far as I could tell. I wondered if that painter was standing on the roof still as he could to fool me. Or was he standing before the door waiting for me to open it?

Only place in the cabin where you could see out was the crack at the eave on the west end. I was too sore to climb on the logs, and they wasn't nothing to stand on. But I had to see out. I had to look in the yard. I put the baby on the bed, and wrapped him up in the quilt Mama had give me. Then I walked over to the corner and reached up high as I could to the top log. My arms trembled as I pulled myself up, but on the third try I made it.

Soon as I put my face to the crack it was like somebody spit at me. Something cold and wet hit my cheek. And then I thought, has Realus plugged the crack with cloth or cotton wool? For it was white outside, and what hit me on the cheek was a snowflake. It was already light and snow covered everything I could see through the crack.

I dropped back and felt my insides sore as a rising. But I had to look outside. I run to the door and lifted the other plank from its bracing. The board fell on my foot but I didn't hardly pay it no mind. I opened the door a crack and looked out, and didn't see no painter. Everything was white and snow was falling steady. They was just the swishing sound of flakes touching and piling up. I stepped out the door to look at the clearing. They was big tracks in the snow getting covered up. You could see where the painter had jumped off the roof and headed out past the shed to the woods, though the tracks was already filling and blurred by new snow.

Your Grandpa didn't get back that day till after dinner time. By then I had slept some, and cleaned up the cabin a little. When the baby got to sleep, I run out to the woodpile and raked the snow off some sticks to carry in. It was a fine, dry snow, like flour or baking soda. I hauled in enough wood to last through the day and night if it had to. I piled wood in the corner where it dripped and run, but I knowed it would be dry enough to burn in a few hours. I was almost too sore to move, and every time I did something I rested a spell. For dinner I reheated my pot of beans and baked a corn pone on the hearth.

When Realus finally come, I couldn't wait for him to see what I had done. I'd be lying if I didn't say I was proud of myself. Any woman is proud of her baby, and I'd done it all by myself. He come in covered with snow looking white as a ghost. He stuck his head in the door, white as one of them polar bears. He had a sack covered with snow too. Snow fell off him in scraps and drops.

"Don't shake that stuff off in here," I said, sounding firm and concerned. "You'll put the fire out." He turned around and brushed snow off his shoulders and off the sack in the doorway.

"And don't let a draft in here," I said. "Some of us could get cold." I wanted to see how long it took him to notice things was different. Your Grandpa was always a quick man, but he had come a long way and was probably stiff from riding, and hungry.

He put the sack down in front of the fire. Then he stomped his boots in the doorway and closed the door. He still hadn't said nothing, though he must have seen the bench was gone except for the one plank. He leaned his gun beside the fireplace.

"Did you find a midwife?" I said.

He turned and looked directly at me. "Don't need a midwife," he said. And his face, though it was stiff and burned by cold, begun to break out all over in a grin. Your Grandpa had that kind of face that when he was happy seemed to grin from the tip of his beard to the ears.

"Don't need no midwife," he said, and pulled me up and kissed me. That was the kind of man he was. You couldn't help but love him. All my anger and resentment trickled away like the snow on the sack. You couldn't stay mad at Realus. When he was away I could work up a rage. But I never could keep it in his presence.

He looked at the baby sleeping on the bed, and then he rubbed his hands before the fire. After his hands was warm he picked up the baby like he'd never seen anything so curious. Men don't take to newborn babies like women does. But he was still proud. And you could see how struck he was. He didn't know how you hold a baby. His big hands could reach all the way around the bundle and the baby looked smaller when your Grandpa was holding him.

"Let's call him Wallace," he said. "After my grandsire on my Mama's side."

That was the first I ever heard of his Grandpa Wallace on his Mama's side. But I didn't say nothing. It was fine with me if we called the baby Wallace. It was a good strong name.

Your Grandpa went out and got two more stumps at the woodpile and put the plank on them for a bench. And we must have set there for two hours, holding the baby and talking. We eat the beans and corn pone, and Realus went out and sliced a piece of deer meat in the shed. I fried that meat over the fire for supper.

"I must have rid fifty miles," he said, "before I come to another settlement. And they wasn't no doctor or midwife there. But they sent me on to a place called Peasticks where they was a store and tavern."

When the baby cried I carried him, and then Realus would carry him. I was waiting for him to ask what happened to the bench, and to the ladder pegs in the wall. I was busting to tell him about the painter, but I wanted him to ask. I think he was teasing me by not asking. Or maybe he was too distracted and happy to notice anything but the baby. Finally, I couldn't wait no longer.

"They was a painter here," I said. He walked in front of the fire with the baby trying to quiet him like I had done all night.

"They was a painter here that tried to get down the chimney."

"I knowed it," he said.

"How could you know it?" I said. "If you was fifty miles away?" He didn't take his eyes off the baby.

"'Cause I seen the top of the chimney was tore up," he said. "Nothing but a painter would do that. I seen it soon as I rode into the clearing."

I didn't know whether to be mad at him, or pleased that he figured it all out from the tore-up chimney.

"Next time he comes around, I'll shoot him," Realus said. And he did.

But that evening he got back, we set by the fire and talked. And he brought out all the things he'd carried in the sack from the store. They was a piece of red cloth for me to make a dress.

"Ain't got nowhere to wear a fancy dress," I said.

"You can wear it here, for me," he said.

Then he brought out a poke of powder, and some shot. And he had a sack of sugar, and some tea. That was the best thing he had brought, really. I hadn't had no tea since our supply run out in the summer, though we sometimes parched bran and made a kind of brew. I boiled some water right then and made a pot. Nothing I ever drunk tasted better. The smell of that tea filled the cabin. It even seemed to make the baby quiet down. And when I drunk a cup, it made the cabin seem bright and realer.

I don't need to tell you how busy I was in the months following, looking after the baby and keeping things clean. I kept the washpot going almost every day that winter. Your Grandpa split wood and got the fire started in the morning, before he went out to clear new ground. He was clearing up a whole section further down the creek and burning up the logs.

Every morning I put my diaper rags and dirty things in the washpot and let them boil. And I strung another line to the shed to dry things on. We put a string up over the fireplace for drying when it rained or snowed. My hands got cracked from all the washing, and I put deer grease on them.

I'd try to find out more about the settlements from your Grandpa, but he wouldn't hardly say nothing. We'd be talking about getting us a hog for next fall, and I'd say, "Why don't you ride into the settlement and buy us a couple of pigs?"

"It's too far to drive pigs," he'd say.

"Couldn't you get little uns and carry them in sacks on the horse?"

"And what would little pigs eat?" he'd say. "They wouldn't be no milk for them."

Another time we'd be talking about getting flower seeds to plant around the cabin come spring. I wanted some big flowers. "Couldn't we go to the settlement and buy some seeds and bulbs and get some more tea?" I said.

"Can't leave you alone," he'd say.

"Then we could go with you."

"It's too far to take the baby."

"The baby can stand anything we can stand," I said.

Along in March your Grandpa did go back to the settlement and buy a new grubbing hoe and some more tea, and some pea seed and cabbage seed. He didn't bring back no flower seeds, but he did carry some chickens in a sack on the horse. That seemed really the beginning of our farming. You can't make a farm without animals. It was a different place with hens clucking and a rooster crowing in the morning.

That spring we kept the chickens in a coop so hawks and foxes couldn't get at them. Even so, a weasel got in and killed one of the hens and sucked her blood. When the other hens started laying eggs, it was the wonderfullest thing. I hadn't had no eggs in a year. A fresh egg for breakfast on occasion made a day seem like a holiday. I'd save up three or four eggs and make a pudding or even a cake. We got used to having eggs again and found it a hardship when the hens started setting. For a few weeks we didn't have nothing but mush in the mornings.

That spring we had trout a lot. I fried trout in corn meal, and baked trout, till we got sick of picking out the bones. Realus could take a few worms and catch an armload of the things.

"Why don't we save up some eggs and some honey and take them into the settlements to trade?" I said.

"We don't have enough of either to make it worthwhile," your Grandpa said. "You just want to go gallivanting. Women always like to socialize."

"Sure, I'm a real society lady," I said, and went back to sewing.

I wasn't lonesome on the creek, especially after Wallace come, and then the rest of the children. Mostly I wanted to buy things in the settlement to fix up our place. I wanted a bigger garden, and flowers, and a guinea hen in the yard. And I wanted a cow so we could have butter. And I wanted hogs for making lard and sausage. And I needed cloth to make new clothes, and sheep so I could spin our own wool.

In time your Grandpa bought all them things. He'd go off to the settlement every four or five months and come back with a calf or a couple of pigs. And one time he brought some young apple trees to set out on the side of the hill. Another time be brought plum and pear trees. He even got a grape vine we set out over there alongside the barn. He got so many things I've lost track of the order in which he brung them. But we gradually begun to push back the woods and make this into a place for people. It's the animals that do it. When you have cattle grazing they keep back the wild things and make room for humans. People on their own can't do it.

Realus even brought back a dog one day, a big cur named Trail, that kept the wolves and painters back on the ridge and let us know if a snake was around. One time we seen Indians at the end of the clearing, but Trail barked at them and they was gone.

"What kind of Indians we got here?" I said.

"Same as in Calinny I reckon," your Grandpa said. "Maybe some Tuscarora too, besides the Cherokee."

The second fall, when Realus took some yellowroot and honey into the settlements to trade, he brought back a Bible. "Every family's got to have a book," he said. "Without a Bible they's no account of folks."

We made ink out of pokeberry juice and he sharpened a goose quill. One night after frost had come he set by the fire and wrote with great pains and thought in the front of the Bible.

"Realus Richards and Petal Jarvis was married in March. . . ."

"What day was we married?" your Grandpa said.

"The night we left the settlement," I said. "You know that."

"But what day of the month was it?"

"It was March 17th," I said. I hadn't thought of that date in a long time. But it come back to me. It was an important day.

So your Grandpa wrote in the new Bible:

"Realus Richards and Petal Jarvis was married March 17, 1772."

You can still see it in the Bible over there. Next he turned a page and wrote:

"Wallace Realus Richards was borned December. . . ."

"When was Wallace borned?" he said.

There he had me stumped, though I knowed Wallace was borned on about the longest night of the year, just before Christmas.

"It was right before Christmas," I said.

Your Grandpa thought for a minute and said the day he come back from the settlement was five days before Christmas. And since Wallace was borned the night before, that would make his birthday the nineteenth.

"Wallace was borned after midnight," I said.

Your Grandpa wrote in the Bible, "Wallace Realus Richards was borned December 20th, 1772."

The very next time he returned to the settlement, your Grandpa bought an almanac that had a calendar in it. And after that we kept account of the days and months. It helped to have a record so we knowed when a hen was set or a cow would freshen. We had our own bull by the next year.

When each of the children come along your Grandpa wrote down in the big book the day they was borned. You can see them there still:

"Lewis Josephus Richards was borned April 26, 1774."

"Eller Jarvis Richards was borned October 14, 1775."

"Willa Elizabeth Richards was borned February 10, 1777."

Them was hard years, but I was too busy nearly to worry about it. By the time Willa was borned, your Grandpa had near forty acres cleared along the creek. Besides the cows, we had at least ten sheep. One of the places we hadn't cleared was the holler back up the branch over there. It was dark and narrow in that draw, but the cows liked to go up there in early spring because it was warm in the holler and out of the wind, and some of the first green stuff come up in open spots below the spring.

We had no way of knowing they was milksick in that holler. They wasn't no warning when Little Eller took sick in the year she was two. It was early spring, before any leaves had come out on the trees. They was just little dabs of green along the branch and up the coves. Your Grandpa was helling off the fields along the creek and coming in smelling like brush fires and ashes. "Don't you burn no poison ash," I said. The smoke of that will break you out all over in blisters.

Soon as he got all the stalks and stubble burned off he would start plowing. The first deadening we made had just a few rotten trunks standing in it, and them was falling down in storms and dropping all the big limbs. Some pine stumps caught fire when he burned the field off.

Wallace said one morning the milk tasted bad. He was always careful about his eating. "Mama, the milk is blinky," he said.

"It can't be blinky," Realus said. "It was milked last night and has set in the spring ever since."

"It tastes funny," Lewis said. He always mocked what Wallace said.

The boys wouldn't drink their milk. But Little Eller went right ahead and drunk a whole cupful. Willa was still nursing then. I didn't even try the milk because I knowed it was fresh. Milk over a day old I put in the churn to clabber. I give the younguns only fresh milk unless they was buttermilk.

It was Sunday, and Realus read some of the Bible to us. It was something he had took to doing after he bought the Bible. We was far away from churches, but he thought the young should hear the Bible read. And once he started, I could see he was right. Later we was going to teach them all to read it for theirselves.

"Mama, my head hurts," Little Eller said when your Grandpa had finished. Wallace and Lewis run outside to play.

"What give you the headache?" I said. I was in a hurry to get things cleaned up around the house, for I wanted to go looking for creesie greens. It was time for them to be out in the fields along the creek. We'd been living on taters and bread and whatever meat your Grandpa brought in from the woods. I thought it would taste mighty good to have some fresh greens for dinner. I'd saved a piece of streaked bacon to cook with the greens.

"Go lay down," I said to Little Eller. "That'll make your headache disappear."

She laid down on the bed while I swept up the ashes and crumbs around the hearth. I had put branch sand on the floor the day before and I was going to sweep it off. Your Grandpa had put in a puncheon floor the year Wallace was born, the year he added the new room and the new loft to the house. Every month or two I polished the floor with sand.

"My head still hurts," Eller said when I started to sweep.

"Go outside in the sweet wind," I said. "It may be smoke inside giving you the headache."

She drug herself out and I swept all the branch sand into the yard. Your Grandpa hadn't built a step yet so you could whisk the dirt right through the door. I wanted to get outside myself. You could tell it was going to warm up in protected places on the south side.

Little Eller stood in the yard shielding her eyes from the sunlight. After a while she come back to the door.

"I hurt all over," she said.

When a youngun gets the all-overs, you know it has a fever. "Come here," I said. I put my hand on her forehead, and sure enough, it was hot.

"I feel all shivery," she said.

Children will run a fever. They's no way you can stop that. They'll get a chill and a sore throat or a bellyache. Especially around the changing time of year, the equinoxes.

"Go back to bed," I said. "I'll put the quilt over you." I made her some sassafras tea. Your Grandpa had dug yellowroot the week before to make spring tonic. I had me a little supply of herbs we'd collected. And we had a jug of liquor he had brought back from the settlement for making tinctures. And the year before we'd made some blackberry wine to drink for stomach trouble. I had sulfur to give the kids for worms.

I give Eller some sassafras tea, hoping she would sweat a little and cool off. It helped her drop off to sleep. Willa was sleeping in the cradle, and I figured I'd run down the creek and pick some creesies while I had a chance.

"Don't let Eller come outside," I hollered to Wallace and Lewis in the yard. I thought Realus was out at the shed looking after the stock. But sometimes on a Sunday morning he would just walk in the woods, far down the creek and up on the ridge, and then around the place, looking for things that needed to be done the coming week. Mostly he held to the Sabbath, unless they was something that had to be done, like fixing up the fence around the garden to keep the deer out, or catching a swarm of bees. On a Sunday he might be out looking for arbutus to bring back to the house. Even then it was hard to find.

I hurried down the creek with my bucket. It was one of them days with sun and clouds passing quick. The clouds throwed shadows like big animals walking by. I did find some greens, but I got my feet awful muddy to reach them. The field dirt had been turned to cream by the freezing and thawing, and it stuck to my shoes. I cropped off my bucket full of greens and headed back, trying to stomp and wipe the mud off as I went. I was coming around the bend by the shed when I heard Wallace hollering. I started running.

"Mama, Eller's having fits," he said. I run all the way to the house, and sure enough Eller was jerking on the bed and staring up like she didn't see nothing. I took hold of her but she didn't stop jerking. They wasn't nothing else I could think of to do, and your Grandpa was nowhere around.

I'd heard of worms giving children fits, but Eller looked too healthy to be wormy. And things like typhoid fever would give people fits, but only near the crisis, after the fever had been bad for several days.

"Get me a wet rag," I said to Wallace. The boys stood there staring. I couldn't hardly see after being out in the sunlight.

Wallace brought me a rag dipped in the water bucket and I put it on Eller's forehead. The twitching and shuddering in her limbs slowed down and finally her eyes blinked and shut. It was another few minutes before she seemed to know I was standing over her. She was hot as a stove and I seen the fever in her eyes. That's when I remembered the milk she had drunk.

Lord, let it not be milksick, I prayed. I kept a cold compress on her forehead, and built up the fire, and waited for your Grandpa to come back.

They's nothing makes you feel helpless as a sick child does. You're responsible, and if they's something wrong it must be your fault. You've got to do something quick but don't know what. You have to be in charge but don't know what to do next, for sickness in a child is mostly a mystery. I knowed they was a remedy, or was supposed to be a remedy, for milksick—if it was milksick—but I couldn't recall it. My Daddy used to tell all kinds of cures, like tincture of lobelia for rattler bites, and tea made from willow bark for a fever. I wished I could ask him.

Realus didn't come back till near dinner time. He walked into the yard carrying arbutus and some spring beauties. He had that shy look men have when they have gathered flowers for a woman. No telling how far back in the mountains he had gone looking for them flowers. The petals looked pure white. It pained me to have to tell him the bad news. But Wallace run up to him and said, "Pa, Eller's took sick."

"How sick?"

"Bad sick, Pa."

Realus put the flowers on the table and run to the bed. "She took sick after breakfast," I said. "I think it was the milk."

Your Grandpa run to the milk pitcher still on the shelf and smelled the spout. Then he come back to the bed and felt Little Eller's forehead. He opened her mouth to look at her tongue.

"She had some kind of fit," I said.

"If it's milksick, you can tell by the color of her tongue," he said. "Ain't but one treatment I know of; that's whiskey and honey. Hot whiskey and honey."

"Is that what the old folks used?" I said.

"That's the only treatment I've heard of."

I got the whiskey jug down from the shelf and poured some into a saucepan to heat on the fire. We still had a little honey left over from the fall, and I scraped around the jar with a spoon trying to get pure sourwood without any comb. It wouldn't do Eller no good to pour beeswax into her.

"How much honey do you put?" I said.

"I don't know no formula," he said. "Four or five big spoons to the drink I guess." He was as scared as I was. It makes a big strong man feel feeble not to be able to help his youngun.

I poured some of the syrup in a cup and Realus held Little Eller up. She was almost asleep with the fever and we tried to wake her. Her face was swelled and red, but her skin was dry.

"Wake up, wake up," Realus said, cradling her head in his big hand.

"Drink this," I said, holding the warm cup to her mouth. I

poured the syrup in slowly, and I think some of it went down. A lot spilled around the corners of her mouth and dripped on the pillow. But they wasn't nothing we could do. I poured about a third of the cup in her and put her back down.

Wallace and Lewis stood in the door watching us. Willa had started crying in the cradle.

"Is Eller going to get well?" Wallace said, and swallowed.

"Shhhh," I said. Fever patients was supposed to have quiet.

That was the longest Sunday evening and night. Your Grandpa and me took turns warming the syrup and pouring some in Eller's mouth. But I don't think she ever knowed what we was doing. She was so fevered and sleepy. In her sleep she fretted and mumbled. I hated to think what kind of dreams she was having.

The children had never had no dinner, so along in the evening I baked some cornbread and washed the creesie greens. I boiled some eggs and we had eggs and creesie greens and bread. We set down at the table, but me and your Grandpa didn't feel like eating, though we nibbled a little at the bread. It showed how worried Realus was. Creesie greens was one of his favoritest things, especially cooked with streaked bacon and a little vinegar sprinkled in.

Finally your Grandpa went out to milk, but he throwed the milk away. He was afraid to give the milk even to the hogs till he knowed for sure it didn't have milksick. "I'll fence off that holler so the cows won't ever go back," he said.

I had made some candles the winter before and I put one on the stand by the bed. I wanted to be able to see Eller, and to give her more syrup. She still hadn't begun to sweat, and she felt hotter than ever. After the other younguns had gone to bed, and Realus had dropped off to sleep in his chair, I heard Eller talking in her fever. I listened to see what she was saying.

At first I didn't know if it was the candle sputtering or her voice. Then I leaned close and seen her lips move.

"Get away, get away from me," she was saying. And it was like she was talking to somebody in the room. "Get back, get away."

And I had this awful feeling, like they was some evil presence in her dream that was there in the room.

"Don't sting me, don't sting me," she said. She was dreaming about the bee that stung her the summer before. She was playing on the bank not too far from the beegums, and one stung her finger. I squeezed the juice of a ragweed on the sting, but her hand still swelled up. And she scratched it for days afterward because it itched so bad.

I felt a little better, knowing she was just dreaming about the bee. It made her seem not quite as sick. My Mama used to say that somebody, when they got awful sick, could feel the shadow of death getting near them. And the strange thing was, the shadow of death was comforting, it was welcome. People in their right mind didn't seem afraid. It was only fevered people, them out of their head, that hollered and took on.

Little Eller stirred and rolled her head side to side like she was trying to dodge the bee. I wondered if I should wake her up and give her more of the syrup. I couldn't do it without Realus to hold her, and I hated to wake him too. If the fever didn't break I should sponge her off with a damp rag. If a fever goes too long it will stop a child's growth, or bake their brain.

I got up to warm the syrup and heard this scratching by the door. It sounded like a puppy clawing to get in, except it was too high on the door. It was just a little sound, nothing big or scary. Your Grandpa's gun was there in the corner.

The scratching stopped, and then continued. I figured if I held the gun when I opened the door, they wouldn't be no danger.

Such a little noise must be made by something small. It sounded like a mouse scratching at the door post, or maybe in the eave.

Lifting the bolt quiet as I could, I swung the door on its greased hinges so it just creaked a little. The gun was in my right hand and I pushed the door with the left. It was so dark out there, and I didn't see nothing at first in the light from the door. Then something fluttered from the roof to the hitching post in front of the door. I strained to see what it was. They was this big passenger pigeon, gray, almost white, on top of the post. It must have been an albino. You don't see many passenger pigeons by theirselves. They stay with their big flocks. But this one had got lost. It was bigger than you would expect.

The bird just set there without making a sound. Its eye blinked. The eye reflected the firelight from inside, and seemed to shine like the eye of a moth that comes close up to light, like a little coal of fire. That bird was used to flying in flocks a mile wide and hundreds of miles long, and there it was setting by itself on the hitching post.

I closed the door quiet as I could, and the bird flapped off into the night.

The syrup had got too hot by the fire, and I had to set it off to cool. I thought most of the spirits must have boiled away so I poured in a little more likker to freshen it. This is all we know to treat sickness, I thought, the sweetness from flowers and the spirits from corn. Both things heated and stimulated the body. That must mean that milksick cooled off and numbed the body. And yet the fever was heating her little body too. I couldn't follow out the truth of it. But it seemed sleeping might be the danger. If she kept on sleeping she might not wake up.

Your Grandpa was slumped in his chair and I shook him. "Wake up," I said. "We've got to give Little Eller some more medicine."

He jerked away and rolled his eyes for a second, like he didn't know where he was. Then he got up and helped me lift Little Eller. I decided not to tell him about the pigeon. It wouldn't do no good to scare him with portents. And besides, it did not seem completely real long as I was the only one that knowed about it.

"We could sponge her off with vinegar," your Grandpa said.

After we tried to pour some more of the syrup in her mouth, and mostly spilled it on the bed, I filled a pan with warm water and poured in vinegar. The vinegar bit right into my nostrils when it was warmed by the water. I thought it might wake up Little Eller, like smelling salts. It would be a good thing if it did wake her up to fight the milksick better.

Your Grandpa rolled back the bedclothes and I lifted her gown and rubbed her body with the cloth soaked in vinegar and water. It felt like touching a stove her skin was so hot. Her little legs was like sticks that had come out of the fire. The vinegar dried almost as soon as I rubbed it on her skin.

"Roll her over on her belly," I said. I knowed a lot of heat left the body through the back. I wiped the vinegar on her back, which was red as a sunburn. I rubbed her all over before we covered her up, but it didn't seem like we had accomplished nothing. She was still hot, and mumbling like she was troubled.

"I've heard of doctors bleeding fever patients," I said. "Reckon it would do any good?"

"Bleeding's for older people," your Grandpa said.

"I've heard of giving boneset tea to break a fever," Realus said. "But this time of year you can't get none."

I watched him setting there looking puzzled and helpless. Doctoring was something we hadn't hardly thought about when we headed off to the wilderness. We was young and thought we would always be healthy. I assumed they would always be doctors and midwives nearby. But I birthed all my children on my own.

Realus had helped with the last three. And we had been lucky all was borned healthy.

I wondered if he was sorry he had brought me to the West. We had had a hard time, but mostly it was a good life. A big strong feller like him could have gone off anywhere he wanted. He could have gone further west, or he could have gone to the city of Charleston or Philadelphia. We had been a loving couple, and we had been hardworking. And we had turned that little clearing by the creek into a home place with fruit trees and grapes and bees. We had more than a dozen head of stock by then, counting the sheep. The next year we was going to add on to the house again.

It's good people can't read each other's thoughts, because all kinds of things pass through a mind that has no right to be spoken. I'll admit I'd had my doubts at times, and not just on the night the painter tried to get in, or when I was scared at the gold diggings. And it wasn't the mystery of our place being so far from anybody else, and us never seeing anybody that bothered me most. No sir, it was that doubt that whispers to you in the middle of the night like a snake suggesting you've done everything wrong. A woman is bothered by the fear she's not loved, even if they's no reason to fear. I got a chill thinking Realus might be sorry he brung me to the Holsten, thinking he wished he'd gone off other ways. But at the same time I knowed they was nothing to it, and that we was happy.

"Maybe we should pray," your Grandpa said.

"The sun sings," Little Eller mumbled. She was way out of her head with the fever. I put my hand on her cheek, but they was still no sweat.

Me and your Grandpa got down on our knees by the bed and we didn't say a word out loud. We didn't need to. What we had to ask the Lord was clear. We had to put things in His hands. I've heard preachers talk of praying through on something and having assurance, and such as that. But me and Realus didn't ask for anything like guarantees. We just asked for help.

When we finally got up, I went to the water bucket and got a dipper of water. I thought if I could make Little Eller drink some it might cool her off. Your Grandpa held her up and I tried to pour water in her mouth a dribble at a time. But most of the water run down the corners of her mouth. I didn't see her swallow none.

I'd always heard people die between midnight and sunrise. Something about the small hours makes that the time the spirit leaves the body. If a sick person lives till sunrise, they'll probably make it through another day. A fever will go down at sunrise. Your Grandpa hadn't bought a clock yet, but we knowed it was past midnight. I prayed Little Eller would see the sunrise.

I set down by Little Eller and held her hand. She was hot as something out in the July sun. I watched her stir and mumble, and before I knowed it I must have dropped off to sleep. Because when I looked up next the fire had died down and the room was quiet. And it was like something had just left. Something had woke me up. Your Grandpa was asleep and the younguns was asleep.

Little Eller was still and not mumbling. But her lips had this black look, and her fingers had turned dark. I've heard milksick does that to folks at the last. I leaned over and tried to feel her breathing. They was no breath from her nostrils. She was still as stone, but her hand was warm in mine. I thought she couldn't be dead because she was still warm. But she must have died at the instant I woke. When I felt her leaving, I woke up.

I thought that instant how little human life means in the big scope of things. A human being can be alive one second and gone the next, and everything else stays just the same. The shock of that froze me for a moment. Already her hand was turning cool. Her flesh that had been hot all night was cooler than mine.

When I woke up your Grandpa, we didn't cry none. It was too bad to cry at first. We was just young folks, and we'd never had much to do with death. No sir, both Realus and me got busy. It was like we took orders to start doing things.

Little Eller was turning blue and all the fever color was draining out of her cheeks. Her body was limp as a sack. Your Grandpa carried her over to the table and I got some warm water and washed her. I'd always heard you washed a corpse so that's what I done. I washed her off and then I rubbed her all over with camphor, for I'd seen people put camphor-soaked cloths over the face of a corpse. Then I put a clean gown on her.

I knowed if I stopped and set down I never would get going again. I had to keep moving. Her hair had got all tangled up and sticky from the spilled syrup. I put more warm water in the pan and washed her hair, pouring water from a cup over the hair.

"What are you doing?" Realus said when he come back. It was getting light out. He had gone to look for planks for a casket.

"I'm washing her hair," I said.

"It don't make no difference where her hair is washed or not."

"It was sticky and all tangled up."

Realus was distracted and tore up as I was. "It don't make no difference," he said.

"It makes a difference to me."

I thought I would remember her always the way I last seen her. I washed her hair and dried it and tied it in a ribbon.

Your Grandpa fretted till after sunrise about material for a casket. There wasn't no sawmill around, so any boards had to be sawed out by him. The buildings was all made of logs, and only a few planks for benches and tables had been hewed out. He didn't have nobody big enough to help out with the saw except me. He went out to the shed to look through the poles and planks there, and come back in and stood by the fire. Then he went out again to the woodpile and spring house. I'd never seen him in such a fret. Everybody has a different way of grieving, and that was his, to stomp and fuss about the lumber for the coffin.

They wasn't nothing on the place fit to make a casket. With time he could have sawed down a wild cherry and hewed boards and polished the wood. But we had to bury Eller that day. We had to get it over with, or we couldn't have stood it no longer.

What your Grandpa done finally was saw off a holler black gum log. He had cut it to make more bee gums. He sawed out a section about four feet long, and then he split it in two pieces. Them pieces he hollowed out with his ax like a cradle. And he smoothed the inside with the adz, and with a piece of glass.

When we laid Little Eller inside that casket in her white gown she looked like a bud inside a nutshell, a baby folded inside a little boat. Realus laid her in there, and I crossed her hands over her chest. I made all the younguns look at her before we pegged it shut. I wanted them to see her looking pretty and at peace, though her ears and lips was already black.

The thing I remember worst about that day was all the crows calling. They fussed and squawked at us from the trees. They circled and regathered down by the creek. I think they was waiting for us to plant corn so they could steal the seeds. I don't know where so many crows come from all at once. The woods seemed to be full of the ugly things. That was the first year your Grandpa put a scarecrow out in the new ground where he planted corn. If he hadn't made the scarecrow, they wouldn't have been any seeds left to grow.

A fter Little Eller died, it was like some colors inside me had been bleached away. As time passed, I had the same feelings and lived in the same patterns I always had, but they wasn't as vivid. Except that I loved my younguns even more, the ones left. I cherished them, and I started taking more time to enjoy them. Hard as we worked, I started taking more opportunities to play with the children.

That summer, after we buried Little Eller, we took long walks in the woods on Sundays, looking for wildflowers. I taught the younguns to recognize all the flowers I knowed. We even found a swamp azalea back in the woods, blooming after the flame azaleas had gone. And we found birdnests in the brush and learned to recognize the eggs without touching them. I was learning myself about herbs from a book Realus had got, and learning the younguns to pick doghobble and yarrow, and sassafras roots and yellowroot.

Some Sundays we took a picnic down to a rock that jutted into the creek beyond the new ground. Your Grandpa even joined us sometimes. I spread a cloth on the rock, and we eat hoecakes and jelly and chicken and hot roastnears. After we eat, the kids would play in the stream. I always did love the sound of water. I could relax there, and it helped the hurt I felt for Little Eller.

In the fall and early spring, when the woods was bare and you could look out from the mountainsides, and didn't have to be afraid of snakes, and the air was cool, we took long walks back on the ridge. Your Grandpa said, "Don't go away so far you're liable to get lost."

"We ain't going to get lost," I said.

"You might get lost or run into Indians," he said. "I don't want you to go too far from the house. I forbid you to go far from the clearing." He sounded harsh and scared. Then he softened, as he always done when he knowed he had gone too far. "Besides, I can't afford to pay no ransom; you might have to stay with the Indians and become a squaw."

But we kept walking in the woods when the weather was good

and I had time. One Sunday we found nearly thirty different flowers and the younguns gathered samples of each. Another time we collected butterflies, and praying mantises and walkingsticks. We collected rock crystals and arrowheads along the creek. We come to a place where the creek joined a river. We walked so far, we found a place we named Pulpit Rock because of the cliff that stuck up over the water. The children climbed on top and pretended to preach to the whole valley.

Another time we crossed over the ridge to the west and come to a real long holler. We followed the branch down to where it opened into a meadow that had lots of ripe strawberries. We all eat strawberries till I thought we was going to be sick. I'd heard too many fresh strawberries can poison a body, but they didn't seem to hurt us.

In that same meadow we come on the remains of a campfire, and we knowed it must be Indians, because they was a broke arrow left in the grass, and pieces of parched corn scattered among the ashes. I knowed Indians lived on parched corn when they traveled. We started back home then, and crossed the ridge to our creek valley, but we didn't see no Indians. When I told Realus he said, "It's only the grace of God you didn't get catched."

Every time we went out on a long walk, we brought something back and put on Little Eller's grave. We put all kinds of flowers on that mound, and pretty stones, and arrowheads. Your Grandpa had set up a smooth slab of rock at the head of the grave, and we made a circle of white rocks around the mound. He kept the weeds cut there. It was something he done for me. I'd go stand on the hill sometimes and look down at the house and the place we had cleared, all the way down to the new fields and the scarecrow he made out of some posts and his old clothes. The scarecrow leaned a little, and I used to think it seemed drunk. It was our drunk scarecrow, standing out there looking crucified in all kinds of weather, watching the corn patch. At times it seemed to be watching me wherever I went. I thought of saying to your Grandpa, take that thing down. It seems too spooky leaning there, with its clothes flapping, watching us all the time. But he would have laughed at me and said we had to keep the crows out of the corn.

One day in October, more than two years after Little Eller died, we decided to go looking for foxgrapes. I wanted to make some jelly, and I knowed they was ripe, for I could smell them in the evening after the sun was gone. In the breeze by the creek, you could smell the grapes ripening and starting to ferment.

We took our buckets and baskets and headed out after breakfast. Realus had built a footlog across the creek just above the bend, and we crossed there and climbed the other ridge. Realus had picked foxgrapes along the river over there before, and I knowed they must be a heavy growth that year. It was a warm day with the leaves drifting off the poplars and maples, a few at a time.

As we climbed up the slope, we could hear the cowbell Realus had got in the settlement and put on Old Daisy. It tinkled up the holler. Since the cows usually stayed together in the woods, he only put a bell on the oldest milker. It was a peaceful sound, but we couldn't hear it anymore after we crossed the ridge.

The foxgrapes was as thick along the river bank as I had hoped they would be. The biggest problem was getting to them. Sometimes I let Wallace shinny up a birch tree and pick some high grapes. But his arms was too short to reach far. And I didn't like him to be high over the water.

A few times I had to step out in the stream to reach a limb. One time I stood on some brush that give way, and I ended up in the water halfway to my knees. The younguns laughed at me. Lewis said, "Mama got her stockings wet, Mama got her stockings wet." But we was having a good time. We had brought along some biscuits and honey and biscuits and ham for our dinner.

As it turned out, we didn't need to worry about reaching the grapes in hard places, because the further up the river we went, the more foxgrapes we found. The air was full of that sweet grape smell where the sun was hitting the ripe bunches. Every grape you touched was tight and full of juice.

"Mama, here's another vine," Wallace called, and we'd follow another hundred yards up the stream to the next lavish of grapes hanging in easy reach. By the time we had picked most of those, he would already have found another tree up ahead.

It was thrilling, but scary, because we didn't look for snakes as careful as we should. And I kept hollering for Lewis to stay out of the branch, and for Willa to keep up, and keep away from brush where they might be a rattler. When you're looking after children and working at the same time, you're split in two.

We kept going further and further up that river. Miles I reckon. And the further we went, the faster we seemed to work. We filled a bucket and left it setting by the stream to pick up on the way back. It looked like we was going to fill every single bucket and basket we had. It would take days to cook down that many grapes into juice and then make jelly. But the grapes was so big and ripe, I didn't want to go back without our buckets full.

"Look, here's a fire," Lewis called.

"What kind of fire?" I said, trying to reach the higher branches above a sandbar in the curve of the stream.

"It's still warm," Lewis said.

I put my bucket down and run over to where he was. They was a clearing above the river, covered with peavines and big weeds.

At first I didn't see Lewis. It was like he had disappeared. The vines was so thick, I was afraid of a snake. I called to Lewis and he answered, not more than a hundred feet away.

Sure enough, he had found what was left of a campfire. Some of the sticks still smoldered a little, so we knowed it had been left that morning. But I couldn't tell if it was Indians or not. They wasn't no parched corn or broke arrows. The vines and weeds had been knocked down where they slept around the fire, but that didn't tell nothing. I reckon both Indians and whites sleep the same way, stretched out in their blankets. And we couldn't tell which way they went neither, or the way they had come.

I called Wallace back and told him to stay close.

"But I'm the scout," he said. "I have to go ahead and find more vines."

"We can find them together," I said. What I didn't say was we had already gone further than your Grandpa wanted us to. I didn't really know how far we had gone, but three forks had split off the river. It was just a creek now you could almost step over.

We crossed in a shallow place and walked a little way up the other side. When we come to a big rock, I suggested we eat our dinner on it. While we was eating, I noticed we was so high up most of the leaves had fell. The poplars was bare, and most of the maples. We was way up on the mountain. A yellow leaf floated onto the rock, and then a yellowjacket appeared, attracted to the honey on our biscuits. I turned away from the jacket, hoping it would go away. That's when I noticed the top of the mountain above. The peak looked like a forehead, and the shape seemed awful familiar. I didn't know where I had seen it before, but I had. Maybe we had passed this way when we come to the cabin years before. They was a lot I didn't remember about that trip. I kept turning away from the yellowjacket and wondering about the knob on the mountain.

And then we heard a cowbell. I didn't know they was any cows that high in the woods. We was far away from our own cows. And they was something familiar about that bell. I had heard it before. It wasn't one of our cows. I wondered if it might be some trick of the Indians.

I'd heard of Indians killing a settler's cow and carrying the bell as they approached the house. That way nobody got suspicious and the sound of their steps was covered by the tinkling. The Indians moved slow through the woods like a cow grazing there.

"Come here," I whispered to Lewis and Willa. I had stood up when I heard that cowbell, and I realized how exposed we was on that rock.

"Come here," I said, and lifted them down to the ground. Wallace had gone off into the woods as soon as he eat his biscuits. He said he was going to get a drink from the stream, but I knowed he was looking for more grapes. We had all we could carry home, but he wanted to look for more. He was all enthused about the search, and his success, and didn't want to stop.

I couldn't holler for him, and tell the Indians, if they was Indians, where we was. Wallace was out of sight, and I couldn't leave Lewis and Willa to go look for him.

"What's wrong, Mama?" Lewis said. I pulled them with me and we crouched out of sight.

"Are we playing hide-and-seek?" Willa said. "Are we hiding from Wallace?" She giggled, thinking it was a game.

"Wallace!" I said, just loud enough so I hoped it would not be heard up on the ridge where the bell sounded.

"Mama, are we going to scare Wallace?" Willa said.

I had left the cloth and the remains of our dinner on top of the rock. I run back and pulled them off as quick and quiet as I could. The thing about Indians is they always see you before you see them. They're like owls that way. Whoever seen an owl that wasn't already watching them?

"I'll go find Wallace," Lewis said.

"No, stay here!" I said. I thought of all the times Realus had warned me not to go too far from the clearing, and not to cross the river. If we ever got back, I would heed his warning.

I could tell by the sun it was getting late in the evening. It wouldn't be long till Realus come back from the field for his supper. He was gathering corn and hauling it on his sled. Soon as the corn was in he'd begin hauling wood for the winter. I wished we could start on back with the grapes. I wished we was already home and I was putting water on to boil and taters in the ashes to bake. It was getting chilly that high up on the mountain.

"Wall-ace," I called again. But we didn't have no choice but to wait for him. If I went looking, it would only attract more attention. When he seen we hadn't followed, he'd come back to tell us what he had found. I was afraid he would holler out.

Then I heard that cowbell again. It was like something I knowed but just couldn't name. It was the sweetest, clearest note. Was it something I had dreamed about? It was like a taste in the air that tingled memory. That made it even more scary, to think some Indian might be tinkling that bell to fool us.

We heard something in the leaves about a hundred feet away. I made the children crouch down even lower, and we listened. Something was stirring in the brush. It would make a noise and then stop. I thought it must be Wallace playing in the leaves. Maybe he was looking for us. I raised up slowly to look out.

At first I didn't see nothing. Then a limb shook and some red sourwood leaves fell. I seen this ugly head poke through, and a turkey come out, scratching and looking around. I was relieved, but disappointed it wasn't Wallace. Made me mad to think he had just wandered off. If I caught him I was going to switch him.

"You stay right here," I said to Willa and Lewis. "I'm going to look for Wallace."

"Can't we come?" Lewis said.

"You stay right here with your sister," I said. "If you move, I'll whip you."

I stood up and eased around the big rock, trying not to disturb even the turkey. But standing up made me dizzy. For a few seconds the world around me seemed bleached and I couldn't remember in what direction the branch was. I couldn't tell much about direction from the woods. Then I seen the peak through the trees and remembered the river was down behind me.

I picked my way through the brush toward the mountain. So many leaves had fell, they was no way to be quiet. I went slow and listened. What I heard was my heart, and the pulse by my ears. Then I heard the cowbell, not more than a hundred feet away.

They was nothing to hide behind but an oak tree, and I stepped back of that. If the Indians had already seen me, it wouldn't do no good to hide anyway. The bell come closer and limbs was being knocked aside. Whatever it was, was coming straight toward me. I thought if the Indians found me, maybe they wouldn't catch the children. Wallace and Lewis and Willa could work their way back down the branch and find their way home.

Something walked right out into the open, ringing the bell. I glanced around the tree thinking I was caught for sure. But it wasn't nothing but a big old Jersey cow looking at me. And it come to me all at once why the cowbell was so familiar. That was my Daddy's favorite cowbell, and that was his old cow Bess. The surprise took my breath away, what I had left. For how could his cow be there in the mountains of the West?

There was the bell my Daddy was so proud of, with its one note clear as an icicle. He would stop what he was doing sometimes and listen to that tinkle off in the woods, the way a foxhunter will listen to his favorite hound. All kinds of things flew through my mind. That the bell had been sold and brought to the Holsten. Or it had been stole. Maybe my Daddy made another bell with the same tone and sold it to a passing settler. But that was Bess I used to drive to the gap and milk every evening. He might have sold the cow, too. Or had her stole and brought over the mountains.

I was puzzling over these mysteries at the same time I was relieved it wasn't Indians hunting us. Something almost come clear in my mind, and then didn't. "Here Bess, here Bess," I said. "Soo cow, soo cow." Of course, it had been years since I left home, and Bess was a young cow then, freshened not more than twice. I tore off some grass and held it out to her. She took the grass in her lips and teeth, just like I was an old friend.

I heard running steps and turned around, still expecting Indians. It was Wallace, dashing around brush and between trees.

"You come back here," I said to him. "I never give you leave to run off up the mountain."

"Mama," he said, out of breath from running. "Mama, they's houses over there."

"Over where?" I said. "I don't see no houses."

"Just over there across the mountain," he said.

"How many houses?" I said.

"A whole bunch of houses." That was when the thing stalled at the edge of my mind begun to come clear, raising into view like the shadow of an outline.

"Is they a church over there?" I said.

"They's a house with a bell on top," he said.

Then I knowed why the shape of the mountain seemed so

familiar. It was the knob at the upper end of the valley where I growed up. And that's why my Daddy's favorite cowbell was here on his favorite cow. We was on the mountain just west of the valley.

"Let's go back and get Willa and Lewis," I said.

"Where is Lewis and Willa?"

"They're hiding back beyond the picnic rock," I said.

I got the children together and we climbed toward the gap. Old Bess followed, and some of the other cows, too. They had been grazing around the huckleberry bushes and rocks of the bald. The cows had all kinds of trails between the laurel bushes and the rock cliffs up there. I had picked berries there many a time.

So much had happened, none of it seemed real. First we had followed the river valley all the way up, picking the foxgrapes, and always finding more further on. One place led to another, to the remains of the fire, and then we crossed the stream and heard the cowbell. We was disobeying your Grandpa more and more. And I seen why he didn't want us to go far from the clearing. I was beginning to see more than I could take in all at once.

By the time we got to the top of the ridge, we was on the Shimer Road. This was the way Realus and me had come when we left that night, and I hadn't even recognized it. It sure looked different from the other direction. It was like the whole world had been turned around.

"Where is this, Mama?" Wallace said. "Where are we going?"

I wasn't ready yet to explain where we was. I was hardly ready to explain it to myself. And how could they understand? Old Bess followed along behind us to the gap, thinking she was going to be fed and milked.

"We're going to see your Grandpa and Grandma," I said, trying not to sound as excited and afraid as I felt.

"We ain't got no Grandpa and Grandma, except way off in Calinny," Wallace said.

"Are we going to Calinny?" Lewis said.

"This is Carolina," I said.

"This ain't Calinny," Wallace said.

Willa was so tired from walking, I picked her up and toted her down into the valley. They was more clearings on the head-branches than before, and more new ground cleared everywhere you looked. I seen at least ten more houses in plain view when we come out onto the bank of the branch above the church. I could hear guinea fowl pottaracking in several parts of the valley. People was gathering corn in the fields and dogs barked at us. I said "how do" to everybody we passed, but they didn't seem to recognize me, and some of them I couldn't place, neither. An old woman set in a chair by a fire shucking corn, and I thought she must be Aunt Mary Lindsay, but I couldn't be sure.

When we got to the house we seen this big strapping feller chopping wood in the yard. It was Henry.

"Don't you recognize me?" I said to him.

"Seems like I do," he said.

"You ought to," I said. "I'm your sister Petal."

I introduced him to the younguns, and while we was talking, Mama come out the front door. She must have been making biscuits or a pie, for she was wiping flour on her apron. I seen how much older she looked, and shorter. It was like the years had pulled her down an inch or two, drawing wrinkles down her face.

"The Lord be praised," she said, and grabbed hold of me. I don't know if I growed after I left home or not, but she seemed like a little person in my arms.

"I never figured on seeing my grand-younguns," she said, and stooped over to look at Wallace and Lewis and Willa.

Henry went off to fetch my Daddy at the blacksmith shop.

It was all happening so fast, I couldn't believe where I was. Everything around the house and valley looked small. It was my memory that played tricks on me, for I hadn't growed none since leaving home, and the house and barn hadn't shrunk.

When my Daddy come from the shop, he had tears in his eyes. I never hardly did see him cry, and he didn't cry then. But his eyes was wet. I don't know if he was sorry he had made such a fuss about me going off with Realus, or he was just purely glad to see me. He was stooped a little now, from bending over his forge. But otherwise he was still a powerful-looking man.

"Ain't this a wondrous sight," he said, looking at the children. He still had his hammer in his hand, he had come so quick. He dropped it on the ground and shook hands with Wallace and Lewis. "Ain't she an angel from heaven," he said, patting Willa's head with his blackened hand.

We stood in the yard talking and didn't even think of going inside. I could see I was going to have to tell my story. They was no other way to explain what we was doing there. Confused as I was, I didn't want to justify my Daddy's low opinion of Realus. But they didn't seem no choice but to tell the facts.

"How did you walk all the way from the Holsten?" Henry said. So I told them what happened that day, without mentioning Realus. I told them about following the river, and hearing the cowbell and fearing it was Indians.

"Indians has been raiding the settlements," my Daddy said. "They've killed people in several valleys."

And I told them about finally recognizing the shape of the mountain after Wallace told me he seen the settlement.

"Things is always a mystery, one way or another," Daddy said.

We finally went into the house, and Mama returned to the pie making. But she couldn't hardly work for looking at the young-uns. Any grandma is crazy about her grand-younguns. But to discover that she had them and see them for the first time all at once must have been almost too much. She would roll a little dough, then turn to talk.

"You mean all this time you've just been living over the moun-tain?" she said.

"It appears that way," I said. "It appears I was tricked into thinking we was in the West."

Neither Henry nor my Daddy said nothing. They looked away from me. Mama was bending over her stew pot on the fire. "Let me help you with that," I said.

"It's just a squirrel stew," she said. "Henry killed a mess of squirrels this morning. I'm making some dumplings to put in."

"We ought to get started for home," I said to Mama. All of a sudden, I wanted to get back and tell your Grandpa what I had found out, just to see the look on his face.

"You can't go back this late in the day," Mama said. "It's too far, and besides the Indians is attacking settlers."

"I want to get home and set this straight," I said. I never was one to put off an argument when I was mad.

"Tomorrow will be just as good," Mama said. "And you'll have more time to think about it. You can't settle eight years' worth of difference in one day."

I seen she was right, but my blood was up and I was stubborn. I wanted to get home and have things out.

"You can't go wandering off in the dark with little children," Mama said. "I won't let you. You and Mr. Richards can settle your argument tomorrow."

When she said "Mr. Richards" I thought of your Grandpa by hisself back at the house, with nobody but Trail for company. I

hated for him to worry, and yet I knowed he deserved to worry.
He'd think the Indians had got us.

Once I made up my mind to stay the night, Mama and me
started talking about all the things that had happened since I left.
I told her about the gold diggings, and she said she had heard
about us being there. My Daddy went looking for me, and got
there the day after we had left. The preacher told him Realus had
stole a lot of gold dust before we slipped away.

"That's a lie," I said. "We just got a few nuggets for all the work
Realus had done."

I told her about the cabin by the creek, and the painter that
come the night Wallace was borned. How I done everything
myself.

"And Mr. Richards never did bring a doctor or midwife?"

"He went looking for one."

"And you never suspected you wasn't in the West?"

"I thought it was mysterious we never seen any other settlers
except that one time."

I told Mama about the long night when Eller was sick, and how
we tried to give her honey and whiskey. "It didn't seem to do no
good," I said. "No matter how much we poured in her."

"Ain't nothing can stop the milksick, once it gets to the fever
stage," Mama said. "You done all you could."

It's silly how people will talk when they're grieved. Far into the
night, after we eat, I told her and Daddy about Little Eller burning
up. And about the passenger pigeon that come to the door. I
remembered the crows at her burial. I told them about the new
ground, and the footlog Realus had put across the creek. I told
them they should see the flowers I had in front of the cabin.

"Now we can visit," Mama said.

"If I go back home," I said.

All that night I kept thinking what I was going to do to pay your Grandpa back for deceiving me. What could I do that would be equal to the wrong he had done? What could I say that would show him how I felt? If I just stayed at the settlement with Mama and Daddy, he would figure it out and come looking for us. Then I would tell him me and the younguns was not coming back to the cabin with such a lying polecat as him.

That was a troubled night, I'm telling you. I was thrilled to see my Mama and Daddy and the old place again. I didn't think they would ever get to see Wallace and Lewis and Willa in their lifetime. We set and talked during supper and afterwards, and I had the sweet feeling of being forgiven, even while I was mad in my mind at Realus. I'd be thinking what I was going to say to him next day while Mama was talking about who had married who and who had died. Many had gone off to fight in the war against the king and some had not come back.

"Henry went to fight in Virginia, but got fever so bad they sent him home," Mama said. "Otherwise he would still be gone."

"This war ain't never going to end," Daddy said. "When the Lord comes again we'll still be fighting the Crown."

"They won't never let us go. Every time we kill a redcoat they send two more," Mama said.

"They's a fight going on south of here now," Henry said. "Bunch of men marched through here the other day on their way to fight Ferguson."

It was strange to think of all the goings on while I had been living on the creek. Stuff I didn't know nothing about was happening all around. I'd just heard a few rumors from your Grandpa after he visited the settlement. It didn't seem hardly possible. It was like I had woke up from more than eight years, and my life with your Grandpa had been a dream.

Mama's friend Florrie Cullen had died of dropsy, and Preacher Reece had a fit while he was up preaching at a revival meeting two Augusts ago. "The preacher didn't even know what hit him," Mama said. "He was up waving his arms and talking about the bounties of the good place, and when his voice stopped his arm just kept waving a second or two until he fell over."

They was families had been run out of town for being Tories. The McBains was one of them. The McBains had been tarred and feathered and carried out of town on poles. But even while they was carrying him Old Man McBain hollered, "Long live the king!"

"Them McBains always was stubborn," Henry said.

"They're living way back to the West," Mama said.

"I've heard tell they're living with Cherokees, "Daddy said.

"Them Cherokees is going to be taught a lesson," Henry said.

By the time I went to bed in my old loft with the boys on a pallet on the floor and Willa beside me, my head was swimming with all the news of war and Indians and General Washington and people that had died. I knowed I was too tired to sleep. I would lay there all night picking foxgrapes and rushing further up the river, listening to the cowbell, the way you do when you're overwrought and overworked. Everytime I closed my eyes, I seen those buckets and baskets of foxgrapes we left along the trail and I kept hearing that cowbell and looking out for Indians.

But when I come back to consciousness a little more, I thought of your Grandpa and what I was going to tell him. As I studied it over in the dark, I thought I had three choices. I could refuse to go back to the cabin, and stay with the younguns at the settlement. That would teach him a lesson, if he had to live on the creek all by hisself and look after the place. Of course, we would have to live all crowded up in my Daddy's house and be dependent on Mama and Daddy. I would be called a grass widow, and everybody would say my man had left me.

Or I could stay with Mama and Daddy a while, say four months, until your Grandpa had learned his lesson. Then I would go back and start where we left off. But the danger of that plan was it would be hard to take up again, after a long spell. People change and ain't never the same.

Of course, I could go back the next day and tell him off and take it from there. What could he say for hisself, when confronted by my news? What kind of excuse could he make for deceiving me?

I must have dropped off to sleep, thinking about the choices, for when I woke in the night, I wondered where I was. First thing I noticed was you couldn't hear the sound of the creek, and that your Grandpa wasn't beside me. And the attic smelled different from the cabin. Then I remembered where I was and what had happened. Suddenly I felt this homesickness for my cabin and for your Grandpa. It come to me he told the lie about the Holsten because he wanted so bad for me to marry him. He was afraid I wouldn't come with him otherwise. Knowing I was a young girl with romantic dreams of the West, he told me what he knowed I wanted to hear. And the truth was I had been happy there on the creek all them years. It had been a good life, even if I didn't have no friends to visit with. I loved the place, and all my flowers and the garden. That was when I knowed I was going back in the morning. I slept a little bit after I had made up my mind.

When we left in the morning, Mama give us a quilt. She always give her guests something when they left, a jar of jelly, a fresh loaf of bread. And she packed some biscuits and jelly and shoulder meat in a lard bucket for our dinner on the way.

"We'll be back at Christmas time," I said.

My Daddy give me a set of tongs for the fireplace. "You see any redcoats you bang them over the head with these," he said.

"Nolachucky Jack and Joe MacDowell and their men will take care of the redcoats," Henry said.

"It's redskins I'd be worried about," Mama said.

I let Wallace carry the dinner bucket and Lewis carry the tongs. I carried the quilt and I knowed I'd have to tote Willa on the steep parts.

They had been a touch of frost overnight, and the valley looked so peaceful, I felt a pang of affection for it. The sun was just turning the fields and trees copper, and smoke lifted from every house. They was shocks of corn in the fields, and a trace of whiteness could be seen in every shadow.

I was sore from the long walk the day before, and stiff from tossing all night wondering what to do. We started out slow and followed the path by the church and up the Shimer Road.

"Why is they a bell on the church?" Wallace said.

"To call people to worship," I said.

"What does worship mean?" Lewis said.

"It means to show respect and honor for God," I said. "Like when your Pa reads from the Bible on Sunday mornings."

"But why does everybody get together?" Wallace said.

"To show they're a community," I said.

We had come to the edge of the woods by then, and when we started climbing, I didn't have no breath for talk. I worked to stretch my sore legs and make them climb. I could work the soreness out, but it might take an hour of climbing and sweating.

When we got almost to the gap, to an open place, we stopped to rest and look back at the valley. The sun was in our eyes and reflecting from the creek. The settlement looked so peaceful, cradled in the valley, the houses all together in a kind of nest of mountains, a few places set back in the mouths of hollers.

As we started down the other side toward the river valley and the mountains to the west, it seemed strange that just yesterday I thought these mountains was in the West, and that I was hundreds of miles from the old settlement. A current of anger washed through me again. I just wanted to witness the look on your Grandpa's face when I told him where we had been. He was the kind of man that sometimes would argue and raise his voice on little things, but would keep quiet when he was really mad. I figured he would just stay silent when I told him he was found out, and his face would turn a little red. He might stomp off to the shed.

We heard the cowbell again, down the ridge toward the river.

"I can hear Old Bess," Lewis said. We stopped to listen to the mellow note of the bell. It come from toward the bank of the river where we had picked the last bucket of grapes and eat our dinner. But something sounded different about the bell.

"Run over there," I said to the younguns. They was no place to hide except some laurel bushes about a hundred feet above the trail. I picked up Willa.

"Where we going?" Lewis said.

I put my finger to my lips and they all seen how scared I was and followed. We got behind the laurels and hunkered down.

"What did you see?" Wallace said.

"Keep quiet," I said.

I couldn't describe what was so different about the cowbell I heard. It was my Daddy's bell all right. But when we stopped to listen, I knowed it wasn't on Old Bess anymore. The bell was too steady. It was quiet, but steady. Cows don't move like that through brush and woods unless they are running, and then it's a hitting and banging sound. This bell was too regular. It had to be carried by a horse or mule, or maybe a walking man.

We crouched down behind the laurels trying not to breathe hard, trying to swallow our breath. I could feel our heat in the cool air, like we was little stoves burning with fear on the sausage Mama had fixed. We waited, and after a few minutes these horses come into view. The first horse had the bell tied to its bridle. The man riding it had on ordinary clothes and a hat, but he was Indian. You could tell by his dark skin and long hair.

I held my breath, and I didn't need to say nothing to the children. Their eyes was big as teacups. Willa started to cough, and I put my hand over her mouth.

The lead Indian stopped just below us, and I seen what happened to Old Bess, 'cause they was big pieces of meat hung from the other horses. They had butchered the cow and was carrying the pieces of her. The horses was hung with all kinds of things, including baskets and buckets. Every horse had at least one bucket hung on it. Some was our buckets and baskets. They had dumped out our grapes along the river.

The first Indians said something in their language, and they talked in low voices. I knowed they was going to spot us behind the laurel bushes. Indians is supposed to have such sharp eyes. They would see our tracks in the leaves, or maybe they could smell us. We wasn't more than forty paces away.

The lead Indian had a rifle in his hand. And then I seen he had something in the other. It was a jug, which he raised to his mouth. The other Indians said something to him, like they wanted a drink too. That was why they hadn't seen us. They was interested in the whiskey.

When the first Indian handed the jug to the one behind him my heart froze, for it looked just like the jug Realus kept the medicine whiskey in. Lots of jugs look like that, I told myself, but this sick pain cut through me. It was the same size jug all right. Each Indian took a drink and passed the jug to the next.

Some of the Indians had on regular clothes, and some was wearing buckskin. One Indian didn't have on nothing at all but a necklace of claws and a cloth around his waist. I didn't see how he could stand to ride on the horse that way. They kept passing the whiskey around. I wondered how they was any more liquor in that jug. Others kept coming into view on their horses, and I reckon they must have been twelve or fourteen all together. I was too scared to count exactly. They circled each other, trying to get another turn at the jug.

When I seen the last one come into sight, my heart stopped for sure. He was wearing a red plaid shirt which I knowed to be your Grandpa's. I had made it out of cloth he got from the settlement last summer, and it was the prettiest shirt he had ever had. I don't know what you would call the pattern, but it was red and yellow, with blue and green lines in it. The cloth was so bright it lit up the woods.

Of course I told myself that Indian could have got the shirt somewhere else. He could have bought the same cloth and made him a fancy red shirt. They might be dozens of shirts made out of that material in the mountains. Then I noticed this black felt hat he was wearing. It was your Grandpa's fine black hat he had bought last year with the honey he took to trade at the settlement. It was still rolled on each of its three sides, and the Indian had stuck a feather in the band.

Wallace pulled my arm and pointed toward the last Indian. He had recognized the shirt and hat same as I had. I wanted to say something to him, like maybe your Pa was not at the cabin when the Indians stole his shirt and hat. Maybe your Pa was out in the woods hunting. I seen how scared Wallace was, and I wished I could comfort him. But they wasn't nothing I could do, except to shake my head, meaning, no, your Pa ain't harmed. I wanted to say we couldn't assume nothing until we knowed for sure. But I couldn't even comfort myself.

The lead Indian swung his leg over the neck of his horse like he was going to get down. But he must have been drunker than he thought, for his foot caught on the horse's mane and he fell off headfirst. All the other Indians laughed at him, and he bounded up quick as a squirrel and swung around with his rifle like he was ready to shoot them. He gestured with his fist, as though daring any of them to get off their horse and fight. They laughed at him. Some stripped leaves off the oaks and flung them at him.

The Indian on the ground swung his fist like he was fighting. Then he stopped and looked at the ground. Everyone got quiet. I wondered what he was doing. He had seemed like the lead Indian for sure. Suddenly he looked up sideways and started laughing. All the others laughed with him.

I wondered if the Indians was going to stay there all day. Willa was gripping my arm so hard her fingernails dug into my skin. Wallace and Lewis was pale where they crouched by the roots of the laurels. It crossed my mind they might already be orphans.

The lead Indian said something to the others and turned toward us. He walked up the slope almost to the laurels and I thought he had seen us. But he stopped about forty feet away and unbuttoned his pants and relieved hisself in the leaves. He seemed to enjoy the sound he made on the dry leaves, and he chuckled as he aimed around, pausing where the noise was loudest.

I thought he must see us hunkered down behind the laurels. Me and the younguns stayed as still as we could. What would I do if he seen us? If we tried to run they would just ride us down. If we all scattered in different directions some of us might get away. But I wanted to stay with my younguns to protect them.

When he finished, that Indian looked right toward where we was, like he had seen something. But maybe he didn't trust his judgment, he had had so much liquor, or maybe he was just thinking absent-mindedly and wasn't looking at all. 'Cause he turned around and walked back toward the group.

It took him several tries to get back on his horse. The third time he stepped back and took a run and leaped all the way over the horse. Everybody laughed at him again. He brushed the leaves off his pants and stomped with anger.

I wondered if we might be able to crawl away from the laurel bushes while the Indians was laughing, and get into the trees around the slope without them seeing us. If we crawled slow and stayed low it might be possible. But them Indians might see us any instant, even through the laurels. I was thinking hard. They wasn't no room for panic. I tried to figure what our choices was.

Suddenly, the lead Indian was back on his horse and they started up the slope the way we had come. Clearly, they was headed toward the settlement. I wished we had some way to warn the people back there. But at least they was enough people in the valley so somebody would see them and warn the others.

Me and the younguns stayed crouched down until they was completely out of sight. We couldn't take no chances.

"Mama, that was Pa's new shirt," Lewis said.

"It was like Pa's new shirt," I said.

"How come he was wearing Pa's shirt and hat?" Wallace said.

"They's lots of shirts like that," I said.

Now that the Indians was out of sight, I felt myself all hot and flustered. We had to get back to the cabin, but what if they was other Indians coming up the river valley? We had seen that campfire the day before. But I didn't know no other way to get home. We could light out across the mountains, but that would take longer, and we stood a good chance of losing ourselves in the laurel hells on the ridge. My thought now was to hurry. The less time we was in the woods, the less likely we would run into other Indians.

"Let's go," I said, and picked up the quilt in one arm and Willa in the other. Wallace was still holding the dinner bucket, but Lewis didn't know where the tongs was. He must have dropped them when we heard the cowbell, or before that on the mountain. We looked around in the leaves and didn't see nothing.

"Let's go," I said.

It was more than a mile till we come to the rock where we had left our last bucket of foxgrapes. The Indians had poured out the grapes and walked their horses over them. The grapes was starting to rot, and yellowjackets buzzed over the mess of hulls and insides. The grapes looked like eyes that had been bursted.

From the rock to the river was another half mile. We crossed the river where it was shallow and then it was easy to follow the tracks of the horses, where the peavines was trampled and the weeds knocked down. I thought we could get back to the cabin by dinner time, if we didn't stop to rest.

We soon come to another pile of grapes. We could tell where they was because of the cloud of yellowjackets swelling and shrinking above them. All them rotting and broken berries made me think how lucky we was only the grapes had been ruined. It wasn't the body of one of the younguns rotting there by the trail. As we hurried through the vines and broken weeds, I kept saying in my mind, "Precious ones, precious ones." Never had the preciousness of loved ones seemed so sweet.

We passed another pile of rotting grapes and come to a bend in the river where they was a kind of pool with vines hanging over it. Wallace was running out ahead and he stopped dead in his tracks. Willa was talking to herself, and I put a finger to her lips. I eased up behind Lewis to see what he had seen.

They was a man standing by the water, leaning on a crutch made from a pole. He had already heard us and turned around.

"How do," he said.

I seen he wasn't no Indian because he had several days growth of beard. His clothes was ragged and stained. His right leg come to an end at the knee, and was all bound up in dirty rags.

"Don't need to fear me," he said. We must have stood there looking at him, white with surprise.

"How do," I said, and held Willa close to me. I motioned for Wallace and Lewis to stay by me.

"I ain't in no shape to hurt nobody," he said.

"Which way have you come?" I said.

He hobbled closer and I seen it was the preacher from the gold diggings. But his hair was gray and so was his beard. Close up I could see the rags on his leg was soaked in blood turning brown.

"Did you pass a clearing by the creek over yonder?" I said.

"I passed a cabin way over by the creek," he said.

"Was anybody there?" I said. He stepped closer. He smelled dirty and sick. I hoped he didn't recognize me.

"They was nobody there," he said. "The door of the cabin was open and looked like somebody had gone through and took what they wanted. But wasn't nobody there."

"You didn't see no Indians?" I said.

"I figured the Indians had been there," he said. "They've been raiding all over. That's why Chucky Jack and his men has gone after them."

"What do you mean?"

He stepped closer and I could smell his foul breath. It was the breath of somebody that's been drunk and is sobering up.

"We fit at Kings Mountain," he said. "That's where I got my leg busted by a Tory musket ball. They had to chop it off with an ax. We kilt Ferguson though. We learnt the redcoats a lesson."

He went on to tell how they had defeated the British, and almost none of the mountain fighters was killed. He said it was like shooting turkeys. Everytime they seed a redcoat they touched him off. When they chopped his leg off all they had to give him was whiskey. They carried him back to the mountains in carts and wagons and he kept a jug by him.

"Now it's beginning to hurt," he said. "Now I can feel the toes they cut off. They hurt like they was half froze and a horse had stepped on them."

He was close enough that it sickened me to smell his breath.

"Don't I know you?" he said. "Why you're Petal Jarvis, that run off with the big feller to the West."

"And you're the preacher," I said. "The preacher that was digging for gold."

"I used to be a preacher," he said. He said he had give up gold mining and become a peddler in the mountains. And then he joined up with John Sevier to fight the Tories.

"They've gone now to fight the Indians," he said. "They left me behind 'cause I wasn't no help. They've gone over to the Tuckasegee to pay them heathen devils back."

I asked him again if he hadn't seen nobody at the clearing.

"Honey, I wish I had," he said. "But it was deserted. Things from inside the cabin was strewed all across the yard."

I wanted to get going again. His words chilled me to the soles of my feet. We divided what we had in the dinner bucket with him, jelly biscuits and shoulder meat. "I'm much obliged," he said. "I'm just grateful to be alive."

That seemed like the longest walk I ever took. Miles stretched out further, the more we tried to hurry. I couldn't believe we had walked that far up the river the day before. No wonder Realus was so sure I'd never wander back to the settlement.

I carried Willa on my hip, and then on my shoulder. Then I put her down and made her walk, but she got tired of me pulling her along and set down on the trail and bawled.

"Come on, darling, we got to hurry," I said.

"Don't want to, don't want to," she hollered.

So I had to pick her up again. I made Wallace carry the quilt, but he let it unfold and drag on the leaves. It was one of Mama's finest quilts.

I kept thinking we had come to the place where we crossed the ridge to the river valley, but every time I was fooled. I tried to remember landmarks. They was a holly bush not too far up the slope from where we started picking foxgrapes. And every time I seen a holly bush, I thought this is where we turn, but it wasn't. When you're in a hurry, landmarks look different. I kept thinking about what the preacher had said about the cabin being deserted and our things scattered over the yard.

Finally we come to a place on the river bank where the weeds had all been trampled down, and Wallace said, "This is where we started picking yesterday." I didn't recognize it, but he pointed to a rock on the bank where I had stood to reach some of the vines and I seen he was right. They was grapes dumped out in the weeds where the Indians had emptied our first basket.

I lit out up the ridge, grabbing saplings with one hand and pulling Willa with the other. I clawed in moss and clutched at rocks and stomped my heels into the steep ground for footholds. Willa cried she was tired, but I didn't stop to comfort her. And I let Wallace and Lewis come along behind as best they could.

They was laurels on the other side and we had to fight our way through the thickets. I kept bumping my head on low branches. Willa tripped several times and I had to pick her up as we come out along the creek, just half a mile below the footlog.

They wasn't a thing moving around the place, except a rooster and a couple of hens in the yard. I looked up and down the clearing, but they wasn't no sign of your Grandpa. I expected to hear Trail's bark, but they was no sign of him. Where we had girdled the first field, the trees had rotted down to trunks that stood like statues among the cornstalks, but Realus wasn't there. And beyond that I could see the new ground, but he wasn't there.

When we got across the footlog I seen what the preacher said was true. The yard was all strewed with our things, quilts and pots and pans, bottles and gourds. The Indians had took what they wanted and throwed the rest away. The baby's cradle had been busted up and cornmeal was scattered around my flowerbed.

"Where's Pa gone to?" Wallace said.

"He must have gone to look for us," I said. It was what I hoped was true, that he had been far out in the woods looking for us when the Indians had come. Or he might have gone to one of the settlements for help.

I seen what had happened to all the chickens and guineas but the rooster and two hens. The Indians had kilt them all and plucked them by the washpot and boiled them. They had had a big feast the night before or that morning. I reckoned it was this morning, since the fire was still smoldering. You could see tracks in the yard where they had run the chickens and guineas down.

Everything in the house was turned over. The beds had been

stripped and the cooking things throwed around. My herbs and spices and all my medicine had been emptied on the floor. That was how they found the whiskey jug, by going through the things on the medicine shelf.

Ain't nothing takes the wind out of you like seeing all your things broke and scattered. The toys and dolls we had made for the children had been throwed out and trampled on. The family Bible had been throwed in the weeds behind the cabin. I felt like setting down on the ground and crying, and would have, except they was so much that had to be done.

The horse was gone from the barn, and I figured either the Indians had took him, or your Grandpa had rode him to look for us. The back end of the crib had been busted open and they had rode their horses over the spilled ears. Realus had picked most of the corn and filled the crib, and a lot of the new corn was ruint. The barn was deserted except for swallows fluttering in the loft and mice swishing around the shucks and hay.

I run to the spring house and opened the door with dread. But the Indians had left the pitchers of milk. The water was rippling as usual around the cider and butter. A panful of late beans was cooling in the water. Spring lizards played in the edges of the pool like nothing had happened.

When I come out of the spring house I heard the cowbell up on the west ridge. The cows and hogs was out in the woods and maybe the Indians had missed them.

"Bring me the milk bucket," I said to Wallace.

"It's gone," he hollered back.

We had carried all our buckets, including the milk bucket, to pick grapes in. I took the lard bucket Mama give us the dinner in and washed it in the branch. Then we run up to the milk gap 'cause I knowed Old Daisy's bag would be busting full if she hadn't been milked since yesterday. It was enough to make her go dry.

They was no sign of your Grandpa at the milk gap either. I carried up some corn to give to Daisy and the heifers. Sure enough, the cow's bag was so full it was sore, and she kicked a few times when I tried to milk. But she wanted to get rid of that milk, and finally she let me squeeze her tits down to the strippings while she bawled and carried on.

When I finished milking, I walked to the brow of the ridge and looked down on the creek valley. Every stump in the fields looked like a man now and cast a long shadow. I thought your Grandpa might be in the woods somewhere and hurt. He might have cut his foot while chopping. Maybe if I hollered, he could hear me. Then I thought if they was Indians in the valley they would hear and come looking for us. A shout would tell them where I was. But I thought of your Grandpa with his leg broke, somewhere in the woods or along the creek, and I didn't care about Indians.

I put the bucket of foaming milk down and placed my hands to the sides of my mouth, and I hollered, "Realus" in all four directions of the wind. When I hollered across the creek an echo come back from that ridge like somebody was answering me. I called a couple of more times, and the reply was an echo. They was nothing else to do but go back to the house.

Before it got dark, we cleaned up the cabin and carried all our stuff back from the yard. It was like a flood had hit the house and poured everything out. The quilts had dirt on them and the cooking pots and pans had to be washed in the creek. They wasn't no way to save many of the herbs and spices poured out. Some of the gourds had been stepped on and crushed. They was just enough salt to keep us for a few days. The can of tea had mostly spilled out, but I saved all I could.

While we worked, the prettiest hunter's moon come up. It was like a big lantern raised above the trees. The light was so bright you could see pumpkins in the fields and shadows from every post and bush. It was a perfect night for coon hunting, or for Indians traveling to the settlements.

Later that night I laid awake, watching the light come through the cracks at the eaves and around the door. The light looked blue where it streaked into the cabin. I thought I heard voices, then decided it was just the creek, or the waterfall up the creek. Or maybe it was a wolf barking. I drifted toward sleep, only to wake again, thinking I had heard something. I thought it might be your Grandpa out in the woods hollering where a tree had fell on him, or the Indians had left him to die in some cove.

I went back to sleep and then woke again, and this time I did hear voices. "Whoa," somebody called, and "Steady there."

Fear shot through me so hard it hurt my bones. They was still a spark in the fireplace and I lit my candle from it. My hands was shaking as I wrapped the quilt around my shoulders, and stood by the door listening. It sounded like a bunch of men coming into the yard on horses. Some was splashing across the creek and others was already in the yard.

"Ho there," somebody hollered. "Anybody home?" I leaned against the door trying to see through a crack.

"We're looking for Indians," the voice said. "Have you seen any Indians?"

At least they are white men, I thought. I remembered what the wounded preacher had told us about Chucky Jack and his men looking for Indians. I pulled out the door bolt and opened it.

In the moonlight you could see riders on horses. They looked twelve feet high in the air and none of them had on uniforms. Some had coonskin caps and some was wearing buckskin. Some had on regular coats and hats, but all carried rifle-guns across their saddles. I stood in the door shielding my candle from the draft.

One of the men rode up close. "Ma'am, we're looking for Indians," he said. "Have you seen a bunch of Indians, ten or twelve of them?"

I told them about the Indians we had seen over on the river. And I told him they had looted our place and took half our things and killed our chickens. And I told him my man had disappeared.

"What was his name?" the man said.

"Realus Richards," I said. "We seen one of the Indians wearing his shirt and hat."

"We ain't seen him," the man said. "We been over on the Tuckasegee doing a little job."

They talked among theirselves for a while, and I pointed across the ridge where the river valley was. Some of the men kept riding around the yard looking at things in the moonlight. They looked in the shed and in the chicken coop, and one rode out to the spring house like they thought we might be hiding Indians. Some of the men had bandages, and one had his arm in a sling.

I was relieved when they finally left, splashing across the creek and heading up the ridge. Maybe they was Chucky Jack's men and they was going to fight the Indians again. Or maybe they was just outlaws. I couldn't tell. But I was happy to see them gone.

"Who was all them?" Wallace said.

"They was soldiers looking for Indians," I said. I didn't know he had woke up, but there he was standing behind me.

"Had they found Pa?" he said.

"They wasn't looking for Pa," I said. "Now go back to bed."

After I put the candle out and laid in the dark for a while, it seemed like I had dreamed about the soldiers coming to the door.

The figures on horseback in the moonlight was like ghosts. They hadn't told me no names. I would look for their tracks the next day, though it would be hard to tell their tracks from the Indian tracks. I laid there a long time, and when I did get to sleep I dreamed your Grandpa was among the soldiers, and that he didn't come forward because he so ashamed. He had took the horse and some tea and his things and rode with the soldiers.

When I woke up, it was daylight and I heard Old Daisy's cowbell on the ridge. It was milking time, and I had a kind of headache from laying awake so much of the night. They was frost outside, not a heavy frost, just a whiteness on the grass and in the shade of the cabin like the moonlight had stayed there.

While I was washing the milk bucket I smelled this rich kind of odor. I thought at first it must be the smell of leaves souring after frost had hit them. When leaves start falling and pile up in ditches they give off a stink. But when I climbed up to the milk gap I didn't smell it no more. Around cows you smell their breath and fresh manure on the cold ground. Old Daisy smelled like the cud she had been chewing.

Not being milked for a whole day had turned her half-dry. At that rate she'd be completely dry before winter started, and she wasn't due to freshen until March. While I milked, I tried to think what we could do to look for your Grandpa. Since the soldiers the night before had come up the creek, they didn't seem much use to go down that way looking.

We could search up the creek in the laurel thickets and in the rocky places over the creek. And I thought maybe me and the younguns could circle the clearing. I figured if we went all the way around the place, from the creek above to the creek bank below the new ground, we might see some sign of where Realus had been. When we left to pick grapes he was gathering corn. He must have picked all the corn that day, judging from the amount spilled by the crib. But they wasn't no sign of the horse and sled. Maybe we could find tracks into the woods and follow them.

Soon as I got back to the cabin and strained the milk and put the pitcher in the spring house, I boiled some grits for the young-uns and told them my plan. They wasn't much butter left but I let them have a little maple sugar to sprinkle on the grits.

"You mean we're going to look for tracks like Indians does?" Lewis said.

"We'll look for any sign we can find," I said. "Maybe they's a track where he drug the sled into the woods. Maybe he was going for more wood."

"Maybe he went hunting," Wallace said. "His gun is gone."

When we stepped outside I caught that sickening smell again. The breeze come right down the creek from the west. "Let's go down the creek and start," I said.

We begun looking above the spring house, at the edge of the laurel thicket. Wallace was solemn and didn't say nothing, but Lewis and Willa thought it was like some kind of game. They darted in and out of the bushes.

"I found a track," Lewis said.

We run to look, but it was just a place where a rock had been dislodged. "That ain't no track," Wallace said.

"I found a track, I found a track," Willa said. She pointed to a place where a weedstalk had been broke. They was a deer track in the soft ground.

"We're looking for people tracks," Wallace said. "We're looking for Pa's tracks."

I tried to keep from feeling hopeless. We went slower and slower along the edge of the woods, examining the ground under dogwoods and young hemlocks. We come to the milk gap on the ridge, and of course they was only cow tracks there. Whatever sign might have been there the day before had been trampled on.

As we come down the ridge toward the fields, Willa tripped over a limb and rolled several times. I run to pick her up, and as I brushed off her coat and hair I seen the sled inside the trees. There the sled set, with several sticks of wood in its bed.

The singletree was hooked to the front of the sled, and the trace chains was still attached. Whoever took the horse had unhooked the chains from the horse collar. The sled was pointed toward the new ground, and the horse tracks went that way. Your Grandpa had sawed wood, and was headed back to the clearing.

We come out of the woods almost at the creek, and looked back toward the cabin. They was some big weeds around the edge of the new ground where your Grandpa hadn't mowed, queen-of-the-meadow and ironweed mostly, but the tops of the corn had been cut, and we could see all the way past the scarecrow to the barn.

"Why's they so many flies around the scarecrow?" Lewis said.

And then we all smelled it. The breeze must have changed, for it hit us suddenly. It was a rich rotten stink, worse than any carrion. It was almost sweet and stifling.

"Shoooo!" Willa said, and held her nose.

"Ugh," Lewis said.

They is some bad smells people actually like. Everybody likes to cherish their own wind and a baby loves to smell its filth until it's cold. But the stench of rotting flesh everybody hates because it is the stink of death. It's the smell of our end. Preachers would say it's the smell of sickness and our fallen condition. I shuddered at the fetor on the breeze.

I seen they was something wrong with the scarecrow. A scarecrow is normally sticks holding up old clothes. But this scarecrow was clothes holding up what was inside them. It was like a body crucified in its rags. Flies swelled and shrunk around its head.

"You all stay back," I said to the children.

"Mama, I'm scared," Willa said and started crying.

"Lewis, you hold Willa," I said. I took a step toward the scarecrow, and Wallace followed. "You stay back too," I said.

I put my apron over my nose the smell was so bad. Somehow I couldn't go up to the scarecrow from behind. It was like slipping up on something. I circled around and edged closer. It was a man all right, put inside the scarecrow's rags and tied to the posts. The body was twisted in the clothes and the straw hat had fell down on the face.

"Get back," I hollered at Wallace, but he didn't pay no attention. He kept follering me.

I stopped and looked away at the ridge. The sun was gold on the many-colored trees. I couldn't bear to look at the face, but knowed I had to. The body slumped there on the poles with its arms crooked and the legs drawed up. They had took its boots and the legs looked whitish green. I got closer and stooped down. They had killed him and tied him up in the scarecrow's rags.

"Get back," I said to Wallace, but he come right up and looked too, before he run away and puked among the cornstalks.

I backed away and held my apron over my nose.

"What's wrong?" Lewis said. "Hush up," I said. "We've got to go back to the cabin." I led them across the fields and hollered for Wallace. He made like he was going to the woods, and then he follered us at a distance.

When I finally got the younguns back to the cabin I told them to stay there. Willa and Lewis begun to cry, and I set with them a few minutes by the fire. But I had work to do.

"You stay here," I said to Wallace. Wallace didn't answer. I took a sheet from the shelf. "You stay here with the little uns," I said. "They's a job you and me will have to do later."

I got some lime in a gourd from the shed and a hatchet the Indians hadn't found. I took the sheet and marched right out through the field to the new ground. I'd lose my courage if I didn't do it directly. They was no leisure to stop and think.

The body was big and I knowed they was no way I could hold it up while I cut the arms free from the scarecrow frame. I'd either have to chop the frame down or cut the body loose and let it slump down. If I chopped the frame, I'd still have to lift the body to cut the arms free. I stood behind the frame and hacked at the ropes till one arm fell free. The body was stiff and swung over like a side of beef. The hat fell off and I tried not to look at the hollow eyes. When I cut the other hand free, the head fell against me, and I jumped back as the body hit the ground.

Children, I've never worked as hard or as fast. Several times I thought I would black out from the smell. I wished the soldiers would come back and help me. I thought of running back to the settlement and getting my Daddy and Henry to come. But that would take another day at least, with the body exposed above ground. They wasn't nothing to do but what I was doing.

As I worked I got mad. It kept going through my mind Realus had deserted me and the younguns. After deceiving me for eight years he had left me to raise the children. Blood rushed to my face from exertion and anger. The resentment give me strength. The sudden hatred of your Grandpa allowed me to do that work.

First thing I done was cut all those scarecrow rags off the body. I couldn't let nobody be buried like that. They had took his own clothes and his body was too stiff and drawed up to put more clothes on anyway. I thought it was better to bury him in the sheet, the way he had come into the world.

I tried not to look at the body when I tore all them rags off. It was turning black as a bruise in places and was light green on the limbs. I didn't look at the face where the birds had pecked.

When the body was bare I sprinkled it all over with lime. Lime will sweeten any smell. Don't know how it works, but the white does make things seem cleaner and dryer. I spread the sheet on the ground, knocking down cornstalks to make room.

It must have took me an hour to get the corpse on the sheet, but finally I did. Then I tied it up with the corners of the cloth and the pieces of rope that had been on the scarecrow. While I worked I had been planning. The easiest thing would have been to dig a hole right there in the field. But I knowed it was better to bury the body up on the hill with Little Eller. That was the graveyard and that was where a body ought to be at rest. It wouldn't be right to bury him under no scarecrow. The problem was how to get the corpse up there. I couldn't hardly roll it over, much less carry it to the top of the ridge.

Then it come to me in my anger that the timber sled was still in the woods where it had been cut loose. If I could pull it by myself to the field, then maybe Wallace and me together could drag it up the trail to the top of the ridge with the body on it. We would have to go slow and do it a little at a time.

I run to the woods where the sled was. It was still partly loaded with sticks of firewood. First I throwed out the wood, then gathered up the cold trace chains in both my hands. The sled felt like it was stuck by its sourwood runners to the leaves. I jerked harder and it give a little. Once the runners had moved a little, it got easier. I pulled the sled through the woods, backing as I went. But soon as I got to the field, I put the chains over my shoulder and hauled by leaning way out forward. I drug the sled to the body and left it.

All the younguns was standing at the barn watching me. They

hadn't stayed in the house like I had told them, but they hadn't come out in the field either. They had half-obeyed me, which is what children generally do.

"Lewis," I said, sounding stern from the work and anger, sounding out of breath. "You stay right here with Willa and don't let me catch you in the field."

Lewis looked solemn and sorry for hisself. Willa didn't hardly know what was going on.

It took most of the day for Wallace and me to roll the body onto the sled, and then drag it across the field and up the trail. I took one chain and Wallace the other, and we'd pull for a few yards then stop. It was just possible to do on the steep places if we pulled for twenty feet and rested. In one rocky place we had to put sticks crossways for the runners to slide on. It was after dinner before we got to the top of the slope.

Willa and Lewis had stood in the yard watching us a long time. Finally they got bored and went back to the cabin to play in the sand by the front door. They had built all kinds of mounds and tunnels there by the time me and Wallace returned. At least they had kept away from the footlog.

"Ain't we going to have no dinner?" Lewis said.

"We'll have dinner later," I said. "I'll make us an apple pie."

I got the shovel and Wallace carried the mattock, and we climbed back up the ridge. The ground there was hard clay. Where Realus had kept the area cleared around Little Eller's grave the dirt was packed hard and baked by the summer heat. I seen it was going to take some mighty work to dig any sort of grave.

Wallace was too little to swing the mattock, so I took it and broke up the ground in a shape as long as a mound and maybe two feet wide. I seen we couldn't dig a proper grave six feet deep.

Besides, we didn't have a casket to go in it. We'd have to dig as deep as we could, enough to be decent, before nightfall, and let it go at that. First thing I hit was a white field rock, and I had to dig around that so we could lift it out. The dirt up there is just red clay. They never is much soil on ridge tops. Maybe that's why graveyards is put on ridges, to keep from taking up good soil. And to keep them away from floods.

When we dug down about a yard and squared out the corners of the hole, I seen that was as far as we could go. I was running out of strength, and the day was almost gone. Me and Wallace throwed our tools aside and took hold of the sheet around the body. It took several tries to roll the body off the sled and into the hole. I tried to do it so the body was facing up, head to the east, but with the legs drawed up and the sheet twisted around I couldn't really tell. We filled the grave halfway before we went back to the cabin for Willa and Lewis.

I was almost give out by then, but I remembered to get your Grandpa's Bible before climbing back up the hill. It was near sundown, and I lined the younguns up beside the grave. Even Willa stood solemn and quiet in the late sun.

I opened the Bible somewhere—I can't remember where—and read a few verses. It seemed the only thing to do. And then we sung a song. The only one the younguns knowed was a Christmas carol and we sung that. All I remember afterwards is filling in the grave with loose dirt and clods while crows was calling in the pines on the hill and down in the field where the scarecrow was just a frame. You don't often hear crows fussing at the end of the day, but I guess we had disturbed them. It was mostly dark and the moon was coming up over the ridge by the time we walked back down to the cabin.

That night after we finished covering up the grave I still had to milk and cook supper. I was so tired I felt drunk. When you're that tired it's like somebody else is going through the motions of work. You feel like you're watching yourself. I drug myself back up the hill in the moonlight to milk and then I strained the milk and put it in the spring house.

After we eat I cleared away the supper things and set down by the fire. The younguns was so tired from the long day they was almost asleep before they finished their buttermilk and pie. Wallace and Lewis climbed up to the loft and Willa went right to sleep on our bed in the living room. I figured I'd just let her stay there for the night.

I thought I'd set by the fire and think about things for a while. I wanted to think about what had happened to me in the past two days, and what had happened to Realus. Too many things had come at once and I needed to study on them. I was mad at your Grandpa, and I was afraid of being left alone. And being afraid made me even madder. I kept rehearsing in my mind what I would say if I seen him. At the same time I was bone-chilled thinking of not seeing him no more.

I kept running over the words that I would say: deceive, seduce, cowardly, unforgivable, blackguard, low-down, sinful, sneaking, infidel. It was like I had a fever and was talking to Realus across the top of the mountain, telling him never to come back, and that he better come back. It was like somebody was calling to me in the woods. I went to look, and though it sounded like a person it turned out to be a snake. That snake was looking me right in the eyes.

With a jerk I come awake. I had almost fell out of my chair. It was like something had shouted at me. But the house was quiet.

They wasn't even a clock ticking. The stillness seemed to push against me, like a pressure in the air.

The door had not been latched, and I got up to bolt it for the night. But before I dropped the hickory bar in place I thought I'd look outside. Moonlight was coming through the crack. I stepped out onto the threshold.

The hunter's moon must have been completely full. It filled the creek with light, but hung so high in the sky it seemed unconnected with the light on the earth. The air was so bright you could almost see the fall colors on trees across the creek. The yard and fields looked clean in the blue light.

They was a figure standing in the field beyond the barn. At first I thought it was a stump from the old deadening, but then I seen it was too close. The figure was hunched over a little, and just stood there. I couldn't focus on it because the light was not good enough. A cold pain shot down through my bones. In the moonlight I couldn't even be sure I seen the figure. I shivered and stepped back into the house and bolted the door.

Now I had to think what to do. If it was an Indian, he was just watching for a chance to attack and rob us. I wondered if it was a soldier that was wounded or lost, coming back from the fight with the Tories, or with the Cherokees. It even crossed my mind it could be a ghost, maybe the ghost of the man that was killed and hung on the scarecrow. It also come to me it could be Realus out there. But it didn't seem like him to just stand in the field and watch the place. It didn't make sense that he would stand there and not come in.

I wished they was a gun in the house. But either the Indians had took it, or Realus had took it. They wasn't even a lantern. I set there by the fire trying to make up my mind. First I thought I should just stay there and keep the house locked up and wait for daylight. Wasn't much else I could do.

I got up and stood by the door listening, to see if anybody had come into the yard. Way off I heard a screech owl and then I could hear the water in the creek. Next I heard a kind of whimper, the kind a dog makes when it comes around after it's been away a long time. It sounded like Trail.

I unbolted the door and opened it a crack, and sure enough there was Trail standing in the moonlight and whimpering. I put out my hand and he sniffed it and licked it. He wagged his whole body with excitement and pleasure of being home.

"Here boy," I said. "Here boy." I stepped outside and looked toward the field. The figure was not where it stood before, but closer. The man stood right by the barn in the moonlight, and I knowed it was your Grandpa.

That made me madder than I was before. It riled me anew that he was afeared to face me. I went back in and got a piece of cornbread and give it to Trail. And then I shut the door and latched it. Let him stand out there and freeze, I thought. Let him shiver till he falls apart like crumbling chalk.

I set down by the fire. I wanted to take a burning stick from the fireplace and go out there and hold the light in his face to see what he would say for hisself. That was always my inclination when they was trouble, to go right to the cause. Wasn't no use to put off trouble. I wanted to see his face when he tried to explain why he had fooled me all them years, and left me alone to birth Wallace with no help on the night of the painter. I wanted to hear what he would say about all those times I had gone without a woman to talk to and my own Mama just across the mountains, no more than fifteen miles away.

I put another stick on the fire and set looking into the flames. Like I said before, I never did see the signs and mysteries in a fire that other people claim is there. I never did see no faces of the dead or the flutter of angels, nor hear the tramp of steps warning of bad things to come. What I always seen was paths that led to distant fields and far mountains. Behind the flames I watched faraway valleys reached by trails that run right up to my feet.

I thought, can I ever live with Realus after what he done? How can I live with a man that would deceive me so? Man and woman can't be one flesh in hatred and suspicion. If I didn't take him back inside I'd have to live on the creek by myself like a widow woman raising her children.

But Realus could go off to the west and start a new place and a new family. A man could just vanish into the wilderness and clear him up a new place and find another wife.

I would take your Grandpa back. Children, I done a lot of thinking that night, and I did a lot of growing up. When we finished burying that poor young man, I was just a girl. By the time that night was over I felt like a grown woman. I don't think a body ever really grows up, but we keep learning. That's part of the interest in getting older, is to learn a little more.

What I seen next was that I was going to have to forgive Realus. And if I forgive him just partly, they would always be that distance between us the Devil hisself seemed to have made in our lives. If I only forgive him in part, that Devil would worm his way back into our lives through that gap and never go away.

No sir, I seen that for my own sake, call it my own selfishness, I had to forgive your Grandpa complete. I couldn't live no other way, and I couldn't live with myself no other way. As I kept thinking I felt myself growing. I seen that I might have a long life, and that I might have grandchildren like you all. I was always a slow learner. It takes me a long time to make sense of things, but I always see eventually where I am, and once I seen how everything had to be the rest was easier.

I must have wandered off in my thinking again, for it was Trail whimpering at the door that called me back to the task at hand. I felt twenty years older. I wrapped my shawl around me and unbolted the door.

Trail whined and licked my hand. I reckon he was so happy to be back home, he was near beside hisself. Dogs love to gallivant but they also love to come home where their people are.

The figure was still standing out there by the barn in the moonlight. It could have been a statue, except it was stooped forward a little. That stoop told me a lot because Realus was never one to slouch. The yard looked like it had been frosted with some kind of blue powder. Even the dirt and the manure pile looked scrubbed and starched. The mountains was shining above the creek in the moonlight. Trail trotted alongside of me, and run circles around me as I walked. But the figure by the barn never moved. Its front and face was dark.

"Realus," I said. "Is that you?" My breath was tight in my throat and chest. But the figure made no more answer than a statue would. I had forgot to bring out a pine knot for a light.

"Ain't no use to stand out here shivering to death," I said. I walked right up to within ten feet of the man but I still couldn't see the face. I knowed it was your Grandpa by the height and shoulders. "You might as well come on in," I said.

Still he didn't say nothing. It was like a big dark ghost standing there. For a second I almost got confused about what I was doing. Had he maybe lost his mind with shame and worry and wandering in the woods? Had he been hit on the head and lost his memory? Was he dead and this was his ghost come back?

Trail was whimpering and jumping between us. He licked my hand and then run to the man. "Calm down, Trail," I said. "Calm yourself."

But I seen what to do then. That dog showed me its wisdom. It was no good to talk. No words could break through the distance between us in the bright frosty air. "I can't see your face," I said, and stepped forward and took his arm in my left hand and his hand in my right hand. His fingers was icy cold.

Now a touch speaks far beyond any words, children. A touch is a little thing, but at the right time it's like a current pours through. People ain't whole unless they're connected, and a touch is the first and true sign of that connection. You can see that in a little baby, how it will delight in being touched and held, how it recognizes affection. They's all kinds of holding and caressing, but I'm just talking about the first touch of friendship and fellowship, the touch of family and kith. Every single person really feels a part of the same family.

I took your Grandpa's arm and hand and held them. His big fingers was froze. I turned him around so he was facing the moonlight. Trail was jumping up on us, and I said, "Get down, Trail. Get down." And I seen Realus's face was wet. It was like dew had settled on it, or the dog had licked it. The moonlight was caught in the drops down his cheeks and in his beard.

"Let's go in to the fire," I said. "You must be awful hungry."

"I ain't hungry," he said.

"You need to warm up anyway," I said. I started leading him toward the house. He put his arm around my shoulders and we walked slowly toward the lighted doorway. He smelled of the damp and cold of the woods, like he had been out for weeks instead of days. Trail whimpered and run in front of us, and then behind us.

When we got inside I was almost blinded by the firelight and candlelight.

"Set down and I'll warm up some cornbread," I said.

"Don't bother," he said. He seen Willa was asleep on the bed and kept his voice low.

"No use to starve," I said. "That won't help nothing."

He bent to the fire and held out his hands. "I always meant to tell you," he said. "I went looking for you and seen you had gone to the settlement."

I didn't say a thing. I put the bread in a pan to warm it on the hearth.

"You need a bath," I said. "It will warm you up."

"I was afraid you would leave me," he said.

"At least you wasn't here when the Indians come," I said. I had the two kittles on boiling.

"I stayed out in the woods with Dan and Trail. I must have rode a hundred and fifty miles."

"What happened to old Dan?" I said.

"He's over yonder by the edge of the field," Realus said. "I thought about riding him further to the west, but I seen I couldn't do that. I had to come back."

"You could be in Kentucky by now," I said. I give him a plate of cornbread and grits and a piece of pie. Don't ever believe a man when he says he's not hungry.

I got out the wooden tub and poured some hot water in it. From standing out there in the cold, he was chilled through to the joints. I knowed he'd be sick if I didn't get him warmed up.

"You've been cold and dirty long enough," I said. "I want you to get in this bath."

Children, they was a pleasure in giving that big strapping man a bath. It was like bathing a great big baby, to make him fresh and clean. I guess in a way men are just babies; at least, they act like babies sometimes. In their shining white skin that don't never see the sun they look tender as babies.

That night, as we laid in bed with the firelight breathing in the room, I knowed I was right. Just touching him told me that. Sometimes you can see far ahead and way back at once. I seen that when I touched your Grandpa with love, it was like I was touching all the people back through the ages, through all their love and affection. And in the same way we touched the future through our love and our children's down through the years. When you grandchildren, and your grandchildren, feel the closeness of a husband or a wife it will be like a part of me and your Grandpa living in you. Don't worry if you don't understand. I don't think the young is meant to. I know I didn't at your age. But I wanted to tell you anyway, so's you'll remember it after I'm long gone. Your Grandpa's gone and he can't tell you. He always had trouble speaking his affections anyway, though he could charm anybody in a friendly way.

Next morning when I woke, Realus was not there. The bed was empty beside me, but soon as I set up I seen they was a fire strutting in the fireplace. It was just daylight, but the bed beside me was cold so your Grandpa had been gone for some time.

I got up and dressed and put on water for tea and grits. I was glad to see the bathtub had been carried out. Willa woke up and stretched. "Is Pa coming home today?" she said.

"Pa come home last night," I said.

"Where did he go?" she said.

"He must have gone to milk," I said. I looked out the door. They was a heavy frost, like the starlight had stayed on the grass, but no sign of your Grandpa. Even Trail was gone. I got the water boiling and made grits and tea. Just as Wallace and Lewis come down from the loft, I heard somebody in the yard. Your Grandpa opened the door. He held his gun in one hand and a limb of something in the other. The light was behind him and I couldn't see what the branch was.

"You was out early," I said.

"Pa, where you been?" Wallace said.

"I went out to get my gun and to feed Dan, and to bring you this," he said. When he closed the door, I seen it was a branch of witch hazel in full bloom. You know how witch hazel seems to blossom right out of the bark along the stems. The blooms was bright yellow.

"Where did you find that?" I said. The limb seemed to fill up the room with its smell. Witch hazel has a sharp smell, a medicine smell, like it is supposed to wake you up.

"I got it over on the branch," he said. "It's the last thing in the year that blooms. It blossoms when everything else has quit for the winter. Sometimes it throws its seeds on snow."

He started to hand me the limb, but I told him to put it on the table. I had to fix breakfast if we was going to have any. But as I worked, I thought how much I liked something that blooms after everything else has, something that shows they's always another chance.

"Put it in the jar of water there," I said, "So they'll be room for everybody at the table and it will keep blooming for a while."

II

THE ROAD
1816

I was always the kind of feller that had to be making something. Never could just sit with my hands empty. Even on a rainy day I had to be fooling around with a piece of wood or tightening up harness. I'd sit on the porch or in the corner by the fire scraping and polishing a piece of walnut for a gun stock or cherry wood for a lap desk.

"Solomon's the makingest youngun I've got," my Mama would say.

"It's the spirit of the creator in him," my Aunt Willa would say. "The maker puts his talent into some more than others."

I took pride in such talk. At least when I was just a youngun. But the truth was I made things because I couldn't stop myself. I liked to be bragged on good as anybody, but mere love of praise would never drive anybody to work hard as I did.

I'd see a piece of pine and have to get my hands on it. It was like the material told me what to do. The grain of the wood, the color and tone, even the smell demanded the block be shaped. It was like wood had its own idea about what it wanted to be.

And once you get into a job, it's like the job itself takes over. You know what I mean, son. The work pulls you along, pulls you into it. And next thing you know, it's like you can't make a wrong cut or measurement. The work takes you over and you just go with it.

Must be why them fellers spend their lives making tables and chairs and such. Now I *could* feel to make chairs every day from the maple and ash and hickory the good Lord has provided. I could do it and be happy. But along when I was just about half-grown, I went on to other kinds of building. I done all the work here on the place Pa told me to. Just like you, I plowed and hoed corn in season, and pulled fodder and picked berries and cleared land in winter. I put my hand to nearly everything you could name, from syrup making to tanning hides. I smoked meat and hunted deer, and carried off taters and hams on my back down the mountain to peddle in Augusta.

They wasn't no road here back then, and you toted on your back or rode a horse wherever you went. Best people had was an old sled they pulled across the holler and along trails. Wasn't no wagons or buggies 'cause they wasn't no place to drive them, except way down in the valleys. And no place you could buy them, except down in Augusta. We was branch people, living here on the high creeks and headstreams.

But it's the hard work that pleases. The kind of work you dread until you start doing, like clearing up new ground or digging a ditch, or trying to figure out how to do something. The figuring may be the hardest of all, studying out a plan, getting the idea to make something. I've seen men break their backs with labor to avoid thinking about how they should do a job. Five minutes of study would have saved them days of sweat.

But son, what I was going to tell you about was how I found another kind of building. I had done some digging before. My Pa would give me a spade and say, "Dig out that tater hole," or "Fill in the gully." And once I helped dig Old Man Cephas Powell's grave on the hill. And I found it was work I could put my hand to, carving the very flesh of earth. Every bit of ground is different in grain and color. Part of the pleasure is cutting into something new, something never before exposed to sun.

One day when I must have been around fifteen, my Pa said, "Solomon, I want you to level out a path from the back yard to the spring." You remember how steep the hill is back of the old place. In wet weather the spring hill got slick and Mama had to carry all her water up the trail on wash day. Pa was afraid she'd slip on the mud and break her leg.

So I started digging. It was about a hundred fifty yards to the spring. You had to go past the woodpile and the washpot and through the steep woods. I had to cut out the brush to make a way for a decent path. The old trail just kind of wound through the trees and didn't go with any plan. It had been there since the place was settled by my Grandpa, Realus.

I'd seen surveyors work, running out a boundary with their rod and chain, and their sighting instruments. Land was being sold off by the speculators back then, and somebody was always running a line and hacking out a right-of-way. I seen I was going to have to figure where my path was going.

The thing about surveying that was interesting was how they set everything to the compass. I didn't have no dial, and I didn't know exactly how it was done. But I knowed they set their compass to the North Pole and sometimes even to the North Star. That was a thrilling thing, to run a line through mud and brush and up a bank and across a ridge even, an unseen line that was set by degrees to something as far away as the North Pole, or a star. I wished I knowed how it was done, but I didn't have no equipment, and nobody to teach me.

When I scoped out the way to the spring I seen in my mind how the trail would go. But soon as I started chopping trees and grubbing up roots, I found how hard it would be to keep going where I wanted to. That was the first time I used an idea about building. I got a spool of red thread from Mama's sewing box—didn't ask her, just took it—and I strung it out through the trees where I wanted the path to go. First thing I learned was you had to line up everything by sight, and to do that you had to cut away brush and limbs to see to the curve in the hill.

You never seen such chopping and grubbing as I did once that string was stretched around the slope. I measured out a zone six feet wide that I cleared, and once I pulled out the roots and dug up the stumps, I started leveling. Of course, I avoided all the stumps and big trees I could.

That's when I discovered the pleasure of hard work, son. I don't mean just that intoxicated feeling when you work up a sweat and have the blood roaring in your ears, though that is one little part of what I am talking about. But I never believed in breaking my back just for the sake of doing it. No, I'm talking about the satisfaction of getting the hard job done right, of accomplishing something. That's the deep-down pleasure of a man's days. To see an idea take form in soil or wood or stone and know that hundreds of people will use your work down the years.

As I was ready to level out the path, Pa come by and said, "Solomon, we don't want no turnpike to the spring. A trail will do."

That made me so mad, I didn't say nothing. Pa always had a way like that to hurt your feelings, just when you was proud of what you had done. He'd say something and just walk away like he hadn't done nothing, didn't mean nothing. That made me madder still. I thought of bashing him over the head with my shovel. That was the bad streak in me, always thinking of revenge. He knowed how to rile me, just as I was getting on with a job.

I watched Pa walk away and thought of burying the shovel in his brain, for an instant, and then I spun back to work, and swung harder and dug deeper. That was the moment the work come to me so bright and clear. I seen what I could do, and what I was going to do. Because I was angry, and because I was guilty of bad thoughts, I seen everything shining and sharp. I seen my path swing out around the hill for the stream of feet. And I seen I would carve the earth for the use of the family, so not only Mama but generations would have the way to the spring.

I cut into that hillside to level out the trail like I was eating the earth with the shovel. The humus under the leaves and roots weaving under the humus and the gritty clay underneath got shifted around by my hands. I felt like the shovel blade was an extension of my arms and every move I made hit its target, like I was finding gold. And I was finding the gold of use, of rightness. Every lick went true.

But I want mostly to tell you about the gap road, and how me and your Grandma got together.

For years they was talk about building a road into the mountains. The state of North Carolina did some surveys, and the state of South Carolina did some. People in Tennessee even promoted the idea of a road across the mountains for driving their stock to Augusta and Columbia. The old settlers of the coves wanted a way out to trade their produce and productions for cash money, and the Low Country people wanted a way into the cool mountains for summer vacations. Everybody that did a study concluded it was too expensive, even too dangerous. They knowed how it could be done, but without the business already to pay for construction, they was no way to finance such a project.

Oh, we had our wagon tracks and cartways even then. Not in these hollers, but further down along the creeks and rivers. They was a kind of slip-and-slide trail down the mountain to Gap

Creek, but it took four oxen to pull an empty wagon back up that way. Anybody carried something in, they packed it on horseback.

After I built that trail to the spring and seen how wide and gentle it was, and how it eased the burden of carrying water back to the washpot, I commenced to study on the problem of a road up the mountain. I was a lad with ideas. I dreamed big dreams. I thought of myself like some boy in the Bible chosen to free his nation. These mountains bound us in, and I was going to split the ridge to let in the light of trade and travel. I didn't know how I would do it. But I guaranteed to myself it would happen.

Now the funny thing was how the vision of building the road become joined with romance in my mind. They got so tangled up I couldn't think of one without the other. No sir, building the road was the same as winning Mary. Marrying your Grandma was the same as finding a roadway into the mountains. This is how it happened.

I went to a funeral over at the meetinghouse in Cedar Mountain. It was not a service for any relative or close acquaintance. Those days we young folks went to every funeral around, not because we had so much reverence for the dead as because they wasn't no better way to meet each other. A funeral brought together the community. They was something thrilling about the occasion. Preachers done their best preaching at funerals. And everybody was there. The dignity of the service was part of the pleasure. You got dressed up, and somebody was being consigned to eternity, honored by kith and kin. It didn't matter if it was a deacon or a drunk, pillar of the community or blackguard. The girls wore their prettiest clothes, and everybody felt raised up a little out of the slowness of their lives.

Me and my brother Charlie had walked up there. We lived about a mile below Cedar Mountain then. It was a Sunday in late summer. The cornfields we passed smelled sweet as milk and the corn was ripe for top cutting and fodder pulling. After the sermon in the little church we walked out to the graveyard. It wasn't nothing but a little clearing with a few rocks and boards over the dozen graves. It had been warm in the meetinghouse and the open air felt good. And then I seen this girl walking with the family up to the grave. She was near tall as me and had this curly brown hair that shined in the sun. And she had red cheeks and brown eyes, like some Irish girls do.

I was going to ask Mike Staton who that was, but the preacher had started praying and I took off my hat and bowed my head. Every time I glanced up during the long prayer I looked at her. And she didn't have her eyes closed either. She was staring down at the grave like she was thinking of something and not listening. The preacher prayed on and on, and virtually preached his sermon all over again as we stood there by the grave. The breeze fumbled with the ribbons and ruffles on her dress but she didn't seem to notice. I seen she had a slim waist and graceful hips. For a tall slim girl she had a generous bosom.

The prayer stretched on and on, and I was burning to ask Charlie and Mike who that was. I stood on one foot and then the other like a little boy. The instant the prayer stopped and they started throwing dirt on the grave Staton said, "You know they made a survey up through the gap?"

"What gap?" I said.

"Douthat's Gap, the gap right here."

"Who made the survey?" I said.

"Some company from Columbia and Augusta. They want to reach Asheville through Douthat's Gap."

"They've made a lot of surveys," I said.

"But this time they run a line with chain and compass."

"Ain't nobody going to build a road through Douthat's Gap," I said.

The girl had moved away from the grave and walked back toward the meetinghouse. Her back was straight as a chair's.

"I'm going to do it," I said.

"You're going to what?" Charlie said.

"I'm going to marry that girl," I said.

"I thought you meant to build a road through the gap," Staton said.

"I mean to do that too." And soon as I got home I told Mama I had seen the girl I was going to marry.

"Who is she?" Mama said.

"I don't know yet, but I seen her today."

I asked around about the girl, and I found her name was Mary MacPherson, and her Daddy was a teacher at the college in town who had come over from Dublin, Ireland, when he was a young man. But he was from Scotland first. I always read every book I could get my hands on, but I never had any formal schooling except for a few weeks at our country school. A few weeks in winter, and a few weeks in summer before fodder-pulling time was all we had.

The MacPhersons had family in Cedar Mountain. That's why they was at the funeral. But they lived in town right near the grounds of the college. I found out where they lived all right, and I studied how to meet that girl. I wasn't no lady's man to speak of. That fall when I was out squirrel hunting, I'd sit and think about my two plans while the gold hickory leaves fell around me. Sometimes I even forgot to look for squirrels, I was thinking so hard. I thought of a hundred plans. I thought of going up to the Mac-Phersons' door and knocking, saying I was peddling honey or firewood. I thought of trying to enroll in the college as a student, studying for the ministry. I thought of attending the First Baptist Church in town just to get a glimpse of her.

Oddly, the solution to my two problems come at almost the same time. It was almost Christmas, and I read in the paper about a Christmas pageant being put on at the church in town. Among those in the program it listed Mary MacPherson and her sister, Elizabeth. I got me a new pair of boots and a new hat and I planned to go to that service. It would take me half a day to walk to town, and half the night to walk back, but that didn't bother me none.

On Christmas Eve I got to town just after dinner, and went right to Kuykendall's store. I knowed the program at the church started around three. I bought me some pickled sardines and a box of soda crackers. All kinds of people was standing around the store. That's where everybody gathered in town, at Kuykendall's. They had all come to get Christmas presents. The railing in front must have had twenty horses tied to it, and the lot behind the store was full of wagons. The air smelled with horses' breath.

I took care not to get any sardine juice on my clothes or hands. It's a terrible smell to get rid of. I didn't want to stink when I finally got to meet Miss MacPherson. It was crowded around the big pot-bellied stove and I leaned against one end of the long counter. My face was burning from the long walk in the cold, and the excitement of the occasion.

I spoke to a boy from up on the mountain, named Camp. I just knowed him slightly. He was talking to a feller I didn't know at all that still had on his army uniform, like he hadn't changed clothes since he got back from New Orleans with General Jackson.

"They say animals is smarter than people," Camp was saying. "They say buffaloes always found the lowest gaps through the mountains. That's why Indian trails follered buffalo trails."

"A dog will find his way home from a hundred miles away," the other man said. "I had a dog in the army that got lost while we was marching. I figure it was stole. But it found us two hundred miles away, where we had come to camp."

"A cow ain't got no sense," Camp said.

"But a horse has. And a hog is the smartest of all. I've heard that overseas they use hogs to find roots and spot quicksand. And a hog knows an earthquake is coming. You watch a hog hunker down and spread its legs and you know a shaker is going to hit."

"Hogs is quick," Camp said.

"A hog will always find the best way to get to its trough," the other man said. "It will find the shortest way every time."

I don't even know if I finished my sardines in that crowded store. The whole place smelled like leather and tobacco and the Christmas oranges Kuykendall had got in. I must have just stood there and stared at the stove while the crowd milled around me. They is nobody stupid as a really happy person, and I must have looked stupid. Somebody spoke to me and I nodded. And I seen my cousin James out of the corner of my eye. "Merry Christmas, Sol," he said, and showed me a bottle under his coat. I may even have stepped outside and had a swaller of his peartening juice. I can't remember. All I was thinking about was how I was going to bust those South Carolina mountains wide open. I was going to let a little light into Dark Corner, and that's a fact.

Ain't good for a man to be that thrilled, much less a boy. I made sure my feet touched the ground as I walked to the First Baptist Church. I reminded myself I still had all the work before me, though I knowed how it was to be done. I had a girl to meet and win, but I thought I knowed how that was to be done too.

The church was already crowded. It was lit by lanterns hung from the ceiling and from the posts, and the room smelled of Christmas greens and wool. Everybody seemed to be wearing their best winter clothes, and they was a scent of cedar chests over everything. I squeezed my way to one of the benches in the back and looked around for Miss MacPherson. I felt so good I knowed something bad was bound to happen.

Things got under way with the preacher praying a long prayer for peace in the world and the defeat of the enemies of Zion. He was a town preacher and you could tell he was educated, but he prayed just as long as the preachers in the country. I looked around but I didn't see the girl nowhere. My eyes was still adjusting to the lantern light and I couldn't see all the rows in front of me. I thought, maybe she's sick, or maybe she's not in the pageant after all. I thought maybe she had knowed somebody was coming to see her and had stayed away.

Then after the prayer somebody pulled this sheet back that was strung across the front of the meetinghouse on a wire and there was the scene of the shepherds sitting under a candle backed by a tinfoil star. And off to the side, where you could just barely see them, was this row of girls and women. Soon as the curtain was opened, they commenced to sing and I seen she was one of them. The shepherds set there looking at the star and the chorus sung this song about Bethlehem. It was so beautiful I found my eyes wet.

After the women sung a man hid by the sheets started reading from the Bible about the Christmas story. That's the way it went all through the program. The shepherds, and then the Wise Men, said a few words, pointing to the star. They was an angel carrying a candle that spoke out of the dark announcing the nativity. And the row of women and girls sung one Christmas carol after another.

When it was all over, the preacher prayed again. They pulled the sheets further back on the right, and they was a Christmas tree all covered with candles. Under the tree was bags of candy and nuts like fruit fell from the tree. They give some of those bags to everybody. The bag I got had an orange and several kinds of nuts and a bundle of peppermint sticks tied in a red ribbon.

When it was all done and everybody stood up to go, I knowed it was time for me to act. Excitement shot through me so hard it hurt the tips of my fingers. I stood in the corner out of the way of the people leaving so I could see Miss MacPherson. She was talking with the other ladies of the chorus, and they seemed to be exchanging little gifts they brought out of their purses. I worked my way to the front of the meetinghouse. The wall behind the altar was covered with pine boughs to look like the hills of Judea, and resin scented the air. And many of the ladies must have been wearing perfume too, and what with oranges and peppermint the whole placed seemed filled with incense.

"Miss MacPherson," I said. I felt my face go hot. But I was thrilled and surprised at myself to be so bold. She turned her brown eyes to me.

"Miss MacPherson, you have the most beautiful voice," I said.

"Thank you, sir," she said.

"I am Solomon Richards, a cousin of your cousins in Cedar Mountain," I said.

"I suppose that makes us kin," she said. She had a school teacher's voice, proper, as though trained in elocution.

I had learned just enough about buckwheat notes and song-books to talk a few minutes about singing. I knowed young ladies wasn't supposed to talk to strangers. Her mother and Professor MacPherson would be somewhere in the room looking at me. I was a little younger than her, and that seemed in my favor.

"I love singing, but I'm a builder by trade," I said.

"What do you build?" she said.

"I build roads. I'm going to build a road up the mountain through Douthat's Gap."

She looked at me closely, for the first time, as though to see what kind of fool or braggart she might be talking to. "I've heard nobody can build a road through that gap," she said.

"But I know it can be done," I said.

"It's always a pleasure to talk to a modest man," she said, and laughed. I thought I had spoiled everything. She wrapped a cloak about her shoulders and packed the little presents she had been give in her purse. I seen two people that must be the professor and her mother standing at the door. All the space of that empty church was threatening to draw the breath out of me. She was as tall as I was, taller with the blue hat on. And she was four years older, I found out later.

"Miss MacPherson," I said, gathering all my melting courage. "I would like to hear you sing."

"You can hear me sing at church," she said.

"I live over near Cedar Mountain," I said. I seen I had lost. I had nothing more to lose. "I would like permission to call on you," I said, trying to talk the way people in town talked.

She was sliding on her black leather gloves. They was shiny and very thin. I knowed she had a right to dismiss me because I was a stranger to her family.

"Mary, we must go," her father called. The professor walked toward us. He offered his arm to his daughter and looked hard at me. The custodian was blowing out the lanterns one by one.

"Papa, this is Mr. Richards," Mary said.

"Howdy do," I said.

"Hello," the professor said.

"Mr. Richards is interested in sacred music, and I have invited him back to the house for sherry," she said. "He is also interested in building a road up to Cedar Mountain."

I went to church in town that winter, and called on Miss MacPherson whenever she permitted me to. I sung hymns and songs around the spinet in their parlor. I talked to Professor MacPherson about the buildings of the ancient Egyptians, and about cathedrals. Back then I remembered everything I read, and at home I spent every free moment reading by the fire or by the lamp, when I wasn't making something. And I talked with Mrs. MacPherson about picking blackberries and huckleberries, and about putting up preserves and methods of drying fruit and pickling sauerkraut. In those days we dried both peaches and apples every summer.

You might wonder why somebody pretty as Miss MacPherson would spark a boy like me from out in the country. I wondered myself sometimes. But I wasn't a bad-looking feller myself back then, and I tried to learn everything I could. I was younger than her, and I knowed she'd had gentleman callers before. But she was not the kind of girl to string boys along. She could flirt with the best of them when she felt like it. But she was too serious for a lot of boys. And she was already past the age when most girls got married back then. You could see why she would scare a lot of boys, with her serious brown eyes and her proper speech.

I was determined, and I was lucky. I proposed to her between Christmas and Easter. I didn't even have any hope she would accept me when I asked the first time.

"I'm honored by your proposal," she said. "But I must ask you to reconsider."

"To reconsider?"

"To wait until you know your own mind."

"I know my own mind," I said. "I've never been more sure of my own mind."

She asked me to wait a month while I reconsidered. "At nine-teen a man may not know his mind," she said.

"I know my heart," I said. "Am I supposed to be an old man to know my heart?"

She agreed to discuss the proposal again in a month. All during that spring the MacPhersons were polite to me. My second cousin John begun courting their daughter Elizabeth, but he was two years older than me and already had his own farm out at Upward. Finally in April, Mary brought up the subject again.

"Papa says we should not marry until you have established yourself in some line of business," she said.

"And what do you say?"

"That we should wait until you have established yourself. Marriage might distract and hinder you."

"Then you agree to marry me?"

"When it is the proper time."

I knowed I had won. Your Grandma was ever a woman to hold to her word.

I figured I couldn't get no backers to build a toll road from the foot of the mountain to Douthat's Gap till I proved I could survey a route. And I couldn't afford to build the road until I had backers to pay for the construction and right of way. With me doing a lot of the work, it wouldn't be more than three or four thousand dollars. But I didn't have but fifty dollars to my name. Cash money was hard to lay a hand on that year, after the 1812 war. They wasn't hardly any money around.

So everything depended on surveying a route up the mountain. I asked everybody I knowed if they would put up a few dollars, if I surveyed a route. Nobody believed I could do it. "Why you'll fall off a cliff at the jump-off," Uncle Cephas said.

"Them blockaders of Dark Corner will shoot you if you don't get rattlesnake bit," Aunt Arrie said.

But I seen their skepticism was to my advantage. "You sign here a pledge for ten dollars if I survey the route," I said. "Then if I don't succeed, you won't have to pay nothing."

I went around with a notebook where I signed up shareholders. "You all want a road out of here, don't you?" I said. "Where you can haul off hams and honey to Augusta." They signed, thinking they would never have to pay a cent, I guess. Mary signed up fifty dollars she'd saved from teaching school. And her papa signed up for a twenty-dollar share. The truth was, if a toll road was opened into the mountains, it would pay them back a hundredfold every year. But at that time none of them expected to pay the money or see any profit, unless it was Mary herself.

I'd always been a worker and a builder, but I'd never sold anything before. I was the kind of feller that would prefer to give away anything rather than to sell it. I tended to apologize rather than to sell. But I found I could do it. I had to get the signatures to raise the money, and without the money they would be no road. And without the road they would be no marriage. And besides that, I wanted to build the road as much as I wanted to marry her. I went around and talked to people in their fields, and had dinners in their houses all up and down the branch valleys and down to the river. I went to the mill and talked to people, and I went to the little store at the crossroads and talked to people. I found that patience was my greatest tool. You talk to people long enough, and mostly they will sign up.

When I got all the pledges I was ready. It was past midsummer and the corn was laid by. I had kept my razorback sow Sue lean that summer, penned up so she couldn't breed or forage on acorns and other mast. One Sunday, I put a rope on her hind foot and led her down to Gap Creek and across to Pumpkintown to Uncle Rufus's and Aunt Willa's house at the foot of the mountains. It was hot weather, and took us all day to make the trip.

"You can't foller a hog from here to Cedar Mountain," Aunt Willa said, raking the hot grits onto my plate. "They's no way through the thickets and across the hollers."

"That's why I'm doing it," I said. "So's I can make a way."

"Solomon's got an idea," Uncle Rufus said. "He reminds me of old Uncle Solomon, who always had an idea."

The grits was almost too hot to eat. I stirred butter into the steaming heap.

"I hear he's got him a girl too," Uncle Rufus said. "Solomon's marrying into quality."

"You're a big stout feller," Aunt Willa said to me. "But you're not going to tear down no mountain with your bare hands to put a road through. Mountains won't step aside to please you."

"I always thought the Blue Ridge could be split with a road," Uncle Rufus said. "But not through Douthat's Gap. You've got Caesar's Head to climb over."

I eat the hot butter and grits fast as I could. It was going to be a long hot day and I couldn't stand on ceremony. I could feel the heat already in the air, like a haint, though the sun hadn't come up over the ridge yet.

"The Indians had a trail," Uncle Rufus went on. "From right here near Pumpkintown all the way to Toxaway and the Tuckasegee."

"They didn't have wheeled vehicles," I said, and washed some of the grits down with Aunt Willa's coffee. Aunt Willa and Uncle Rufus was awful good to me. I would walk down and stay with them a week at a time when I was a boy. They didn't have no children, and Uncle Rufus liked to coon hunt. We'd take his dogs on a moonlit night and run all over the mountains of upper South Carolina. Hunting in the moonlight is another world. I wish I had took you more, son, like I did your Daddy, back when I was still able to tramp all night through brush.

"You stay on another day and we'll go to the singing," Aunt Willa said.

"Much obliged," I said, and stood up. "But I got to bust the ridge by sundown. They'll expect me home by dark."

"Your hog ain't fed," Uncle Rufus said.

"I don't want her fed. That way she'll hurry home faster."

I had drove Sue all the way down Saluda Gap and through the Winding Stairs the day before without feeding her. I wanted her good and hungry. We had took the long way by North Fork.

"You'll get a mess of chiggers up there," Aunt Willa said. "And spiders in your face and eyes."

"I wouldn't go in them mountains without a gun," Uncle Rufus said. "Too many painters. And somebody said they seen Tracker Thomas up there."

"Everybody claims they've seen Tracker Thomas," I said. "He's been dead probably twenty years."

"They's haints up in the hollers," Aunt Willa said. "People has heard all kinds of Indian spooks and wails coming from deep hollers under Caesar's Head."

"That's just blockaders talking to scare people," I said. "They don't want no road for the law to come in and find them."

"I wouldn't fool with no blockaders," Uncle Rufus said. "You might end up wrong end of a musket."

"Them cove people will do you dirt," Aunt Willa said. "Some of them is half Indian."

"You can't see where you're going with all the leaves on the trees," Uncle Rufus said. "It was me, I'd wait till fall."

"Can't wait till fall," I said. "We've got to do our clearing and digging in the fall before it gets too cold. I've got to blaze a route now, before fodder-pulling time."

"You'll get mighty hot climbing that far," Aunt Willa said. "It must be twenty miles straight to Cedar Mountain, not counting the hollers and go-rounds. You take some biscuits and a canteen."

"I can't carry nothing but my hatchet," I said. "I'll be running too fast and trying to hold onto old Sue."

The truth was I didn't know how I was going to hold onto Sue except by her tail. I didn't even know if I could run bending down like that. But it was the only way I had thought of to foller and let her have her lead. Wouldn't do no good if I held her back, or if I lost her. It was going to be an experiment. I had no certainty my plan would work. The whole thing was based on what I'd heard at Kuykendall's store on Christmas Eve.

I made sure my suspenders was buttoned, and I got my hatchet from beside the door. "Much obliged," I said to Aunt Willa.

"Don't gouge out your eye on no locust limb," Aunt Willa said.

When I got to the pen, the sow was squealing with excitement and hope. She expected to be fed. But Sue was also like a good dog: she was always ready for adventure, ready to go someplace.

I had the sense a great event was about to happen. You know, son, how we all grandify things, imagine that on any given day we will do some little thing that will become history, that we are acting out a grand role even going to the outhouse or draining a puddle. I told myself I was in the hands of the future and what I did that day would be writ large across the mountains for decades if not centuries. Vanity is the weakness of all of us, and the downfall of many. But I don't reckon anybody ever pushed hisself beyond the usual ruts without a certain amount of vanity. I was acting for my own memory, and I don't think I would have worked so hard if I hadn't been. I was working for love of your

Grandma too, but they was some vanity bound up in that, and it wouldn't be too far wrong to say they was all part of the same bundle.

As soon as I pushed the palings aside, Sue shot through fast as only a pig can be fast. I just had time to grab her tail and foller, half stumbling and half running.

"You come back and see us," Uncle Rufus called. But I didn't have time to answer because it was all I could do to hold onto the sow with my left hand and grip the hatchet in my right as Sue trotted past the woodshed and outhouse. Chickens scattered out of our way and a guinea set up its racket. We run right over Aunt Willa's flowerbeds, and I felt my boots crush stems and petals. I'd have to apologize later, for they was no way I could stop.

Running half bent over, everything seemed a blur. They's a menace and glory to late summer weeds, and they just seemed to be swirling and swishing around me, getting taller as we left the yard. Ironweed reached higher with its purple than the hogweeds, and thistle and Spanish needle reached higher than ironweed. Above them all was queen-of-the-meadow, just beginning to bloom. We swung through the tall weeds, knocking down stems big as cornstalks. I felt like I was being dragged through riots and explosions of green. Even the early light seemed green as it flew by me, tangled in leaves and stalks. I knowed the weed hell was full of snakes, and hoped Sue was scaring them away ahead of me.

Sue busted out at the edge of the cornfield and swerved in and out of the first row, knocking down a few half-grown stalks. For an instant I thought she was going to head back the way we had come the day before. After all, that was the way she knowed to go. And I couldn't turn her away, if she did start toward Gap Creek and Chestnut Springs. My project would be ruined and I'd have to think of another way to survey my road. But at the end of the field, at the last moment, she plunged into the woods going north in the direction I assumed was Cedar Mountain.

"Whoa," I said, hoping to slow her down a little. But she didn't respond. She hadn't been trained like no horse. I seen the trouble I was in. She could slide under the poplar limbs without slowing, and slip under brush that slapped me in the face. I ducked low as I could, still holding onto the tail. Limbs smacked me across the cheeks and ears. I was glad I had not wore a hat, for it would have been lost in the first hundred yards.

"Whoa," I said, trying to shield my face with the hatchet in my right hand. Limbs rushed at me and I closed my eyes. A briar raked my knee, but I didn't have time to look down to see if it tore my pants.

Them first few hundred yards was part of Uncle Rufus's growed-up field. You know how bastard pines and blackberry briars will take over a patch when you turn it out. The stiff needles on the pines stung my neck and face. I was starting to get mad. It was like Sue was punishing me for driving her so far the day before. I thought she was like a woman that waited till she had you just the right place to get even with you, pay you back for a slight. She had me bent over and holding on. I was so mad I forgot and didn't blaze a single tree until we reached the deeper, older woods where they was less undergrowth.

My plan was to mark the trees with the hatchet every few yards. Later I would come back and stake out the right-of-way. Even if I blazed one tree out of a hundred, I figured I could find the path we had follered. It was the general route I wanted to mark, not the foot by foot and step by step way Sue had gone.

Leaning over to keep my grasp on the sow's tail, I couldn't reach high on the trees to make my marks. All I needed was to make some noticeable cut. But it dizzied me to run bent over, and to reach up to hack the bark. I seen it was going to be harder than I had guessed.

"Whoa," I said to Sue. "We've got all day." But she didn't pay no attention. She seemed to trot even faster to punish me. I had starved her and driv her near thirty miles, and now I was holding onto her tail. She lunged ahead like a horse in harness. With every step she grunted and broke wind, and I had no choice but to hold on and smell her. I hoped she would empty herself out.

The hog lunged even faster into the brush. They was a clump of laurel bushes ahead and I wanted her to go around it. But she dove right through the limbs. It was all I could do to hold on and keep the branches from stabbing me in the eye. I didn't have time to make no slashes on the laurels, but I didn't need to, for we broke enough limbs just getting through to mark our passage.

They was an Old Field ahead. At least that's what everybody called it. It was just a clearing of wore-out clay that had been there since anybody could remember. The Old Fields was here when the first settlers arrived. We used to say they had been farmed by the Indians and then washed away. Maybe they was places that had been struck by lightning too many times, or had poor soil to begin with. Or maybe they had been burned over in firehunting and washed away. The Indians hunted deer with fire. The dirt was just red clay covered with pebbles on stems of dirt and patches of broomsedge. They was a grave in the corner with rocks piled on top that was thought to be an Indian grave.

As we run through the brambles, the sow suddenly jerked to one side and flung me after her. I almost fell in the briars. Then I seen the head of a rattler, raising through the vines and broom-sedge. It was a big old head, the shape of a tomahawk. I seen them eyes just gleaming. Without even thinking, I swung the hatchet and the snake's head flew off into the weeds squirting blood and venom.

But we was running too fast to stop, and as we passed the coiled body the stub of the neck struck my leg hard as a man's kick. I guess it was already aimed and the length of the body just continued the strike. It was like the body acted on its own.

The coiled snake would have filled a half-bushel hamper. Its middle was thick as the calf of my leg.

What's that? No, I don't think the Indians worshipped no rattlesnake or left the snake there to guard the field. No, sir. People talk all kinds of rot such as that. I've heard Indians respected rattlers because they give you warning. They had a story explaining it was an agreement made with the king of the rattlers, that they never would bite an Indian without giving fair warning. Not like the sneaky copperheads. The rattlers, they said, had a noble nature.

Where my leg was hit by that snake it was sore, and I wanted even more to slow down. "Whoa," I called to Sue, but she didn't pay no attention. I wondered how much longer I could foller her. The sun was just coming up over the Gap Creek mountains.

I seen that even if I was to last the first hour, I'd have to do something different. I couldn't keep going all bent over and jerked around, and flailing out to blaze the trees. I was already getting swim-head from the slinging around with my head down.

It wasn't no good to pull back on that sow's tail. It must have hurt her a little bit but she didn't seem to care. She could jerk me along fast as she wanted. I run to one side, and I pulled back, and then I run to the other side. And I found out the hog run slower when I didn't pull back. If I quit pulling, she stopped running so hard. By running faster, I encouraged her to go slower.

Son, you'll find a lot of things works that way. The more you want something, the less the world wants to give it to you. By striving, you seem to turn the tide against you. It's just human nature, and maybe a pig's nature, to resist. People and hogs are a lot alike. I pulled and pulled back on that sow, and the instant I relaxed my hold she slowed. Otherwise I couldn't have gone on another mile. The heat was starting to build and my neck and face itched from cobwebs and the rasp of limbs.

I tried to remind myself of the project I was undertaking, of the way we would level out a road on the route we was going. But it was hard to remember what I was up to in the heat of running and dodging limbs, that in the future wagons and carriages would be rolling by where we stumbled.

I heard dogs barking to my left, but I couldn't see a thing when I turned that way. Dogs was one of the things I was most afraid of. Now a hog will defend itself against a dog. A wild hog, especially, will turn on a dog and cut almost any hound with its tushes. A hog has thick skin on its neck and shoulders a dog can't hardly bite through, and a hog is so rounded a dog can't hardly get a bite on it anyway.

Dogs can run a hog to bay. Though it wasn't dogs hurting Sue that worried me most. After all, I had the hatchet and a man's presence will make a difference. But if dogs started harassing her, she would be distracted from her path. My project would go all to pieces if she veered away, or turned to fight and forgot our purpose.

The dogs was getting closer and I wondered if they was on our trail. They sounded still off to the left, like they was coming to meet us. They was yips and rattling complaints, more like beagles than hounds.

When that pack of dogs come out of the trees, the first thing I seen was the dapple color of a beagle rushing in the undergrowth. The dog run right to Sue's side and yelped.

Sue swerved and slung me after her.

"Get away from here!" I hollered. "Be gone."

Two more beagles appeared out of the bushes. They ignored me and run right up to the sow yipping and bellering at her side. She turned and lunged at them and sent one of the dogs spinning with her shoulder. The others drawed back too.

"Get away, get away!" I yelled.

Three more dogs arrived and they was all under my feet as I run. I was afraid I was going to trip over them. I kicked out at the one nearest and caught him in the ribs. The beagles yelped and hollered like a gaggle of geese. They seemed to have forgot about whatever rabbit or fox they had been running. I wondered if they was a hunter with them. I didn't relish being seen kicking somebody's dogs, even if they was bothering me.

"Hie, hie!" I hollered. "Get away from here, get away." But the dogs didn't pay no more attention to me than if I was a gnat. I swung my hatchet but tried not to hit the dogs.

Sue was already veering off course. She was bearing right, away from the dogs. She would swing back to snap at a beagle and then bear further to the right. I wished I had a stick to beat the dogs away. If I hit one with the hatchet, it might kill it.

I had to think quick what to do. If we got too far off course, I'd have to give up the survey and try later. It would be a week before I could rest the sow for another attempt. And I was running the risk of ridicule anyway. I would be the laughing stock of the community if me and the sow got lost and had to wander out of the woods with no path blazed. No one would invest in a road if I was known as the "sow man" or the "hog follower."

How could I face Mary and her Papa if my plan was ruined by a few beagles? How foolish it would sound to people, that a man had tried to let a hog show him the path of a highway. I swung my hatchet and hit a beagle on the back with the blunt side. It squealed and run off into the brush, but the others continued to harry Sue. I thought if we stopped, the dogs might back away. It was the fact that we was running away that made them chase Sue.

But I couldn't stop Sue just by pulling her tail. I couldn't even make her slow down. And she never responded to my voice. With the dogs at her heels she was running faster than ever. I was streaming with sweat and out of breath.

"Get away, get away!" I hollered at the beagles. I thought of killing them one at a time with the hatchet. But I couldn't reach most of them without letting loose of Sue. Once I turned loose she would be gone. She would head off into the thickets and I would never catch up. And I wouldn't know what route she took back to Cedar Mountain. She might not return. She might head out into the wilderness and go wild on the chestnuts and acorns.

All my plans seemed to be collapsing around those infernal beagles.

Suddenly Sue wheeled around, flinging me against a poplar. I hadn't marked a tree in a quarter mile. She bared her tushes and faced the beagles. They was took by surprise and pulled back. They circled and barked as Sue lunged at one and knocked it yelping away. She wheeled and leaped at another. The others pulled out of range.

The beagles acted utterly shocked. They hadn't expected to fight. They had been running for the thrill of chasing an animal that seemed to be fleeing.

Sue lunged again, then stood back to face her attackers. The beagles yelped and crossed in front of each other at a safe distance. Gradually the dogs quieted as we stood and watched them. Now we seemed entirely different. They couldn't bear to look at us with their wet, sad eyes. After a few awkward minutes they shivered nervously, sniffing the air, and slipped away one by one into the trees.

Sue watched in triumph as the beagles retreated and vanished. She looked at the bushes to see if the dogs would come back. We was still in pretty level country and you could hear things moving in the undergrowth. She raised her ears and listened, still panting. Now everybody knows a hog sweats through its nose. Her nose was covered with drops big as dew on a fall morning. I never knowed how the drops on a hog's nose could be so big and still hold together. They stood out round as marbles. Sue snorted and sweat flung off in all directions.

She had to make up her mind to keep going. They was no way I could prod her. I was tired already, and I figured she was tired. They was a little whisper in my ear that said to call it off and try again another day. Wait until the leaves has fell off and you can see further. Wait until the weather is cooler and the climb up the ridge will be easy. They hasn't been a road up the Blue Ridge all these thousands of years, it said. It wouldn't hurt to wait a couple more months. They's no shame in turning back if you know you'll try again in a few weeks.

If I turned back, I could be at Uncle Rufus's in time for dinner. We'd set down to some new corn and new potatoes. It would feel good just to sit down. I felt like I'd spent a hard morning in the field, bent over to pull weeds or thin out hills of corn.

Sue looked from side to side of the little clearing we stood in. Things scratched in the leaves and rustled in the brush. It could be ground squirrels or birds, or the beagles still circling around us. Sue could smell what was out there if the air was moving. I was soaked with sweat, and sweat dripped in my eyes. When you stop running you always feel hotter than when you're moving. It's like the heat builds and catches up with you once you stop. It's like the heat raises through your guts and bones into your head. I was boiling inside.

Sue looked to the left, and to the right. Then it was like she remembered in a flash what she had been doing. She wheeled around, jerking me behind her. I almost lost my hold. Maybe she satisfied herself the dogs was finally gone. Or maybe she remembered her pen on Cedar Mountain and the trough of cornmeal and slop.

She swung around and it looked like she had forgot the direction up the mountain. I couldn't remember which way we was supposed to go without looking at the sun and looking through the trees for landmarks. The woods seemed the same on all sides. But after a couple of turns Sue straightened out and kept going. It was like it all come back to her, where she had been heading when the beagles appeared. She picked up speed and I followed, slashing a poplar with the hatchet as I run past. My tiredness and sweatiness seemed to fall away. It was like a headache had disappeared in a cool breeze. The woods stretched out toward home, and Sue seemed to know exactly where she was going.

The Bible says man was give dominion over the things of the earth, and I reckon that includes the soil itself. Even red clay can be carved and shifted around. Since I was a boy I had loved to make terraces in the field, to level out a band around the hill by cutting into the steepness and piling the dirt on the down side. We plowed a deep furrow and then plowed it again. And you had something level and regular in the uneven spill of the terrain. I love that look of something flat where everything else is rough and changing with the lay of the land.

A road is just a terrace across a slope, or across a swamp. It has to be wide enough and level enough for wagon wheels, and the grade has to be gentle enough for horses to pull big loads up, and hold back going down. A road is a kind of lever for moving a mountain, I used to say to myself. With the right grade the tallest mountain can be conquered. By swinging around and back the heaviest load can be pulled right to the sky itself and brought down on the other side.

A good road is so tender, it seems to hurt as it reaches into the night or the shade of woods. I had seen the old Pike where it goes down through Saluda Gap and the Winding Stairs, and I had seen the road from Old Fort up to Asheville, and it thrilled me to think I could make something that useful.

When I think of new roads, I think of some preacher riding along them and building new churches and congregations on the way. I see young people going to singings and baptizings and dinner on the grounds. The young folks meet each other and fall in love and unite families scattered in the coves and hollers. Roads is like fresh water on dry ground. Along them people arrive, ground is cleared and towns get started in the valleys.

I had a feeling I could make a road anywhere, from any place on the face of the earth to another. All I needed was to level dirt a foot at a time, a step at a time. The soil will take you to the highest peak or the furthest point of the continent. The method is to haul dirt from the high places and put it in the low places, with spade and mattock, pick and shovel, dragpan and plow, with powder and fire-and-dowsing. All rocks can be broke or pried and rolled out of the way. It's a matter of pitch or connection. All paths and little roads tap into a turnpike like feeder streams fill and draw off a canal.

I didn't think I could hold on much longer. My left hand was already stiff from gripping the sow's tail, the way it gets from holding an ax handle for hours. My palm was sore and sweating. I wanted to change hands, but even if I could have, it would be awkward to blaze the trees with my left. Maybe Sue would stop for a rest when we started climbing.

We had come to steeper ground. In South Carolina the hills start rolling higher as you approach the mountains. But the hills don't rise gradually toward the mountains; they canter along and hit the wall of the ridge head-on. It was in the steep country I really needed the sow. Anybody can lay off a road in flat country, in gentle hills. But how do you find the best grade for going around mountain flanks and crossing coves and winding up to a gap? Is it better to go across a ridge or around it?

Sue seemed to speed up as we started climbing. A hog climbs not in jumps and humps but in little steps running like a spider. A hog moves its big weight a little bit at a time.

The grits felt uneasy in my stomach. Having to run bent over was the worst. Several times the brash come up in my throat and I tasted the sour butter and coffee. I swallowed hard to sweeten the taste with spit. I hoped I didn't get sick at my stomach. If I got to throwing up, I'd have to let go of Sue. They's no worse feeling than that. A man will wish he is dead if he gets sick enough at his stomach. Bending over was putting pressure on my belly. And getting hot will make you sick too. I was used to heavy work, but the running was worser than anything I'd done.

The sow turned up the slope at a steeper angle than I would have took. We had come around a hill right to the foot of the mountain. I wondered why she was going to the top of the rise. She trotted, stirring up the dry leaves. I felt itchy with sweat and scratchy with spiders and gnats. But I could not scratch with the hatchet in my right hand.

It was only when we reached the top of the rise and walked panting through the thinner trees that I saw the reason she had come that way. The creek below was lined with big boulders. It would take months, even years, to bust up the rocks to make a way through there. Sue had took the only route that bypassed the boulders. How had she knowed they was there? For the second time that day I felt a thrill of satisfaction and confidence in what I was doing. What the boy at Kuykendall's store said about a hog's instinct was turning out to be true.

My left hand felt like it was bleeding, but I could not release my hold to look at it. If the sow ever tired and stopped, I'd change hands and wrap my palm with a rag tore off my shirt.

But in the open woods on top of the rise she trotted even faster. I run beside her to stay upright, and that rested my back some. But to run beside her I had to go faster, and that made her increase her speed again. She seemed to have demons in her. I thought of the swine the demons was cast into and how they plunged into the sea. I was glad they was no ocean nearby.

It wasn't till we come down off the rise further on that I seen why she had been hurrying so. They was a ford across the creek. The creek up there was getting small and poured right through the leaves under the laurels. It was shallow with a rocky bottom. Sue stopped right in the middle. The current was so cold it burned my sweaty feet and legs but it felt good. She's giving me a rest, I thought.

And then I seen why she really stopped. It wasn't just that she wanted a drink. They was a kind of pulpy paste washed up on the rocks and she begun licking it like it was the finest slop. It looked and smelled like something rotten, something soured or vomited up. At first I couldn't see what it was. I bent closer and got a good whiff, and then I recognized the scent.

That pulp smelled like apples under a tree after they've been frostbit and thawed a few times. It was a sweet-sour smell. Somebody up the creek was making liquor, and they had throwed out the mash after the beer was done. They was probably boiling the beer at that moment, while the mess washed downstream. I knowed they was nothing a hog loved better than half-rotten mash.

What is mash? Why, mash is what you have left after you get the juice out of fermented malt. What is malt? That's sprouted corn you've kept warm and wet and then ground up to ferment.

No, I've never made liquor. That is, I never made it to sell. But I've seen it made. I've even helped make a little in my time, for my own use. For medicine, you might say. Everybody used to make a little whiskey back then. It was necessary to have alcohol for tinctures and medicines. Everybody kept a jug or a keg. We didn't figure it was the giverment's business, what we done with our corn and peaches and apples. The giverment was after the revenue. They wanted us to make the liquor and pay taxes and then buy it back from them.

South Carolina even then was full of blockaders that made hundreds and thousands of gallons to sell in the flat country. Dark Corner was wild as anybody could want. It was full of Howards and Gosnells, Revises and Morgans, people that was always fussing and feuding. My Pa always said, "Stay away from the blockaders in Dark Corner. In a fight they'll cut a man from head to belly before he can wink."

"Get out of there, go on!" I shouted to Sue, and shoved her flanks. But she only stepped forward to gobble another cake of mash stuck on the bank. That was like both wine and dessert to a hog, I reckon. The blockaders often fed their mash to hogs, if they was close enough to the pen. And their hogs stayed drunk half the time, grunting happy and fat.

The sow eat all the mash in sight and then scrambled up into the laurels. I hoped she wouldn't head upstream. The still must be somewhere up there, probably not too far away. Some blockaders guard their works and shoot anybody that comes in sight. Others just hide if they hear somebody coming. Since it was day, I thought they might have throwed out the mash and gone home with the night's work. But what would they think of a man that come running along holding a hog's tail? How could I explain myself and Sue to men with guns pointed at me?

The sow turned and followed the bank of the stream, probably smelling more mash further up. That was one thing I had not planned for the day. I had feared that we might run into blockaders, but I hadn't thought Sue would seek them out in the holler, and I hadn't considered the sow might get drunk.

I couldn't see a thing through the laurels. They growed right down to the bank of the stream. We ducked around the bushes and under them. In such a cover a man could be bushwhacked and never know what hit him. I didn't have time to look around. I was too busy dodging limbs and holding on to Sue with my left hand. Everywhere I looked it seemed somebody was watching us behind the thickets. A chill went through my guts and bones.

I thought again of letting go, of giving up the survey, of coming back in the fall like Uncle Rufus suggested. It wouldn't be no good if I was shot dead trying to find a road.

I could let Sue go and she'd wander back on her own. She would fatten up on the mast and I would catch her at hog-killing time. They was other roads I could build, other jobs, and even other occupations. I was young enough to foller any trade I chose. I could be a carpenter, learn masonry. It would take a while to get started and build up a business. Even Professor MacPherson couldn't object to a change of trade. He would probably welcome something more practical than the dream of building turnpikes.

My grand design for the road seemed ludicrous there in the laurel thicket with blockaders lurking in the shadows. How had I come to that hideous situation? Streaming with sweat and covered with bark soot and gnats, my hand gripping a hog's rear end? I could smell myself in the close air; I smelled raw and afraid, running scared.

I would have turned back then, except for the thought that it was probably too late. The trees above leaned over as though threatening to smother me. The sky and sun was hid away. The laurel bushes poked at me and twigs stabbed at my eyes as I run past. They was already watching me, most like, and I couldn't get away. I smelled like sweat and hog farts. I couldn't see no way out of the trap I'd come to.

I would have let go and run off into the thickets and hid, except for the thought I'd have nothing if I chickened out. I wouldn't have no job, and I wouldn't have no Mary. And I wouldn't have no confidence in myself. A man has got to have confidence, or he is lost. And to have confidence, you've got to have a plan.

The survey was my main plan, my only plan. All the obstacles didn't change that. Obstacles could be crawled over and around and pushed out of the way.

Sue paused long enough to swill a gob of mash lodged against a laurel root. She was beginning to swing her head and step different, like the mash was affecting her. It's hard to say how a hog shows the signs of drunkenness. But you could tell she wasn't herself exactly. Not that she staggered. They was a new looseness in her steps. She turned a little slower, and grunted easier. It was her pace and manner, though you couldn't have pointed to one thing and said, "There, only a drunk hog would have done that."

"Hey there!" somebody hollered ahead. A man stood by the bank with a rifle in the crook of his arm. They was a fire going somewhere behind him because I could see smoke swaying out into the trees. I didn't know how long he had been watching us.

"Whoa there," I said and pulled back on Sue's tail. But that seemed to make her mad and she speeded up, jerking me after her. As we approached the man he raised his rifle, but Sue veered around him, like he was just another tree.

"Whoa there!" I hollered again, trying to show the stranger I meant to cooperate, that it wasn't me wanted to barge into his camp. They was nothing I could do. The man looked in wonder at me as we run past. I reckon he would have shot a man alone already, but a man pulled by a sow so astonished him, he just watched.

As we swung around him I seen a tent strung between two oak trees. It was a ragged, faded tent that blended so well with the shadows you didn't notice it at first. It was held down by stakes and twine. Sue must not have seen the cords for she headed right at them. As she tripped on the strings, the stobs pulled out of the ground. She fell on the tent and I stumbled on top of her. As I rolled off one of the stakes punched me in the side. Sue squealed like her throat was being cut. The tent come wilting down as canvas will when its lines break.

"Hey there, hey there!" the man with the gun hollered. He come running after me, his gun aimed first at Sue, then at me.

As the tent sagged two men jumped out of it. They must have been sleeping, for their hair was wild and their galluses was down. They must have worked all night making liquor and was taking a rest before they worked again. They likely had been sound asleep, for their eyes looked swole up and they blinked in the morning light.

"Where the hell?" one man said. "Where the hell you going?" I never felt so foolish. My side was bleeding where I had hit the tent stob, and I still gripped the hatchet in my right hand as I scrambled to grab Sue's tail again.

Sue rolled over on the tent and the rest of it come down with a kind of whoosh that sent dust and leaves boiling up. They was a wild look in her eyes as she squealed with confusion. If she hadn't been partly drunk she would have got away. But I lunged for her tail and grabbed it firm just as she got to her feet.

"You stop right there," the man with the gun called. But I couldn't look back. A bullet whizzed over my shoulder like a mad honey bee.

Sue clambered right through the middle of the fallen tent and I followed, knocking my shins on pots and things under the canvas. She didn't see the shelf loaded with pans and buckets and kittles until she hit it with her shoulder. Pots come banging and ringing down on top of me. I felt like I was being hit from every side. They was such a racket, I couldn't tell what nobody was saying. They might have been another shot fired, for all I know. I held onto her tail, and let everything bang and roll behind me.

When everything's happening at once, it's like you're both aware of it and not. I knowed the men was hollering at me and follering and threatening to kill me, but I knowed I had to hold on to Sue or all would be lost. If I stopped to explain, I'd just get killed and nothing would be accomplished. If I kept going, I might get away.

They was a tub full of mash and a dozen or so jugs near to the fire. Sue skirted the jugs with a delicacy that seemed impossible in the situation and stuck her snout in the tub to gulp some mash. But it must have been hot for she squealed and shook her head, pulp streaming from her jaws, and run on.

I looked back over my shoulder, in that pause. The three men was watching us with a mixture of awe and confusion. They had never seen anything as crazy as a man holding a sow's tail. The fact that I seemed crazy was my best protection.

"I'm going to build a road," I hollered back at them. "We're surveying out a right-of-way."

"This ain't no right-of-way," the man with the rifle called. "This is the wrong way."

They had the biggest doubler I had ever seen. It must have been a hundred-gallon still, maybe two-hundred, of shining copper, like it was new made. They had the fire going under it. And even as I run past in all that panic and confusion, I seen the clear liquor dripping from the eye of the worm in shining drops.

Another bullet sung by me as we run out past the woodpile. But I figured if they was going to shoot me, they already would have. I figured they was obliged to do something, so they fired them shots to scare me.

What's that? How could we build a road right through the still? I was pretty sure when we come through again that still would have moved. The blockaders would take their outfit to another holler after they had been found. Since I hadn't been killed and since I had seen their operation, they would just take everything to another branch.

As we passed the fire, the heat almost blistered me. No wonder them fellers was sleepy, after working in that blaze all night. Maybe the fumes had got to me, for the whole place seemed to spin around, the big barrel with its slop of mash, and the copper worm like a big tendril of a grapevine with the jug at the end of it catching lit tears of liquor. And we had passed a pile of wood that seems in memory to be higher than my head. It must have been a month's supply of split oak. And they was a quilt hanging somewhere among the saplings, but I didn't know what it was for. Maybe it wasn't even there; maybe I imagined the quilt.

I expected any second for a bullet to hiss by my ear. I stayed bent over as I run. My best hope was just to keep going. Like, if you seem to know where you're going, people will hesitate to bother you. But over the sound of Sue's grunting and panting, and my own short breath, I could hear the sounds of birds, and dogs barking. But the strangest thing was, it sounded like men making them noises. As we slipped into the laurels, I glanced back just once, and those three fellers was running after us. They follered us baying like dogs, and calling between their hands like birds, and making every kind of sound you could think of.

That was the most unsettling thing that had happened to me. It was like them fellers decided they couldn't shoot me 'cause I was crazy. But they wanted to scare me and make me never come back, and they had found just the right thing to do.

I kept hearing their calls and painter screams after we got deep in the laurels. But with us shaking the bushes and kicking up the leaves, I wasn't sure when I quit hearing their whistles and woofs and just thought I did. They seemed to be halloos and growls in the air, but I couldn't be sure.

Among the rattle of the leaves and the shivering of the bushes, I soon heard another noise. They was a kind of hum ahead. It was like I could place the sound but couldn't name it. It was a buzz like a fire or a swarm of bees, and we was running directly toward it. I knowed what the sound was but couldn't think of it. It was a roar like a fireplace will make when you get a big fire going with hickory and the draft gets stronger and stronger.

I couldn't hear the cries of the whiskey men behind, but ahead was this roar. And then I knowed it must be a waterfall on the creek, for I could smell mist in the air. Sue was staggering a little from all the mash she had eat, and she seemed to be losing her sense of direction. We plunged deeper into the holler, right toward the sound. If they was a waterfall, it looked like we would be blocked and have to go back toward the still.

I started to feel the mist in the air like a cool breath. It felt good, like I was changing from one to another season, in just a few minutes. I was soaked with sweat already, and cobwebs stuck to my clothes. For some reason the spray made me feel the scratches and bits of bark and cobwebs on my skin worse than the heat did. Big drops clung to webs strung between laurels. A drop hit me in the eye like a soft egg busting. The drops running down my neck and back felt like spiders.

Maybe it was the roar of the waterfall that made me itchy and nervous. I was sure we'd have to turn back, yet Sue kept trotting further and further. The sound of falling water got louder. The leaves and rocks dripped with mist. Maybe the hog was so drunk she did not even notice the roar and crashing. At least when we reached the dead end I could catch my breath.

Sue busted out of the laurels, and there was the pool into which the long, white tongue of water was plunging. The water boiled up crazy where it hit, and the pool looked dark and deep. I thought Sue was going to head straight into the water. The cold pool would feel good, but I wanted to stay away from the pounding foot of the falls.

I looked up and seen water coming over the lip and at me like tons spit out of the sky. It must have been fifty feet up to where the creek bent and broke over the rim. Rags and chains of spray tore off and whipped around. Falling water seems to shout at you. It sounds like it's warning you of doom and destruction. It puts a fear in your gut, but you don't know why. I thought we had come to the end of our survey.

But Sue did not slow down. She darted right at the falls, through the fine mist gilded by spots of sun coming through the trees. She splashed along the rocks at the edge of the pool. The water burned my ankles like dark flames. It took my breath as we stepped in. The freezing water seemed to peel away my skin.

Sue was heading straight toward the shaft of crashing water, and it looked like I'd have to turn her loose if I didn't want to be crushed and drowned. The pounding water could knock a body senseless. The sow seemed bent on suicide. Maybe she was trying to shake me loose, or maybe she wanted to cool off in the falling creek water.

I was ready to turn loose, but suddenly she darted *behind* the curtain of the falls. The heavy power of the water smashed my left hand as I held onto her tail.

It was dark behind the sheet of exploding water, and it took me a few seconds to see the cave of wet overhanging rock. It looked like they was signs on the rock, all kinds of markings on the walls, Indian signs and maybe names and dates cut by hunters and trappers. I squinted to see better. I wondered if the Spaniards had lived there. I knowed the Spaniards had climbed into the mountains looking for gold, and they made the Indians dig like slaves in their mines. But I didn't know where the Spaniards lived, and how long. I wanted to look close at all the signs, in the gloom of the dripping cave, but the hog kept going, her hooves clicking on the rock, right to the other side.

We broke through the far edge of the curtain of water and suddenly come back into bright light. I couldn't wipe the spray out of my eyes because the hatchet was in my hand. I blinked away the drops as Sue swerved to the right and started climbing. I couldn't see well, but it looked like they was nothing but a wall of ferns and moss. Sue leaped right up the slope, and the ground under the ferns was moldy leaves that my feet sunk deep into.

As we started laboring up the mountainside it seemed like I had imagined the cave behind the waterfall. That dark room of writings on the rock was just something I had dreamed. I tried to remember if they had been anything else in the cave. Had I seen any pots or arrowheads in the gloom? Was they any bones of animals or humans?

They was all kinds of rumors of a lost lead mine of the Cherokee. Some of the early settlers, like the McBains, was supposed to know where it was. The legend was the entrance to the mine was near water. Could the entrance be behind that waterfall? I was beginning to imagine I had seen all kinds of things. That's the way it is when you want to believe something. It just seems to be so. I imagined I'd seen a pile of coins in one corner. Some was gold and some was green corroded copper, and some was silver black as soot. Or maybe I had seen bags and Indian beads, and maybe a skeleton in those few seconds in the cave? If they was enough treasure there, I wouldn't even have to build a road.

The slope was so steep even Sue was beginning to slow down. I had to think on the work at hand. I could return to my fantasies later. As our feet plunged and slid in the soft dirt I saw a road could be dug there. It wasn't rock like I had feared. If the whole ridge was dirt a road could be zigzagged right up its side. Usually around a waterfall the ridge was rock. That's why the waterfall was there. But the slope here had a covering of dirt.

As the mountainside got steeper I stuck the hatchet into the dirt for a grip. I marked the trees best I could as we climbed, but mostly I held on to keep from falling off the ridge. We switched back, and then switched back again, levering right up the soft face of the mountain. With pick and shovel I could level out a road to the top of the ridge above the waterfall. Sue had knowed where she was going after all.

As we sweated up the steepness I thought of all the people in history that had crossed terrible mountains. In school we had heard about Hannibal that crossed the Alps with an army of elephants to attack Rome. They was a drawing in the teacher's book of elephants slipping and sliding through snow. And some elephants lost their footholds and went sliding over cliffs into the valleys below. And the teacher read us about Caesar crossing the Alps with his army, pulling their supplies in carts and ox wagons. And she read us about Pizarro and his pack mules carrying gold out of the Andes. Moses had to climb up on Mount Pisgah in the Bible to look over into the Promised Land. And when I was little, the newspaper was full of stories about Lewis and Clark crossing the Rockies and finding the Pacific.

Where we come out on top of the ridge the waterfall was just a whisper far below. I could tell from the angle of the sun falling on the poplars it was late morning. Jarflies sung in the trees, or maybe it was rattlers. With the blood thumping in my ears I could not be sure.

Sweat was pouring into my eyes and I couldn't blink it away. I tried to wipe my forehead with my sleeve, but my shirt was wet and stuck with bits of dirt and leaves. I must have got a piece of trash in my eye, because suddenly it hurt like somebody had jabbed a stick in it. It was my right eye, and whatever had stuck in it lodged like a briar or piece of glass.

"Whoa," I said to Sue. But she didn't pay no attention to me. She didn't even pause. I blinked my eye quick as I could, but it didn't do no good. Tears practically squirted out of my eye, it hurt so much. I couldn't let go, and I couldn't drop the hatchet. The hurt stabbed through my eyeball and through my head.

I tried to roll my eyeball, because that worked sometimes to dislodge things. But it was hard to roll my eyes and see where I was going at the same time. You have to roll both your eyes and

Sue was running right through the poplars. If I didn't look, I could crash into a tree or limb and gouge my eye out, as Aunt Willa had warned me. My eye hurt so bad, I couldn't hardly stand it. Whatever it was, was turned wrong under my eyelid. With all the tears and sweat I couldn't see that well anyway.

"Whoa," I said again to the sow. But I didn't expect her to slow down. I was talking to soothe myself. I was close to panicking, son. A man can't stand something cutting into his eye. It will terrify him that he can't see, that the world is crashing in on him, and he must get the hurting thing out of his eye.

Sometimes when you have a great pain and you can't do nothing about it, you try to think of something else. You try to forget the pain into control. I tried to think of the path ahead, and the road we would build, but it didn't do no good. I tried to think of the blockaders we had passed and what they was doing that very minute, whether they was already moving their still.

I tried to think of Mary and what she was doing. I figured she was sitting on a cool porch somewhere in town, teaching little children to draw. She knowed I was going to make the survey that day, but I told her she might as well stay in town. Later she might go to her room and write a letter, and have lemonade before lunch. She would be cool and calm, and she would be appalled at the sweaty, bloody, bruised condition I was in. I tried to imagine how she would look in her summer dress. But it wasn't no good. The pain in my eye was too bad. I couldn't think of anything but the hurting. If I didn't do something quick, I would have to let Sue go and call the whole thing off.

I tried to look down while holding my head up, and at the same time look out for limbs and trees. But my eye stung so bad it kept blinking and my face winced. I couldn't look long in any one direction. I kept turning my head like that would sling the piece out of my eye. The turning seemed to help the pain a little. The more I turned my head the less the eye seemed to hurt.

The problem was I couldn't keep my eye on where we was going. Sue brushed me past a black oak tree and the bark raked my shoulder and cheek like a rasp. More soot was sticking to my sweaty skin. I stumbled across my own feet a couple of times. The pain in my eye made me reckless, and it made me lose my balance.

What happened next I don't know. But I figured later my head must have hit a big limb, because they was a knot on my forehead big as a guinea egg. But I seen stars flung every which way, and it was like the air turned to flame and then dark, flame and then dark. It was like I heard echoes off the mountains and rumbles in the ground under my feet.

But the oddest thing was, I must have kept walking right along after the sow. I guess I had been walking so long my legs just kept going while the whole night sky was shooting around in my head, and the Milky Way run through my mind like a rag pulled through a wringer. I just kept hoofing as before.

When I opened my eyes again, the vision in my right eye was foggy, the way it is after you rub your eye a long time, or when you have a fever in it. It was like they was a veil on the light, or I was looking through waxed paper or a piece of onionskin. But whatever had caught in my eye was gone. It had been knocked out, or washed out, by the lick on my forehead. I later found something black and round in the corner of my eye. It looked like a hard beetle that had been smashed. I guess what hurt so much was its shell that had broke, or maybe its sharp claws. My eye was sore as if it had been stuck with a briar. And it felt like it had grown a scum over it.

When I opened my eyes, I seen somebody standing on the rise

above me. I just caught him out of the corner of my left eye. It was an Indian dressed in homespun pants and a buckskin shirt. The Indian's long hair was tied to a feather at the back. He looked like a Cherokee, but I didn't really have a chance to examine him. He stood there without making a gesture or offering a greeting. I wasn't even sure I seen him, because the sow didn't seem to take notice. Maybe it was a trick of the sweat, or the tears drying in my eye. Or maybe the hit on my head, or the pain in my eye, that made me a little beside myself.

When I turned to glance back where he had stood, they was trees in the way and I couldn't see nobody at all. Maybe it was just a dream. But the figure had been as real as daylight. The Indian stood there watching us go past. He didn't threaten or make any sign he had seen us. I would have liked to look back to see where he went but I couldn't stop Sue. I wondered if they was some trick to his disappearance, a hole he had dropped in, or a bush he hid behind. But Sue kept running and I couldn't even turn around, much less search for him. I was beginning to wonder if the heat had got to my brain.

My homespun shirt and pants was so wet with sweat they weighed like iron. Where the cloth pulled tight I wanted to shift it around to prevent binding, but my hands wasn't free. Holding the hatchet, I could only make clumsy attempts to straighten my trousers and suspenders.

How far had I come? So much had happened already to take my mind off the survey that I had no way of knowing if we was still headed toward Cedar Mountain. It seemed like we was still in the right direction, but I couldn't be sure. The truth was we could have been halfway to Wall Holler, or walking in a curve back toward Pumpkintown. The sun was close enough to the middle of the sky that I knowed it was near dinner time. But I couldn't tell what was north and south, much less east and west, we had made so many turns and switchbacks. The sun still seemed a little bit behind me, but I couldn't tell for sure.

If they had been a trail before, we had lost it. It seemed like we was high up on a mountain in some flat woods. It seemed like we was approaching the end of the world. I could see nothing behind the trees but sky. I was always confused by a place so flat you couldn't tell which way the water runs. Where runoff can't make up its mind which way to go, how can people? Was we on top of the highest ridge? At Cedar Mountain we should be able to see the Pisgah mountains to the north, blue and hazy ahead.

My vision was so clouded from the hurt eye and sweat I couldn't trust it. But it looked like they was some kind of lake ahead, or maybe just a zone of fog around the edge of the moun-tain. You don't usually see fog on the mountains on a summer day with the sun shining. But that was what it seemed like through the trees, except for a sparkle here and there like water. If I could have stopped and looked better I might have figured it out. But stumbling and panting, trying to mark a tree every hundred feet, I could only glance ahead. Sometimes it looked like the sky coming to meet us, like we was going to run out on the sky. And some-times the view would be lost behind laurels and it didn't seem like they was nothing ahead at all.

I even thought I could smell water, but when you're panting and streaming sweat and follering a hog you can't be certain of your sense of smell either.

We come to an open place in the trees, and sure enough, they was water ahead of us. It looked like a stream, or a pond with tall pines on the far side. It was the prettiest little pool you ever seen, with trees right at the edge and a meadow on the near side. I'd never heard of any pond near Cedar Mountain. It was like some place you would dream about. I knowed I was lost.

Sue did not slow down, but headed straight toward the meadow and the sheet of water. A breeze was coming off the pond. Maybe we could at least cool off, whatever kind of apparition this was.

I had once heard Old Man Jarvis tell about a Cherokee story of a lake on a mountaintop. But Jarvis said the lake was supposed to be on top of the Smokies or the Plott Balsams. Anyway they was supposed to be a lake on top of the mountain that nobody could see normally. But if a man was in pain, or had been wounded, he could find that lake and be healed in its water. The lake would be revealed to him but nobody else. And after he was cured by its water the lake would disappear and he couldn't remember where it was. It was just a tale Old Man Jarvis told, about the ancient bear that lived by the lake, and the spirits of ancestors that guarded the healing waters. Jarvis was always talking on about ghosts and such, and I never believed any of his stories, but the pond reminded me of what he had said.

I thought I heard voices, and somebody screaming, but Sue kept running and I couldn't be sure. It seemed like they was high pitches and shrieks. Maybe it was birds. Sue come around a clump of shumake bushes and there was this meadow. And beyond the meadow was a group of girls playing in the water. Somebody had dammed up the creek with mud and brush, and these girls without a stitch of clothes was playing in the water. They was dark skinned like Indians, and you never seen such a pretty sight.

I felt even shorter of breath than before, and would have pulled back and stopped but Sue kept right on going. They's nothing startles or scares a man much as the sight of a naked woman when he don't expect it. A woman without her clothes will stop you in your tracks every time.

But I couldn't stop. The sow paid no attention to the bathing girls at all. I knowed it was rude to rush up to them with no warning, but they was nothing else I could do. Sue would not even slow down, and we come stumbling across the meadow.

The girls was so busy splashing the creek water, chasing each other and screaming they didn't even see us. Their hair was black and glistened in the sun. Some was so young, they didn't even have hair down at their crotch, but others was older and mature. I remember thinking in my rush how big their legs was at their thighs. The dammed water was strange, like a beaver pond, but the girls playing there was even stranger. They shrieked and pushed each other into the water. Others run along the grass and jumped into the shallows. A few laid in the grass sunning theirselves.

I don't know which one seen us first. Sue come trotting along straight at them, and it flashed in my mind how I must look, a crazed man in sweat and filth running at them swinging a hatchet. But they was no way I could pause and reassure them.

"Eeeeee!" one screamed. The others thought she was still playing.

Now it was an even prettier sight. They was the golden color of gypsies, and not a one had a thread of clothes on. Some just had little breasts that was beginning to swell, but the older girls had big round breasts with nipples the color of coffee. I'd never seen but one naked woman in my life, and I'd never seen a naked Indian girl. They was laughing and splashing and their titties was bouncing and swinging around. I couldn't look right at them, and I couldn't keep from looking.

They was one in particular that was taller than the rest. She was tall and slim and had this long black hair that went down over her shoulder. She was not playing with the others but seemed to be looking at something in the shallows near shore. Maybe she was searching for some kind of shells or rocks, or watching minnows. Her hair fell down around her face as she bent over. She had the most perfect large breasts I ever seen till this day.

Some things you carry with you all your life, and I tell you the sight of that girl is something I never forgot. Some sights make life worth living. They give you a lift every time you recall them. They are things you remember when everything else goes wrong.

She looked up and seen me just as the other girl screamed. But the tall woman didn't seem startled or scared at all. She didn't even seem embarrassed. In fact, she smiled at me—I must have been a sight—like she was pleased that I seen her there in the water, happy that I seen how beautiful she looked. It seemed so natural, the way she looked at me.

It seemed like she was going to step forward and say hello to me, come wading to the bank and shake my hand. Her hips was narrow and rounded perfectly to her thighs. It was like I had walked into another world. All the running and straining, the sweating and dirtiness seemed fell away. For once Sue slowed, maybe in astonishment at the sight of all them golden bodies, maybe because she was considering plunging into the water too.

In the instant as the tall girl smiled at me and the first girl screamed, a breeze seemed to dry the sweat on my forehead and clear my sight. The rocks in the shallows of the creek shined like nuggets and nuts of metal. The grass by the water was purple branch grass.

The girl that screamed first screamed again, and pointed at Sue and me. Everybody stopped and stood in the water watching us. It felt like the sun got dark that instant. There I was, walking along the bank with my hand on a sow's tail in front of thirty naked girls. I tried to wave with the hatchet, but it was an odd gesture. I tried to smile and say hello, as I had just smiled at the tall girl a second before. I wanted to turn my head and keep walking to show them I hadn't meant to surprise them, to spy on them. But I didn't know how to say that to them.

In that moment when everybody froze, I noticed something even more astonishing about the girls. They did not have Indian features. They had skins dark as Indians or mulattoes, but their features was neither black nor Indian. They had white features, with dark skin and straight black hair. And it come to me they was Melungeons. They was the lost tribe of Israel I'd always heard about. They was supposed to live in the mountains toward Tennessee, but I'd never seen any. They lived like gypsies in the remote coves, and the preachers said they was the lost tribe.

Just then an old woman run shouting out of the trees. She wore a bandana around her hair and she pointed a finger at me. I seen her over my shoulder as we trotted on. She was screaming at me but I couldn't understand what she was saying.

"Harashawi!" she seemed to be shouting.

All the girls was watching Sue and me run along the grass. I couldn't stop even if I wanted to. I figured that old woman was the person in charge of all them young girls, maybe some kind of teacher or guardian. I knowed the Melungeons lived off by theirselves in the high mountains, but nobody knowed much about them. They was just the lost tribe, and nobody knowed about their religion or private ways. They was tales about them mingling with the Cherokee. These people looked like whites, except for the color of their skin.

"Harashawi!" the old woman hollered. She run right up to me and shook her finger in my face. Then she pointed back to all the naked girls in the water. It was clear what she was saying. She was shaming me for surprising the girls during their swim. Whatever kind of people they was, men wasn't supposed to bother the girls while they was bathing. It struck me how much people was alike everywhere, even the strangest people.

"Harashawi," the old woman said, and crossed her arms and uncrossed them. I guess everybody in the world has the same gestures for saying something is forbidden.

She run in front of me and Sue and the sow stopped, turned to go around. But the old woman headed us off again. She was faster than you would expect an old woman to be. She was not going to let us get away until she had had her say.

"Harashawi," she kept saying, like shame on you, shame on you. Sue and me backed around, but the girls had come up behind us. The sow turned in confusion, looking for a way to escape from the closing circle. Now the old woman begun hollering at the girls. Some was holding clothes up to their chests and some others had slipped their skirts on. But the tall girl stood back at the edge of the water and watched. The girls was all dripping wet and their skin shined in the sunlight.

The old woman kept screaming at them, and one by one they slipped back to where their clothes was piled in the grass. The dresses had big stripes and all kinds of colors. I had never seen clothes like that, even in pictures.

The girls put the many-colored dresses over their heads and slipped them on their wet bodies. The last to put on clothes was the tall girl, who never had come close. When she stood out of the water, you could see how strong she was in her legs and hips.

"Harashawi!" the old woman shouted. The tall girl waited a few moments before going to get her dress. She was older than the others, and must have been some kind of assistant teacher or leader. I could see she was not afraid of the old woman as the others were. She slipped into her dress slow and deliberate.

"We was just passing through," I said to the old woman, and to the girls. "We are surveying a way for a turnpike across the mountain." It sounded foolish, explaining to them what I was doing, all sweaty and tired, following a sow through the woods. But it was even stranger because I could see they didn't understand. They only knowed their own tongue apparently, and I had no way of showing them what I meant. I held up my hatchet and they backed away, then crowded in closer to look at the pig. I let the hatchet drop down to my side to show them how harmless I was. They seemed curious to get a closer look at us. Hemmed in like that, they wasn't nowhere me and Sue could go.

But the old woman wasn't mollified a bit. She kept hollering and pushing her finger in my face. It was clear I had committed a sin in their society. Or maybe it was the sow that upset her. Maybe they had a law against hogs or pork. She come up close and I seen my reflection in her black eyes. She smelled like garlic or some other strong seasoning and she looked right in my face.

Before I knowed it, she had slapped me right in the straddle on my privates. It didn't hurt too much, but I was took by surprise. It was like a warning slap. I'd heard stories of boys being attacked by women in houses of ill repute down in Columbia or Augusta when they forgot or refused to pay. This old woman slapped me like she was making a threat.

"Hold on there!" I hollered. Sue was twisting around nervously looking for a way out. The circle of half-clothed wet girls seemed to tighten. I couldn't tell if they was just curious, or trying to keep me from running away. They was something ridiculous about my situation, but nothing ridiculous about the old woman. She was still pointing her finger and hollering at me.

"I'm just surveying a road," I said. "I'm just passing through, not bothering nobody."

I wondered if she thought I owned the land and was going to run them off. And it occurred to me she thought I had used the sow as an excuse to spy on the girls.

"What kind of people are you?" I said. But she didn't understand. The old woman just kept hollering. I looked around at the girls, and they wasn't laughing anymore. They watched me and Sue with fear and fascination. I had the hatchet in my hand and the old woman was pointing at that. I raised my hand to show her it was just an ordinary kindling splitter and she jerked away. And the girls backed away too. Sue turned in the open space.

The old woman pointed to the hatchet and then to herself. She meant me to give it to her. She was going to take away my hatchet. She wanted to believe I was dangerous.

"I need this for marking trees," I said. "I'm just blazing out a way for a road. I want to split the Blue Ridge with a road." But it wasn't no use. She didn't understand a thing I said, and she didn't want to understand. Every time I raised the hatchet to explain or gesture, they backed away, then moved in closer. I tried to think of a way to show them what I was trying to do.

The old woman was telling them to do something. I didn't like the changed look on their faces. They was afraid of me now and getting scareder. Things can get dangerous, when somebody is afraid of you.

"I'll just be on my way," I said, and pointed toward the mountains where I was headed. I thought I could see Caesar's Head up there in the haze. I wouldn't mind the heat and strain if I could just get away, get back to work. My hard journey seemed sweet and certain compared to what I had got myself into.

The old woman screamed when I raised the hatchet to point, like I had tried to hit her.

"I just want to get going," I said. "Don't want to hurt nobody."

And just then I seen where the girls had come from. They had some tents in the trees at the edge of the meadow. The tents was red and blue and not shaped like any tents I had ever seen. They had rounded tops, like the cloth was stretched on hoops of a covered wagon. They was all bright colors. I didn't see no men-folks, and I didn't see no horses. I couldn't imagine where the men of their tribe had gone.

"Where you all from?" I said to the old woman. "How did you bring these tents up here?" But she didn't pay no attention to me. She was still haranguing the girls and hollering at me by turns. It was beginning to look bad.

The girls would step in closer, then move away when I turned, like I was some kind of animal they was afraid of. Some had their clothes only half on.

"Just let me go," I said. "I don't mean to bother nobody."

The old woman had found a stick somewhere. It was like a walking stick but heavier. It looked like something that might be used for troubling clothes in a washpot. I didn't like the way she looked at me, like she was trying to figure out how to finish off a treed bear or painter.

"We wasn't trying to hurt nobody," I said.

But the old woman wasn't listening and she didn't see no fun in anything. She was giving orders to the girls, but of course I couldn't understand them. I guess she was telling each to grab hold of me somewhere so I couldn't hit them with the hatchet.

Sue was squealing with nervousness. She was still panting from the run and slobber was hanging from her jaws and nose. She was squealing and grunting with panic, the way I felt like doing.

"Just let us go and we'll be on our way," I said, and pointed toward the mountains yonder. The old woman swung the stick at me and I jerked my arm back.

You say, what did they want with me? I didn't know what they wanted or what they intended, and I still don't. I knowed the old woman was mad because I had seen her girls naked, and I guessed she wanted to punish me. But I couldn't be sure of anything. For all I knowed, them girls was princesses and any man that seen them bathing would be put to death. Maybe they was part of a harem. They was no telling what I had run into.

"I never meant to harm nobody," I said again. As I turned with the sow in the tightening circle, I knowed I was most vulnerable from behind. I turned with Sue to face my accusers and attackers, but I couldn't cover my back. And sure enough, the first hands that touched me grabbed from behind. They was soft girl hands, but they was so many they gripped my arms fast. I thrashed to break free. It's a reflex: somebody grabs you and you jerk to get loose.

Even as I thrashed I made sure I didn't hit nobody with the hatchet. Scared as I was, I seen my only hope was not to hurt anybody.

I held onto Sue's tail, and I held onto the hatchet, and I tried to knock them away with my elbows. I lunged back and suddenly found myself off balance. They was grabbing my feet and I was lifted up and turned away. It didn't seem possible delicate young girls could have such strength. It was like the sky whirled around as they lifted me. I floated in a pool of hands.

Before I knowed it, the pig's tail was twisted out of my grasp, and fingernails was biting into my right hand to free it from the hatchet. I held the handle hard as I could but it was twisted from my grip. I don't know how so many of them could have grabbed my wrist and fingers. The hatchet come loose and a dozen hands was holding my right arm.

"You let me go," I hollered. "I ain't done no harm." I couldn't see where we was going. They didn't carry me on their shoulders, and I was surrounded by scared and curious girls. Each of them had a hand on me, on my arms and back, in my hair.

"Put me down and I'll go on," I said.

They seemed to be carrying me toward the tents in the trees. I wondered if they was cannibals, or performed human sacrifices. I'd heard Melungeons had their own religion and didn't practice any of our beliefs. I didn't know when the lost tribe give up its practices of the Bible of Israel.

"I'll forget I ever seen any of you," I said.

Some of the girls started giggling in their nervousness, and then all of them begun giggling. They poked and pinched me as they carried me. I didn't make any sound like I was hurt, for I figured that would make them prod and pinch more. I didn't want to make them think it would be easy to torture me.

The old woman screamed at them for laughing. I guess she wanted to make it a solemn ceremony of sacrifice or execution. But once they started giggling, they couldn't seem to stop.

One girl pointed to my belly button where my shirt had tore open, and they all laughed. A lot of dust and bits of bark had stuck to the sweat there and my navel was black. Another one pinched me on the nipple, and they all laughed again. The old woman shouted something and they got quiet.

"People will come looking for me," I said. "If anything happens they will be a search party." I said it but they didn't understand, and I didn't even believe it. I didn't know where I was or who they was, and it all seemed like a dream. I wondered if I'd had a heat stroke and died along the trail, and this was the hereafter. The

secret of death might be that it was hard to tell where life ended
and death started.

Whack! Something hit me on the side of the head and my ears
rung and fire shot under my eyelids. It was the old woman's stick.
The spot she hit was numb for an instant and then begun to burn.
It felt like it might be bleeding, but I couldn't tell.

I didn't even know they was lowering me until I felt the ground
at my head. I expected them to leave me there and stand back, but
they all knelt around me. They was just young girls, scared of
what they was doing, but even more scared of the old woman.
They held me down and the old woman stood at my feet. She
spoke to one of the girls who then run to the tents and come back
with something she handed to the old woman. It was little and I
couldn't tell what it was. The old woman held up a string that had
glittering things on it. I couldn't make any sense of it. It was a fine
string of silk or flax with bits of broken glass wove or tied into it. I
wondered if it was some kind of necklace.

Then the old woman handed her stick to one of the girls and
took something out of her dress. It looked like a big needle or an
awl. It was sharp as a needle but fat at the back like it was used for
punching holes. The old woman held up the awl and string of
slivered glass in the sun. Suddenly it come to me what she was
about. She was going to punch a hole through me, through my
hand or skin or tongue, or some other place, and pull the string of
broken glass through the hole. It was their kind of torture.

"No!" I hollered. The girls held me tighter as they slipped my
shirt off. I had always heard how Indians stripped their victims
before they tortured them. And when a woman was humiliated
and run out of town they always stripped her and shaved her
head. And people to be tarred and feathered was stripped naked.

"No!" I hollered again. I seen they was going to make me naked like I had seen them. But they had ceremonies and punishments I didn't know nothing about. The old woman held the big needle and the sparkling string up to the sun for me to see.

"I am a United States citizen," I said, thinking they must belong to some foreign nation. Maybe they was Spaniards or Frenchies. I'd heard they was still traders and settlers speaking foreign tongues in the Southwest. Maybe they had wandered into the mountains by mistake.

"They's laws in this country," I said. "People will look for me." It added to the horror that they was such pretty girls holding me down, pinching and squeezing me. They had to do whatever the old woman told them, but they had their own curiosity too.

What passed through my mind? Why, I seen I was a goner. They wasn't nothing I could do or say that would make any difference. But even at that moment when I seemed to be finished, I was thinking about the road too, about how it would never be built until some time way in the future. Sometime they would have better equipment for making roads, and they would be so many people coming into the Blue Ridge they would have to build a road through Douthat's Gap to Cedar Mountain. But because they wasn't a road now, it would be harder to settle that part of the mountains. And people would be more lost in their coves and hollers for fifty years, closed off from the rest of the world. Scared as I was, all that went through my mind.

Sure, I thought of your Grandma. I was glad Mary wasn't there to see me humiliated by them girls. Some things are so embarrassing they can destroy love, and I was glad she would never know how I come to my end. People would just assume I got lost in the coves and was eat by a painter.

"You all will be ashamed," I said. I said anything that come to mind. I don't know what all I said. I probably said things I wouldn't even want to repeat.

The old woman knelt down among them with the needle in her right hand, and I thought at first she was going to poke it in my eye. They held me so I couldn't move. I screamed loud as I could, until I seen she was going to run the needle through my tongue. That's when I clamped my mouth shut. She hesitated for a moment, then tried to work my jaws loose with her fingers. But I clamped even tighter. Then she took hold of my lower lip to run the big needle through it. She attached the string to the needle, to pull the string of broken glass through my lip.

Son, they's something about extreme pain and fear. It's like they take you back to the beginning, to something you had forgot. It's like you're in touch with some bedrock truth of pain. Maybe it's because you remember the time you was born in pain, and you remember your mama's pain. Or maybe even the moment you was conceived in the grunt of pain and pleasure. The pain cuts back through the shame of our flesh and filth. And maybe it goes back to something even further, to the sin in the Garden of Eden, or the pain in the creation of this dust and worlds.

My pain and fear was so great I felt close to something, maybe to the relief of death. The old woman started threading her needle with the glittering string, and I could already feel it being pulled through my lip, just a little jerk at a time to prolong the pain. She would tug the string sideways to make it hurt worse, and then she would sit back to observe the effects of her work. I must have been screaming at the limits of my lungs, but I can't remember. I know my mouth and face was wet with blood from the needle wound, and with sweat and spit. I didn't think I could stand it if she pulled the needle through and the bits of glass begun to cut my lip a little at a time.

Suddenly somebody else was standing over the old woman. I didn't recognize the face at first. "Hishnagawi," the face seemed to be saying. The old woman stopped and looked up at her accuser.

"Hishnagawi," the face said again. The old woman pulled away and I seen it was the tall girl. She had her clothes on now. All the other girls turned me loose. My mouth was full of blood and I could feel the needle against my teeth.

"Hishnagawi," the tall girl said again. She bent over me and pulled the needle out of my lip. She handed the string back to the old woman. My lip bled like it had been sliced.

She helped me to my feet and handed me my clothes. I pulled my pants up and buttoned my suspenders. She must be some kind of princess or priestess I thought, if she could order the old woman that way. But once she handed me my hatchet, I didn't stop to inquire or even thank her, for she pointed to the woods. I didn't even finish with buttoning my shirt, but took the hatchet and started limping toward the trees fast as I could.

I don't know how the tall girl was able to free me. Maybe she had some special power. Or maybe they was one favor she could ask and they had to oblige her. Or maybe she was a priestess of their religion. She led me a few yards from the circle of girls and pointed toward the trees. She was taller than I was and her black hair sparkled in the sun.

When I was about halfway to the trees, I stopped and slipped my boots on. My socks had holes wore in them and my feet was blistered, but I tried to walk without limping. My boots was wet from sweat and the creek water at the falls, and they pinched and bound my feet in the sore places.

Back then we went barefoot in the summer. But I wore boots out in snaky woods, and when I worked with a shovel. You can't push a shovel with a bare foot. But for hoeing corn and working on the place I didn't wear no shoes from May till October. My feet was tough, but they had swole up.

My lip hurt like it was on fire. I wiped the blood off my chin several times with my arm. My wrist and forearm was covered with drying blood. I held the back of my hand over my lip to stop the bleeding, and smelled the pig smell on my palm. But I knowed my lip would be a lot worse if they had pulled that string of glass slivers through it. It would have tore my lip half off.

Sue is probably halfway to Cedar Mountain by now, I thought. This mission was ill-starred from the first. Maybe I would try again when the leaves was gone, and I would get somebody to go with me. Or maybe I would just give it up. Maybe the mountains was never meant to have a road built into them. If the good Lord had wanted a road here, he would have built it hisself. But then I thought, maybe the Lord does want a road into the Blue Ridge and I am his chosen instrument.

Once I got into the woods and found a spring I'd wash the blood off my face and hands. I would feel better if I was cleaned up a little. And then I'd find my way as best I could to Cedar Mountain. I didn't know where I was, but surely I couldn't be more than eight or ten miles off the track.

If I had strength, I would climb a tree to get my bearings. That's what explorers and hunters used to do. They'd pick the tallest pine or poplar and climb up to the tip to survey the valley. But I was too tired and too weak to do any climbing.

I seen a flash of white go bobbing out through the trees. It was a deer. I watched it go, and seen the head going up and down as it run. That meant it was a doe. A buck runs with his head held erect. The doe must have been grazing at the edge of the meadow even with all the girls frolicking there.

Soon as I got into the bushes at the edge of the clearing I looked back to align my sight with the way I had come. But the girls had gone. They must have disappeared into the tents because the meadow was all bare. And I couldn't hardly see the pond either.

They was just the meadow and the mountains beyond. The mountains looked like the South Carolina mountains all right. I tried to judge which was the last gap I had come through.

The sun was about in the middle of the sky, and it was so hot it made me shiver. Or maybe I was so weak I shuddered. Every bit of shade felt good. I figured I was going generally north and all I had to do was keep walking. If I come to a holler, I could look for moss on the north side of stumps. And when it got past dinner time, I could tell by the sun which way to go. In the meantime I had to get as far as I could from them Melungeon girls and that old woman. I wouldn't mind putting miles between us in ever-what direction.

I picked my way through the undergrowth watching every step. Copperheads like to lay under bushes. Without Sue in front of me I felt naked. At the edge of a little draw I heard something in the leaves below. It sounded like a bear wallering or a dog fighting with a coon. I stood still and listened. Leaves was being kicked up and they was all kinds of grunts and panting.

I thought of turning aside and walking along the rim of the draw to avoid whatever trouble it was. I was too weak to fight my way through any more obstacles. Whatever it was I didn't want to bother with it.

Then I heard a squeal, and another. It was a hog all right. Maybe it was a wild hog. I listened again. It sounded so much like Sue I couldn't go on without looking. The banks of the draw was covered with laurels and sweet shrub. I couldn't see a thing as I picked my way down the side. The fussing and grunting continued. I was too stiff to go fast among the bushes. Besides being sore and stiff I had that hollered-out and dried feeling you get when you're really tired. You feel like something has sucked the marrow out of your bones, and you have gone brittle in your legs and belly.

I slowed down to a tiptoe on the floor of the draw and parted the limbs of a laurel to see what the commotion was. Sure enough, it was Sue, and she had this big copperhead in her mouth and was flinging the snake around all over the place.

It filled my heart with a great big barrel of honey just to see that razorback. Never thought I'd be so happy to see a hog. She was turning and thrashing to bite through that snake and bash its head against a tree. It was the biggest pilot I ever seen.

When I grabbed hold of her tail, I don't think she ever knowed it. She kept slinging around and smacking that snake against the ground and on saplings as it tried to bite her. A hog's skin around the shoulders is almost too thick for a snake to bite through. I don't know if it struck her or not. They say hogs is almost immune to copperhead bites, though I never seen it proved.

I held her tail and moved to her side as best I could with all the brush around. Several times I swung at the snake's head with the hatchet and missed. I was afraid I would cut the sow. She flung her head this way and that way and the pilot curled and thrashed. I couldn't hit the snake without hitting her snout.

To tell the truth, I didn't mind standing there a minute while she worried with the copperhead. My lip was still bleeding and sweat was getting into the wound. My whole chin hurt and stung.

They was blood on the hog's chin also. She was biting through the snake as she shook and banged it on the ground. She was chewing the body through and the snake's twisting and writhing probably helped her bite through the scaley back and bones.

Suddenly the half of the snake with the head flew off into the leaves and Sue gobbled up the half still in her mouth. A hog will eat faster than anything you ever seen and it wasn't half a minute till she swallowed. I looked around for the head but couldn't find it. A copperhead is so close to the color of old leaves and sticks and trash anyway you can't see them most of the time. Sue looked for the rest of her dinner and couldn't see it any more than I could. I figured her nose would find the snake.

Instead she looked back and seen me holding onto her tail. And it was like she all at once remembered where we was headed. She seemed to forget the rest of the snake. Maybe snake heads ain't tasty compared to bellies and tails. Maybe the poison in a snake's head don't taste good, even if it don't hurt a hog.

She looked at me for an instant, then lunged forward. It was like everything that happened before was just a pause, a little interruption, and she stepped over the obstacle and hurried to make up for lost time. She was like a human in the way she recalled what her purpose was. We was starting all over again.

Sue went right up the other side of the draw. I had to duck limbs and crawl under laurels. I wasn't going to let go again. I wasn't going to let sore legs and bleeding lip slow me down.

Where we come out of the gully, they was a little open patch and I seen my shadow falling on the hog in front of me. That meant we was still heading north, if it was noon, or just after noon. We might have got a little off track, but Sue seemed to know exactly where she was pointed. Though she must have run fifteen miles already that day, she didn't seem a bit slower. To my tired legs and back she seemed to be going faster. I starting marking trees again every thirty steps. It hurt my sore arm to raise the hatchet, but I was pleased to be at my work again.

The woods was almost level for the better part of a mile, which was lucky, because I don't think I could have done no climbing till I regained my strength. The big, dark ridge was looming ahead. It looked like a wall of black smoke hanging up there. I thought it must be Caesar's Head, but couldn't tell for sure through the summer trees. It seemed impossible we could bust through such a ridge, much less build a road through it. No wonder nobody had done it before.

The sow dropped out of the undergrowth onto a trail. It must be one of the old trader paths from South Carolina into the mountains, I thought. All the trader trails follered Indian trails, war trails for reaching the Low Country. And the Indian paths follered the traces made by buffaloes in even earlier times. Maybe this trace would take us right up toward the gap.

Or maybe we had wandered onto the old Estatoe Trail that led through Oconee and up toward the Little Tennessee. If so we had wandered far off our way. But it was certainly easier going on the old trail without limbs hitting me in the face every other step. The sow trotted faster. It was all I could do to stretch out and mark the trees from time to time, though I guess it didn't matter much since we was just follering the path.

I didn't see the man dressed all in black until we was almost at him. He stood in the bushes off to one side of the trail and wore a wide black hat. He clutched a big Bible in his hands.

"Hold on there," the stranger said as the hog approached him.

"She's got her head and I can't stop her," I called.

The man pulled back into the bushes as though afraid of being touched by dripping sweat and blood. I nodded in greeting.

"Only the prodigal would follow a swine," the man said.

"I'm surveying a road," I answered. "Across the Blue Ridge to Cedar Mountain."

"Maybe the Lord don't want a road," the man said as we stumbled past. "A road is a channel for the Devil to bring in more wickedness to the settlements."

Now son, I was never disrespectful to a preacher. I've always tried to be courteous to a man of the cloth. I've done some bad things, and I ain't always been the man I ought to be, but I never give preachers no trouble like some boys did. But it always made me mad when preachers talked against things, like they didn't want nothing new or good to happen. Like they didn't want nobody doing anything except them. Nothing makes you feel bad like a preacher talking against you. It's like they just want mournfulness and misery. That's how they keep their power over people, through unhappiness and sickness. It's worries and troubles keeps preachers in business. If people was happy they might not need so many preachers and revival meetings.

"If the Lord wanted a road he would have made it hisself," the preacher said.

"So we shouldn't wear clothes, 'cause if the Lord wanted us to he'd have made us with pants on?" I said over my shoulder as we went past. Sue hadn't slowed down at all.

"The Devil works through sarcasm and a hard tongue."

"You see the Devil in everything but yourself," I hollered back. I was surprised to hear myself argue with a preacher. It was just something that come out. Must have been the state I was in, dizzy with exertion and the hurt in my lip.

"The Devil is the prince of this world," the preacher called. He fell in behind me and follered, like he was already going that way. But I figured he needed somebody to talk to. Preachers would be out of work if they couldn't find people to shame.

"People need a road," I hollered back at him. "I'm Solomon Richards and I'm going to make one."

"I'm the Reverend Billy Taylor," the man called. "And I foller the call of the spirit, not the guidance of a hog."

I was too out of breath to want to answer, but my blood was up from all the running and straining. Things kept crowding into my head that I had to say.

"Are you looking for misery?" I hollered.

"You look like a man in misery," he called.

"I'm making a good road for people to use," I said.

"You look like a man that's suffering the degradations of the flesh," he said. "I never seen a man that looked worser."

I knowed I looked bad, but it was because I had been working. I had been trying to carry through my plan. Instead of helping he wanted to make me feel ashamed.

"All you want is misery wrapped up in shit," I hollered.

"Profanity is a sign of a weak and troubled mind," he said.

"Profanity is a sign of disgust," I said.

But suddenly I didn't want to argue anymore. It don't do no good to argue. Nobody ever changed somebody's opinion with a fuss. Preachers think they've got all the wisdom. And I didn't need to argue with him. I had to argue with the hollers and steep mountain, and the thickets ahead of me. But the preacher wasn't tired of talking. He was just getting warmed up.

"It's not roads people need," he shouted. "It's the blood of redemption they need. And the blood is the new testament."

I didn't answer him no more.

"I can bring the word on foot or on horseback, or on my knees if I have to," the preacher said. The preacher had got started and I seen he was going to preach to me. As long as he follered, I was his congregation. But my resentment was all gone. He could have his say and it didn't bother me no more.

"I carry the witness of song," he said. "Music will soften the heart of the sinner. You start singing and first thing you know the sinner's whistling along, and then he's humming. And next thing you know he's singing hisself. That's why I teach singing schools. That's why I carry the sacred harp to the hinterlands and far settlements. The buckwheat notes are like seeds sown over the coves and ridges, planting the words in people's hearts."

I was beginning to listen to the preacher's voice with interest. All us Richardses loves music, and I liked his idea that the pleasure of music could help lead people right. That seemed a better message than grief and condemnation.

Suddenly Sue turned off the path and run right up the ridge through a stand of chestnut trees. The leaves was so deep we made a racket through them. It sounded like the preacher was calling after us, but it might have been the rattling of the leaves. I was too busy dodging limbs and looking for trees to blaze to look back, and when I did get a chance, they was no sign of the preacher behind. But when we got to the top, I heard a voice singing far below. It was a slow, sad hymn, and I knowed it was the preacher going along the trail practicing his psalmody.

It seemed I could hear the preacher's voice for several minutes beyond the noise of the leaves and our panting, and the snap and shudder of limbs. The voice seemed in tune with the sounds we made, and with the breeze on top of the ridge. And it was like I could hear the voice long after we had crossed the ridge and the preacher must have been two valleys away.

Son, there is always somebody inside us saying we can't accomplish anything, that all our ambitions is nothing but vanity and pride, that our determination is just the love of vainglory, that we might as well lay down and die and get it over with. But the only real argument is hard work, to foller out our idea and plan as far as we can go.

Beyond the chestnut woods they was a rock flat in the ground so long and wide it made a clearing. It was so long it looked like a city street, except for the humps and ripples in the surface and pools of rainwater standing in pockets. Sue run right out onto the rock and across it the long way. The pools was green in places and had little snails in them.

The edge of the rock was lined with huckleberry bushes. I could smell the ripe berries in the sun. If I'd had time I would like to have picked a mouthful. Maybe I'd come back with a basket sometime. There ain't nothing in the woods smells better than ripe huckleberries in the sun mixed with scent of pine resin.

Something whirled in the bushes ahead. I couldn't see a thing but trembling limbs and swaying tops of saplings. Whatever it was made an awful fuss. If I could have stopped Sue, I would have. I didn't want to run into any more Melungeons or blockaders. The day was more than half over, and I was far from Cedar Mountain.

I seen something black in the shaking limbs, but couldn't tell if it was shadows between the bushes, or something doing the shaking. I was going to holler at Sue, but any racket I made would only attract the attention of whatever it was. "Whoa," I said under my breath. Whoa, I whispered to myself. But the hog kept running. Her hooves clicked on the rock. Her feet had been polished in the leaves and they shined like ivory. Whoa, I whispered, but she didn't pay no attention.

The limbs of a bush parted and I seen a paw poke through. It had a lot of fingers ending in claws. It was a bear reaching through the bushes. I would have stopped if I could, but it wasn't no use. Sue hadn't seen nothing, or smelled nothing, and she kept click-click-clicking right along the rock. If the bear attacked, it would attack Sue.

I seen another paw reach up and pull down a limb. That bear was eating highbush huckleberries. It hadn't seemed to notice us. But I didn't see how we could go clicking across the rock and not disturb it. I knowed bears was real near-sighted and depended mostly on scent. It would smell us, if nothing else. No telling how bad I smelled myself, of sweat and dirt, and blood.

And I had the stink of strain and worry, and the raw smell of fear on me.

We was within twenty yards of the shaking bushes and still the bear hadn't noticed us. It was so busy eating berries, I hoped it would not sniff the air. And maybe the noise of the leaves was so loud close to its ear it wouldn't hear Sue trotting on the rock.

I found myself actually tiptoeing as I run, but Sue didn't hesitate. She just kept clopping along, happy to have open space and a level path in front of her. I hoped maybe the bear would not notice us at all, if we just kept going at a steady pace.

They was marks all over the rock where hunters had carved their initials, and they was picture-like marks that must have been made by Indians. Nobody knowed how to read such signs, but they looked like they was meant to say something. A lot of marks had been rubbed off by weather and passing feet, and lichens and moss had growed over some. Here and there hunters had built fires on the rock and they was charred logs and ashes scattered around. People coming up there to pick berries had cooked their dinner too, and left corn shucks and chicken bones on the rock.

They ain't no end to my troubles, I thought. First you run into a preacher in black, and then a black bear. It was one bad omen after another. I don't know how much I believed in luck, but I thought maybe if I had all my bad luck on the survey I'd have good luck building the road. I had forgot my buckeye. Feller carried a buckeye in his pocket back then both for luck and to keep away rheumatism. I wasn't worried about rheumatism at that age, but I could have used some luck.

I didn't believe much in luck then. But now I'm not so sure. Some things you can't explain except by good luck or bad. Everything just seems a chain of happens. Take meeting your Grandma. I never would have seen her if I hadn't gone to that funeral. I never would have gone to the funeral if I hadn't seen Staton the day before at the mill. And I wouldn't have gone to mill that day except we give some extra meal to the Short family that was sick. And I never would have heard about using a hog to survey a road if I hadn't gone to Kuykendall's store that day before Christmas. It goes on and on, one thing leading to another. One thing happens because something else has. You can die for the merest twist of bad luck, or live to be ninety.

As we got closer to the bear, I tried to make a plan. I figured if he smelt us or seen us it would take him a minute to decide what to do. Bears don't think fast. And then if he started to come at us, he most like would attack Sue. Bears prefer not to attack people, unless it's an ill sow with cubs to protect. It's the fact that people stand upright that seems to scare them. Bears is like hogs; they'll do things the easy way if they can.

If the bear come at Sue, I'd hit it with the hatchet. A bear has such a little head and such thick fur it's hard to hurt one with something little like a hatchet. But a bear has a low forehead and a pretty soft skull, and I thought, if I hit it with the hatchet just behind the eyes, it will go down. The problem would be to land a lick there if the bear was rassling with Sue and jerking around.

The closer we got, the busier the bear seemed with the berries. It must have been a hungry bear. Them big paws was twisting and knocking around the bushes every which way. Of course a bear can't pick them little berries. It don't have nothing but claws on its hands. It pulls the limbs to its mouth and eats the berries right off the bushes, biting leaves and twigs too.

Because I was watching the brute, I didn't see the big puddle of rainwater catched on the rock with sticks and leaves floating in it. You couldn't tell how deep it was, 'cause sunlight was reflected off the skin. Sue darted to the right to surround the water, toward the bear. I was jerked along and before I knowed it we was headed at the bushes.

I don't know exactly when Sue seen the bear or the bear seen us. We come stumbling and clicking over the rock. It all happened so fast. By the time we got to the side of the puddle we couldn't have been more than six feet from the bushes. Sue swerved again through the edge of the water. And I think it was the splash that caught the bear's attention. Water sprayed out from our feet into the bushes.

I looked right into that bear's face as it was gobbling berries, and it seen me. We often think animals are like people and make up silly things about their feelings. But I'd swear that bear was caught by surprise with its mouth full of berries. I could tell the instant it seen me, a man with hair going every which way and blood down my chin, looking him in the eye.

It was close enough to reach out and slap me with a big paw. I could have spit in his face. It had a look of panic, and confusion, trying to make up its mind whether to attack or run. I raised the hatchet, assuming it was going to jump at me.

But the bear turned loose of the bushes and dropped to its feet. I twisted to see where Sue was heading, so as not to stumble, and when I looked back the bear was still standing there, trying to make up its mind. That bear had the look of a man caught with his pants down.

I thought maybe if I hollered at the bear I could scare it. Sometimes if you surprise a wild animal, it will turn tail before it has time to get mad and think. Bears is naturally shy and will run, soon as they get wind of people coming. You'll find their warm bed and the leaves all kicked up where they run away.

Close up, that bear looked more brown or red than black. I'd noticed that before, when a bear was killed, its face and hair had some gold and red in it. Its eyes was kind of yellow. A bear has little old eyes. You can tell it can't see nothing.

"Hie!" I hollered at the bear after we had passed. "Hie!" I figured we could be no worse off than we was. "Hie!" I said again. That bear backed like I'd hit him on the nose, tearing down some of the bushes he had been holding.

"Hie!" I hollered again. He started forward and then backed up like he had made a mistake and couldn't remember which way he wanted to go. That bear was embarrassed to be caught that way, and he was plumb rattled. But I knowed a bear that mixed-up could soon get riled, and then he would be more dangerous than ever.

For once I wouldn't have cared if Sue had speeded up. She had been surprised by the bear too and was running a little sideways, glancing back to see what the bear was doing. Hogs like to look out for theirselves. They don't want to be attacked from behind. She run sideways for several hundred yards.

I know that bear scared her worse than anything else had because it released her bowels. Suddenly I was having to look back at the bear and at the same time trying to dodge the filth Sue was dropping just under my hand.

"Hie!" I yelled at the bear again. It looked at me through the bushes for an instant, and then, pretending to be bored with the whole business, it turned around and headed back into the trees. It was like that bear made a decision to recover its dignity in the face of absurdity and insult. It turned at exactly the speed that told me it was not hurrying. It would not be rushed by no foolishness. The bear lumbered off into the shadows, swinging his big belly full of huckleberries from side to side, like it was going into the woods for a noon nap. If bears could whistle, it would have been whistling.

I was only too glad to get on down that rock myself. The stink of the bear and the stink of the sow's mess was something to leave behind. Sue's hooves clicked and she trotted back into the middle of the long rock. The rock altogether was about half a mile long, and we was halfway across it.

When we was out there in the open, I tried to judge the time again by the height of the sun. My sense of time had been ruined by all the strain and exertion. My shadow fell a little bit further over Sue, but I couldn't tell how much it had advanced. It could have been one o'clock, or two o'clock, or even three o'clock, for all I knowed. It was much hotter in the open sun. The rock sent up heat like a stove. The puddles felt scalding when I stepped in them. When I glanced back I thought I seen a thunderhead low on the southern horizon.

Suddenly it come to me how hungry I was. I hadn't eat a thing since the grits at dawn and I had been running on an empty stomach for hours. Now what I thought of was gritted bread. You know what gritted bread is, boy? People don't fix it much anymore. But back in the old days in mid- to late summer, that's what you had. When the corn was in its milk you had creamed corn and regular roastnears. But after the corn got too hard and tough to eat off the cob you picked it and grated it. Just a grater made by driving nails through a piece of tin. The kernels was still a little soft, and not hard enough to grind up as meal. They wasn't many mills back then anyway. And even if we had cornmeal it was gone by July and August. Long as the corn was in its milk we had it fresh every day. Ain't nothing better than new taters and beans and fresh corn.

But once you gritted the hardening corn and mixed it with buttermilk and salt, you put the batter in a skillet and baked it over the fireplace like regular bread. When it got all brown on the outside, you had something special.

I looked back over my shoulder at the thundercloud. It was looming higher, even while we was still on the long rock. The thunderhead sparkled on top like a snowy woods where the sun touched it. But underneath, the cloud was sooty and ink black. It was coming up fast. I could feel the change in the air, the closeness. Sweat drops clung to me like little snails.

I tried to brush the sweat out of my eyes with my sleeve. How much sweat could there be in me, for I hadn't had a drink since the coffee at Aunt Willa's? My sleeve was all brown from dried blood. Every time I wiped away the sweat it seemed to start my lip bleeding again. And the sweat stung the wound.

At the far end of the rock they was even more ashes and burned sticks scattered where bonfires had been. As we run the last hundred yards I thought how hard it would be to smooth a road on the wavy surface. The road would have to go around the edges, unless we wanted to spend a year cutting through the uneven dips and rises. Moving rock is the hardest part of road making, even if it's just little loaf-bread size rocks that have to be dug and carried away. But if you have boulders to shove around, it means every kind of shoveling and straining and prying.

But the worst is where you have a dyke of solid rock. Back then we didn't have nothing but black powder for blasting. And most of the time we couldn't afford black powder for road building. But if you did have powder, it took a whole day just to drill a hole for it. Took two men to drill, one hammering and one turning. And they had to keep washing the dust and grit out of the hole. If you had a rock of any size, it could take weeks to bust a way through.

Don't tell me you've heard all this before? It gets on my mind how we used to do things, and I want to tell you. An old man likes to talk. It relieves his mind, especially when he can't get out and work no more. And I'm telling you about the old days so you will know. Soon they won't be nobody who remembers those times.

They was a trail in the bushes at the north end of the rock leading straight down the slope. It must have been a hunter's trail, or the berry-pickers trail. Sue turned right onto the path and I was relieved not to have to fight through the zone of bushes. The track was well used, and I wondered who would come this far to pick berries. We must be ten miles from anywhere. And then I smelled smoke.

The smell got stronger. It was like we was follering a trail of smoke. It was like the smoke was crawling along the path, or something going ahead was leaving the smoke. And the further we went, the stronger the smell got. They was people at the source of that smoke, for it didn't smell like no leaf fire or grass fire burning on its own.

The first thing I seen ahead was clothes spread on bushes. They was linens and scarves, britches and stockings laid over bushes by the trail. They looked like tents or kites fell in the woods. I hoped it wasn't no more Melungeons, but I couldn't even slow Sue down. Then I seen the washpot over the fire in the clearing. A woman wearing nothing but rags was bent over a tub. Her hair fell in tangles all over her shoulders and face as she scrubbed clothes on a washboard. The woman seen Sue and me coming and stood up by the tub, her hands dripping. Except for the rags hanging around her gaunt frame she was practically naked.

As Sue run by the washpot I seen the children. They emerged from beside bushes and posts and logs like little partridges. None had on a shred of clothes. I guess she was washing whatever clothes they had. They watched me like I was a ghost dropped from thin air. Thunder cracked in the sky. The clearing smelled like smoke and ashes, and the heavy soap the woman was using.

"Howdy," I hollered, and waved my hand with the hatchet in it.

Then I seen the house at the same time I seen the man. The building was made of poles and was low as a stable. The reason I knowed it was a house was it had a stick and clay chimney at one end. At the other end was a pen of palings, and chickens was pecking in the dirt there. But they was chickens all around the yard and guineas too. The guineas started hollering when they seen me, and it was like ten saws was sawing on nails.

"Howdy," I said to the man. He was red-headed and terrible fat. He set on a stump in front of the building whittling a stick. His knife stopped in a curl of wood when he seen me and Sue coming around the washpot. I don't know if he hollered to the children, or if the woman did. But all of a sudden those naked little young-uns was running along side and around me. They must have been five or six of them, and they run right past me yelling "Soooy, soooy," and "Get back, get back, old hog."

I couldn't tell what they was doing at first, and then it come to me the man had told them to catch Sue. He must have thought she was run away and I was trying to catch her. Every time one of the kids got close to Sue and tried to grab her she jerked to the other side and pulled me with her.

"Stand back," I said. "Just let her go." But they just ignored me. Maybe they thought if they could catch the hog they could claim her. One of the boys tried to grab Sue's ear, but he fell down. I hoped he didn't get hurt, for they would blame me.

Two of the children got in front and headed Sue off again, this time closer to the shackly cabin. Chickens squawked out of the way and the guineas kept up their pottaracking. I didn't see how I was going to get through with the paling fence on one side and the children crowding on the other.

The dirty little younguns closed in and Sue either had to knock down the fence palings or come to a halt. "Get back, hog, get back, hog!" the children shouted.

"We don't want to stop; we're surveying a road," I said. But again they didn't seem to hear me. Thunder cracked in the sky behind and above me.

"Stand back," I said. "We want to go before the storm breaks." But the kids watched the hog like it was a prize they had chased down in the woods. Sue turned this way and that, looking for an opening. The wind had pulled the smoke around our way and I could smell the ashes and steam off the dirty clothes. I wondered if the family had itch was why they was boiling their clothes. The woman called something but I couldn't tell what it was above the racket. The whole clearing smelled like chickens and rancid fat.

The sow wheeled around to lunge sideways, but the fat red-headed man was blocking her way. He had his knife in one hand and a stick in the other. He moved slow, but his vast bulk shut off our way of escape. He wore a rough kind of overalls and no shirt and seemed almost as naked as the kids. The red hair on his chest looked stiff as wires. None of them seemed like they had left the clearing in a long time or seen anybody.

"We are surveying a road," I said to the man. But he just watched me without speaking. I wondered if he and all of them might be deaf. I knowed I looked a sight, with my hair and beard flying every which way and blood all over my chin and shirt, and dried on my wrist and sleeve.

"We just want to go on," I said. "I'm going to build a road through to Douthat's Gap so you all will have a way to market."

"Don't want no market," the man said. "We just want this hog that's invaded our yard."

The man's eyes was green as the slime in a ditch. He didn't smile and he didn't blink when he talked. He reached out to prod Sue with the stick.

I didn't have no proof of who I was or what I was doing. I was twenty miles from any law or help. And I was tired. If they wanted to take Sue, I reckoned they could. I wasn't going to hit naked children with no hatchet. They pressed around the sow.

"You'll get paid for the right-of-way," I said. "When the road is built and tolls are charged."

They was a blast of thunder above all the hollering, and the air was now cool. It was the damp air of a storm. I wanted to get out of the yard before the rain hit.

Sue turned to run through the fat man's legs, but he caught her with his stick. He was quick as a hog hisself, at least with his hands. He pressed closer and reached into his hip pocket for a string. "Tie that hog's legs with this," he said to the bigger boy. The man was sweating and panting, and his face was the color of pokeberry juice.

It looked like Sue was done for. The woman had come up behind me and closed off any retreat that way. She held her long troubling stick pointed at my back, its end bleached by soap and hot water. They was nothing to do but give in. Them people seemed hungry enough to eat me. I figured I'd be lucky if they let me go and just kept Sue. I could come back with the sheriff some day and charge them, but it wouldn't help me survey the road.

The boy made a loop in the twine and bent over to put it on Sue's front foot.

"You're making a mistake," I said. But the man looked at me with those green eyes and didn't answer. You could hear a wheeze in his lungs. Thunder broke out again in the air straight above.

As the boy knelt to put the twine on her hoof, Sue seen the opening in the circle and jumped through it. She brushed two of the children aside and shot forward like from a cannon. I jerked after her and felt the children clawing at me. The man whacked my back with his stick. I felt the end of the woman's troubling stick as she swung at my head but hit my shoulder instead.

Once me and Sue broke out of that circle, we run like the Devil hisself was after us. Lightning lit up the yard, and we leaped across chickens and piles of trash, filth from the kitchen, and guineas screeching like fiends. People like that never have horses or outhouses, and their yards are like sewers. I don't think we touched ground more than twice as we aimed toward the woods.

They was a garden of pole beans at the end of the yard. The sticks was thin and crooked and bent every which way. It looked like a brushpile the vines was crawling over. I don't know how they got in there to pick them. But the biggest poles had vines going all the way to the top, ten or twelve feet high. The patch looked like a hanging jungle. I was glad Sue picked her way around the edge and didn't try tearing through the vines. I don't think we could have got through. Them people would have caught us in that mess and killed us for ruining their garden.

The shareholders I had got had agreed to pay small fees for the right-of-way through cleared property. We was going to try to get free use to open woods. Where possible, we would go around any clearings. But even the small fees couldn't be paid until the road was open and tolls was coming in. I didn't know how we would deal with this family.

Sue surrounded the beanfield and entered the woods just as they was another blast of thunder straight overhead. You would have thought it was a war and shells was bursting. They have the awfullest lightning storms in South Carolina on a hot day. It's like the whole sky turns to fire and explosions. If you reached out a finger lightning would hit it.

If they was a path out of the clearing, we had missed it. You know how the woods will put up a solid front against a clearing, plugging each chink to claim every inch to reach the light. The undergrowth will fill up the gaps, and they seems no way into the woods. I guess every bush is trying to crowd out the others.

Sue plunged right through the wall of bushes and, though my face got slapped and scratched, it felt good to be in woods again. It was dark, except for lightning flashes. The people was hollering and the guineas screeched behind, but nobody follered into the woods. It was like we had gone from day to night.

Then everything lit up, and the woods was all flickering in shadows, like blue dust had been throwed on the air. Hogs are afraid of thunderstorms, but Sue seemed to ignore the crashes. The next clap echoed off the mountains ahead and behind. They was a roar back there, but I couldn't tell if it was wind or heavy rain. If you stop in woods before a storm, you can hear the rain advancing like an army. But we couldn't stop, and I was out of breath and mostly heard the blood in my ears and my own panting.

In the humid air gnats stuck to my neck and forehead. I tried to rub them away with my wrist. I thought of turning loose of Sue's tail and letting her go on her own as the storm descended. We was so far off the way, it probably didn't make no difference. At least I could sit down and rest and maybe crawl into a laurel thicket out of the storm.

A shadow shot over me and they was a crack in the air like a whip had been popped, and a second later the ground and air shook. The torment of the heat was unleashing its power. I had heard that hogs draw lightning like dogs, because of their hair. Sue trotted straight ahead through the dark woods.

The first cold drops hit limbs above and dripped on my neck and arms like little feet walking. My shirt was already wet with sweat. I shivered and kept running. The big drops tapped my hair and ears, and I wondered if they was hail in the storm. Something

stung my neck like fine birdshot. The woods sounded like somebody was shaking rock salt down through the leaves.

They was a lick, like a dry stick had snapped in the air ahead. I
saw a trough of lightning jerk down the sky and swarm through
an oak tree a hundred feet in front. With a hiss the tree busted
into steam and smoke, and you could hear the sap seethe and
foam in the terrible heat. Pieces of wood and bark flew around
me. A sliver pricked my cheek and a long splinter of the tree
landed in the sapling beside me. The sound was so loud I didn't
hear it. It was like the air shoved me so I lost my breath. Sue
turned in confusion. My ears rung and I smelled this funny smell
like something had been singed and froze at once. Where the oak
had been was just a shred of shining stump.

I pushed the sow toward the shelter of a sourwood tree. Just as
we dropped to the ground the rain come in curtains and fine hail
pecked the leaves under the flimsy protection of the sourwood.
Sue crowded up against me, grunting with fear, and laid her head
in my lap. She was tired out as I was, and just as scared too, I
reckon. The ground shook, and lightning popped in the trees on
all sides. She trembled and squealed.

They is nothing like the sense of privacy you get in the middle
of a storm. You are exposed to the elements so you make a cave, a
shelter of yourself, and close yourself off to the wind and water.
You hunker down into a little nut of warmth and life against the
threat of the storm. Nothing feels as precious as your own flesh
under the lash and shiver of rain. But even as you resist the
wetness, the dry places on your belly and under your arms are
shrinking, and eventually you are cold and wet all over.

I got to thinking then about how much trouble I had gone to
that day. It was a joke against me that I had labored so and been
hurt and threatened and had strained too much. And so far I
didn't know if we had even follered the right path.

But then I thought, that's what work really is, something diffi-cult, something to fill up the time. Every day is a long day if you don't have work to do. Every hour is long unless you have some-thing that has to be done. The best thing's to feel work's a must, and they's no way around it.

Of course, we think all the time we want to rest, that we just want to finish the job at hand so we can sit down and do nothing. But loafering is better to think about than actually do. What people call leisure is mostly a bore. Nothing is as dreary as a holiday. You've got to watch out for the long Sunday afternoons when they's no meeting and you can't do no work. We all talk about how much we'd like to go fishing and how much we'd like to sit around and daydream. But that seems wonderful because you're busy, because you have work that must be done.

You say have ever I laid back and give up the struggle? I reckon not. I reckon I never will. We'll sure enough get rest in time. My guess is what we're all working for, what we want most, is the rest and surrender at the end of life. They is no pleasure like that final laying back and giving up the struggle. All our lives we're at a strain to get this and that. You know how it is when sleep throws its dust in your veins and you feel the sweetness spreading through you. I bet that's the way death feels, like something seeping through us that scratches the itch we've always felt, like soothing cool air on the fever of our blood. I bet the pain of our wanting is salved and soothed away.

You hear preachers talk about people like they're either good or bad. But there ain't nobody but what's some of both. It depends on who's doing the judging, and how they want to look at it. Anybody might do most anything, if the circumstances was right. They is no one way somebody is and just has to be. We can all be different people at different times.

Look at the ways people seen me that day Sue and me made the survey. To Aunt Willa and Uncle Rufus I was just a hopeful boy that had grand ambitions and no practical experience. I must have seemed foolish but harmless. Uncle Rufus had an expression for people whose ambition was too big for their means. He said they "liked to bore with a big auger." I think he even admired that kind of hope and ambition, but thought it bound to fail, as most things is bound to fail.

To the blockaders I must have seemed like the craziest man they ever met up with in the woods. I come running out of the laurels holding a sow by the tail and crashed right through their camp without saying so much as "kiss my ass." Even when they shot after me, I didn't stop, and they didn't try to foller me because even blockaders don't hurt lunatics.

To the Indian I must have appeared as just another strange white man on his hunting ground. Cherokees by then didn't have no hope of keeping us out. They just appeared here and there like ghosties of theirselves, and watched the wilderness disappear before the ax. One more white man with a sow probably didn't seem that much different from all the others.

I can only guess what them Melungeon girls thought I was. They acted like I was a spy, or a degenerate devil. The old woman sure seen me as the enemy of whatever she was trying to do. They was camping there by the pond, but I don't know to this day where they come from or where they was going.

That family in the clearing that didn't have hardly no clothes must have seen me as somebody to rob. They was hungry and looking to steal anything that come along. Their house wasn't more than a sty. I reckon they didn't care much who I was.

I've heard people talk about how you should live so that when you come to die you'll be proud of what you've done, take satisfaction in the things accomplished. That sounds good, but when you think about it, it don't make sense. When you come to die, you might be in such pain you're not thinking about nothing, or you're just confused. If you don't get satisfaction all along you probably won't get none at the end. It would be silly to think of struggling all that time for just some moment of rightness at the last.

Me and Sue set there in the middle of the storm and it felt like an ocean had dropped on top of us. I ain't never seen such rain before or since. You couldn't see more than fifty feet. It was like in a snowstorm where all the air is filled with flakes. Trees was bending every which way, and I don't think it was just a high wind. It was the force of the water hitting the trees, like you throwed a bucket of water on a weed. Trees was breaking and limbs flying. A big limb hit the ground not more than six feet away. The sourwood wasn't no protection, but I didn't see any reason to move, for every other place was just as exposed.

Thunder banged around like somebody was hitting a roof with hammers. Every time they was a crack, Sue jerked and squealed. I never seen an animal so scared. She pushed up against me like a girl in love. We stuck together and made a little tent of warmth inside the rain. I scratched her back and belly, and rubbed behind her ears which she liked best. Me and Sue had come a long way that day.

How will we ever know which way to go now? I thought. We will be so washed out and tired after the storm passes we won't never be able to get back on track. And if the sun don't come out we won't know which way is north.

Right then the rain slacked and the wind quieted. I felt all the strength had drained out of me. I didn't feel like standing up and going on. I figured I'd just wait a few minutes, and then rouse the sow. Why not rest for a spell, maybe half an hour to regain my get up and go? Why not collect my wits and rest my back? Sue didn't make any move. She just laid there with her head in my lap and grunted. The woods got quiet so you could hear the trees dripping and thunder in the distance. A bluejay squawked, and flew overhead. Maybe that's why they are called raincrows, I thought. I wondered then, and still wonder, where birds go in heavy rain and high wind. You would think they'd get washed away and drowned. After a storm you see dead birds that got bashed on a tree or smothered in the downpour. But most of the birds come out chirping and flying soon as the storm is over.

I told myself to stand up and get started. But I put it off a few more seconds. The woods was full of trees knocked over and broke limbs all around. It would be even harder to find our way through that hurricane of twisted up roots and wind-throw-downs. Green leaves had been knocked down like it was already fall.

Then a roar come suddenly from behind us, and I wondered if the storm was coming back. I've heard bad storms do that, will circle back and hit you again.

The roar we heard turned into wind and rain in just a few seconds. You never saw nothing come so fast. It was like the rain was waiting behind a wall to jump over and surprise us. Both rain and hail hit from behind and Sue jerked awake. Something stung the air like a razor strop on your face and balls of fire run all over the woods. I'd always heard about ball lightning but never seen any. Instead of a bolt, it was balls the size of melons shooting among the trees. It was like sparks the size of tubs flying from all points. One went by within ten feet and I could hear the hiss. It was all these little suns bouncing and shooting all over, and when the crash of thunder come they disappeared.

The rain this time seemed even harder than before. Drops

mixed with hail lashed across my face. Sue pushed closer and I hunkered down out of the attack, turning away. You wouldn't have thought the air could hold so much water. Trees rassled around and above us, turned white and cracked.

I noticed something I'd never seen before or since. I guess you have to be in the middle of a storm to witness it. After a lightning flash, it was like the air was sucked away, like it was burnt up, and my ears would hurt from inside. Then with the thunder air come pounding back. It was like lightning just took away the air, took away breath, and thunder sent some back to fill its place. My ears hurt both ways, from inside and outside.

Something else that happened during the second part of the storm was I seen this light all over the trees above us. It was like lightning got stuck on the limbs and glowed there, shining around the limbs and leaves in haloes and wreaths. I've heard of things like that happening at sea, where the mast and rigging of a ship glowed in a storm. But here we was in the mountains and the trees was shining in this yellow and pink light. I felt like the place was spooked, or blessed, and I couldn't tell which. Everything gleamed and the rain was still heavy. I wasn't sure but what I seen ghosts and witches, or maybe angels, flying through the sky. But it was probably an effect of the lightning.

"Are we ever going to get out of this?" I said to Sue, just like she was another person. She grunted and broke wind. "We still got a long way to go," I said. "A long way."

Out in that storm I felt I was just an impulse, a desire to make a road, and to marry your Grandma. I was just an idea with a little fat stuck to it. Compared to the storm, and the rotting strength of time, I was nothing but my desire. The storm would cover me in leaves and nobody would ever find me, wasn't for my will to go on, and my memory of who I was.

When the rain begun to slack a little I seen things moving in the leaves and puddles. Something crawled up against me and jumped and I seen it was a little toad frog. The leaves was full of toad frogs. They was the same color as the leaves and crawling and hopping every which way. They was everywhere you looked. That last heavy rain had been a frog rain. Now don't laugh at me. I know people will dispute my word. But back then it come frog rains and sometimes worm rains. Where else could all them toad frogs come from except the sky? People will say they's nothing to it, but I've seen them myself. I've seen frog rains and I've seen snail rains. You go out after a rain and the ground is covered with frogs, where else did they come from? Answer me that. I've heard of fish rains, but I never seen one myself. But people say they've gone out after a heavy storm and the ground was covered with fish. A storm just sucks things up one place and drops them another. And this time they was toad frogs crawling among the hailstones and puddles. Where else did they come from? I ask you that.

When the rain finally stopped, I felt all the strength had been scrubbed out of me. I was stiff and weak, and sore like I had been beat. The woods was dripping and the ground was covered with pools and little gullies where the leaves had washed away. Hailstones smoked a little where they was piled up and melting. And then I smelled the sour of the scorched oak's sap.

Sue opened her eyes and scrambled to her feet. The hog seemed to remember she was far from home and from her slop trough. I just had time to grab her tail and pick up my wet hatchet. She must have been stiff as I was, for she stepped awkward and slow among the splinters and limbs of the blasted oak.

The lightning had even run out the roots of the tree, exploding them and leaving trenches in the dirt.

The hatchet had little coins of rust on the blade, in outlines of red on the steel. Rain water must rust things faster than regular water, I thought. The rust was bright as gold dust, growing there on the blade like some kind of mold.

That was when I felt the tiredest, because I didn't know how far I was from home. And I felt drowned in my clothes. Every bush and sapling we touched showered me with more water. The hailstones winked and hissed as they melted in the leaves when the sun come back out. I had to blink the drops out of my eyes, as my face got sprayed with the aftershowers.

The sow begun to pick up speed once we got around the blasted tree. You take one step and then just one more, and another, and another, and first thing you know the kinks are loosening in your legs and back. I don't know who loosed up first, Sue or me, but we kept going with our lurch and stumble around the fallen limbs and wind-throw trees, picking our way among bird nests and saplings bent over and half-broke by the wind.

I had to remind myself to blaze the trees. Among all the splinters and hurricane of oaks and maples it would be hard to spot the marks. But they was nothing else to do. At least some of the trees would already be down when we cut the right-of-way.

When I raised my arm to slash the bush, I found my shoulder was even stiffer than my legs. Something stung in the socket and I couldn't raise my arm no higher than my chest. It was like my arm was paralyzed with pain if I tried to reach higher. I thought I must have dislocated it, or been hurt worse than I had noticed. The shoulder hurt with a stabbing heat. That was my introduction to rheumatism. I was young and I'd never dreamed of such a thing. It was the exposure to cold rain and wind on the hot tired shoulder that done it. Any time you expose a shoulder like that it can give you rheumatism. I reckon it's some kind of fever that gets in the joint. And unlike the stiffness it didn't work itself out as we went along. I had to blaze the trees lower down, and it was hard to swing the hatchet at all. Rheumatism will go away in a day or two fast as it comes, but it won't go away just because you are exercising your arm, like a muscle cramp will.

Ahead of us was a rock ledge, one of those that looks like the wall of a castle or some big battlement in a fairy tale. It rose way up through the trees. And they was a hollowed place at the bottom that looked like a den. The ledge reared so high I expected to see a flag flying on top. When we was almost under the wall I looked way up and seen this big cat on the rim looking down. At first I didn't believe what I seen. It must be sweat or a drop of rain in my eye. Since I couldn't stop, a limb interfered with my view, but the next second I could see again and that painter sure enough was up there, looking down on us.

You almost never seen a painter in the daytime, even back then. I'd heard of black painters, but every one I'd seen killed was kind of tawny yeller. The cat on that cliff looked smoky, like it was shadowy and black at the tips of tail and feet. I knowed it had been watching us since long before I seen it.

I don't think Sue had any idea the cat was up there. She wasn't looking that way, and the smell couldn't have drifted down. She charged through the brush finding her way at the base of the overhang. I think the cave there had been used by wild hogs. They was hog rocks all over the mountains back then. The dirt was all stirred up. Whatever it was had been scared away or eat by the painter. I didn't have time to look for tracks.

What's a hog rock? Why it's a place in the woods where hogs gather, either wild hogs or hogs that are ranging for roots and mast before killing time. Hogs like a place that has some protection from sun and cold and wolves or painters. They like to find a overhang below a cliff where they can rest out of wind and partly shielded from rain. I guess every valley from here to Georgia had a hog rock back when so many hogs run loose.

But if Sue smelled any other hogs near the den, she didn't show no sign. Maybe she did smell the painter and just hurried on.

I looked up again and didn't see the cat at first. And then I seen it had moved along the rim of the cliff and was follering us, walking as we walked. It was pacing us. This was even more dangerous than the bear back at the long rock, not only because painters is more dangerous than bears, but because we was tireder. With the rheumatism in my shoulder I didn't even know if I could lift the hatchet to hit anything. I was so tired it was like my feet was running on their own. They wasn't nothing I could do to speed them up or make them stop. For once I was glad Sue didn't want to slow down.

It must have been two hundred yards along the bottom of the cliff. At the far end they was a slick of laurel bushes. Once we got into that I couldn't see nothing anyhow. And they was no way we could be quiet, knocking limbs and sending showers down on our backs. If the painter attacked, I figured he would go after Sue, and I could either hit him with the hatchet or run. If I hit him on the head maybe I could knock him cold, but who could hit a painter in the head with a hatchet, especially if it was rassling around with a sow? Uncle Rufus was right: I should have brought a gun. I should have tied a rope around Sue's foot and the other end around my waist, and carried both the hatchet and a gun. But it was too late. I could have even asked somebody to accompany me with a gun. But I was embarrassed to ask anybody to come on that crazy expedition. And besides, it seemed better to do the survey myself and then announce that it had been done.

A painter likes to stalk its prey. I've heard of them follering a lone hunter or stray cow for miles before attacking. Painters like to wait for the right vantage from which to jump. I guess the cliff was too high. It was going to foller us and wait for a better opportunity.

You hear all these stories about a painter follering a hunter once he's got blood on him, stepping in his tracks, running along the ridge above, climbing trees to look down on him until it's ready to pounce. They used to be a story I've heard Uncle Rufus tell, about a pretty girl that had helped her aunt with hog killing, rendering out lard and making souse meat. After she worked all day, the aunt give her a new quilt, because she was betrothed to be married, and a package of fresh ribs and tenderloin for her family. It was coming on dark, and when she got up the trail she heard this painter on the mountain. It squalled, and jumped from tree to tree on the ridge above. She knowed it smelled the meat and the scent of cooking lard on her clothes.

First she dropped the meat on the trail, a piece at a time, but after the cat eat all that it still follered her. Next she dropped a handkerchief, and she could hear the handkerchief being tore to pieces. Then she dropped a sweater, and the big cat stopped to rip that to pieces while she hurried up the trail. She dropped one thing after another, and still that painter kept coming on after it tore the fabric to shreds. She thought the cat was going to get her finally, and was going to drop the new quilt. But just then the dogs run out from the clearing and she seen she was home. She dashed to the house while the dogs fought with the painter, but realized after she was inside by the fire where her family and fiancé waited that she didn't have a stitch of clothes left. She wrapped herself in the new quilt.

It looked like all of creation was opposed to me building the road up through Douthat's Gap. All day I had been confronting one difficulty after another. It looked like they wasn't no hope I would ever be able to just survey the road. It was like God hisself had decided I didn't have enough trouble. Like the preacher said, maybe God didn't want no road into the mountains.

I would have give up then, except the very danger made giving up impossible. With the painter stalking I had no choice but to keep moving, and to hope that cat would turn back. Probably the painter had smelled the blood on my chin and beard and shirt.

You see a painter out in daytime so rarely they must have been something wrong. I don't think I ever heard of anyone confronting one in the middle of the day. The storm must have woke it out of its den and riled it, or lightning touched it and made it crazy. Lightning had hit near and the big cat had been addled. That's what I thought. That painter didn't act normal.

They was sweet shrubs all around the end of the ledge, and Sue plowed right through them. The bushes was loaded with rain and bathed me again in cold water, waking me a little from my dread. I tried to tell myself that if the painter was going to attack it would have while we was under the ledge. Now that we was out in the open, it would have to run up behind us.

I heard a growl and looked back. The painter was follering us about fifty feet behind. It growled and whipped its tail side to side. They seemed to be slobber hanging from its jaws, and for the first time I thought it might have been bit by a mad dog. You don't think of cats going mad. You think of dogs and squirrels and coons getting bit and going rabid. But that don't mean cats can't get bit too. I thought of a mad dog because of the way the cat walked. They was something about its lurch, about the way it walked partly sideways that reminded me of a mad dog. It looked curved somehow, like it was tending to go in a circle but stumbling to correct itself. I wondered if it had been blinded by the lightning and couldn't see the trees and bushes, and was follering us by smell or maybe by sound.

If we stopped and didn't make any noise would it stop too? It would have been worth trying to find out, but they was no way I could make Sue pause. She trotted on.

We crossed a little opening in the woods about seventy feet long. When we got almost across, in the sunlight that was now bright as ever, I looked back and seen the painter gaining on us. The cat run up to within ten yards of me. I raised the hatchet to defend myself, ignoring the pain of rheumatism. I thought if I could hit it between the eyes we might get away.

But the cat stayed about ten yards away. I kept walking and it was right behind. Its eyes looked crazy, like they was fevered and not focused. I've seen the eyes of drunk men look like that, like they're looking off in all directions at once. I couldn't even tell if it seen me or not.

I've heard people say if you peer into the eyes of a mad dog you can see the devil looking out at you. My Mama used to say a mad dog was demon-possessed and Satan was inside it. That's why a mad dog couldn't cross a stream. That's why a mad dog was afraid of water. It was suffering the fires and fevers of hell and wasn't allowed to quench its thirst.

If that cat scratched me, or bit me, it wouldn't matter if I killed it or not. I would get the rabies too. They would be no way to save myself if the slobber got into my blood.

I banged into a tree looking round and seen the cat had dropped back again. Then it fell on its belly and rolled over having some kind of fit. It wallowed in the leaves and kicked out in all directions, its paws brushing leaves and twigs.

Sue and me stumbled on through the undergrowth. I hoped the painter wouldn't be able to get up, that it would be so confused it wouldn't remember which direction we had gone. I knowed that a mad dog couldn't cross a branch or stream of any kind. I've heard that even a mud puddle will stop a mad dog and it will lay down and have fits. I don't know if it's the smell of water that makes the animal go crazy or the look of it. It's dying of thirst, and yet it's terrified of water. But I thought if we could reach some kind of branch we would be all right. Even if it was just a spring, or a standing pool after the storm, it might work.

The problem was we was way up on the ridge and it might be half a mile before we come down to any spring. Even if Sue broke out of her path and we run right down the mountain the cat might foller and fall on top of us. If we just kept going, it might lose our trail if we could get far enough ahead.

I kept glancing back, hoping not to see any head or tail above the bushes. And it really looked like we might get away, like we might gain enough distance. But then I seen the tawny head raise up and look around, like it had come to its senses and the fit was over. The cat looked like it was waking from a daze and trying to get its bearings. Just then I stepped on a twig that broke and Sue brushed a wet bush, and the head turned toward the sounds. It was follering us by sound. It lurched to its feet and started coming after us faster than before. It run into trees and bushes and halted to listen. Then it come on again.

If they was not so much water on the bushes we might have got away. But every time you touched a limb or sapling it rained a little storm on us and the leaves. If we could just get to a open place where we didn't make any noise we could get out of hearing.

But they was nothing but heavy undergrowth ahead. Sue and me kept knocking into limbs and the painter come on again, lurching and brushing against trees, gaining on us. This time it got so close I could hear it panting. They was a rattle and seethe in its throat, like somebody with pneumony. It sounded like the painter was about to choke itself on its own congestion.

I couldn't do more than glance back or I would bang into the brush. But I seen the spit hanging from the cat's mouth. They was foam around the lower lip dripping down like soap suds. I thought of venom in a snake's mouth. And I could smell the sickness on the animal.

I couldn't tell if the painter was going to die in its tracks or leap. If only we could come to a stream, a little branch, it would stop. But I didn't see nothing ahead but bushes.

Then I heard a dog bark up ahead. It must have been a little dog and a good way off, but I heard the bark clear. If only the dog would come closer, would run after us and bark at Sue. Never had a greeting seemed more welcome. I'd heard even a little dog could scare away a painter. I didn't care if it was a blockader ahead guarding his still. I hoped it was a hunter in the woods. If the dog would come bounding after us maybe the hunter could shoot the painter. Cats don't want nothing to do with dogs.

But the painter didn't seem to hear the dog. Or if it heard the barks it just ignored them. The cat might have been too sick to care. Or maybe it was thinking of me and Sue and not of anything else. It reached out a paw and slapped at me. The claws tore my shirt but didn't break the skin. It stumbled after the swing and paused for an instant then come running again.

This time I seen the stuff around it eyes. It was like a sugar crust on a cake, or snot around a baby's nose. It's eyes had run and the matter dried like bits of hominy. I couldn't tell if the painter seen me at all, but this time it was going to jump on me. I raised the hatchet to hit just when it leaped. But the hatchet caught on a sassafras limb. The limb broke my swing and I knowed I was a goner. I felt the sick breath of that painter. The sassafras limb was loaded with water and it shook a shower of drops right into that cat's face. You've never seen such a reaction out of any beast. You would have thought I throwed burning oil on its face. The drops splashed its eyes and the painter rared back like it was scalded. It jumped backward and flopped on the ground. It squalled in a hoarse way, suffering terrible. And I seen it shivering and writhing on the ground like a worm, or a cut snake. You never heard such groans and squalls. The woods sounded like they was full of sick painters.

If I had had a gun and could have turned loose of Sue I would have gone back and put that cat out of its misery. Nothing is as dangerous as a hurt animal, though. They was nothing to do but go on and let the painter die as it was, choking in its fever.

I heard the barks again, but they seemed a good way off. They was short yipes like a little dog makes, not a hunting hound and not a cur dog like so many mountain people had back then. It sounded like a squirrel dog, or some kind of terrier. If Sue heard the dog she didn't show no sign. She kept trotting.

Sue run straight in the direction of the barking. We had got into much deeper woods while running away from the painter. We had entered a forest so thick it was dark as twilight.

Sue trotted on for several hundred yards in that near darkness. I blazed a tree here and there, and listened for the barks. Had I imagined the dog in the first place? Maybe I wanted to hear a dog so bad I just made it up, hoping the painter would hear the barks too. I was so tired I might imagine anything. Or the dog could be running away in the direction we was going. Or maybe it had been a fox barking. Things had gone so strange that day I didn't trust my senses no longer.

The trees was bigger than any I had ever seen. It seemed like their trunks was wide as houses. And they was so many trees Sue had to weave back and forth through them. That was why they blocked out all the light. The trees was like pillars in a palace. They seemed to be supporting a dark roof up there. I couldn't tell what kind of trees they was. They didn't look like any oaks or hickories I had ever seen. But even in the gloom I could see the bark was all covered with moss and sooty mold. They wasn't no undergrowth, just the big trees standing like masonry columns. If the painter had chased us into these woods he would have caught us.

They was another yip ahead, and then another. Sue and me was winding back and forth between the trees. It seemed like the barks was off to my left, and then they seemed to come from my right. I hoped we wasn't going in circles.

It got lighter up ahead. In the woods it didn't seem the sun could be shining nowhere. It was like we'd been inside all day, in a cellar or attic, and thought it was overcast. And then we walked out to find the sky clear and sun pouring out its warmth.

Sue busted into a little opening, and I blinked with the sudden brightness. The sun was out in spots on the ground, and blinding where it shined from wet leaves and little puddles in cupped leaves. They was a yipe from the bushes nearby. I jerked around to find the dog but seen instead a man in buckskin standing in the laurels watching us. He looked like he was growing right out of the laurel bushes. A little dog growled in the brush beside him, its hackles raised.

The man appeared never to have shaved in his life or had his hair cut. His hair might have been blond at one time, but flowed gray and white down his shoulders. Never had I seen a wilder-looking human. Hair growed out of his ears and out of his nose. He wore an old black hat that appeared to be three-cornered, the kind my Grandpappy wore in the Revolution. But it was so wrecked you couldn't really tell. It was frayed on all the edges, but had a gold badge pinned to the side. He had leather strings over his shoulders and around his neck, and he leaned on a long musket, the kind you didn't see much anymore even then. His eyes glittered under the wrinkles and bushy brows.

"Is this the way to Cedar Mountain?" I blurted out. I couldn't think of nothing else to say. And it seemed like years since I had talked to a human. My voice surprised me.

"Some say it is," the man said, and never took his eyes off me.

His dog run out in front of Sue and cut her off. Instead of wheeling to go around the little terrier, or just running right over her, Sue paused. She must have wanted a rest, to be so easy stopped. It was just a little clearing in the laurel bushes. She could have plunged into the brush. But she stood her ground. The hackles was raised on the little dog's back.

"Will she bite?" I said. The dog was too little to do more than nip the hog, but I had to say something to break the old man's stare.

"She might," he said. "She might if she didn't know a body." The man looked steady at me, like he was asking me to explain. They was spots on his skin, a sign of real old age. But he stood so straight and alert he didn't seem that old. I realized how I must look with the dried blood on my chin and beard and shirt, and my clothes all wet and tore. I must have looked like an escaped prisoner, or somebody who run from his sick bed or grave.

"I'm surveying a road to Cedar Mountain," I said.

The little dog kept yiping and Sue backed up against my leg.

"Friend, you look like you been to war," the old man said.

"I'm just trying to make a road," I said. "And it seems nobody wants me to."

"A road just leads faster to the grave," the stranger said. "I want to go where no roads go." He had a quaint but cultivated speech, like they had in the last century, like they had brought from Virginny. It seemed odd to hear a buckskin talk that way.

"I want to take the way that winds around some through the woods," he said. "They's roads aplenty if people can see them."

Was the old man Tracker Thomas? They was stories he was still alive somewhere in the mountains, that he still hunted in the Indian country to the west. Tracker was supposed to have come into the mountains at the time of Daniel Boone. But instead of going north to Kentucky, he stayed in the high mountains of Carolina and Tennessee.

They was all kinds of tales about Thomas and another trapper named Muskrat Maybin. They was stories about how they was rivals over an Indian girl, and about how they seen who could trap the most furs, and who got the most would win the girl. Muskrat caught five hundred muskrats and thought he had won for sure, but Tracker showed up with fifty mink pelts worth more than all the rat hides put together.

People like to make things up, if they can find a hero, a name to pin their stories on. Some names just seem to stir the imagination and attract liars. We want to believe they done extraordinary things. It's like we need people to act out our lies. Ginseng hunters and trappers in the mountains beyond Brevard said for years they seen Tracker Thomas there. Others claimed to have spotted him in the Long Holler and near the Sal Raeburn Gap. But I never had believed such tales. If Tracker Thomas was still alive, he'd be eighty-five years old. What eighty-five-year-old could live on his own in the mountains? Nobody could live in the wilderness like they done in the old days anyway.

"Did you notice the orchard around you?" the stranger said.

"This is wilderness," I said. "I don't see no orchard."

The old man pointed to his left, and then to the right, and for the first time I seen the apple trees. They was little trees, spread out like wild apples will. Their bark was blacker than other trees. Whoever had planted the orchard had left it, and the other trees had grown between the fruit trees, above them. The orchard was buried in shadows, but each tree had apples on it. Some was gold and some was streaked and some was turning bright red.

"Who could have planted these trees?" I said. "Never heard of Indians growing apples."

"They's more things we don't know than we do," the man said.

"These trees look old as the Garden of Eden," I said.

The old man's eyes glittered with the pleasure of showing me the apple trees. It was like when he pointed them out, they just appeared, for I hadn't seen them before. Of course I hadn't been looking there either, what with trying to foller Sue and see where the barking dog was.

The little dog kept jumping sideways in front of Sue as she turned to face it. But she didn't go on. She would swing her head at the dog and it would step out of the way and then hop closer again. I think she needed a rest as bad as I did.

Seemed like it had turned to autumn around the stranger. It was the oddest thing, but I had the impression of yellow leaves on some trees, and red leaves on the shumake bush. Maybe it was just the colors of the apples and the dapple of spotlights from the sun. But it seemed the woods was full of fall colors and the air was thinner and cooler.

"How come these apple trees are here?" I said. "Ain't nobody been here to set them out?"

"How do you know who has been here and who ain't?" the old man said.

"Wasn't nobody in the mountains but the Cherokee," I said.

"But who was here before the Cherokee?" he said, smiling and leaning on his rifle.

"Don't rightly know," I said. "But I've heard of the lost tribe of Israel, and I seen some Melungeons back down the trail."

"Friend, we are all the lost tribe of Israel," the old man said. "And we don't know what all has been here since creation."

He took pleasure in telling me, and in surprising me. We old fellers always like to tell the young things they couldn't have dreamed of. It's one of the pleasures of being old.

"For all we know, this was the Garden of Eden," he said. "It looks kindly like paradise, don't it?" He looked both young and old at the same time. And he seemed to think he might be in paradise. A yellow leaf floated to rest on his hat and another rested on his shoulder. He smiled at me out of the shadows.

"How do you live in the woods and not get lonesome?" I said. "This is far back in the mountains."

"The trees are my company," he said. "And the change of seasons. I have the fellowship of time."

I wanted to ask if he was Tracker Thomas. But I couldn't bring myself to out and say it. He seemed so peaceful and happy, and I didn't want to offend him. If he didn't want to tell me he was Tracker Thomas, I couldn't ask him.

"I've never been lonely but once," he said. "That was when I took a load of furs to Charleston. In the town and taverns I begun to feel awful lonesome. My ears felt like they was going to burst in the Low Country. Once we started back through the pine woods and got to Fort Ninety-Six, I begun to feel better. And the closer we got to the mountains, the better I felt. And when I seen the ridges again, I thought I was going to jump out of my skin with joy. These blue slopes looked like the ramparts of heaven itself."

He ignored his little terrier that kept Sue at bay. She stood still, like she was unaware of the tormenter. But I knowed she was stiff with fatigue like I was. We was soaking up the moments of rest like a thirsty man would cold spring water.

"Sometimes I just sing to myself and Powder," the old man said, and pointed to the dog. "I sing the old hymns and tavern songs for the joy of it. And the mountains echo the song back to me. A rock cliff will answer you word for word."

"Is Cedar Mountain straight head?" I said after a pause. It was past the middle of the afternoon. The shadows was bigger and reaching to join over the laurel bushes and trees.

"Some say it is," the old man said, like he had said at first.

"I don't want to get lost," I said. "Not this late in the day, after coming this far."

"I want you to get lost," the stranger said. "Can't really see where we are till we get lost."

"I've got to get home, and I've got to build a road."

"You don't have to do a thing," he said. "You're free to go where you please."

"I have promised to build a road across Douthat's Gap."

"You don't have to build a road," he said. "Of course, somebody will eventually. And next thing we'll have is wagons and dust, peddlers, new ground cleared and gullies washing every holler. The game will be gone, like the Indians is gone."

"It's just a matter of time," I said. "Somebody will build a road."

"I hope it's more time than I have," he said. But he didn't sound mad. He sounded peaceful and sad. It was like he was already grieving over the wilderness that would be gone.

Sue begun to lunge at the dog again. She side-stepped and suddenly darted around the terrier, like she had rested and got her spirit back. I just had time to grab her tail.

"Here, have this," the old man said. He held out a thick gold coin, which I took in my hatchet hand. It was the fattest, brightest gold you ever seen, thick as a biscuit.

"I found it," the stranger called as we was leaving. "It might be some use to you."

That gold piece felt heavy and soft as clay. I looked at it the best I could while running and dodging limbs. They was a picture of a king on one side and some foreign writing. But I couldn't look no more for I had to mark trees. The little dog was barking after us, but then dropped back. When I glanced back the stranger seemed to have gone.

"Much obliged," I hollered back.

The heavy gold coin warmed my hand as I swung the hatchet again and again, marking pines and poplars, cucumber trees and white oaks. The sun got hot again as we left the deep woods and run out the slope. The shadows was stretching on the open places. The big coin felt like it had a fire in it.

I glanced through the trees to see the mountains ahead. I had thought I had seen Caesar's Head way up there. But now they wasn't a thing familiar. It didn't seem like we had gone down hill. We was running out the same ridge. I couldn't figure out what had happened to the mountains there.

But Sue didn't seem confused at all. It was like she had got a second wind after breaking away from the terrier called Powder. She trotted fast as she had that morning. She darted around trees and stepped aside to miss a rock or stump. She run like she had had a night's rest, or like she'd had a lot of syrup and coffee.

"Slow down, old girl," I said.

But my voice seemed to spur her on, like I'd said "giddup," or "hie." I wondered if she would outrun me yet, if after all the way we'd come I'd have to give up and let go near at the end. It made me mad just to think of it, how people would laugh at me if the pig showed up in Cedar Mountain by herself and I had to come stumbling in the next day with my hatchet and my torn clothes.

"Whoa there," I said. "Whoa there."

But the widening shadows must have made her think of feeding time. As she approached the day-down, she thought of the end of her ordeal. The thought of rest and a trough full of slop made her run in spite of herself. But I wondered if she knowed where she was going anymore. I couldn't see nothing ahead when they was a break in the trees. I couldn't imagine where the mountains had gone. Mountains don't just up and melt away.

Then I thought maybe we had turned and was headed a different direction. Sue had swerved and lost the trail. I glanced around to see through the trees, and sure enough, it seemed like they was mountains off to my left. They looked further away than before. They had that misty look of faraway mountains. The ridge must have swung to the right as we was follering it.

"Whoa there," I said. But it didn't do no good. Sue was splitting through the trees faster than ever. Her legs was a blur as she found the quickest way through brush and around a big tree. Her hooves hit sure places in the leaves and found just the right paths between rocks and wind-throws.

Tracker Thomas had said he wanted me to get lost. It was like his suggestion put a spell on me. Because he said it, it was bound to happen. He didn't want no road across the gap, and he was still the ruling spirit of these woods. Had he give me the coin to confuse me, to distract me? The big coin shined in my hand like the reddest, newest gold.

Don't talk foolishness, I said to myself. If you got lost, you done it on your own. Had nothing to do with the old man or anything he said. But if we was lost, Sue didn't seem to realize it. She had her head and seemed to know know where she wanted to go. I couldn't hold her back now, any more than I could before.

We went under a big white pine where it was already dark. I felt something touch the back of my hand and thought it must be a pine needle or a cobweb. But when we come out in the light again I seen it was a black spider. It had a red spot on its belly like a black widow. I was going to fling my hand to throw it off, but seen it was gripping the hair on my skin. I was afraid if I shook it, it would bite me. Black widows can jump three or four feet and I was afraid it might hop right into my face. Didn't seem nothing to do but hold my hand out like I needed it for balance. I couldn't afford to rile the spider. A black widow bite won't kill you unless you're already sick or weak. Except the bite will kill a youngun or an old person. I was so tired I didn't know what the bite would do to me. I couldn't fling it off and I couldn't brush it off on a tree without getting bit.

We had come out on some kind of shelf-land, a level place that run out along the mountain above any creek or branch. I couldn't recognize a single landmark. I could see the ridge, but it didn't look familiar. I didn't see a thing I'd noticed before, back before I seen Tracker Thomas and his dog. It was like somebody had turned the country around and rearranged the slopes and trees. Either that, or my eyes was playing tricks. Or my memory was all twisted by the excitements and strain of the day.

"Where are you going?" I hollered at Sue.

But the woods soaked up my voice, and the hog sure didn't answer. She didn't slow down a bit. The fat coin burned in my hand against the hatchet, and I couldn't hack trees for a swing would make the spider bite. I thought of running my hand under leaves to knock it off, but it could bite the instant something touched it. It clung to the hair on the back of my hand.

I'd have to remember where we was going, since I couldn't make any blazes. Sue was pulling me rod after rod and chain after chain, and I couldn't mark the way. If I lived through this day, I would have to come back and mark that stretch better.

But I was lost, and I was tired. They was nothing I could do with the spider except not disturb it, and hold my hand far from my face as possible.

I begun to think strange thoughts. It seemed I couldn't tell uphill from down, and that I might be running to South Carolina, not up into the mountains. I imagined somebody was running under me, upside down, like a reflection, and every time my boots touched ground, they touched his boots. The earth was thin as the surface of water, and he was running on the underside.

And I thought of strange contraptions, of wagons that moved under sail like ships. And these wind wagons got all tangled up in the woods because they was good only in open country. And I seen a plow that was pulled by sails. It was a big turning plow, bigger than any I had ever seen. It turned over the dirt a foot down, twisting up a shiny belly of soil. And the plow was pulled by a thing on wheels, like a wagon, with a big sail on it that could be adjusted this way and that. A man rode in the wagon adjusting the canvas and guiding the big plow.

Then I thought of a gun that could be played like a trumpet. And the barrel could be filled up with whiskey and corked for a long trip. In my fatigue I seemed to remember it was the blockaders that caught me beside the pond and tried to torture me. And it was the Melungeon girls that was making whiskey and throwing out the mash that Sue drunk. It seemed like it was the old Melungeon woman that put the spider on my hand.

I blinked to wake up. The spider wasn't no dream at all. It was right there on the back of my hand, and it hadn't moved. I had to clear my head. I needed a dash of cold water in my face, but they wasn't any water and I couldn't reach my hand to it even if they was. I needed a cup of coffee and a hot biscuit. I needed some salve on my lip. I needed to sit down and rest and sleep. I could feel the sleep wanting to rise in me, like some kind of powders through my blood. The sleep was rising like a flood that wanted to float me away.

The spider looked like a shiny black jewel set on the back of my hand, spotted with red enamel. And it clung there as an extra big tick or flea would. But out of the corner of my eye it seemed like a drop of blood, a clot that had hardened and blackened.

Sue kept running along the shelf-land. She turned beyond a clump of laurels, and cut through an open space below some oak trees. Sometimes it seemed we was going in a northeast direction, and sometimes in a northwest. I tried to examine the shadows behind trees, but I couldn't stop, and couldn't look away from the spider on my hand for more than an instant. We seemed to be lost and getting loster.

But the black widow didn't move at all. I wasn't sure I could feel it. But I seen it there like a black eye surrounded by lashes. I tried to remember about black widows. Was they attracted to heat, the way rattlesnakes are? Did they like wet places, or dry places? Maybe it was the smell of exhaustion that attracted the spider. Maybe a spider can smell when a body is about to die. Like buzzards, they're drawed to a body near the breaking point. It's the same instinct that pulls a wolf to a sick buffalo or deer. Maybe the spider thought if it stuck to my hand a few minutes more it could feed to its heart's content.

I wondered if insects was attracted to the smell of metal. Was they a perfume coming off the coin that drawed the spider? Was my sweat mixing with the gold to make an aroma? Maybe the brightness of the coin fascinated the spider. But it didn't make any move to touch the gold. It stayed still on the back of my hand. I wondered if I flicked my wrist it would just drop off.

Just then the spider started crawling. It felt like a drop of water running on the back of my hand. The skin itched where the little feet moved. It walked out to the knuckles and around like it was looking for something. A spider moves not like it is rowing on its long legs, but like it is being poled by one leg after another, fast and separate. The black widow circled back and rested just below the wrist. I thought it was maybe going to jump. But I couldn't focus on it long because we had reached the end of open oak woods and was entering brush and weaving our way between saplings and sassafras bushes.

"Whoa there," I said in a low voice. But Sue didn't pay me no mind more than she ever had. I didn't want to holler loud because I thought it might upset the black widow.

It seemed like we was heading east now. I couldn't see anything ahead but deeper woods. I couldn't see how we was going to get through. The spider started crawling up my wrist. I wondered if it would crawl inside or outside my sleeve. If it crawled outside I could slap it off. If it crawled under the cloth I didn't know what I would do. I'd have to turn loose of Sue's tail. People get bit if a spider goes under their clothes. Just the binding of the cloth will make the spider bite.

In my confusion I stumbled against a chinquapin bush and those flame-shaped leaves must have been loaded with rain for they sent a shower down like somebody had throwed a bucket of water. When I looked I seen the spider had been washed off, but I couldn't see where it had gone. Had it jumped somewhere else on me? Sue kept right on going, and I didn't have time to stop and look.

I thought I seen that spider on my pants leg. Maybe it was just another drop of rain, but it shined like the drop at a thermometer's bottom. Then it was gone and I had to keep going. Every chance I got I looked down at my britches, but it was gone. Had it bit me and in the rush I had not felt the sting? I was already numb with fatigue. The rheumatism didn't feel as sore. Maybe the poison was spreading and I didn't even know it.

You're wondering why I kept going? It seemed like I had been running for a year. It seemed like I couldn't remember a time I hadn't been running. I wondered why I had ever even thought of building a road. I couldn't remember why it had seemed so important. They comes a point when ambition just seems to wash out of a man. It's like something changes in you and instead of looking ahead and bracing for projects and enterprise you see the sweetness of rest and modesty. You are ashamed or at least amused by your grand ambitions. You want to grow a quiet garden. You want to sit on the porch and talk to neighbors. You want to savor the minutes and hours, and protect yourself against age and weather. It's like they's some change deep in your makeup and a stream has been diverted way back up the valley.

But once I got rid of the black widow spider it wasn't just fatigue and loss of ambition that troubled me. It wasn't even shame at the foolishness of my scheme. The day was almost over. It was near four or five o'clock, and we was lost. We was loster than we had been all day. I didn't have no sense of direction anymore and Sue seemed to be going this way and that. When I got a chance to look for the sun, it was first over one shoulder and then over the other. I couldn't recognize anything, and the woods ahead just went on and on and got deeper and deeper.

"Where you going?" I said to Sue. But she didn't slow down. She was running on habit now. She had been running so long she couldn't stop. It was like she still had speed and it carried her forward. She run like it was easier to go forward than to quit. She run like she didn't care where she was going, like a dog that's been hunting all night and keeps trotting along because it's so far from home.

Everybody's life is hard. You show me somebody whose life ain't hard and I'll show you a dead man. The only thing that can get you through so much messiness and grief is a plan. Only trashy people just drift, and though they's a certain wisdom in drifting I don't see how they can stand it. How can anybody just loll around all day, with nothing to look forward to?

But I was so tired, I wasn't hardly at myself. The woods went on forever, with more trees, more thickets. The shelf-land was endless, and the mountains went on and on.

Boom! boom! boom! I heard off to my left. It sounded like a drum. I wondered if it was far-off thunder. Maybe they was going to be another storm. But Sue didn't seem to hear nothing, and she didn't slow down.

I heard it again, boom! boom! boom!, slow like somebody shooting pistols, a second or two between shots. It was like somebody had a dozen pistols, and was shooting them one after another. The sounds stopped and I wasn't sure I had heard them.

The leaves was drying out and rattling a little, covering up any sound in the distance. I couldn't see any clouds that would indicate another storm. And the air didn't feel like it was going to rain. In fact, the sky had cleared completely, and the air was getting warm again. I hit a laurel bush with my shoulder and it rattled and did not wet me.

The boom-boom-boom come again from the distance. It really sounded like a drum. But who would be beating a drum this far back in the mountains? The blows sounded like echoes, but timed so even it was hard to imagine thunder or even pistols making the noise. Could the Cherokee have come back and be having a war dance? a corn dance? Could they be having a rally for an attack?

Boom-boom-boom-boom, the sound come again. It was so regular it was scary. It was timed exactly to the blood beating in my ears. Could I be imagining the sound? Could it be a stroke coming on, or might it be a sound in the mountain? I'd heard of mountains that made noises, that groaned and knocked at certain times like they was having bad dreams. Singing mountains they was called. People thought they had caverns and waterfalls inside, or rocks that shifted around with the phases of the moon.

Boom-boom-boom-boom come over the horizon again, and then a couple of echoes follered up. Could they be an army marching through the mountains? I tried to think of the last militia that had been mustered. Not since the Battle of New Orleans had local folks marched under colors. The sound was ghostly. It was like something knocking against the sky. But I didn't believe no ghost army could be marching through the coves and hollers.

It come to me why the sound was so spooky. It was like somebody knocking at a door or gatepost. You hear knocking and you have to go see what it is. If somebody is rapping, you can't ignore it. But this was a big hitting, like something inside the mountain or inside the earth. And the sound filled the sky, running from one horizon to the other.

"Whoa," I said to Sue, because I wanted to stop and listen. "Slow down, old girl," I said. If I could stop and quiet my heart and the thumping in my ears I might be able to figure out the racket. I might make sense of it.

But Sue just kept trotting. And it sounded like the noise was getting louder and we was getting closer. But I couldn't be sure, because the bangs come from all around.

Maybe they's a war going on, I said to myself. Or maybe it's a shoot-out. Maybe they's a duel taking place. But I never heard any guns shoot so much or so steady. People come to the South Carolina line to fight duels, so they could run in either direction if the law showed up. But whatever it was, it wasn't regular gun shots, unless they was a brigade on each side.

I was so busy thinking about the big knocks I hadn't noticed we come to the end of the shelf-land. Suddenly Sue run into an open space under some big maples. The ridge bent around over what looked like a creek holler. I thought I could hear the seethe of water, though I wasn't sure, with the leaves rattling and the booming from over the ridge. That was when I realized we had been resting on the shelf-land. The level ground had made me forget how hard it was to run uphill. Without knowing it, I had been resting for the climb ahead.

Finally even Sue slowed down a little. The uneven ground cut her pace in half. She grunted and swung her weight from side to side. Boom-boom-boom-boom. The sound was even bigger, and much closer. It was just ahead of us somewhere, down near the creek. And now I could hear another sound. Besides the booms, they was a grinding noise, like something was being broke or crushed. I tried to guess what could make such a racket. I'd heard of fulling hammers that pounded cloth to make the weave closer and tighter. But nobody was weaving cloth back in the coves and beating it in a fulling mill.

The noise was so loud Sue paid attention now. She cocked her ears to the sound, and then flattened them the noise was so painful. It hurt my ears too. Each knock pressed on my head like a gust of wind. The knocks was so loud they seemed to ring inside my head.

"Whoa there," I said to Sue. She slowed down more but didn't stop. She seemed to want to turn away from the noise, but the only way to turn was further up the ridge. She was too tired to climb if she didn't have to. We kept going generally toward the awful sound.

T he hammering was so loud it seemed in my head. The ridges caused the booms to bounce back and magnify and multiply. When you're in the middle of a loud sound it feels like you're smothering. I don't know why a big noise will suck your breath away, like it squeezes your chest in a vise.

Suddenly we come around the ridge into sunlight, and Sue stopped at the rim of a high bank. I thought it was a cliff at first, we was up so high, but I seen it was just a high bank of rocks and dirt. Somebody had dug way back into the mountainside and left this blinding wall of rocks and dirt. You never seen such a mess of muddy rocks, mud holes and dirty logs and heaps of gravel as they was at the foot of the cut.

I was so busy looking for the source of the noise I didn't see the men at first. They was the color of the yellow dirt and mud, and I was half blinded by the glare of the sound. I noticed one, two, three of the men moving around the spoil of gravel and mud. They was coated with mud and dust, and when I looked closer, I seen they didn't have a stitch of clothes on.

It was hard to tell anything about the men, they was so covered in dirt. But it looked like one of them had long, blond hair, and the other two might be dark, Indians or gypsies maybe. They had shovels and hammers, and they was boxes and wheelbarrows filled with rocks. I figured they had to be mining something, but it was impossible to tell what. It didn't appear to be gold for they was no cradle and toms, and no sign of panning or washing gravel.

They didn't see me and Sue, standing way up on the rim of the cut. We had come to the end of our journey, for Sue didn't make any move to backtrack and they was no way to go forward. Half the hole below was in shadow, and I had trouble seeing into the darkest part. One of the men was rolling a barrow up to the head of the clearing, and I shielded my brow with the hatchet to see where he was going. Slowly my eyes adjusted, and I seen where the terrible noise was coming from.

It was a big waterwheel, but the crudest-built one you ever seen. It was made out of rough logs and saplings pegged and tied together. The wheel creaked as it turned and the buckets streamed water like white hair. But the wheel turned steady, lurching as it went round. And what it turned was this big wheel of wooden spokes, like a wagon wheel without a rim. Each spoke would push down the end of this log and raise the other end. On the other end was a big hammer. The hammer raised up and fell down with a deafening boom. That's what made the awful noise.

It was a triphammer, raising and falling as the spoke let it go. It was crude beyond describing, but it seemed to work. They put their rocks on that hammer and it smashed them to gravel. It come to me they had to be mining lead, or lead and silver, since the two almost always go together. And if they was mining lead, they had to be a furnace nearby where they melted it down.

Sure enough, smoke was rising through the trees further up the holler. I couldn't see no fire, but something was hot up there. You could smell the smoke and the heated rock. And it come to me if they was a furnace running, they must be more than three men at the works. Right then I got a bad feeling at having stumbled on the secret mine. No prospector likes his diggings discovered.

And I seen something else, just before I tried to get Sue to back away from the lip of the cut into the woods. I seen these old washpots and ladders throwed off to the side, and they looked like things made a hundred, or two hundred years ago. They had rusted and rotted, but you could tell they had laid there a long time. I'd always heard rumors that Spaniards had dug mines in these mountains, that they forced the Cherokees to dig for gold and silver. That reminded me of the thick coin in my right hand. Quick I pushed the big coin in my pocket. I didn't want nobody to see that money until I'd had a better chance to examine it myself. And I didn't want to lose the gift from Tracker Thomas.

"Back away, let's back away, old girl," I said to Sue. I pulled at her tail and she swung her head with irritation. "Whoa back," I said. But she was tired and stubborn, and she didn't want to backtrack. Maybe she was curious about what was going on below, or maybe she smelled the smoke and thought something must be cooking. She figured where they's men they will be something to eat. Men don't go into the woods to work without their rations.

"Back away, back away," I said. "We ain't got no business here." I grabbed her leg and pulled. But it's hard to move a hog. She had gone as far as she wanted to go and jerked away from my grip. I thought she might budge when the rheumatism stung my shoulder. And at the same moment I seen one of the men below pointing at us. I dropped to the ground, but Sue was pulling so hard she tipped right over the rim of the cut and jerked me after her. Next thing I knowed, the breath was knocked out of me. I rolled down that steep bank, ass over head, with the sky whirling and the hog first on top and then under me. All the woods and walls and mud was spinning. It felt like we rolled for miles on the sharp rocks before coming to rest in the mud with the dirty naked men standing over us.

Both Sue and me stumbled and lurched to our feet. After such a

fall and tumble, it felt my ribs was broke and every inch of my
body had a bruise on it. I was groggy as if it was three in the
morning. The men closed in, but it wasn't me they was grabbing
for. The three of them grabbed Sue as she struggled to stand up.

"She's a tame hog," I said, gasping to find my breath. "We was
surveying a road."

"We're surveying us some tenderloin," the tall man with the
blond beard said. "We're surveying us some ribs and ham roast."

"That hog is my property," I said. "And we're on our way to
Cedar Mountain."

"You ain't on your way nowhere but hell," the tall man said. He
and the Indians held Sue, one on each ear, one on the tail.

"Do you steal from anybody that comes along?" I said. I tried to
think of something to make them let us go. I owed it to Sue to not
let her be killed, even if we didn't get the road laid out. I don't
think nothing is as important as loyalty, even to a hog if it comes
to that. All law and order is based on loyalty.

"Ain't nobody else come along," the tall man said. "And we ain't
stealing; we're just borrowing, you might say."

I reached for Sue, but they pushed me away. I still had the
hatchet, but them fellers could see how weak I was. I was covered
with mud now as well as blood and sweat.

"Turn that hog loose," I said, trying to sound strong.

"You ain't in no shape to give orders, chief," the tall man said.
The two Indians laughed.

But I seen what their problem was. They couldn't secure Sue
unless they had a rope. But if one turned her loose to get a rope
then I might attack the others and she would get loose. To do
what they needed to, one had to attack me first and subdue me. I
watched to see how long it would take them to figure that out.

If the man at the furnace was to come back to the diggings,

their problem was solved. But the hammer made such a racket it wasn't no good to call him. I had the hatchet and could attack, but then they would kill me for sure, though Sue might get away.

"Here, chief, give me that hatchet," the tall man said. With the hatchet they could kill Sue and not need to go for a rope. "That hatchet won't do you no good," he said. "But it will do us a lot of good."

If I attacked them and they had to defend theirselves, they would lose the hog. And they was no advantage to killing me if they lost the sow. They was hungry men working out there in the woods, probably around the clock to get the lead and silver quick as they could. Under the dirt their ribs was showing.

"Let's discuss this with common sense," the tall man said. He kept looking up the creek to see if the fourth man might be coming. The shadows had now covered most of the pit, though the sun was still bright on the walls and woods above. It was a long, summer day and they would be two or three more hours of light. The banging hammer made the air seem crooked. Or maybe that was just the way I felt, that the air was all twisted and tangled up.

"What's your name?" the tall man hollered.

"I'm Solomon Richards," I said. "And I'm building a road through Douthat's Gap to Cedar Mountain."

"Solomon," he said. "You ain't going to build a road nowhere, not over this ridge. You're tired out and wounded. Give us that hatchet and we'll pay for the hog. We got plenty of silver."

But I knowed they'd kill me no matter what, because I had found their mine and could go back and tell where they was.

"I know what you're doing here," I said.

"Give us the hatchet and we'll give you a share," the blond man said. The Indians hadn't said nothing. I didn't even know if they spoke English or not.

I had to think of something quick. The fourth man might appear any second, or they might figure out they had to kill me before they could eat the hog. If one come for me, I'd have to kill him with the hatchet. Only one idea occurred to me.

I looked around the shadows of the clearing to see where they kept things. They was only heaps of mud and gravel, puddles and boxes, and paths made by the crude wheelbarrows. I couldn't see no tent, but it looked like a bark and brush lean-to stood at the edge of the trees. I figured that's where they kept the silver, and whatever guns they had. The silver might be buried in the leaves, but I figured it would be near where they slept.

I started running toward the edge of the woods. The mud was so deep I sunk to my ankles. The tall man come running after me. The mud sucked and spit where a foot touched. I was too tired to outrun anybody. Normally I could sprint fast as the next one, but I had gone too far, and too much had happened to me that day. I made my legs run, but it was like they belonged to somebody else.

"You can't get away," the tall man called after me. I didn't answer for I needed all my breath.

"They's no way out except up the cliff," the tall man hollered. At least that's what I thought he said. The hammer was banging so close my ears hurt and I couldn't be sure what I heard. But the naked man was gaining on me. I had on my boots and sweaty clothes and I was near wore out.

They was a bank at the edge of the woods where the shed was. You never seen such a crude camp, even among hunters or new settlers. They was just a fire with a stick over it for roasting turkeys or squirrels. And they was dirty pans laying around on the dirt. Some had cornbread in them and some had mush or grits. Didn't look like they had nothing to eat but cornmeal.

The lean-to was a kind of brush arbor, open where it faced the fire and clearing. They hadn't took the trouble to construct it.

They just piled brush and bark on a rough frame. Their blankets and stuff was scattered inside. It was so shadowy there, I couldn't see much. I was looking for a gun or rifle. I knowed they would have one somewhere. Nobody would go out into the woods like that without a gun to shoot game and defend their claim.

But what I seen was something else. They was a fringe of roots hanging on the edge of the lean-to. I thought at first they was rags, or maybe ramps. But they was shiny roots swollen as little sweet taters, some shaped like dolls and others like the private parts of a man. I knowed right then that was ginseng. They must have been two hundred roots there. These fellers was sang diggers that stumbled on the lead mine. That's why they had such crude equipment. They wasn't really miners at all.

The woods was full of sang diggers back then. In late summer they would start scouring the ridges and hollers, especially in the Flat Woods, and upper edge of South Carolina beyond the Big Springs. You had to find it while the leaves and berries was still on to recognize it.

Everybody that dug ginseng kept a little for theirselves. It was supposed to be a general tonic. It was supposed to pick you up. And some people said the Chinese took it to make them sexually powerful. That's why it was shaped like a man's private parts, to show what it was good for.

I knocked the roots aside to look into the shed, and one of the roots come off in my hand. But I didn't even think about it. I was too busy looking for a musket or rifle. They was clothes and a coffee pot, tow sacks and knives scattered. They was even a coffee mill. The tall man wasn't more than ten steps behind me.

Sure enough, they was a gun leaning in the corner and a powder horn and shot bag beside it. I grabbed the gun and pointed it at the blond man. I seen from his face it was loaded. Don't nobody keep a gun in the woods that ain't loaded.

"Chief, it wouldn't do no good to shoot me," he said, out of breath. "You would never get out of this hole alive."

"And neither would you." I had him there. I knowed he didn't care what happened to me if he was going to be dead first.

"Might as well talk," he said.

I aimed the gun low down, like it was pointed right at his naked crotch. I knowed that would make him more willing to talk. The Indians held Sue by the ears back at the bottom of the bank.

"We'll give you a share," the naked man said.

"Don't want no share," I said.

"Put down the gun and we'll just let you go, you and your hog," he said.

"No, you wouldn't," I said. My hands was so trembly I couldn't hardly hold the gun steady. "You got to make a better deal than that," I said. "You let my hog go and then we'll talk."

"We'll buy your hog," he said. "We's nigh starved here."

"Hog ain't for sale," I said.

I couldn't hardly hold the gun up no longer, but I hoped he didn't see my hands shaking. The musket was long and heavy.

"You let the hog go or I shoot," I said.

This was a mean feller, but he was worked down and stupid with hunger hisself. He wasn't in much better shape than I was.

"Let the dang hawg go," he hollered. The two Indians didn't do anything for a few seconds. They wanted the hog bad as he did.

"Let the hawg go," he hollered again, between hammer booms.

The Indians let Sue loose and she run right toward the woods upstream. She was headed toward the furnace and didn't know it.

"You stay right here," I hollered to the blond man. I wanted to catch up with Sue and grab her tail. But I had to hold the hatchet and the gun to cover myself. And I still had the piece of ginseng in my left hand. "You stay right there," I shouted.

"Ain't going nowhere, chief," he said. "And you ain't neither."

I run sideways, pointing the gun back at the tall man. He stood there dressed only in filth and watched Sue vanish into the trees like it was his last chance. He was saying something else, but I couldn't hear with the noise of the hammer. I noticed the two Indians had started edging around the clearing toward the woods. I guess they wanted to reach the trees before I did and cut me off. Or maybe they wanted to get up to the furnace and warn the man there. For all I knowed, he had a gun too.

Those men didn't have no privy down in the clearing and they had been using the edge of the woods. Everywhere I stepped was more filth. My feet couldn't avoid their dirt. I wanted to keep Sue in sight, but I had to keep the gun pointed at the tall man too. I walked as fast as I could and still keep him covered. The pounding of the hammer made my ears and head ache.

When I glanced ahead, I seen the fires of the furnace deep in the holler. It looked like an eye of light in the side of the mountain, two hundred yards up the stream. I could smell the smoke and the stench of fumes from the melting ore. A shadow passed in front of the fire.

The blond man was follering me into the woods. I hollered to him to stay back, but my voice was buried by the crash of the hammer. And I was too weak to gesture with the long musket. It was all I could do to hold the gun out level and not stumble.

As I got closer to the furnace, the flames was blinding. I seen figures running around, and it appeared the two Indians was trying to head off Sue. The place was such a mess it was hard to tell what was going on. They was piles of wood, and mounds of dirt where they had been making charcoal. It was charcoal they used in the furnace because the fire burned blue and white-hot.

The furnace was just a pit lined with rock, with a kind of shelf above where they loaded the ore. The fire was so hot it was like you could see ghosts in it. I thought of the three Hebrews in the fiery furnace. The heat pulsed and swelled and flowed like a stream over the coals out of some distant place.

They had made their equipment out of what appeared to be mud and clay. It was the crudest outfit you could imagine. They had molded a cauldron and spillway through which the melted metal run. It was a little stream of light pouring down a clay trough to the forms, also made out of mud. The furnace was going full blast, and the liquid fire flowed fast down to the molds in the dirt where they made bricks of silver and lead.

The three men had caught Sue and was holding her in the trees by the pile of wood. The tall man was still follering me. I was in a worse situation than I was before, 'cause now they was four of them. If I shot the blond man the others would still come after me. Or one would come after me, while the others held Sue. If I shot one of those holding the sow, I would still have to fight off the blond man. I was half-blinded by the furnace, and half-deafened by the hammer, and wasn't even sure what I was seeing.

As the tall man got closer I had to think quick. The heat from the furnace dazed me. The creek sparkled below the furnace and I wondered if I should dash across it and leave Sue to be eat by the miners. It was so dark in the woods beyond the creek, I might get away. It seemed like a laurel slick.

But I seen something below the furnace and beside the creek. It was a pile of shiny bricks. It must have been eighteen inches square and a foot high. It was the silver they had melted and molded. The molds was just above the pile, and the creek below.

The blond man was no more than twenty feet away. He seen the fix I was in and he must have knowed I didn't want to shoot nobody. "Give me that gun!" he shouted.

"Stand back," I said.

"Give me that gun," he ordered. "You can't get out of here."

I didn't have no idea what to do. I was blinded by the glare of the furnace and blistered by the heat from the charcoal. Without really thinking I swung the musket and aimed at the trough where the glowing metal was rushing into the molds. When I pulled the trigger, the spillway cracked and the fiery soup splashed out of the groove and spread on the ground. The hot ore run right to the stack of bullion and set leaves and sticks on fire wherever it touched. Surrounding the stack of bricks, it dashed on to the creek and exploded. The hot metal hitting the water turned to steam and spit scalding drops and beads of redhot silver every direction. I felt a pin or two of fire hit me and shielded my eyes.

The blond man run toward his pile of bullion and then hit the ground. I don't know if he was stung by flying metal or overcome with scalding steam. I didn't wait to see but dropped the gun and run around the charcoal pile and straight toward the dark woods. I didn't notice what had happened to Sue, but seen the three other men had dropped to the ground too. The air was full of flying drops as more metal poured into the creek.

I splashed across the stream above the furnace and tore my way into the laurels. My head hit limbs and I tore my pants but I kept running. I didn't know if they was coming after me, or if they was any way out of the draw, but I figured the more distance I put behind me the better it was.

Gradually my eyes adjusted to the dark thicket, and I could see to avoid brush and branches. With the hatchet in one hand and the piece of ginseng still in the other, I knocked limbs out of the way and ducked between big bushes. As the ground got steeper I found footholds on rocks and hooked my arm around saplings to pull up on. I used strength I didn't have to climb up out of that holler. I wormed under the worst bushes, and pulled myself up sideways in places. When I finally got to the top, I paused to listen. At first I couldn't hear anything but my breathing, and the boom of the hammer below. Then I heard a grunting and scratching in the leaves about a hundred feet below me.

The laurels was so thick I couldn't see a thing. But the scratching and growling continued. I was so tired from the climb it felt like my body was glowing. You know that feeling you get when you've strained, like all your muscles are humming and hot, and would shine in the dark like hot iron. I wasn't sure I could make my legs do what I wanted them to anymore.

The root of dried ginseng was still in my left hand. It had got dirt on it when I had grabbed hold of the ridge to pull myself up. All my life I'd heard how sang would give you energy, how it would make the old feel young again, how it acted like a stimulant and tonic. I was hungry enough to eat anything. I rubbed the dirt off with my sleeve and bit into it. I expected it to taste like it looked, like a dried sweet tater. But the taste was at once sharper and milder. It was a mixture of tastes and smells. The flesh was dry and tough, but it made my tongue and jaws feel better, once the fiber mixed with spit. I tore off a little with my teeth and chewed it like birch bark. It occurred to me I was eating a dollar's worth of sang root.

The scratching and grunting got closer, and sure enough Sue come heaving out of the laurels. I was so glad to see her tears come. "You couldn't leave old Solomon to go home by hisself," I said. "No sir, you couldn't let me do it by myself." But I knowed she was just trying to get out of that pit, same as I was.

When Sue got close, I put the sang root in my mouth like it was a cigar and grabbed her tail with my left hand. We was near the top of the ridge. I thought she might stop at the ridge comb in confusion, but she didn't even pause. She turned to the right just like she was on a familiar path, and we was off again.

When I started walking, I felt the awful soreness and stiffness in my knees. But it was like a fact that didn't matter no more. A warmth and lightness spread through me right to the tips of my toes and fingertips. I knowed it must be the sang. It was not a feeling of intoxication. It was more like a good meal after you're tired and hungry. I could feel my strength coming back.

As I run behind Sue I chewed on the piece of ginseng, holding it in my lips and teeth. I would suck spit through the end. That spit tasted at once like pepper and musk and ginger. Every time I swallered I felt the heat flowing out through me. The strength spread to my arms and legs. I starting blazing trees again. I wished I could give Sue a bite of the sang, but they wasn't no way. She seemed to be getting a second wind herself, and picking up speed as we run along the top of the ridge.

"That's a girl, that's a girl," I said as we run. I chewed and sucked the end of the root like it was a sugartit, like it held mother's milk. The more I sucked the better I felt. Maybe the Chinamen know what they're talking about, I thought. It come to me that there *was* wisdom in the East. They knowed about ginseng like the Arabs knowed about coffee. I thought, you could learn a little bit on your own, but you could learn the most from other people, if you listened to what they told you. Everybody together knowed more than any one person could.

We come down out of the woods into a pennyroyal meadow. Upper end of the clearing was what is called a ramp cove, and I could smell the wild onions as our feet crushed the tops. People like to climb up into ramp coves and dig them in the spring, though I always thought they was too strong for my taste.

Around the edges of the clearing was wild peavines. Used to be whole mountainsides was covered with wild peas. You couldn't get through them in the spring, so many bees was on the blooms. I don't know what happened to all them vines, unless where they growed over was the first places cleared up. The earliest settlers must have set fire to the dried vines in the winter and had a ready-cleared field. I think the vines growed up where the Indians had burned over the woods doing their firehunting. Where the ground was cleared, I guess the peavines just took over.

They was a little group of people out in the middle of the meadow. I didn't see them at first in the thickening shadows. The sun was near the top of the ridge to the northwest and much of the opening was in shadow. They was three people in the group, an older man and two boys. They stood around a cloth laid on the pennyroyal, and they was so intent on something on the cloth they didn't notice me and Sue coming. The sow headed right toward them and of course they wasn't nothing I could do to stop her.

"Whoa," I said, to give them warning when we was about seventy-five feet away. "Whoa, old girl."

The boys and man spun around like they expected Indians. Sue run right to them, going toward the cloth. She must have thought they had a picnic spread there. I wondered if they was having some kind of ceremony. Something attracted Sue's nose.

"Stop that hog," the man said.

"She ain't going to hurt nothing," I hollered.

"Stop that hog," he said again.

The two boys grabbed Sue, one on each ear, just as she reached the cloth.

"She wants to get the honey," the man said.

Sure enough, they was a little bowl of honey on the cloth. These was bee hunters, trying to corner bees.

"Do you see it?" the old man said.

"Yeah, I see it," the older boy said.

They was a bee flying up over the bowl of honey. You could see it clear against the white cloth. It danced around in the light.

"Watch him now," the old man said.

After the bee rose away from the sheet it was harder to see. But once the bee got up into the late sunlight it looked like a black and gold bullet. It turned this way and that, its wings blurring like little puffs of breath.

"There, he's going," the younger boy said.

"No, he ain't," the old man said. "He ain't ready yet." The bee flew in half circles, stabbing one direction then the other.

"Maybe the sun's in his eyes," the older boy said.

"Hush up," the man said. "We've got to watch close."

The bee swung to the left and to the right, and I seen a daytime moon behind it. The moon looked like a piece of ice floating under water way up there. It made me shiver in my sweat.

"There he goes," the man hollered. He pointed to the trees and up the ridge. "You foller him," he said to the taller boy. "You foller him past that poplar yonder on the ridge."

"You want me to let aloose the hog?" the older boy said.

"Forget the hog," the man shouted.

The boy lit out across the meadow the way his grandpappy pointed. The man started gathering up the honey bowl and sheet and the ax that laid in the weeds. "Here, help me," he said.

The younger boy turned loose of Sue's ear. She hesitated a moment, not realizing she was free.

"You get that hog away from here," the old man said.

"I don't want to bother you all," I said. "I'm busting out a way for a road."

"You look like you been busted out yourself," the man said. He reached into one of the buckets and handed me a piece of honey-comb. The comb was dripping with golden honey. I took the piece in my hatchet hand. "I thank you," I said.

"Ain't nothing but clover honey," the boy said.

I licked the comb and sucked off as much honey as I could. The honey was so sweet it burned my mouth. Maybe the ginseng had left my mouth a little raw, and my lip was sorer than ever. The honey tasted so good it hurt. The spit in my mouth ached.

Just then Sue realized she was free and jumped ahead, jerking me along. I smeared honey in my beard but I didn't drop the comb and I didn't stumble. I had to skip a few times to keep up.

The man and boy headed across the pennyroyal meadow with their buckets and cloth to take aim from another corner.

"I thank you," I said again, as Sue started running for the woods. I found myself stepping as though by habit. The ginseng had took away some of the pain and soreness. But I felt like I was a puppet and my legs was pulled by strings. I could run but I was no longer in control of my running. I could only foller the habit we had set. Sue trotted straight for the woods, right of the place the taller boy had gone.

I wished I had asked the bee hunters where we had come to. That showed how tired I was. I wasn't hardly at myself anymore. Here I was, completely lost, and I hadn't thought to ask the way to Cedar Mountain. Maybe I was afraid they'd say I was close to the Georgia line, or that they never heard of Cedar Mountain. But we was already headed into the woods and it was too late.

My feet was sore and I wondered if the skin had been rubbed off by all my walking and running. It felt like my socks was just shreds. My boots had been wet all day, and grit had got in them when I rolled into the muddy pit. Sand was cutting into the balls of my feet, but they wasn't a thing I could do about it.

I put the rest of the honeycomb in my mouth and sucked the marrow from the cells. Honey run down my chin, and I licked my lips, tasting the salt of sweat and dried blood. But the honey was so sweet and powerful I could feel it working inside me. It was like I had swallowed a light, and could feel the shine going through me, follering the ginseng. I was so empty my body had nothing to go on. The honey lit its way right through my belly and chest, and out into my legs and arms and fingertips.

The belly feels good if it has timber to warm it, something to work on. I don't think I had a peppercorn of energy left when I eat that honey. Even after the honey was sucked out, I kept chewing the comb.

"Where you going, old girl?" I said to Sue. She was running a little sideways again. I wondered if one of her hooves was cracked. She seemed to be favoring her right front foot. But she was trotting so fast I couldn't see nothing. I fancied I seen blood on her hoof, but it could have been my imagination, or my tired eyes. I didn't trust my eyes anymore.

"You done got us lost," I said to the sow. I was talking to myself, like you do when you're real tired, or half asleep. "You've done got us lost and the day is almost over."

I tried to think of some way to get my bearings. The sun was off to my left, but I only seen it when we come to an opening and light laid a floor of gold between the shadows. It was too dark to notice moss on the sides of trees. I tried to remember if they was some rule about where the moon would be in the sky. It depended on the time of year, but I couldn't think clear about it. Everything was running together in my head.

The woods was darker and stranger than ever. It seemed like they was a black wall ahead of us; a few more hundred feet and we wouldn't be able to go no further. I couldn't tell if it was a ridge or a line of trees. But it seemed like we had come to a wall and they was nothing beyond it.

I didn't even care if we had to stop. If we come to a final barrier, we could just sink down and rest in the leaves. I would lay down and sleep all night and then find my way in the morning. Nothing seemed as sweet as just to settle into the leaves and earth. To give up the sweating and panting, seemed the best thought I could dream of.

But Sue didn't slow down. If they was a wall ahead, she didn't seem to know it. She run on and on and the wall seemed to retreat, keeping its distance as we run toward it. Was it a cloud? Was it a further range of mountains?

Then suddenly we come out of the hardwoods into a line of white pines. The brittle lower limbs looked impossible to get through, but Sue plunged right between them and let me prick and lash myself on the stiff twigs. You don't see a grove of white pines generally out in the mountains. They grow in stands where a field has been cleared and then growed up. In the deep woods you'll see a white pine here and there, but not a great grove of them. Pines can't spread like that in a standing oak woods.

Sue jerked me into the musky bristling dark. It was shadowy as night under the great trees. I could just barely see the trunks ahead, but the sow darted among them like she had cat eyes. The trees was so tall and dark it seemed like running through caverns under the earth, or mines held up by posts. I could hear wind sighing in the limbs above.

Son, it's mostly our fancies that keep us going. We have to believe we can do great things even to accomplish little things.

But in them pine woods I couldn't recall clearly what my fancy was, or why I thought I could build a road. Neither the impulse nor the image would come back to me. I couldn't remember who I thought I was to do such a thing. They had always been a voice in my head telling me what I could do, but I couldn't hear it no more. The sow was grunting, and they was my own grunts, and the moaning in the trees overhead. It was like I was under an ocean.

I was so lost in my thoughts and my desire to quit and rest, I didn't even notice we had come to the end of the pine woods until Sue burst out of the shadows into a little clearing. It looked like a field that had been mowed and was growing up again in a second cover of hay, a rowen some people call it.

Somebody hollered at us across the opening. A girl was running at us across the grass. "Help," she hollered, out of breath. She was barefoot and running with her arms full of weeds, and her fiery red hair flew in all directions.

"He's been snakebit," she panted, running up to me.

"Who's snakebit?" I said. She run alongside of me.

"It's my brother," she said. "He got bit."

"Where is he?" I said.

"Over yonder with Sallie," she said and pointed toward the end of the field. "He's with my sister Sallie." I seen another girl way over there bent above somebody sitting on the ground. Sue's path was in that direction but off to the side.

"Did you cut the bite?" I said.

"We ain't got no knife," she said. "We was gathering simples today. Mama sent us out to get some yarrow. Sam was pulling up yarrows in the weeds and the snake bit him."

"What kind of snake?"

"A rattler. Sam didn't hear it I reckon, 'cause he's deaf."

"How long ago did he get bit?" I said, trying to make up my mind what to do. I didn't have a knife neither. All I had was the hatchet.

"Just a few minutes," she said. "Please help Sam."

Sue was tending to the right of the figures in the field. If she kept going straight, we would miss them by a hundred feet.

"Please help," the girl said. She had her arms full of yarrow which people then gathered and sold to medicine companies. She held onto the bundle of weeds like it was a baby.

"See if you can stop Sue," I said.

"Stop who?"

"See if you can stop the hog," I said.

I seen that girl hesitate for a second, and then she throwed down the yarrow and run in front of Sue. But the sow darted to one side. The girl run alongside and grabbed Sue's ear. I pulled on the tail, and thought for an instant it was going to work.

But Sue jerked her head and flung the girl off. The girl tripped on her own feet and went rolling in the grass, her skirt getting tangled up around her waist and hips.

I had to decide quick. A few minutes before, I had been thinking of quitting all together, of just sinking down to rest and letting the hog go on. But now that somebody was demanding I stop, it was hard to let Sue go. After all I had gone through, it seemed impossible I couldn't finish the survey, or at least try to finish it, before sundown. They might be another hour of light.

The girl gathered herself up from the grass and run after me again. "Could you let me borrow your knife?" she said.

"Ain't got a knife," I said.

"Then let me borrow your hatchet," she said. When I started out that morning the hatchet had been sharp enough to shave with. But after slashing at bark all day and hitting into the dirt and rocks I doubted it would slice skin over a snake bite. We was getting toward the closest point I would to the other girl and the snakebit boy. I thought about my road and my plans and I seen they wouldn't be worth nothing if I couldn't stop and help somebody bit by a rattler. They wasn't no road that important.

And it come to me in that instant that Mary wouldn't marry me just because I surveyed and built a road. That was a young boy's fantasy. That was the way we think in daydreams. If she married me, it would be because she wanted me. What woman would marry a man just because he built a road? I seen that building the road was my condition, on myself. Even Professor MacPherson wouldn't much care whether I built the road or not. And didn't matter if he did. People that pegged their approval on whether you done this or that didn't matter either. If the road was meant to be built, it would be, and if Mary meant to be my wife, she would be. I let loose of Sue's tail and run over to the boy in the grass.

His hair was red as his sister's, and it fell all over the place in curls. But his face was white as a saucer, and sweat stood out on his forehead big as blisters.

"Where is the bite?" I said, looking at his bare feet.

He held out his arm and I seen the two fang marks on the back of his hand. His wrist had turned red and was beginning to swell.

"I'm gonna die," he said.

"You ain't going to die," I said. "The bite is far from your heart and far from your head."

"Are you a doctor?" Sallie said.

"No, I ain't a doctor," I said. "But I'm a Richards, and Richardses all have medicine in their blood." I wiped the hatchet on my shirt and felt along the blade. The steel had been dulled and dented. They was only one place, right at the bottom corner, that was still sharp. I didn't know if it was sharp enough to cut the boy's skin, but I didn't have time to hesitate.

It's harder to cut right into human flesh than it seems. If you think about it, you can't do it. It must take doctors and surgeons a long time to learn to slice somebody's flesh without trembling. I took the boy's hand and pushed down hard with the corner of the blade. He screamed and tried to jerk his hand away.

"Hold him down," I said to his sisters. Their yarrows was scattered all around, and they stood watching me. They bent down and held him, one on each shoulder. My arm was trembling it was so tired and sore with rheumatism.

"Hold him down hard," I said. "Hold tight to both his shoulders and arms. Don't let him jerk."

I pushed the corner of the blade down on Sam's hand and this time the skin broke. Quick, I made three more cuts, a little deeper than scratches. Blood begun to darken the marks and ooze out. I had to decide if I was going to suck the wound or not. If you don't have a sore in your mouth and you spit the blood out, it won't hurt to suck a snakebite. But if you have a sore, it will poison you, same as the person bit. I had the hole in my lip but I thought I could cover it with my tongue and spit quick. I put my mouth to the back of Sam's hand and sucked till I tasted blood. Then I spit in the grass. I sucked two more times.

The hand was red and swole up even bigger, but it looked white around where I had sucked. Blood kept oozing out of the cuts.

"I can tear a rag off my dress and tie it around his hand," the older sister said. All the children was red-haired. They had hair of the darkest copper.

"No, let it bleed," I said, "to rid of more poison."

But some of the venom must have already got into the rest of Sam's body for he said he felt numb and cold.

"Don't you go to sleep," I said. I could see that his eyes was closing a little. But he couldn't hear nothing you said.

"I feel sleepy all over," he said, and shivered. He felt hot, like he had took a fever. Maybe that's what poison does to a body, gives you a fever like any infection does, the way pain makes you feel hot.

"Stay awake," I said. "You've got to stay awake."

"What we need is some liquor," I said to the sisters.

"I can run to get some," the younger sister said.

"Don't we want some snakeroot?" the older sister said.

"You have to make tea from it," I said.

"Mama will boil some tea," the younger sister said.

And it come to me, what the old-timers talked about for rattlesnake bite. It was tincture of lobelia. That's what they give people, lobelia leaves soaked in whiskey. Everybody kept a bottle. Lobelia cut the fever and the swelling.

"Run get some tincture of lobelia," I said.

"Tincture of what?"

"Of lobelia. Just ask for lobelia."

The younger sister run off across the meadow the way Sue had gone. She had forgot her yarrows, and run as only a kid can run, like she could reach the ends of the earth in a few minutes.

"Let's get him up," I said. I tried to lift Sam, and seen how weak I was. It was like my muscles had been glued stiff.

"You get his other arm," I said. With great effort we lifted him. It's always shocking just how heavy a body is.

"Can you stand up?" I said loud in Sam's ear. But he seemed groggier than ever. "You help us to walk," I said.

With me practically carrying him on one side and the older sister on the other we started across the field a step at a time. Sam was almost asleep on his feet. "Keep walking," I said. "You're doing good."

I assumed we wanted to go the same way the younger sister had run, and we started off in that direction moving a few inches at a time. I left the hatchet in the grass with their piles of yarrow. I needed both my hands to hold up Sam.

"Where did he get bit?" I said.

"Right over there by the woods," the older sister said. "Where we was pulling up yarrows. He was so scared he run out here."

"And Sam don't hear good?" I said, gasping with the strain.

"He don't hear at all in his left ear. Ever since he had the fever, he's been half deef. He had the fever same time Pa did, except it killed Pa."

"Who was your Pa?"

"He was Ewell Maybin, the song leader. After he died, Mama and us started gathering simples. It was something us younguns could do besides hoe corn. At first we gathered stuff that wasn't worth nothing. Then we learned the shape of leaves. We get weeds and roots and dry them and Mama sells them to a man from Asheville."

Sam was getting heavier with each step, and the woods at the end of the field didn't seem much closer.

"Does anybody have a wagon?" I said. I couldn't carry Sam much further. He was near asleep and leaning his head on my shoulder.

"Mama don't have no wagon," the sister said. "We don't even have a horse no more. We borrow a horse to break the ground and then we make a crop with the hoe. And we get in simples."

We stopped to rest for a little. "Stay awake, Sam," I said. "Sam, can you hear?" His head lolled over on my shoulder.

"How far is it to your house?" I said.

"It ain't too far, after we get to the end of the Blue Field."

"The Blue Field?" I looked around the meadow and I seen it really was the Blue Field. I hadn't recognized the place before.

That showed how tired and dull I was. And then, I had never come at the Blue Field from the south. It looked strange in the late sun. But sure enough, it was the Blue Field, now that I noticed it. It was about a mile below Douthat's Gap. It was the last clearing before the wilderness of upper South Carolina.

They called it the Blue Field because somebody had once growed indigo there, way back in the time of the first settlements. I still remember some of the blue pots they used to boil the stuff down. They was big washpots. Along in late summer, about this time of year, they would cut the stalks and boil them in these pots. What they had left, after they took the fiber out, was this black-looking water. When they boiled the water down, it left nothing but powder hardening to bricks. All you had to carry out to market was those black bricks. Indigo was black as soot in its boiled-down form. But one of those bricks would dye hundreds of yards of material. When I was a boy I used to think the blue of the indigo come from the mountains. These was called the Blue Ridge, and I figured the roots of indigo went down into the soil and sucked up the ink that give the mountains their color.

Since I knowed now where we was, it was just a matter of going for help. But the Blue Field is on the other side of the gap from Cedar Mountain. If somebody closer didn't have no tincture of lobelia, it might take an hour to run down to the settlement and back. It was a long, uphill walk to the Maybin house.

Sam had quit walking and was dragging his feet. His head leaned all its weight on my shoulder. "Sam," I said. "You got to stay awake." I shook him and he opened his eyes a little.

"Want to sleep," he said.

We stopped a minute to rest ourselves. If I had not been so tired, I would have carried him up the hill.

"Why is he so sleepy?" his sister asked.

"It's like he's had a lot of bee stings," I said. "You've heard how somebody stung by a swarm of bees will sleep thirty hours. It's the poison I guess." I didn't say they often go to sleep and don't wake up.

The sun was getting so low, the weeds and grass seemed lit from underneath. It was like we was walking on a field of light. I shook Sam again. "Look at the grass," I said.

He rolled his eyes and muttered.

We got slower and slower, but finally come to the edge of the field. It was all in shadows, and I couldn't see after having the sun in my face. "Where's the trail?" I said.

"It's right up here, sir," the sister said. They was a rut through the weeds and underbrush into the woods. I didn't see how we could walk one on each side of Sam, the trail was so narrow.

"We're liable to get bit by a copperhead," I said. "They're crawling blind this time of year."

I tried to think of some other way to carry him. I wondered if I could walk in front and hold his arms over my shoulders while he leaned on my back. Maybe she could hold him up from behind. "Let me get in front," I said. "You hold him from the back."

But he was leaning so limp I had to bend forward and pull him onto my back like he was a sack of cornmeal. I leaned over and carried him a ways, but they wasn't much the sister could do to help. I seen I couldn't go far that way. I was too sore and wore out myself, and the rheumatism in my shoulder hurt too much. I was straining my blood and marrow for strength I didn't have. I went a few more steps and stopped, off balance and about to fall.

"I have to rest," I said. "See if you can keep him from falling."

She caught Sam under his shoulders and we just managed to lay him down on the trail without falling ourselves. "Wake up,

Sam," I said, and shook him. Just then we heard steps on the trail ahead and here comes the younger sister with a jar in her hand.

"All Mama's got is this liquor," she said. "She sent to see if Old Man Stamey had any of that other stuff."

"Give me the jar," I said.

I unscrewed the lid and held the jar to Sam's lips. He had gone back to sleep soon as we laid him on the trail. "Wake up, wake up," I said. "You've got to drink this." I held his head up with my left hand and tipped the jar to his lips. It was corn liquor and had an oily look, like they was things coiling around in it. But they wasn't much of a bead on the liquid when I shook it. Somebody had sold Mrs. Maybin weak liquor.

"Take a sip of peartening juice," I said. Some of the liquor slopped into Sam's mouth and his eyes popped open. I guess the whiskey burned his mouth and throat.

"Drink all you can," I said. "It will make you feel better."

"Is he drinking any?" the younger sister said. She was bent over with her hands on her knees trying to catch her breath. Sam started coughing. Maybe he got some of the liquor in his wind pipe, or maybe the liquor made his throat raw. His whole body stiffened with the effort of coughing and his face turned red.

"Don't let him get strangled," the older sister said.

"At least the coughing will help wake him up," I said. I looked up and the woods had got darker. The only light was in the tops of the trees. Dew was forming on the weeds and grass.

"Maybe all three of us can carry him," I said. "You both can take his feet and I'll carry his head and shoulders."

"You don't look able to carry nothing," the older sister said.

When Sam stopped coughing, I give him another drink from the jar. "Do you think you can walk?" I said.

But he laughed like I had said something funny.

"He don't know what you're saying," the older sister said.

"Give me some more of that God-blessed good medicine," Sam said. I tipped the jar for him to take another swaller.

"That's what Mama gives for the croup," the older sister said. "Whiskey and honey."

"Give him some of this," a voice said. A woman followed by an old man walked out of the shadows on the trail.

The old man had what looked like a wine bottle or a blueing bottle full of murky liquid. "Give him a swaller of this," he said, and pulled the cork out. "This is tincture of lobelia."

I held the bottle to Sam's lips and he drunk a little, but I could see he didn't like the taste.

"Drink it," Mrs. Maybin said. "It'll fight the snake poison."

"I even put a little laudanum in it," Old Man Stamey said. "That'll make him feel better. They say more people die of fright from snakebite than die of the venom."

They was no doubt Sam was feeling better.

"Son, can you walk?" Mrs. Maybin said.

"I want to kill that rattler," Sam said.

"That snake is long gone," Old Man Stamey said.

"Had sixteen rattles," Sam said. "Sixteen and a button."

We raised him on his feet and he swayed like a willow limb. Mrs. Maybin took him by the shoulder and pushed me aside. "You don't look in no shape to hold anybody," she said. The two girls and his Mama held up Sam and we started up the path.

"We'll probably step on a copperhead," Old Man Stamey said.

"I'll walk in front to scare the snakes," I said.

"You'll rile them up so they will bite me," he said.

The path was dark now, but they was still light in the trees above, and in the sky where stars was seeping out like grains of salt away from the moon. I held the jar of whiskey in the hand that was sore from gripping the hatchet all day.

"I know who you are," Old Man Stamey said behind me. "You're Solomon Richards, the feller that wants to build a road through Douthat's Gap. We seen your hog come through about an hour ago."

"Where was she headed?" I said.

"Looked like she was hoofing it for Cedar Mountain."

The weeds was wet with dew. My boots swished the damp leaves.

"Nobody thought you'd make it back here," Old Man Stamey said. "You follered that sow all the way across Dark Corner?"

That was the first time it come to me we had made it back. I had been so worried looking after Sam, I had forgot about the survey. And I was so give-out, I wasn't hardly at myself. It didn't seem to matter. The project didn't seem hardly real anymore, there in the dark, for I had give up. When you give up something you ain't prepared for success.

"You seen my razorback named Sue?" I said over my shoulder.

"Like I said, she come through about an hour ago just heading lickety for Cedar Mountain," Old Man Stamey said.

"Then she knowed her way," I said.

"She knowed her way to Cedar Mountain. Everybody that seen her wondered what happened. They thought maybe you got lost."

I walked slow and steady through the leaves. I figured I'd give any copperhead time to get out of my way.

"Wake up, Sam. Wake up, son," Mrs. Maybin said behind me. They had stopped in the trail and I had to go back to them.

"Wake up, Sam," Mrs. Maybin said. She slapped her son's cheek.

"He can't keep his eyes open," the older sister said.

"Maybe it's the liquor," Mrs. Maybin said.

"Is he sweating?" Old Man Stamey said.

Mrs. Maybin put her hand on his forehead. "He's a little damp," she said. "He's beginning to sweat."

"That's the lobelia," Old Man Stamey said. "He's sweating out the poison."

But Sam was so weak and sleepy, it was clear he couldn't walk no further. It was about dark and we still had almost a mile to go. "We'll have to carry him," I said. "Me and Mrs. Maybin will get his shoulders, and the rest of you hold his waist and feet."

It was awkward. My arms was trembly and my knees too sore to carry any burden. But we heaved him up and started. I had to grit my teeth with the effort. I shouldn't have been able to help after what I had done that day. But I guess it was the thought of making it back after everything that kept me straining. When you think you can't go no further, it turns out you can. And then you find you can go further still. Nobody knows what they can do till they have to. I could smell myself in the dark and I had a rank smell of work and exhaustion. It was a sweet smell.

We carried Sam to the little Maybin house beside the trail, and I headed on to the gap.

"You can rest the night at my house," Old Man Stamey said.

"I'm too close to stop now," I said.

The moon throwed some light on the trail ahead. And I could see the steep sides of the gap going up like walls to the sky. I thought of the butterflies that come through the gap on certain years. They come in so many millions of orange and black they looked like leaves flying through the narrow passageway. It would take them hours to get through. The moon made me think of the big gold coin in my pocket. It was still there, though gritty with dirt and sticky with sweat. I took it out and the gold flashed in the moonlight.

III

THE TURNPIKE
1845

oney, it was always hard for me to come to the end of a job. It was getting up toward dark and I still couldn't bring myself to leave the cut where we had worked so many months. A few yellow leaves floated down into the turnpike from the poplars way up on the ridge, beyond the top terrace and shelf we had dug. I picked splinters of meat off the bones of the pig and eat the last morsel of the barbecue. And then I throwed all the mess of bones and sticks and half-burned wood over the bank and watched them slide far into the weeds and brush below. The ridge down there looked like the scar of a landslide, like the guts of the mountain had give way and spilled all the way to Terry Creek and dried to a scab.

I found more sticks to pick up, and papers people had dropped at the ceremony. I wanted the turnpike to look perfect when it was opened for traffic the next morning. My hands was sticky with the grease of the pig, and I tried to wipe them on the new grass. I wanted to keep the grease off my good suit of clothes. I climbed up one of the terraces to see how the cribwork and walls of wattles and gabions was holding. Everything was tight as a barrel and weeds and grass was beginning to grow on the new dirt. By the next spring pine seedlings would begin to spark the shelves. Every foot of space we had measured and shoveled with the chaingangs would be covered in a few years by trees.

The sun was low over Corbin Mountain and edging into Painter Gap. And still I couldn't bring myself to leave the site. I guess I was savoring the end of the job. The pleasure of walking through the cut with the gold rattling in my pocket was too sweet to end. The mountain had fought me all summer, and I was tickled to be standing in victory over the finished cut. The weather had not beat me, and the mud had not beat me, and Mr. Lance and his crooked ways had not beat me. Most important, the mountain had not beat me. I looked down at the holler where the old turnpike went. The new road swung like a king's procession through the cut and around the mountain in an easy grade.

Finally I knowed I would have to go, if I was to get back to the Lewis house in time for supper. Me and Miss Lewis was going to tell her parents that night we was to be married. And I would pay Mrs. Lewis mine and Noble's bill for the summer.

I thought to take the trail one last time back to the Lewis house. For the rest of my life I would be traveling the new turnpike through the gap. The trail was a kind of shortcut through the woods, and I could gain some time by going that way. All my tools was already back at the house.

Part of the trail was covered up with spoil dirt, and I slipped around the brush and blackberry briars, trying not to pick my good clothes on the stickers. The trail, once I reached it, dropped quick out of the sunlight. I couldn't even see at first, and had to let my eyes get used to the shadows. Ain't nothing darker than a laurel thicket, unless it's a cave. The bushes growed right over the trail, shading out whatever light got through the trees above. The woods smelled sour the way leaves do right after frost has hit them.

I was going down the steep zigzag of the trail, jumping from side to side, when I heard this terrible scream in the trees above. It sounded like a woman in childbirth. It was the kind of squall that tears through you and hurts the middles of your bones. I knowed it was a painter, a big painter.

I stopped for a second and heard it drop heavy out of the trees, and pad along the ground in an odd pattern of steps. It come to me that was a three-footed animal. A painter with four legs runs like any other cat, but this one sounded one, two-three, one, two-three. A shudder went through me. It was Old Tryfoot that I had caught in a trap four years before, way over on the yon side of Pinnacle.

Painters don't never attack grown people in daylight. But it was already dark in the holler. I could just see to find my steps. I started walking, and the pad of feet follered me, one, two-three, one, two-three. The painter was coming on steady. I tried to think what to do. Was it better to run, or slow down and make the painter think I wasn't afraid of it? Dogs could be bluffed that way, but I didn't know about a painter.

The grease was sticky on my hands and I seen it was the smell of meat that had drawed the cat. I reckon I had the smell of barbecue all over me. I eat barbecue like a youngun eats watermelon. It had got on my clothes and in my hair, like as not.

The painter climbed up in a tree behind me and shook it like they was a big storm. I wondered if it was going to jump from tree to tree right down on me. Could be Old Tryfoot remembered me. I couldn't see nothing but the laurel bushes right around me, but I knowed cats can see in the dark good as in daytime.

The painter was after the smell of meat, and I didn't have no meat to give it except that on my own bones. The smell that drawed it was mostly on my hands. I took the handkerchief out of my coat pocket. It was a silk handkerchief that had been give me by Miss Lewis. She had embroidered my initials on the corner. I wiped my hands on the silk and throwed it on the trail.

Don't reckon I had gone more than thirty or forty feet when I heard the painter snarl and start ripping that handkerchief. Sounded like it tore the fabric to pieces with its teeth. While it was ripping the cloth, I hurried on and got maybe a hundred yards further down the trail. The path went deep into the holler past a spring and across a branch. I didn't want to start running yet. That would seem too much like panic. But I walked fast as I could and started climbing toward the tableland.

The painter may have eat the handkerchief or just tore it to shreds. But after a few more seconds I heard the thud of paws on the trail, one, two-three, one, two-three. It was gaining. I didn't even have a knife with me. I wished I had my squirrel rifle, or the shotgun I always carried on my trap line. But you don't carry a knife or rifle to a ceremony wearing your new suit.

Sweetheart, let me stop here and go back a little. I'll come around to that old three-legged cat again. I want to tell you about them days. You know how a grandpa likes to talk about the old times.

It was the beginning of change back then in these mountains. We had lived so far back in the hollers and coves, and high on the ridges, we didn't pay no attention to what happened in Raleigh or Columbia. Politics was for flatlanders, for the cities of the plain, you might say. Our county seat was way off in Asheville, and all it done was collect taxes and send out the sheriff to bust up a still from time to time. We tried to leave government alone, and make it leave us alone.

Then about 1838 everything changed around all at once. It was like something touched the elements, and the light and air was different. They broke off the south end of Buncombe and started a new county. We didn't care, for it was closer to pay our taxes and we could go to court on Decoration Day and listen to the lawyers.

It always was a pleasure to hear lawyers string out their big words and glittering lies. Then they got to fussing about where the county seat was supposed to be. They was the River Party that wanted it by the French Broad, and they was the Road Party that wanted it on a hill just north of Flat Rock, along the Buncombe Turnpike. The rich farmers of Mills River wanted the town near them and said they'd be steamboat traffic on the river. The flat-landers in Flat Rock said no, the seat should be near them, in the center of the county. Old Judge King said he'd even give the land on the hill there free for the courthouse.

The parties got to feuding, and they was fistfights and shouting and lawsuits in Asheville and torchlight rallies. Finally the legislature down in Raleigh stepped in and said they wouldn't be no new county if they didn't shut up. I reckon the uppity-ups in Flat Rock finally got the town put on the hill by the Buncombe Pike where it is today. But they was hard feelings all around for a long time.

Right in the middle of the mess was a politician from Asheville named Lance. He was a short man, and he had been crippled since he was a boy, and he walked with a cane. He had a terrible temper and a loud voice. Lance had made a pile of money in one thing and another. He had a bunch of wagons and teams that carried freight up from Old Fort and Greenville to Asheville, and across the mountains to Tennessee on the old turnpike. And he owned several taverns and drovers' stands. And they said he had bought thousands of acres of speculation land and was selling it off in squares and quarters. He also loaned money at high interest to folks in trouble.

How come I got to know Lance was he cabbaged the contract to build the new turnpike. They was so many hogs and cattle and wagons and stages coming over the old road, it was wore out and had almost washed away. In places it wasn't fit for use. The old road come through the gap, and it hadn't been kept up at all. They was places the old pike wasn't much more than a ditch.

Lance was on the committee that let out contracts for construction in both North and South Carolina, and I reckon he give the biggest one to hisself. Whoever got to rebuild the road could collect tolls for the first five years. And whoever started collecting them would probably just go on collecting them.

What's that? Why girl, even in 1845 it cost a dollar for a wagon to drive across the pike. Even to ride a horse cost two bits. And they charged a penny a head for hogs driv along the road. In the fall when stock was took to market a toll house collected hundreds of dollars a week.

I had built roads with Pa ever since I was a boy. After he made the way up through Douthat's Gap to Cedar Mountain, people everywhere asked him to build roadways for them. When I was younger than you are now, I started helping him survey routes. We dug out the road up on Hebron, and we made a road along the Blue Ridge out past Upward to Dana and Hickory Nut Gap. We even built a road up on Mount Olivet, though it wasn't a very wide one.

But I never thought of myself as no builder when I was young. I wanted to tramp through the woods and trap fur. Road building was what Pa done. I wanted to get away from roads, back to the creeks and high branches where the muskrats and mink was. It was like they was gold and treasure in the woods and high mountains, scattered in dens and along streams. A mink pelt is so soft you just want to rub your hand on it. In a cold year their fur gets thick and warm and almost black.

Fur was what I seen when I was sixteen and looked at the mountains to the west, at the creek valleys and Flat Woods and the rim of mountains over toward South Carolina. It was a thing that thrilled the first settlers, and beyond them it drawed the hunters and traders and explorers, and before that the Indians had loved to catch and trade fur. I thought of the sparkling pelts of red foxes and gray foxes and coons with rings on their eyes and tails. It was the shining wealth and song of these mountains.

It was always hard to catch a fox or a mink. Don't let nobody tell you different. I reckon the Indians caught them in deadfalls and snares, and they shot foxes with bows and arrows most like. They was awfully good trappers. But with a steel trap you've got to catch a mink in water where it drowns or it'll gnaw the foot off and get loose. You put the trap in water just deep enough so the mink will step in it, not swim over it.

Now a fox will outsmart you every time. A fox will find your trap and spring it. A fox will steal your bait and leave the trap untouched. They can smell your scent on the metal and stay away. To catch a fox, you've got to boil your traps and handle them with gloves and put scent on them to cover any human smell. And you hide the trap under just enough dirt and leaves so they can't see it. Put it too deep and it won't spring fast enough.

But you say you want to hear about the painter? I'm coming back to that. Be patient. What folks want most to do is what is hardest. You'll find that true with near everybody. A girl that is hard to get is most wanted. Something you can't hardly get, you try every way to secure. Something is scarce and has to be brung a long way the price goes up. That's one of the mysteries of people, how much they like to strive and worry.

When I was a boy, Pa made me work with him, building little roads and big roads. But because it was what I had to do, I didn't take to it then. I had to work around the place too, hoeing corn and milking the cows, but I never took much to that either. I couldn't think of nothing but trapping and hunting. Every chance I got, I was off in the woods with my gun and traps.

In them days I knowed every valley and ridge between here and Dark Corner. I tromped the woods to Big Springs and the Long Holler, and back to the Sal Raeburn Gap and the mountains toward Brevard. I felt like I knowed every tree along the trails and along the trap line. I knowed the trees so well I could remember what I was thinking when I passed one the time before.

A trap line is like a net throwed out over the mountains. But nobody is supposed to see it except the person that set the traps. A good trapper hides his traps so you could walk right over them and not see them. And you remember where every set is, no matter if they is dozens, strung out over twenty miles of branches and trails. You're like a peddler that knows all the places in a region.

I don't reckon they's no finer feeling than coming home with four or five pelts and one of them is mink. Even if you was cold, you could come in and set by the fire and skin off the hides and stretch them on boards. Mama complained about me skinning animals by the fire, but she let me do it. And I always cleared away the mess and wiped up the blood. I hung the stretched hides on the back side of the crib, out of reach of dogs while they dried and cured.

Some days, if I had run into a polecat, they could smell me coming all the way down the valley. If the wind was right the stink carried for miles. A skunk gets in your trap you have to take it out, and when it's riled, it throws the stink on you before you can kill it.

When I come home smelling like a polecat, Mama would meet me out at the barn with clean clothes and a piece of lye soap. I had to wash up in the branch and then burn my dirty pants and shirt.

I never did think a polecat smells as bad as other people do, but maybe I got used to them.

I'm *coming* to the painter, girl. Every winter I made a little money selling furs that was mailed off to the St. Louis Fur Company, and to Chicago, and to a place in Baltimore. And most of these companies had catalogs and sold you guns and ammunition and traps and bottles of scent to attract mink. I bought a mackinaw coat and a new rifle. But every year I come out with a few dollars extra. The pelts of twenty miles of creeks and branches could be changed into a handful of silver dollars. But I done it for the fun of tramping back in the mountains.

Besides trapping, I done my share of hunting too. The valleys was full of deer back then, and they was wild turkeys in almost every holler. They was bear in the Flat Woods, and over in South Carolina. And sometimes somebody would lose a pig or a calf to a painter. You never did see a painter in the daytime, hardly, but you heard them squalling in the night and they would come into your yard and kill a dog if they felt like it.

You always heard stories about painters. The mountain over here at the state line was called Painter Mountain. Since I was a little youngun I heard stories about Great-grandma Petal Richards staying up all night to keep a painter from coming down the chimney. That was the night my Grandpa was born. She burned up half the furniture to keep the fire going.

One time I seen some coonhunters come out of Gap Creek with a big cat stretched on a pole. I reckon it was six feet long, and it was the color of a Jersey calf, except the tip of its tail, and its ears and paws, was almost black. It was so heavy it wore out the two men carrying it up the mountain.

I had a fox trap on the yon side of Pinnacle. It was at a place called the Sand Gap where the dirt is loose and gritty. I had caught three foxes there, and one morning I come along to check the trap and heard something growling. I thought a fox must have been caught and something was eating it. And I heard this thrashing around in the leaves and brush like they was a fight. I eased around the bend in the trail and didn't see nothing at first. The trap was wired to a pine tree and the pine was shaking like a wind had hit it.

Suddenly something rared up from the other side, and I seen it was a big yeller cat. People are always talking about black painters, but all I ever seen was tan with maybe some black on them. This painter rared up like it was going to jump on me. But its paw was caught in the trap. Now a normal fox trap wouldn't hold a painter. The painter would just pull out of it. But I had used a bigger trap, a number four beaver trap I had ordered special to see how it would work for foxes and coons. And I had seen the tracks of an otter on Grassy Creek and wanted to catch it.

I raised my gun to shoot, and just then the painter broke away. It tore the trap right off the pine and run away limping, dragging the trap. Before I could even fire a shot, it was gone.

I wasn't more than about sixteen then. I reckon the trap rotted the painter's foot off, for I started hearing stories about a three-legged painter. Hunters in the Flat Woods would say they seen a big cat that was missing a foot. You know how stories like that will start on their own and grow. A feller named Ballard was camping back there one night and the cat attacked him. It raked him across the eyes with a big paw and the last thing he ever seen was this painter missing a foot. It clawed his eyes out and he took a week to make his way back to the settlement. He done it by finding a branch and follering it.

You started hearing stories about Old Tryfoot. That's what they named the painter. People up on the mountain said the painter took their lambs, and killed their pigs. They said it could smell a mother's milk for miles, and always knowed when a cow had freshened or a sow had a new brood. Some of these stories I believed and some I didn't. People said they seen Old Tryfoot looking in the window at night, and they seen him on top of the church one time in the moonlight. Boys said they seen that cat diving into the river catching fish, but I think what they seen was their own faces reflected in moonshine.

But the story I did believe was the one Alice Jeter told. She had a new baby named Sarah. It wasn't more than ten weeks old. She went out to her garden and picked some peas in a basket and was shelling them on the porch. Baby Sarah was laying on a pallet on the puncheons. Alice had heard a painter squall the night before. But in the daytime she didn't think they was no cause to worry. When she went inside to get another pan to wash the peas in she heard a rush and thud on the porch. The baby cried for just an instant and then they was the pad of feet across the yard. By the time she got to the door she just seen the painter slip into the woods.

Alice screamed so people heard her all up and down the valley. She was near beside herself. She run after the painter but it was gone. She run down to her brother's house and told him what happened. Then she hurried back to the house and looked on the porch like she thought the cat might have brung the baby back. She went inside and looked in the cradle but it was still empty.

They got together a pack of dogs and tracked the cat right up the side of the mountain to these rocks just under the top. And they seen this crevice where the cat must have crawled. The dogs set up a howl outside the cave, and the men gathered with their guns trying to figure what to do. They listened to see if they could hear the baby cry. They didn't want to smoke the cat out for fear of smothering the baby. They talked and waited, and they couldn't hear nothing from the cave.

Finally they pulled the dogs away from the entrance and somebody took a long stick and poked around inside. They couldn't feel a thing, though the dogs was yipping and carrying on like they could still smell the painter. One of the Smart boys lit a pine knot and pushed it inside, and he didn't see nothing at first. The painter was gone. It had left before they arrived, backtracked on itself and leaped up a tree and was gone. But what the Smart boy did see was bones in the corner of that cave, white as if they had been gnawed clean, or eat and then puked up. And among the pile was the bones of little Sarah.

Honey, what you end up doing may be the last thing you ever planned. I didn't go to be no builder, mostly, like I said, because that's what my Pa done. He was knowed far and wide as "the Roadbuilder." From the time I was a shirt-tail youngun I had to help him lay off right of ways and dig out roadways on mountainsides. I might have liked doing it except it was what I was expected to do. Everybody said, "You're just like your Pa." I was always sweaty and bent over a dragpan or wheelbarr. But all I was thinking about was how I'd like to be off in the cool woods looking for sign of mink or fox.

I didn't want to be no schoolteacher like my Grandpa MacPherson either. Mama would talk about how he had worked at the little college in town and how poor he was paid. And he had to do everything from teaching handwriting to directing the chorus. Mama would say, "Maybe David wants to be a professor, like his Grandpa," and I would make it up in my mind that I would never be no teacher either, much as I liked to read books and find out about things.

But it's like we know what our destiny is and we try to avoid it. Like somebody is called to preach and they get drunk and try to prove how mean and sinful they are, till they can't resist the call no longer. And sometimes when a boy falls in love, he'll not even mention the girl he's struck on and will avoid looking at her or even going near her house, until he can't stand it no more. He'll talk about every girl in the county except the one he's in love with. The truth is, he is struck so deep he can't talk about it. Then one day, when something happens that means he can't wait no longer, like sickness or a death in the family, he goes and confesses to her. And she has knowed all along how he felt and what a fool he is, but couldn't do nothing about it.

I told myself all I wanted to do was trap and hunt and gallivant around the ridges. I told Pa I didn't want no more roads into the mountains. I wanted people to stay to the woods and trails, like Pa said Tracker Thomas told him they should. I learned to use a dial and leveler, better than Pa ever had. But I told myself I was learning so I could work quick and get a job over with and go back to the woods. I told myself I didn't care how a road was made, as long as I could get it done and take my pay and buy a few more steel traps.

I knowed about grades and soils and how to build a simple bridge, and I read books on civil and military engineering which I bought at the store in Augusta when we drove down to trade in the fall. But I told myself I was doing it to support myself, and to make people leave me alone. I thought I just wanted to do my work and get back into the woods.

Then Pa had his stroke and everything changed. I was took by surprise, for Pa had always been so healthy and full of ideas. When he was on a job, all he thought of was how to get a road made. He expected everybody to fall in and help him. He give orders and he couldn't believe the rest of us wasn't as keen as him to get on with the job.

So here this big strong man that hadn't never been sick before couldn't move his left side, and he couldn't talk fast, the side of his mouth was drawed so. It was like something had got inside him and held him. And he was in pain too. Wherever the stroke had hit, I reckon it hurt something awful. He was a strong man that had always done whatever he wanted to, and he couldn't stand to be helpless. He was mad that he couldn't get out of his chair.

Pa kicked and rared and lashed out at whoever tried to help him. He talked ugly to Mama for the first time I ever heard him. He hollered like a little kid and he cussed at Doctor Wilkes when he come to examine him. It didn't seem like Pa at all. I told the doctor I was sorry, and he said not to worry about it. He said Solomon wasn't hisself, and after a stroke it was natural to blame a doctor if he couldn't make you walk again and feel better.

I seen Pa do things I never would have dreamed of, like slap pills out of the way and knock a bowl of soup out of Mama's hands when she was trying to feed him. But the thing that showed me how much he had changed was when Lance the politician from Asheville that got the contract for the new turnpike come to the house.

"Mr. Richards, I want you to lay out the new road through the gap," Lance said.

But Pa wouldn't even try to answer him. His head was turned to the side and he didn't speak. I reckon he was ashamed he couldn't work like he used to. He didn't seem to care about the new road. He just looked at the floor like a little youngun that ain't used to strangers. It made me sick inside to see him do that.

"Solomon is getting better," Mama said. "He is getting better use of himself every day."

"But Pa has to rest a lot still," I said.

When Mr. Lance stood up to go, his fine beaver hat in his hand, he drawed me aside. "David," he said, "could you survey the right-of-way over the gap? You've been helping your Pa, ain't you?"

Even before Pa took sick, I had done a few little jobs on my own, building roads out at Flat Rock and doing most of the labor myself with my cousin Noble and my brother John. I done it of course to make money to buy more traps.

"I'll give you the contract for the gap," Mr. Lance said. "Howard and his chaingangs from South Carolina will build the road up to the foot of the mountain."

This was the most important job in upper Carolina. Pa was too sick to take it on, and Mama was already worried about money. It seemed like I didn't have no choice. I was scared to take the job on, and even scareder to refuse it.

"David can build a road any place," Mama said to Mr. Lance.

"I'll start the survey for Pa," I said. "Then when he's better, he can build the road." It seemed like the only decent thing for me to say. And right then, in a few seconds, the rest of my life was changed. And the strange thing was I knowed it, though I didn't know it exactly either. What I did know for certain was it would be a long time before I could go back to the creek banks and my trap lines in the woods.

Well, my child, I've always been one to stay with a job once I start it. It don't do no good to jump into something and then quit. Some people will give up a job before they've learned how to do it. If I have a talent, it is a talent for sticking with things. A lot of people will get tired of a hard task and leave. They can't wait to get things over so they can be gone. Everybody wants to move on to something new.

But I found out a long time ago it's staying with a job that gives the true satisfaction. I get the urge to quit and move on, same as anybody. But if you resist the restlessness, and stay and see things is done right, you get a satisfaction you don't find no other way. Even Pa was always one to move on to the next job, the next road contract, before the present one was finished. He liked to lay out and start new things. He wanted the thrill of seeing where a new track would go. When it was mostly built, he lost interest.

He left me, even as a boy, to stay there and see the ditches and drains was dug right, that gravel was spread on the steep places, that big rocks got pounded into low wet places. I found they was pleasure in staying on a job till the very end, till the last rock was hammered in and the last shovel of dirt throwed. That was a pleasure I don't think Pa ever learned. I learned it because he made me do it. He made me finish up for him, and I found they was a thrill in completeness after everybody else has gone.

I liked to do the same thing at corn shuckings and barn raisings. I liked to stay there till the whole thing was done and everybody else had gone off to eat and sing. Ain't nothing so sweet as staying with the work till the bitter end. When I was a boy I would hang around the school yard after the last class of term. The other younguns run off home, and I lingered while the teacher packed up his things and locked the schoolhouse. I felt such a contentment to have got through the term I didn't want to leave. After the whippings and recitations and spelling bees it was wonderful to see the schoolhouse quiet.

It was a wisdom I learned by accident. Yet maybe I was born that way too. It just suits me to finish what I start, while other people have to run off to fresh things, which they will probably leave to start something else. In building they's a special ease in seeing things through. You might call it the rewards of patience.

But whatever you call it, the feeling is real and important, and I hope it will be important to you.

Honey, I want you to be patient. It may look now like you won't ever have another chance to get married. But they will be another boy come to love you, and your baby. You've got to see this through. To see things through is the best we can do. They ain't no escape and I don't believe they is no higher purpose than to finish a task right down to the end without giving up and without turning away from the grief that is give us.

My girl, though I hated to work for Pa, I loved to find an easy way through thickets and big rocks and split the mountain so folks could get across. It was a pleasure to make a level track through steep slopes, to move dirt and rocks around for people's use. The gentle grade of a road is like a lever that moves a mountain out of your way, a foot at a time. If you make a road right, you can take any load anywhere. Switchbacks up a ridge are like threads on a screw that twist right up to the highest summit. I hated it, and I loved it.

A road brings order to the wildest country and makes a flow of people and wealth into the wilderness. A road is like the blood and breath to farback valleys and dark coves. I hated to do it, and I thrilled to do it. Now I ain't sure how I feel.

"Richards," Mr. Lance said, "we're going to build the first real road these mountains ever seen, and we're going to build it cheap."

"Cheap ain't always the best business," I said.

"We got convict labor," he said. "We don't have to pay them hardly nothing, except a fee to Mr. Howard, the warden."

"I can get my own crew," I said.

"Who you hire comes out of your pay," Mr. Lance said. "The

heavy work will be done by Howard's gangs." Mr. Lance winked when he talked. He leaned on his cane and sweated from the strain of standing.

"We'll build a plank road over the low places," Mr. Lance said, "so there won't be no mud. And we'll make a grade so gentle the finest carriages can drive up from Greenville without a pause and the horses won't fart on the pretty ladies."

Honey, sometimes you come to a place and it seems like they's no way to get beyond it. The more you worry and fuss the worser everything gets. I know how you feel. That's why I'm telling you this. When your heart is about broke, ain't nothing helps but knowing other people have their troubles too. That, and getting on with your work. Here, don't cry.

The jump-off into South Carolina is the steepest place I know. You've seen it yourself. If you set down on the leaves at the top you could scoot all the way to Chestnut Springs. When people took their wagons that way on the old turnpike, loaded with hams and maple syrup and such, they had to tie the wheels back with rope on one side and hickory withes on the other. It was all a horse could do to hold the wagon back and men got on each side and helped. Coming back with a load from Greenville or Augusta, they had to make several trips up through the gap, or carry most of it on their backs. But coming up wasn't nigh as scary as going down. Climbing up was bone-wrenching, gut-busting work. But going down, it was like the earth fell away and left you nothing to hold to. Even if you wasn't afraid of high places it felt like the ground was tipping way down toward the treetops in Dark Corner and they was nothing between you and the trapdoor of hell.

The old turnpike had been graded up the side of the mountain, but was too steep for all but the lighter wagons and coaches. Most people had to get out and walk at the worst places. And every time it come a bad rain, the road washed away a little more. Runoff would cut across the turns and leave ditches and rocks exposed. The curves had never been drained right, and in the low spots the road was a swamp in rainy weather and a trough of dust and manure in dry times.

I got out my dial and leveler and tromped across the gap. I done some measuring and some figuring, and I seen what we was up against. I worked it out on paper and showed the numbers to Mr. Lance. "Best way to make the grade is to swing around between Corbin and Painter Mountain," I said.

"How much longer will that make the road?" he said.

"About three miles," I said.

"That's too expensive," he said.

I should have pulled out of the project right there, but I was too young and ignorant to know it. Lance didn't care about nothing but money. His face glistened with sweat as he tapped his finger on my page of figures. "Build it shorter," he said. "It ain't that far to Greenville." He was worried about paying for right-of-ways.

"Only way to make it shorter is to cut away half the mountain," I said.

"Then cut it away," Lance said. "The convicts will do the digging anyway."

"We'll have to move a whole lot of dirt," I said.

"Then move it, son," he said, like he didn't have time for the likes of me.

"Yes, sir," I said. And felt silly for agreeing. I should have quit right there, except I wanted to start that big job for Pa, so he could build the road for Mama's sake. It was my first contract, and if Pa didn't get well enough to make the road, I would never have that good a chance to show what I could do myself. Some things seem meant to be, no matter how hard or painful they are. It was like I *had* to build that cut through the gap; I didn't even choose to do it. From the time I heard about the new turnpike, it was like that mountain chose me. We don't understand most of the things that happen. They come at us, and we handle them the best we can. I knowed Mr. Lance and his contract was going to be trouble, but I couldn't back down. It was like this job and grief had been give to me, and it was my job and my grief. Honey, that's what makes the difference. It's like having children; you'll do anything to protect them and raise them, because they're yourn. A task is the same way. If we see a labor has to be ourn, we'll do it, no matter how hard or dangerous. I think that must be what a soldier feels when the bullets start flying, that they's nobody else there to do what he has to do.

All along I kept Pa up to date about the job and about the survey I had done. Of course he knowed how steep the gap was. He knowed all the mountain gaps by heart. "I hope you have to cut through rock," he said. Right then I knowed he wasn't going to do this job.

"Thanks for your good wishes," I said. I was mad enough to hit him, except he was a sick old man. He had been running things so long, he was bitter because he knowed, better than me, he couldn't do the job, because he knowed he had to set in his chair and let me do it.

We didn't have nothing but black powder to blast with back then, and it took two men a day to drill a hole for one charge, one turning the drill and the other swinging the hammer. Up on the gap it was too high to get water for heating and dousing to break the rock, unless you carried it up in buckets. Until the road was built they wasn't no way to carry it up. Blasting through rock was the hardest work to be found, and the most dangerous. Somebody was always being killed by a short fuse or a flying rock. Pa seemed to wish me misery and failure. "Thanks for your help," I said, and stomped out of the house.

It's one thing to brag what you will do, and another to get out and do it. A mountainside ain't nothing but trees and rocks and thickets, and you have to figure where a road has to be. You have to have what carpenters call "the idea," to see the road as it will be, when leaves and logs and briars are out of the way. The mountain at the gap is so steep, you have to dig your heels in the leaves to keep from falling.

I took my leveler and my compass and my ax, and me and my younger brother, John, and my cousin Noble—we always worked together—started hacking out a right-of-way. Other crews working from South Carolina had already laid out the turnpike from the foothills to the bottom of the mountain. And they was coming right along with the building. We could look down the mountain and see the gangs hammering little bridges over creeks and laying down logs in the low spots and nailing boards on them for the plank road. The convicts sung as they worked, and their voices echoed off the hollers below. The old turnpike had been built by slaves, but these was a gang of white convicts and a small gang of black convicts Mr. Howard was in charge of. The gangs worked on the same roads, but they lived in separate prisons and they worked apart. Back then, the warden of a prison didn't get no pay. He took what he could collect for the labor of his prisoners. In South Carolina the gangs built railroads as well as roads, and they even worked on farms, and digging sewers in Greenville.

It didn't seem possible to grade the road gentle enough from where they worked to where we stood. If the grade was steeper than eight feet to the hundred, a heavy wagon couldn't be pulled up it with a team. If we couldn't get an easy pitch it wouldn't be no better than the old road.

"Comes a rain, we could use the slope as a muskrat slide," Noble said. We was always joking while we worked, but I didn't feel like laughing that morning. I stood right on the South Carolina line and it come to me why Mr. Lance had hired me. He didn't care if the turnpike was a good road or not. He just wanted it built quick and cheap. He figured I was so young and ignorant I'd do whatever he said.

Ain't nothing on a mountain straight or regular. That's one thing I knowed about laying it off. You draw a straight line, or a smooth curve, right through the roughness and roll of a ridge. You cut a road out where it needs to be, not where it's easiest to make. You shovel ditches and lead water where you want it to go. You take out trees and rocks and shape the dirt like you think it should be shaped. The Bible says man was give dominion over the earth. But you have to work with the soil and rock and slope you find. If a mountain is in the way, you bust through it. You make the lay of the land fit your idea and purpose. But you also make your idea fit the place you're working on.

"Drive a stake here, and here," I hollered to Noble and John. Holding onto trees and bushes they drove stakes and tied white rags where the road was to be cut. I made the right-of-way extra wide, knowing the cut would be deep at the top. "There, and there," I shouted, aiming my leveler to get the right pitch. It didn't seem possible they could be a roadbed under us, deep in the mountain. But I knowed it could be done. They was a perfect grade inside that ridge and I was going to reach it. "Yonder, and yonder," I said, pointing to places for John and Noble to make ax marks on trees and drive more stakes. I slashed laurel bushes aside to see where I needed to go. This mountain ain't been fit for nothing but ginseng and blockade liquor, I said, and I'm going to make a way here. As I worked up a sweat I felt like tearing the mountain apart with my hands. Saluda Gap had stood in the way long enough. I wanted to sweep away the trees and laurel slicks and rocks and rake out a road the way a youngun makes things in sand. I looked at the trees like a farmer looks at weeds. I'm going to improve this ridge a little, I said.

I knocked away spider webs to get my sightings. Once I seen a copperhead in the leaves and kicked it with my boot halfway down the mountain. We come on a hornet's nest in a chestnut bush and I broke off the limb it hung from and throwed the whole thing down the ridge, and only got one sting. When I come to a rock or boulder I rolled it out of the way. "There," I hollered, "and there," pointing to places for them to drive more stakes.

"Is this the place?" John said, standing by a flame azalea in bloom.

"It's the only place," I said.

The mountainside in spring was still a tender green. Some laurels was blooming yet and the azaleas was busting out. We broke limbs of flowers out of our line of sight and chopped down saplings. Twice I got out my compass to make sure of the angle I had figured. In the heat of work it seemed strange to be checking our direction with the North Pole so far away. But we was right on course. I knowed we had to come into the gap at an angle of twelve degrees off the straight north, or almost north-northeast, as it's called. I was going to hit it exactly. All the brush and trees on the ridge was trying to get in my way, but the compass could see right through them. "There, and there," I hollered to John and Noble.

By dinnertime we had marked out near quarter of a mile. "I

ain't never been so rushed," Noble said, when we set down on a log and opened our dinner buckets.

"You ain't never had such a big job," I said.

"Hurry won't make it easier," John said. "Pa always said hurry's sign of being scared."

"You ain't working for Pa no more," I said. I don't know what come over me. I guess I was afraid that if I didn't get the survey and the job done quick I would lose my chance. I was scared maybe Mr. Lance would give the contract to somebody else, or that the government would decide not to build the new turnpike. I don't know what I was afraid of. I had to prove I could do the job, and if things went wrong I didn't want nobody to blame me.

"I ain't busting a gut for nobody," John said.

"This is my job and you'll do what I say," I said.

"I ain't working for you," John said. He picked up his dinner bucket and ax and started climbing back up the way we had come.

"You walk off now, you can't come back!" I hollered after him. "I don't pay no quitters." But he didn't answer. He just kept on walking till he got out of sight over the lip of the gap. I felt even worser then, for I had never done a job without John. We had always worked together for Pa. But I didn't call to him or run after him to bring him back.

With nobody but me and Noble working, the job went slower that evening. We slapped at flies and brushed mosquitoes out of our eyes. Limbs whipped back and stung me in the face, and I smacked them out of my way. One time the leveler fell over and slid down the mountain till it lodged against an oak. I had to climb down to get it. We was getting closer to the work gangs, and their singing and hollering made me nervous, I guess. It seemed like I could smell the sweat of the convicts below.

As soon as we finished marking the right-of-way, they would start sawing down the trees and clearing it. And then we would begin digging the cut. I wasn't used to bossing over men, except for John and Noble. Mr. Lance said the convicts had their own guards and warden. "Just tell them where to dig and drill," he said, "and Mr. Howard will make sure they do it right."

It was almost dark when me and Noble got to the place where the highway from the foothills stopped, down close to Chestnut Springs. The convicts had already quit work and gone to their camp. We could hear them hollering and banging pots, and smell their cooking. It was dark in the holler, though the trees up on the ridge was still lit. A shot was fired and a bullet sung through the air like a sick banjo string. Me and Noble started back up the mountain.

It was too far to walk from Cedar Mountain every day, and me and Noble and John had took a room at the Lewis house just north of the state line. The Lewises had a big house with porches on both stories, and they kept boarders from the Low Country in summer and stock drovers and any other travelers too. Captain Lewis had several thousand acres there on the line, and he owned property in South Carolina also. They had slaves that worked around the house and served at the table.

Soon as I seen your Grandma, I was attracted to her. She was the oldest daughter of the Lewises and helped her Ma run the place. I flirted with all the girls back then. I seen her in her long, white, summer dress going around to make sure everything was ready for supper, and I couldn't take my eyes off her. I talked to her a few times, like the young will if they get a chance. But I didn't really fall in love until we sung together. Us Richardses always could raise a song, in church and at home, at infares, and even by ourselves out in the woods. Somebody said music is the food of love, and I believe it.

They was a big parlor in the front of the house with a fireplace at both ends, and they was a little organ against the wall away from the window. Evenings they lit the lamps above the organ and I would play it after I washed up and had supper. After the rough work of surveying and digging, it was a pleasure to work the white keys, and pump the peddles like I was dancing or marching somewhere. One night the second week I stayed there, the guests was gathered in that big room. Some was reading the papers, and some was smoking their pipes, and some was arguing about the president and all the crooks and thieves in Washington, and whether we ought to go to war with Mexico. It was a cool evening, and the flames in the fireplaces looked red as roosters that stretched and crowed on the logs.

"Can you play this?" Miss Lewis said, and handed me a songbook.

"I'll try my best," I said. I had always loved the old songs from Scotland. They are sweet and pure in their sadness. I begun peddling and playing the first chords and Miss Lewis started to sing the first line. By the time she reached the second line I knowed I was in love. Her chin and throat looked so white and perfect in the lamplight I couldn't quit looking at them. And her voice touched me in a way I had never been moved before. They is a point before which you can resist love and think you are just being playful. But after that point is reached, they is no turning back. I felt the pain and thrill and jolt that instant.

That evening we read through most of the numbers in the songbook. The light from the lamps seemed bright as a sunrise. I forgot about the time and the other guests and the worry of road building. Noble was off smoking his pipe by hisself, I reckon. I watched Miss Lewis's eyes and lips while she sung. When our eyes met it was as though the light was coming from her.

I had sparked a number of girls back in Cedar Mountain, both while I was in school and after. But I was too busy working with Pa on roads and walking my trap line to ever really fall for one. Now Miss Lewis had a lot of beaux among the local boys. They was boys from South Carolina that come up to see her, and boys from town too. If I had any advantage it was because I was working on the turnpike that went by her house, and because we sung together.

While I stayed at the Lewises, I went to church more than I ever had before. I walked with Miss Lewis to the regular services, and to a singing school at Crossroads. Nothing softens your outlook like love. I felt like I had discovered music and Miss Lewis and goodness at the same time. Everything that summer seemed to have the face and voice of love, Miss Lewis, the hymns and songs, the words we said, every cricket chirp and sunset. Even the hard work on the cut, the harshness of the mud and cussing and sweat of the convicts, seemed part of the new plan of things. Every evening I walked the trail from the gap and washed up on the back porch and put on my clean clothes. "Ain't never seen you so primpy before," Noble said as I splashed cologne on my neck and cheeks.

"I ain't never heard such jealousy," I said.

Miss Lewis and me took walks in the evening, when it was still light. We walked past the big cribs where they stored grain to sell to the drovers in the fall. We walked past the distillery and the indigo vats. Katydids was already singing in trees. They was crickets in the grass and a jarfly somewhere in the orchard. We walked down the trail that was the shortcut to the gap.

"Everything is making music," I said. The evening star had

come out and was sparkling like the note of the crickets. Far off we heard a church bell and the sound of a waterfall. When you can hear a waterfall like that, it is a sign of rain.

"We're making the best music," Miss Lewis said, "just us together."

After me and Noble marked out the right-of-way, the chaingangs cut down all the trees to the top. They used crosscuts and axes and buck saws. When a tree was felled, they rolled the logs off down the mountainside. "Don't you want to save the wood?" I said to the warden.

"Got no use for more logs," he said. They had already finished the plank road to the bottom of the mountain. The big logs knocked down little trees and piled up against each other all down the mountainside. It looked like somebody had poured scalding water on a bank of lush weeds. You never seen such a mess of laps and broke-down poplars and timber going every which way like logjams high in the air. The dead oaks soured and the broke limbs wilted.

"We could saw up the logs and pile them to cure," I said to Mr. Howard.

"Ain't got time," he said. I think he resented that Mr. Lance had put me in charge of the cut, and him so much older than me. He showed me quick he wasn't taking no orders from me. Mr. Howard carried a gun on the job, like the guards and foremen. And he told everybody what to do. He was used to building roads in the piedmont and flat country. He talked like a flatlander, and he hadn't especially wanted to come up here and dig a road out of the belly of the mountain.

"My men ain't used to climbing rock cliffs," he said, and spit.

"A road has to be built right," I said.

"Any way you can build a road is right," he said. He leaned down toward my face. "Ain't that right?" he said.

"I guess it is," I said. I didn't have no choice but to work with him, Mr. Lance had said. Just tell them where to dig and where to drill and where to stop.

After they got through clearing the right-of-way, it looked like a storm had hit the mountain and broke off all the trees. I had heard of blow-downs, where one big tree fell in wind and all the little trees would go down too, in a line up the mountain, because they had no protection once the opening was made. That's what it looked like, except the trees spilled below was all crisscrossed and twisted up. And the ground looked ugly as the mange where it was exposed.

Once the trees was down, that left the stumps, all through the gap and down the mountain. Howard's gangs had a stump puller they could use on flat ground. But the gap was too steep for it. You never heard of a stump puller? Why honey, it's on wheels like a big cart, wheels higher than a man's head. And it has a chain wrapped around a big spool. You hook the chain to a stump and pull the whole thing with ten or twelve oxen. The spool turns and jerks the stump out of the ground.

Ain't nothing harder than working stumps out. You take a shovel and mattock and dig out around them and then chop the roots. But every stump is different. Some you can split down the middle and pull out. And some has a taproot like a big carrot that goes straight down and you have to dig the whole thing out to get to it. Pine stumps is easy, but hickory and oak and sometimes chestnut is nigh impossible to dig loose.

Howard put the convicts to working and they chopped and heaved and rolled stumps off down the mountain. The stumps with all their roots looked like big ticks pulled out of skin. The convicts sweated and shined in the sun. They hollered and cussed as they strained. But they didn't sing much while they was pulling up stumps, neither the black chaingang or the white chaingang. They always worked about half a mile apart.

"Boss, this is *bad* work," one said.

"These stumps don't never give up."

"These stumps was put here at creation, and they'll be here till Doomsday," another said.

The biggest stumps Howard blasted out with black powder. Every time a stump blowed up in pieces and sailed down the mountainside all the convicts cheered.

The third stump they blowed must have had a bad fuse, for the convict that lit it didn't have time to get away. I guess the spark jumped the fuse, for he hadn't run more than twenty feet before the stump exploded. A piece hit him in the back, and down he went in the leaves. Howard took a dipper of water from the bucket and throwed it on the man's face. "Carry him over to the shade," the warden said.

"Maybe his back is broke," I said.

"He'll be all right," Howard said.

Where I got real sick of Howard was when two convicts started to fight. I don't know what they quarreled about, but they got to kicking and hitting with their chains. One knocked the other down and was kicking him in the head. Howard had the winner tied over a log and his clothes pulled off. "Boss, don't whip me," the man said. But Howard cut a hickory withe about six feet long and stripped the leaves off. He whipped the man on his back and on his white butt while he screamed. He beat the convict till his back was bloody and he messed all over hisself. And after the man passed out, Howard left him laying there in the sun, with flies buzzing in the blood on his back and where it had run down in

his hair. I wanted the job to be over with right then. I didn't want
to have no more to do with Howard and his chaingangs.

Where the stumps had come out the red dirt showed through
the leaves and trash and topsoil. The dirt was so red the holes
looked like sores, and when it rained they started bleeding down
the mountain.

When the gangs started digging the cut I got a shovel and
helped them. I never could stand to see people work in dirt
without pitching in. Why is moving dirt around so thrilling? To
carve and shape a mountainside makes you feel good, and to open
a ridge for a road makes you feel worth something. Just by shoveling dirt in the right places you let light into hidden coves and
farback hollers, like sunlight touching raw dirt that's been hid for
thousands of years. It was almost painful to do.

"You don't need to work with prisoners," Noble said.

But I couldn't stop myself. I stood around with my compass
and chain and leveler for a while, like I was inspecting the gangs'
work as they started loosening the right-of-way with picks and
mattocks. But I seen how rough they was cutting along the upper
line we had laid off.

"Let's make a clean cut," I said to Howard.

"Won't make no difference how clean it is to start with," he said,
and spit ambeer.

"People work better if they're doing it right," I said.

I got a shovel and dug along the upper boundary to make a
neat cut. The woods dirt broke easy until you hit a root. Then you
had to chop the root with an ax or mattock, or big grub hoe.
Roots streamed with sap when they was sliced, and they smelled
like seeds or sour fruit. I dug through leaves and rot and black
dirt, and in a few inches turned up yellow and red subsoil. The

black dirt on mountaintops is never thick. I dug the line across the top straight as a rifle shot to show the convicts how to do it. I wanted them to take pride in their work.

The gangs labored without shirts, and they was dirty and shiny with sweat. Their backs glistened as they swung the picks. Looking down from the top, it was like watching a crowd of locusts and grub worms attack the ridge and eat down into the red quick. They hollered and cussed, and Howard's slave boy carried water among them. "Hey, Henry," they called to him. And when he come they drunk from the dipper and ruffled his hair and slapped him on the backside. "Hey, Henry," they called, "bring us some of that sweet water."

One of the pleasures of opening dirt is it's different in every place, and it keeps changing. Every shovelful has different grains and smell. Some deep dirt is gritty as sugar and sparkles in the sun like little mirrors. Some is dull as rotten rocks way down in the ground. Some dirt is gray and some yellow and some orange. Soon as you get away from topsoil you don't find no black dirt, or even brown dirt. The soil you move out of a mountain is always red or light-colored. And it has a smell when it's exposed to air, sometimes like liquor or camphor, sometimes like water that ain't seen light in a long time and blinks. When you dig, every shovelful seems to touch a secret, like they's treasure, or a big snake, or passage down there. You get down to grave level and spring level, and feel the mystery of deep soil. And when you bring it up into light it's already starting to dry and go stale. In a day or two dirt starts to form a crust.

I have dug into soil that was like bread, and dirt stiff as the meat of a chestnut. And sometimes you reach into mealy dirt that is almost green and has specks of mica in it like little fish scales. And sometimes you touch into clay pure as butter. When I dig, I am curious to see what the next shovelful will show.

"I hope we don't hit no big rocks," I said to Noble as we dug the upper edge of the cut. I didn't want to slow down to drill and blast, or to carry water for fire and dousing. But all along the cut my shovel never hit a rock bigger than a mushmelon.

When the gangs got the surface of the right-of-way loosened up with picks they brought the barrows and sleds and started shoveling out the spoil. I figured they was maybe five hundred tons of dirt to be moved, and that they would carry it down to be used as fill in the low places. But they dumped the spoil right over the side of the mountain.

"Ain't you going to use the dirt as fill?" I said to Howard.

"Too far to carry," he said.

"You'll kill the trees below," I said. They was dumping the dirt on the great mess and tangle of trees and stumps already spilled down the mountainside.

"Ain't got time to carry dirt halfway to Greenville," Howard said. "What do you want to build, a flower garden?"

"I'll tell Mr. Lance to put a stop to it," I said.

"Tell Lance what you please," Howard said.

But Mr. Lance was way off in Asheville that day, and by the time I seen him it was too late. Tons of spoil had been dumped over the side of the mountain, smothering bushes and bending saplings, covering a lot of the stumps and logs down there. The whole mountain begun to look like it had been hit by a landslide or flood.

Because we found no rocks to speak of, and because they didn't have to carry dirt but to the lower side of the cut, the work went faster than I expected. By early July the gangs had shoveled down twenty-five or thirty feet into the gap. Most of the dirt was bright red, but deep down it got yellow, and in the saddle of the gap itself it was gold. It looked like we had shoveled out half the mountain and throwed it on the trees below.

"You throwed a lot of North Carolina into South Carolina," Lance said when he seen what we had done. "Maybe we should charge the Sandlappers."

He was sweating from having to walk up to the cut from his buggy. He leaned on his cane and wiped his face with a silk handkerchief. "Richards," he said, "you've done good."

"I didn't mean for them to throw the dirt down on the trees," I said.

"Won't hurt nothing," he said. "Trees will always grow back."

"Mr. Lance," I said. "When will I get my pay?" I was staying at the Lewis house and I had not paid them any board. And I was courting your Grandma and wanted some good clothes. And I hadn't paid Noble a cent neither.

"When you finish the job, Richards," Mr. Lance said. "You have a contract, boy. You're not working for wages anymore."

That burned me up, that we would have to work all summer and not get a cent. And what would I say to Noble, that he had to sweat till Dog Days with no wages? Mr. Lance could say I had a contract, but I had never seen no piece of paper. We had just shook hands and agreed that I would lay out the cut.

"Of course, I can lend you some money if you're short," Mr. Lance said, wiping his face again with the shiny handkerchief. I had heard Lance made a lot of his money by loaning to poor people at high interest. Rumor was he had took land from people that couldn't pay him back.

"I can get by," I heard myself say, though I didn't know how I would do it, unless I borrowed some from Pa.

"You'll be finished by the end of Dog Days," Mr. Lance said.

"If all goes well and we don't hit no rocks," I said.

The deeper we dug, the more I expected to find rock. I had thought all mountains was rock inside, that that was what made them stand up and last. I thought if you raked the dirt and trees off any mountain you would find the soil was just the rotted and crumbled outside of the rock. The rock was the bones of the mountain that give it its shape. But in the gap we dug down twenty-five, thirty feet, and except for a few boulders and veins of loosened quartz they was nothing but more dirt. It looked like we would finish early. By August I would have my money, and I wouldn't have to work with Howard and his convicts no more. I could talk to Miss Lewis about getting married.

People come from all around to inspect the cut, and said it was the biggest thing ever built in the mountains. The upper bank was almost forty feet high, and I had sloped it back to the trees on the lip of the cut. I knowed that when it rained the bank would wash a little. But they was a ditch on the inside to carry away runoff. The bank would grow up in weeds when another summer come. I thought about setting out little white pines there once the hot weather was over.

One Friday evening, right at the beginning of Dog Days, it commenced to rain. We'd had showers and thunderstorms all summer. You know how clouds coming in from South Carolina hit the Blue Ridge and dump their water on a hot evening. But the ground would dry out in the sun by the next day. Sometimes we worked right through the rain. When you're sweaty and dirty the rain feels good on your back. The drops run like cold little feet on your neck. A summer rain is clean as a bath if they ain't no lightning. But when it thundered on a hot day, we got away from the gap. Every tree on the ridge had been striped down its bark by a lightning hit. Lightning started walking around up there, we got away in a hurry.

At the beginning of Dog Days it come this slow, steady rain that went on all night, a she-rain people called it then. It's the long soft rain that soaks the ground, that don't run off but sinks in and melts the dirt. Every day I expected it to stop, but it rained again. When they was a break, me and Noble walked the trail over to the cut and tried to work a little, but it was like shoveling cream and mush. The gangs stayed in their camp at the foot of the mountain. We was digging the highest, deepest part of the cut. Even though they was a break in the clouds when we started, it was raining again before I had filled a wheelbarr. The clouds moved in from the south and hung there like ghosts around the gap. Me and Noble walked back to the Lewis house.

You know how it gets in a wet summer. Soon they was mushrooms in the pastures and orchards. The roads was nothing but mire and water stood in every low place. The creek was a dirty spate. The woods smelled like mold and mildew. It seemed the ground was rotting and the woods was in darkness. It didn't look like the sun would ever shine again.

"We might as well go home," Noble said when it kept raining the second week.

"The minute we get back to Cedar Mountain it will clear up," I said. Of course, I spent every minute I could with Miss Lewis. When she wasn't helping her Ma run the place I set with her in the parlor while she sewed. And sometimes we set on the porch and eat watermelon while we watched it rain. Every time we went for a walk we got wet, but we didn't care. Her Ma scolded her for getting her shawl wet. Young people in love don't care what they do to pass the time. All they want is to be together. We sung at the organ at night. We could stand out in the rain and kiss and not ever notice the dampness. Tell the truth, I didn't mind not working them first days.

But Noble didn't have nothing to occupy him. "It ain't never going to stop," he said.

"Let it rain," I said.

Near the end of the second week I seen Mr. Howard come riding into the yard. I was setting on the porch with Miss Lewis drinking tea when he rode up all covered with a big black coat. I couldn't even tell who he was till he reached the hitching rail.

"Have you been to the cut?" he said.

"Not today I haven't," I said.

"It might pay you to go look," he said.

I got my coat and hat and me and Noble took the trail over to the gap. At first I couldn't tell what had happened. It was like the cut we had dug had disappeared. In its place was a pile of dirt and trees and roots. Muddy water was streaming out of the mess. The roadway was gone.

The high bank above the road had caved off in a slide. The mountain had melted and run like it was candle wax. It was like the dirt we had cut through bulged out and ruptured. The mountain had pulled away from itself in clots and gouts. Trees leaned over from the top, their roots sticking out in air. Wet weather springs had opened in the side of the spill and poured down on the soupy mush. All our summer's work was covered up.

And it come to me what Pa had said, about hoping we would hit some rock in the gap. They wasn't nothing to hold the mountain back when it got soaked. They wasn't no firmness, no strength inside the mountain, once rain started pouring on it. The raw dirt had turned to jelly, and then syrup.

"This mountain don't want no road across it," Noble said. And I felt it was true. Here, at the highest point on the turnpike, it was like the mountain had decided to stop us. It was like the guts of the mountain had voided theirselves on our roadway. It seemed the mountain was cussing me for cutting through it. It had put a hex on the project, and was fouling over my work.

It did finally stop raining the next week, and Mr. Howard brought his gangs back up the mountain and we waded into the edge of the slide. First the stumps and trees had to be chopped out of the mud. And then we started shoveling and carrying the muck out of the way. Soon we was all covered with the paint and paste of the red mush. Only clean place was out in the woods, away from the road. My clothes and my boots and hands got caked with the batter.

"If I had knowed this, I'd have let Lance build his own road," Mr. Howard said.

Mr. Lance come to inspect the landslide. He huffed and puffed up the hill from his buggy. "Richards," he said, "you could have avoided this."

"I can't stop the rain," I said.

"You must have built it wrong," he said. That made me so mad I couldn't get my breath for a few seconds. For he was right, something had been done wrong. All our work that summer had been wasted. I was so blind with anger I couldn't think of nothing to say.

"You ain't paid me a cent," I said, as though I meant the bad luck happened because he hadn't paid me.

"And you won't get a cent until this mess is cleaned up and the road finished," he said.

He walked off like I wasn't worth arguing with. He limped down the hill with his cane, swinging his fat frame from side to side. I was so mad I was shaking. I thought of pushing his face down in the mud and drowning him. I thought of him coughing and choking on mud and manure in the road. I seen myself pushing his face deeper in the manure and letting him smother on gobs of muck.

I couldn't work no more. I had to get away, and I walked above the road and climbed into the wet woods. My boots was all caked with red clay that scraped off like turds on the leaves. I walked out through the wet underbrush, smearing and tracking the woods floor. Never had the green leaves looked so clean, and the bark of trees was pure as spice. The sticks and leaves on the ground looked scrubbed and polished. Water standing on leaves was clear as magnifying glasses.

When I turned back toward the road I climbed to the top of the high bank and looked down on the roadway. Shelves would have to be dug in the mountain above the cut. A steep bank would just slide away again when it rained. We would have to dig steps back into the mountain to make terraces.

The convicts worked like maggots in a carcass. They was dumping load after load over the edge of the cut and it spilled like pus down the mountainside. Everything was smeared and tore up. It seemed impossible this was the beautiful gap where we had started working a few months before. The whole mountain was filth and waste, like a wound festering and running its corruption down the slope. It made me mad all over again just to look at what we had done.

After about a week we had dug most of the roadbed out again. And by the time that was done, Noble and me had surveyed out a new line at the top of the cut and started them chopping trees and digging again. We dug out a flight of shelves in the mountain, to keep it from crumbling off into the gap. It was a bigger job than cutting the road in the first place.

"I didn't go to do no such extra work as this," Mr. Howard said. He had the gangs dump the spoil on either side of the mountain, spreading the mess on the North Carolina side. Now it looked like the whole mountain had been tore out and gutted. It didn't even look like the gap anymore.

When the terraces was about half finished, it commenced to rain again. I woke up in the night and heard the drops on the cedar roof, and thought of all the fresh exposed dirt, and the shovels and mattocks and all the other tools rusting in the dark. I said to Noble, "Here we go again," but he didn't wake up. He kept snoring and I listened to the rain. Eventually, when I got back to sleep, I dreamed about floundering around in the mud up to my armpits. But it was bright yellow mud, and sour like clots of clabber. The mountain was trying to drown me in its filth.

It kept raining for a week, as it will in summer once it starts, and the mountain broke loose again. The shelves we had cut melted and slumped away. The whole mess come sliding down into the cut, like brown sugar that had been wet. The roadway was filled again. It was like the mountain was laughing at me. It didn't want to be split by no road, and it was slapping my work out of the way. More trees and roots and rocks fell into the gap.

By the third week of rain, it looked like the mountain was trying to heal itself. The slides filled in and smoothed over the cut. Tiny weeds had started to grow on the fresh dirt. If we left it alone, briars and seedlings would take on the slides by the end of summer. In a few years, nobody would know the cut over the mountain had ever been made.

So, my dear, to round a long story off, it kept raining all through Dog Days into late summer. We dug the cut out three times, and every time the bank caved off and filled it again. And Mr. Howard threatened to take his gangs back to Greenville and leave the turnpike be. Mr. Lance would talk to him and then we would shovel the shelves wider and further back into the ridge. The bank was now fifty to sixty feet high in the gap.

"You won't get no pay till it's finished, till you build it right," Mr. Lance said to me. I wouldn't answer him no more. I thought of hitting him over the head with a shovel, and I thought of just walking away from the job and never coming back. I thought of going to Texas, and I thought of going to the Rocky Mountains and being a trapper there. Only thing kept me from running away was your Grandma. I was going to stay and marry her, and I couldn't look like no quitter in front of her. And I couldn't let the mountain beat me if I wanted to build roads in the future, no matter how much I hated Mr. Lance and his crooked ways. I was embarrassed to face Mrs. Lewis too, for I hadn't paid her a cent for my room and board. I tried every way not to see her, which was hard since I was living in her house.

Darling, it was like that muddy cut was where our family had come to. Our road went back to Cedar Mountain and Douthat's Gap, and it went back through all the work your Great-grandpa had done. It went back to Saluda and the place your great-great-great-grandparents had cleared after they left the settlement at Mountain Creek in Rutherford County, and beyond that it went back to Virginia, and Pennsylvania, and Wales. But it all stopped there at that muddy mountain, and it seemed like I couldn't go beyond it. I had to finish the turnpike, or it looked like they wouldn't be no future at all, for me or the family. Do you see what I'm saying? It had all come down to that one cut through the gap. And it depended on me. Wasn't nobody else could help.

Finally, I figured out what had to be done to the Mud Cut, as people had come to call it. I dug the terraces even wider and deeper, reaching way back up the ridge. And I had the convicts bust up rocks to put on the shelves. It was work they hated, but Mr. Howard made them do it. I guess he wanted to get the job over with and it seemed the only way. For the lower tiers, I built cribwork of logs and planks to hold back the dirt walls. Higher up, me and Noble fixed what is called wattles and gabions by military engineers. I had read about how they protect earthworks by a kind of wicker made of osiers and saplings. We drove posts in front of the terraces and wove withes and sticks in mats to hold the dirt back. And we wove what looked like big baskets out of withes of hickory and willow, and filled them full of dirt. It took another month longer to finish that. And Mr. Howard and Mr. Lance both cussed and threatened me. But when me and Noble was done, the cut through the gap was tight as a corncrib. The last thing we done was dig a ditch along the top, to keep water from running down on the cut. You can still see the terraces there above the turnpike, though trees has growed on the shelves now.

When we finished the turnpike Mr. Lance give a barbecue at the gap on the stateline. He invited bigwigs and politicians and their wives from Asheville and Greenville. He sweated in the hot October sun and he wiped his face with a handkerchief and made a speech. "Ladies and gentlemen," he said, "this is the greatest project ever completed in upper Carolina. It unites our states forever in common enterprise."

They roasted a whole pig on a spit, and they was plenty of sweet cakes and punch. And they was champagne for Mr. Lance and the politicians. The chaingangs that done the digging wasn't there, but their boss, Mr. Howard, was. Everybody eat a plate of barbecue and had a good time. And then they got in their carriages and buggies and started back down to Greenville on the new turnpike, or north to Asheville. I stood where the crowd had been in the gap and listened to the carriage wheels rumble on the plank road below.

Noble had already gone back to Cedar Mountain, and your Grandma hadn't come to the ceremony. She said she didn't want to hear a lot of politicians make speeches and take credit for our work. She said she wouldn't stand out in the hot autumn sun to listen to them liars congratulate theirselves.

I was feeling good, 'cause Mr. Lance had give me two hundred dollars in twenty-dollar gold pieces. They weighed in my pocket and tinkled when I walked. I wanted to get back home and put them in my bag before they wore smooth at the edges. I wanted to get back and tell Miss Lewis about the bonus I had been give. And I wanted to pay her Ma for mine and Noble's room and board so I would feel free to ask for Miss Lewis's hand in marriage.

But I lingered there in the cut where me and Noble had worked so many months. Grass and weeds was beginning to grow on the terraces. They had built the fire for the barbecue right in the road and I wanted to sweep the ashes and burned sticks out of sight. Slivers of meat still stuck to the bones of the roasted pig. I picked off the best pieces and eat them, looking way down the cut toward Chestnut Springs and the foothills of South Carolina.

I couldn't think of nothing to distract the painter but to take my coat off and rub my hands on the cloth. I tried to smear whatever grease and smell was still on my fingers into the wool. It was the only suit I had. I took my comb out of the breast pocket and stuck it in my trousers. I run my hands through my hair to get oil on them, and wiped that on the coat too. Then I throwed the jacket behind me and hurried on.

It was getting dark even in the woods above the holler. The trail was nothing but a gray hole between the bushes. I tried to think of what I had heard about painters. Was they afraid if a man turned to face them, the way dogs is and a black bear is? Or was they like a bull that comes right toward whatever stood in front of it? Did they like to run down things, and running away would make them more dangerous? I knowed they run down deer and calves. I made myself slow down. I figured the cat might hesitate to leap on somebody going brave about his business. I thought of your Grandma and all her family waiting supper for me. I told myself I would never go into the woods again without my gun. And I would never go into the night without a lantern. Painters was afraid of fire, but I didn't have no way to make a fire.

In the dark I could smell pine needles on the slope, still warm from the evening sun. They is no sweeter smell than pine straw that has been heated up.

It sounded like the crack of a whip when the painter tore my coat in two. It was like thunder ripping the sky. Old Tryfoot tore the cloth, and tore it again. I guess he was mad 'cause they was nothing to eat except wool with the smell of barbecue on it. It sounded like he was clawing the jacket into threads, snarling and panting.

As I hurried on, I pulled down my galluses and wiped my sweating hands on my shirt. The dark had got hot as a toothache. I undone the black ribbon of my tie and flung it behind me. And then I fumbled to unbutton the shirt. It was like my hands could find the buttons in the dark but the fingers couldn't unbutton them. My fingers was so sticky with sweat they caught on the cloth. It was my only boiled shirt and I didn't want to tear it.

My fingers felt like they was melting at the tips, and sweat and barbecue juice stuck them together. The painter had dropped the rags of the coat and was running up the trail again. It made the awfullest squall, the scream of somebody tortured. It was like a scream I had heard from the house in Greenville where they keep afflicted people. I reckon the painter would already have caught me except it was three-legged and had to run sideways a little.

I tore open my shirt and heard the buttons fly off into the leaves. They was mother of pearl, and Mama had ordered them special from a place in Atlanta. Then I remembered the shirt had cufflinks. I got the right one out, but the left one was tight on my wrist and wouldn't budge. I picked at it with my fingernails, but the head was stuck in the buttonhole. They was the only cufflinks I had.

Old Tryfoot was practically on top of me. He was so close I could hear him breathing. The shirt fluttered in the dark like a big white bird on my wrist. I give the shirt a jerk with my right hand and tore it off the cuff. I pitched the cloth behind me and doubt it hardly touched the ground before the painter snatched it.

Painters don't growl like dogs. They have their own kind of snarl. Old Tryfoot chewed at the white cloth of the shirt and growled like a glutton jealous of his meat. I could hear teeth gnashing on the fabric, and ripping the seams Mama had sewed so careful.

It looked like I wasn't going to make it. The trail up to the Lewis place runs for about half a mile through the laurel thicket and then through some oak and poplar and sassafras woods before it reaches the clearing. If somebody seen me coming they might grab a gun and shoot the painter. But it was already dark and they wouldn't be nobody on the porch. If the dogs was in the yard they might bark and come running after the painter. But the dogs would be eating their supper in the shed behind the kitchen where Alfred, the Lewises' house slave, fed them.

I didn't have nothing left to throw down but my trousers and the galluses. Without the galluses my pants would soon fall down anyway. I couldn't slip my trousers off without taking my boots off either. It's hard enough to pull your pants off in the dark, much less while you're running.

Slowing a little I reached down and tried to jerk a boot off. But all I done was trip myself and go sprawling in the dirt. It was dark and everything seemed to be whirling around. The trees and the stars above flew past my head. A bird somewhere in the woods was squawking. Down the trail the painter quit tearing the shirt and come running again, padding the ground, one, two-three, one, two-three. I wasn't even sure which way the trail went no more. But while I was stopped, I pulled both boots off and throwed one behind me. The other one I held onto.

The first boot must have hit the painter in the face, for it sounded like he slid to a stop in the leaves to turn and rassle the boot with his paws. I reckon a three-legged cat can't reach out and grab something as easy as a four-legged one. I heard the boot knocked around in the leaves and the cat snarling as it bit and slapped the leather. The boot must have been too tough to rip.

As I got up and started running again I knocked into limbs and saplings before finding the trail. I stubbed my toes on rocks and roots, and crashed through a bush or two. But my feet, hurt as they was, found the dirt of the path and I begun to run faster. I tried to think, was they some way to slow the cat down so I could get to the house, or at least to the clearing? It just seemed I was a goner.

But I run harder than ever. It was like my feet didn't hardly touch the ground. When I heard Old Tryfoot close behind, I hurled the other boot back in his face. He paused to slap that boot into the brush and then bite it like it was a lamb or pig.

They wasn't nothing left to throw at the painter but my trousers. And in the pocket of my pants rattled the ten gold pieces. It was everything I had from the whole summer's work, for all the sweat and laying off and digging out the landslides, cutting the terraces and tearing out the innards of the mountain again and again. I had took not only the cussing of Mr. Lance and Mr. Howard, but the cussing of the mountain too. It was like the mountain had tried to put a curse on me, and had a personal grudge against me, and I had won. And now the mountain had sent Old Tryfoot to get revenge. The ten coins was all I had to show for the misery and worry. It looked like the gap was going to win after all, or at least I was going to lose. I had read about victories so hard the winners lost in the long run.

I had to take the gold pieces out of my pocket. And I had to use both hands to pull my trousers off. If I dropped the money in the dark I might never find it, or somebody else might find it. It was all I had to pay Mrs. Lewis and to pay Noble, and for me and Miss Lewis to start housekeeping with. I took the ten hot coins out of my pocket and put them in my mouth. They tasted like sweat and barbecue, and the metal tasted old and new at once.

I stopped and pulled the pants over my feet, one leg at a time. The cat was thudding so fast up the trail I expected the slash of its claws in my neck and shoulders. I could almost feel its teeth on my face. When I flung the pants back I think they must have covered the painter's eyes for he growled and turned sideways into the brush. I started running even faster.

With the coins in my mouth I had to breathe through my nose. And I couldn't holler out for nobody to come help. I held my head up and run like I was reaching for the edge of the world. I run like I was rounding the curve of the earth in the dark. I run so hard it was all a blur as I brushed limbs and hit bushes with my knees. I was so busy running I didn't hardly notice when the dogs come out of the shed and started barking. I guess they had finished their supper or had smelled the painter on the wind, for they met me where I come out of the woods and started snarling at Old Tryfoot until he stopped and turned back into the trees.

I didn't stop running till I got to the porch. There I flung open the door and run right into the parlor. In the lamplight they was

all standing there, waiting for supper to be served. They was Mr.
and Mrs. Lewis and Miss Lewis and about ten overnight guests.
Miss Lewis was standing by the organ, and she looked startled,
like she had seen a headless ghost bust through the door. But your
Grandma ever did have a cool head. She reached up and tore a
curtain off the wall and brung it to me. It was only when she had
wrapped the drapery around me that I realized I was naked except
for my drawers and the cuff still on my left wrist. I was out of
breath, and I wanted to tell her and all the others I had run from
Old Tryfoot. But my mouth was full of gold coins, and when I
opened it to speak I felt one of the twenty-dollar pieces slide right
down my throat. The funny thing was that as the coin slipped
down I felt a laugh rising in my chest. I couldn't help but laugh,
seeing the look on everybody's face. It was like I had run a thousand miles, only to arrive in my birthday suit. I had moved a
mountain that summer, and here I stood like a baby in a diaper.
Miss Lewis and me would go on many hundreds of miles together
and thousands of days together, but I wouldn't never be as scared,
or feel as silly again. They wasn't nothing to do but laugh about it.
Nothing else would get us through that moment. I seen your
Grandma starting to laugh too, and already I was beginning to feel
better.